Praise for Erica Ridley and The Wild Wynchesters

"Erica Ridley is a delight!"

—Julia Quinn, *New York Times* bestselling author of *Bridgerton*

"Erica Ridley's love stories are warm, witty and irresistible. I want to be a Wynchester!"

—Eloisa James, *New York Times* bestselling author of *My Last Duchess*

"Ridley's motley crew of Wynchester siblings is as charming as it is unforgettable." —*BookPage*

The Duke Heist

"This entrancing Regency...is a knockout."

—*Publishers Weekly*, starred review

"Schemes, heists, and forgeries abound in this charming series starter. This unconventional and quirky Regency will have readers falling for the plucky family and rooting for Chloe and Lawrence to buck tradition." —*Library Journal*

The Perks of Loving a Wallflower

"A plot full of mystery, high jinks and tender personal revelations."
—*New York Times*

"A feminist fairy tale readers will rejoice in."
—*Publishers Weekly*, starred review

"Completely enchanting." —*Kirkus*, starred review

"Pure reading bliss." —*Booklist*, starred review

"This clever novel will delight readers."
—*Library Journal*, starred review

Nobody's Princess

"Ridley hits the sweet spot of tickling readers' funny bones and pulling on their heartstrings in equal measure. This is a joy."
—*Publishers Weekly*, starred review

"Another perfect dose of reading joy." —*Booklist*, starred review

"Ridley is fast becoming an auto-buy author and makes a good read-alike suggestion for fans of Lisa Kleypas, Grace Burrowes, and Elizabeth Hoyt." —*Library Journal*

My Rogue to Ruin

"This Regency romance will have readers speeding through the pages and smiling all the while." —*BookPage*

Hot Earl Summer

"Plenty of charm...Ridley once again showcases her skills crafting interesting characters and fun-reading plots, which stress accepting and supporting people in the ways they want." —*Library Journal*

"[A] dazzling romance to ensure maximum reading enjoyment."
—*Booklist*

"A delightful Regency romance that isn't afraid to go over the top."
—*BookPage*

A Waltz on the Wild Side

Books by Erica Ridley

The Wild Wynchesters
The Duke Heist
The Perks of Loving a Wallflower
Nobody's Princess
My Rogue to Ruin
Hot Earl Summer

The Dukes of War
The Viscount's Tempting Minx
The Earl's Defiant Wallflower
The Captain's Bluestocking Mistress
The Major's Faux Fiancée
The Brigadier's Runaway Bride
The Pirate's Tempting Stowaway
The Duke's Accidental Wife
A Match, Unmasked

Rogues to Riches
Lord of Chance
Lord of Pleasure
Lord of Night
Lord of Temptation
Lord of Secrets
Lord of Vice
Lord of the Masquerade

Magic & Mayhem
Kissed by Magic
Must Love Magic
Smitten by Magic

Heist Club
The Rake Mistake
The Modiste Mishap

Regency Fairy Tales
Bianca & the Huntsman
Her Princess at Midnight

The 12 Dukes of Christmas
Once Upon a Duke
Kiss of a Duke
Wish Upon a Duke
Never Say Duke
Dukes, Actually
The Duke's Bride
The Duke's Embrace
The Duke's Desire
Dawn with a Duke
One Night with a Duke
Ten Days with a Duke
Forever Your Duke
Making Merry

Gothic Love Stories
Too Wicked to Kiss
Too Sinful to Deny
Too Tempting to Resist
Too Wanton to Wed
Too Brazen to Bite

Heart & Soul
Defying the Earl
Chasing the Bride
Taming the Rake
Undressing the Duke

Young Adult Novels
The Protégée
Insatiable

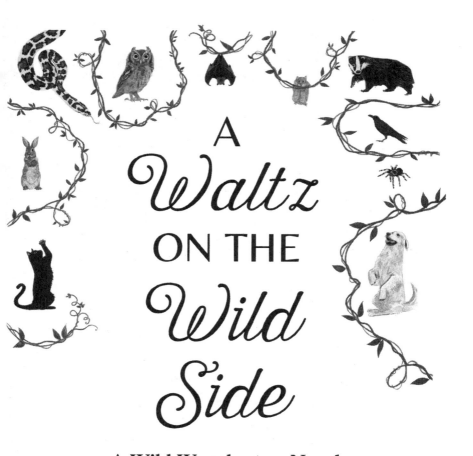

A Waltz on the Wild Side

A Wild Wynchesters Novel

ERICA RIDLEY

FOREVER
New York   Boston

This book is a work of fiction. Names, characters, places, and incidents are the product of the author's imagination or are used fictitiously. Any resemblance to actual events, locales, or persons, living or dead, is coincidental.

Copyright © 2025 by Erica Ridley

Cover illustration and design by Caitlin Sacks. Cover copyright © 2025 by Hachette Book Group, Inc.

Hachette Book Group supports the right to free expression and the value of copyright. The purpose of copyright is to encourage writers and artists to produce the creative works that enrich our culture.

The scanning, uploading, and distribution of this book without permission is a theft of the author's intellectual property. If you would like permission to use material from the book (other than for review purposes), please contact permissions@hbgusa.com. Thank you for your support of the author's rights.

Forever
Hachette Book Group
1290 Avenue of the Americas, New York, NY 10104
read-forever.com
@readforeverpub

First Edition: August 2025

Forever is an imprint of Grand Central Publishing. The Forever name and logo are registered trademarks of Hachette Book Group, Inc.

The publisher is not responsible for websites (or their content) that are not owned by the publisher.

The Hachette Speakers Bureau provides a wide range of authors for speaking events. To find out more, go to hachettespeakersbureau.com or email HachetteSpeakers@hbgusa.com.

Forever books may be purchased in bulk for business, educational, or promotional use. For information, please contact your local bookseller or the Hachette Book Group Special Markets Department at special.markets@hbgusa.com.

Library of Congress Cataloging-in-Publication Data

Names: Ridley, Erica, author.
Title: A waltz on the wild side / Erica Ridley.
Description: First edition. | New York: Forever, 2025. | Series: The wild Wynchesters; [6]
Identifiers: LCCN 2025008606 | ISBN 9781538726136 (trade paperback) | ISBN 9781538726143 (ebook)
Subjects: LCGFT: Romance fiction. | Novels.
Classification: LCC PS3618.I392255 W35 2025 | DDC 813/.6—dc23/eng/20250318
LC record available at https://lccn.loc.gov/2025008606

ISBNs: 978-1-5387-2613-6 (trade paperback), 978-1-5387-2614-3 (ebook)

Printed in the United States of America

LSC-C

Printing 1, 2025

*To anyone who has ever
stood strong against injustice*

*And to Roy,
for everything*

1

Whilst Miss Vivian Henry's mind was busy plotting how best to steal the Crown Jewels, she fried a pan of bubble and squeak with her left hand, pulled down cups and saucers with her right hand, knocked the silverware drawer shut with her left hip, and kicked her cousin's round leather football out of the kitchen with a well-practiced swing of her right boot.

In other words, it was an utterly ordinary Sunday.

"Breakfast is ready," Viv yelled as she set the table.

"Coming!" came her cousin's muffled voice through the thin walls. "Have you seen my daggers?"

"On the mantel, between your faux spectacles and the pile of rope," she called back, refraining from additional comment.

The long-running jest that Viv was the only one who learned anything from Quentin's special-interest tutors had stopped being funny for both of them. Perhaps today was the day her cousin would finally practice. She hoped he didn't hurt himself.

"Aha!" came Quentin's triumphant shout. "Found you."

Someone brown, furry, and impatient darted beneath Viv's skirts and between her legs.

"Not now, Rufus, you roly-poly glutton," Viv scolded him as she served bubble and squeak onto two porcelain plates. It wasn't how she'd broken her fast when she lived in Demerara, but it would do.

Even Rufus thought it smelled tasty. She rubbed his furry head with her toe. "Sorry, sugar. You must wait until supper for more."

Quentin darted into the room. He flung his arms wide with dramatic flair. "What do you think?"

Viv kicked a chair in his direction as she poured the tea. "What the devil is in your hair?"

"Chalk," he answered happily. "It's to make me look older."

"It makes you look ridiculous. Do you know how long it took me to set all those twists in your hair just so?"

"Hours," he replied with feeling. "I was there."

"Then why would you spoil all of my effort with powdered chalk?"

"I'm Godfather Wynchester today," he explained. "The white hair is to make me look distinguished."

Quentin looked like an eighteen-year-old itinerant with powdered sugar in his curly black twists and inexpertly drawn "wrinkles" on his golden-brown forehead. Nonetheless, Viv knew from experience that if she voiced such observations, she would be the one tasked with improving the disguise. This morning, she simply had no time to spare.

"Eat," she commanded her cousin. "Grandfather Wynchester can't save the day if he passes out from malnutrition."

"Godfather," Quentin corrected her with his mouth full. "You could be Grandmother Wynchester."

"I'm ten years older than you, not fifty." Though sometimes eight-and-twenty *did* feel like a lifetime.

Her young cousin pointed to his head. "Try chalk dust."

"Try again. I refuse to have anything to do with that family. As should you. Won't you please let the Wynchesters perform their own skullduggery?"

Quentin flashed hurt eyes at her. "I've told you a hundred times; my secret club and I have sworn a solemn oath to help them."

And Viv had pointed out a hundred times that the real Wynchesters had no idea Quentin and his costumed friends existed. Not that inconvenient facts had ever stopped her cousin from spending his days in search of adventure.

"Please remember to say 'friends,' not 'secret club,'" she reminded him. "The newest Seditious Meetings Act explicitly forbids secret societies. No solemn oath will save you from the noose."

"We're being careful," he promised her. "That's why we use false names and disguises, just like the Wynchesters."

"That's not enough protection. Do you have a powerful duke for a brother-in-law, like they do? Or access to the Wynchesters' lawyers and endless piles of gold?"

Quentin shoved eggs into his mouth rather than respond.

As Viv turned back to the sink, Rufus burrowed between her skirts again. She hiked her hem up to her shins. "Summon your creature. He's in my way."

"Maybe he wants you to sit down, too. Eat something. You're always doing a thousand things at once."

"If I don't do them all, who will?" she pointed out.

But Viv's belly chose that moment to let out a lusty growl. In surrender, she set the pans she was scouring aside and took her seat at the breakfast table.

Rufus immediately tried and failed to hop up into her lap.

"By all that's holy, Quentin, if you do not call your creature away from me—"

"He's not mine anymore and you know it. Anyone can see he's adopted you. You're his pet now."

"Did I ask to be anyone's pet?" She nudged the toast and blackberry preserves toward her cousin.

"Well, I don't know what I'm supposed to do about the matter," Quentin said peevishly. "Rufus hates me, just like Sally does."

"You can't keep acquiring animals and pawning them off on me," Viv began.

"I'll raise your pin money," he interrupted, chewing with his mouth open. "Sally feeds herself anyway. I'm too busy fighting crimes."

As far as Viv was concerned, the worst crime was the horror Quentin had committed against his hair. She would be the one spending her evening washing and restyling it instead of penning Act Two of her play, in which her villain *du jour* made an attempt upon the Crown Jewels.

Perhaps if she could finish this bloody script, she could earn enough income not to *need* to siphon any pin money from her younger cousin's limited quarterly trust.

"Oof." Quentin slumped backward in his seat and patted his nonexistent belly. "That was good."

Viv scooped up the dishes and headed for the sink. "Can you see if the newspaper has arrived?"

He brightened. "Perhaps there are more articles about the Wynchesters!"

"What is left to say about them? Six orphans adopted by a rich foreign baron, who had nothing better to do than spoil them rotten—"

"—and instill lifelong values of empathy and philanthropy. He gave them a purpose in life: helping those who have nowhere else to turn. Of course they're mentioned in every newspaper! Everyone loves to read about the powerless beating the powerful, and the oppressed triumphing over their oppressors."

Viv couldn't argue with the last part. Many of her plays featured unlikely protagonists rising out of hopeless circumstances. She swung a heavy pot filled with simmering water from the stove to the sink, so she could soak the soiled dishes and scour them clean.

Her cousin soon returned with the newspaper and a stack of correspondence.

"More post than usual today," Quentin said cheerily, then waggled his eyebrows. "Are you receiving love letters from your adoring fans?"

"I'm not known for my sweet and warm personality. Lately, it's been mostly comedians and a few nutcakes wanting help with their crimes. No one adores me but you."

"Someone out there will appreciate your sharp edges," Quentin assured her. "And isn't your reputation the newspaper's fault, anyway? They specifically asked you to be harsh and direct, because it generates bigger reactions from subscribers."

"They didn't have to ask," she said dryly. "Plain-spoken and brutally honest is the only way I know how to be."

This was also one of the many reasons why a suitor was not in Viv's foreseeable future. Her minimum requirements were high. If a man did not meet her qualifications, she would not waste either of their time with a prolonged courtship. Telling him he didn't suit would be the first words out of her mouth.

Which unfortunately meant, she didn't meet the average gentleman's minimum requirements, either.

It didn't matter. Viv didn't want *average*. She expected more from a partner, and from herself. Besides, she was far too busy managing her own affairs to worry about an alleged phenomenon as unlikely as true love.

Quentin glanced up from the newspaper with a sour expression. "Only a tiny little paragraph on the front page today. What a travesty. Their successes are so inspiring."

Viv said gently, "I admire your big heart, and your friends' unflagging compassion, but living the same lives as the rich and well-connected isn't an attainable goal."

"They're role models," Quentin said stubbornly. "And they're mostly not aristocrats. Many started out poor. Several are Black, like us, or have other characteristics that society spurns. But they made a name and a place for themselves anyway! They're *respected*. They have value."

That was his usual response to any criticism against his idols, but something was different today. There was an unusual tenseness in his shoulders. A vein she'd never seen before pulsed at his temple. As if whatever they were talking about was no longer just about the Wynchesters.

"I respect you," she said hastily. "You have value."

Exasperation flickered in his eyes. "We're not talking about you and me."

Weren't they? Then what? Viv prided herself on always knowing exactly what was going on around her. Quentin had never kept anything from her before—or even possessed any secrets to keep. When dissatisfied, her well-meaning cousin was no stranger to rash actions. For the first time in her life, she hoped she was reading someone wrong.

He was also a good lad, she reminded herself. Whatever he was not yet ready to confide wouldn't turn out to be anything major. There was no sense getting worked up over nothing. Especially when there were real dangers afoot.

"The Wynchester family criminally disregards the auxiliary effects of their privilege," she said. "They not only instill the false belief that it's easy to be just like them, but also perpetuate an impossible standard for the less privileged. The upper classes can point at them and say, '*They* came from humble origins and became educated and wealthy. If the lower classes are poor and disadvantaged, it's their own lazy fault, and not a problem *we* need to address.'"

Quentin crossed his arms. "I don't care about the upper classes. The world needs more Wynchesters."

He had never known a world without the infamous family. Their portentous group adoption had taken place four years before his birth.

By the time her young cousin had learned to read, their daring exploits were already in every scandal paper. He never questioned their fame, or what they did with it, because he'd never known anything different. Viv knew. And like it or not, she'd keep trying to make him see.

"Your wild Wynchesters may never suffer consequences, but it doesn't work like that for you and me. Their successes don't mitigate our barriers. You may think they're heroes, but what I see are smug, rich brats who believe laws apply to everyone but them."

Quentin let out a groan. "That's *how* they help their clients. You write plays for a living, don't you? Haven't you ever heard of Robin Hood?"

Viv did not in fact write plays for a living. Despite his frustration with her, Quentin was being very charitable with that characterization. Viv wrote a thousand words without fail, every single day, but had yet to sell a single script.

"All I'm saying..." She took a deep breath and stopped herself from making the situation worse.

From the time her younger cousin was a child, she'd been his companion, then his guardian. Though he did not yet have his majority, Quentin was grown now. She had better start treating him like it, if he was to learn how to be his own man.

Even if old habits were hard to break, and past nightmares impossible to shake.

As an olive branch, she jabbed a soapy finger at the newspaper. "Just read me the important bits."

His posture relaxed. "Your column?"

"No, I already know what *I* wrote. What's on the front page?"

He scanned the lines while she scrubbed. "The voices agitating for voting reform have dwindled to nothing. Even the group of ladies over in Bath who think all *women* should have the vote have ceased making noise."

"Can you blame them?" she asked. "The Peterloo Massacre was just a few months ago. After their own government sent armed soldiers to attack peaceful protesters hoping for voting reform, it's more dangerous than ever to stick your neck out unnecessarily."

He turned a page. "Do you think it'll ever happen?"

"Hard to say. Thirty years ago in Sierra Leone all heads of household voted—even unmarried African women, like me. That's a British colony. Why not here?"

"Because England doesn't even give all *men* the right to vote." Quentin snorted at something in the paper. "Just obnoxious aristocrats, like these buffoons."

"Which ones are the buffoons today?"

"The Marquess of Leisterdale and his heir, the Earl of Uppington. It seems they settled everyone's tabs at their club last night and are now the favorites of the ton. The pair were out celebrating Uppington's recent return from spending several months overseeing their Caribbean holdings. Leisterdale is quoted as saying, 'Owning a sugar plantation is like having access to an endless pot of gold.'"

"Is that right?" Viv's stomach twisted. She knew exactly what it was like to be a Black woman tethered to some white aristocrat's sugar plantation. "Where in the Caribbean?"

"Demerara. Where you were kept." His fingers shook, rattling the paper. "These men weren't the ones who..."

Viv's hands stilled in the dishwater. "No."

"Did...my mother..." He swallowed audibly.

Viv closed her eyes and fought the tidal wave of memories. "Not with them."

Quentin was quiet for a long moment, then cleared his throat. "It says here, the marquess's heir—Lord Uppington—has been boasting that he keeps the highest-paid mistress in London."

"How does he know, if he just got here? Are other lords required to submit their receipts to him?"

"He's had her on the line for years, apparently. Mistresses count on gifts as much as wages, and since Uppington is gone so often, he can't be showering her with jewelry, so he pays her an exorbitant stipend instead."

"I'll wager the mistresses he keeps in Demerara don't see a bloody penny," Viv muttered.

Quentin glanced up sharply. "What?"

"Nothing. Keep reading. I'm almost done washing up."

"The rest of the news is boring. Some lady snubbed some lord at Almack's. The Prince Regent is remodeling one of his palaces yet again. And…oh, this is interesting. A politician in the House of Commons was burgled last night."

"Why is that so interesting? What did they steal?"

"He refuses to say, which is intriguing enough. But apparently, the robbery involved balloons, shepherd's pie, and a whooper swan. What in the world is a whooper swan?"

Viv stopped cleaning dishes. She turned around slowly, wiping her hands on her apron. "*Anas cygnus*, as described by famed zoologist Carl Linnaeus in his 1758 tome on natural systems. You're certain the robbery utilized those specific items? Balloons, shepherd's pie, whooper swan?"

"Mad, isn't it? Who would even come up with something like that?"

Viv would have. And did. Last week she'd finished a comedic play in which the malefactors stole an ancient scroll in just that manner. But it hadn't fully been her idea.

Instead of the usual domestic concerns, one of the more preposterous letters sent to her daily ask-me-anything advice column had enquired how to steal a treasure map from an aristocratic Mayfair town house. Viv never responded to such ludicrous queries, but she did use their absurd contents as fodder for future manuscripts.

Well, bollocks. Now theater managers would think she'd copied the idea from the real-life case, rather than believe her imagination had come up with these twists on its own.

Except...had she?

"Gah." Viv slumped her hips against the wet sink. "Now I'll *never* be able to sell that play."

Sometimes unique ideas seemed to float in the air, occurring to multiple people at once. However, these unlikely crimes were too similar to be a coincidence.

Perhaps she and the thief had both been inspired by the same source material. Or perhaps what had happened was—

"You wrote about a robbery?" Her cousin reached for Viv's notebook on the table.

"Quentin, no!" She tried to snatch her journal out of the way, but she was too late. A perfect blackberry-preserves-stained thumbprint now marred the bookmarked page she had been revising. "How many times do I have to ask you to wash your hands before touching my things?"

"Sorry," he said sheepishly. Quentin rose from his chair and trudged over to the sink, where the wet bar of soap shot from his hands and nearly whacked Viv in the eye.

She caught it with her left hand seconds before impact and handed it back in silence.

When his hands were clean, Quentin consulted his pocket watch. "I must hurry. The club is waiting on me. Don't worry, I already collected the new advice column responses from the table. Anything else you need me to post for you whilst I'm out?"

"That'll do." She glanced toward tall stacks containing copies of the play she'd finished the month before. "I have to pen the perfect letters to accompany my latest script."

"You're absolutely brilliant, cousin." Quentin seemed his sunny self again. Perhaps her overactive imagination had exaggerated the earlier tension. "Someone will recognize your genius soon."

"I certainly hope so," she muttered, dipping her hands back beneath the sudsy water. "I'm getting tired of—ow!"

His eyes went wild with panic. "What? What happened?"

"Nothing." She held up her finger, upon which a single bright red bubble of blood protruded. "Nicked myself on the paring knife."

Quentin's eyes went glassy and his knees buckled.

Viv wiped the blood on her apron and dashed forward just in time to catch him. "You haven't changed a bit. What kind of would-be Wynchester faints at the sight of blood?"

"Can't let anything happen to you," he mumbled. "Don't scare me."

"I'm fit as a fiddle," she assured him as she settled him back on his feet. "Have fun, and don't break any laws. The Wynchesters may live outside of society's rules, but people like us cannot. Please be safe. And come back home in time for dinner."

"Wouldn't miss it." Quentin kissed her cheek. "I'm beating you at cards afterward."

She snorted. "That *would* be an improbable twist, wouldn't it."

2

$\mathcal{M}$r. Jacob Wynchester spent all morning scowling at the same handwritten poem. Immersed in the worn leather-bound notebook in his hand, he exited the rear of his family's three-story house and glanced up just in time to avoid being decapitated by a pair of large, very sharp swords.

"Watch out!" yelled his sister Elizabeth as she danced to the right.

"Isn't the person swinging the sword the one who ought to be watching what they're doing?" Jacob asked.

His sister-in-law Kuni parried, her long black braids swinging. She and Elizabeth zigzagged across the rear lawn amid a clatter of curses and clanging blades.

Jacob headed left, toward a big, whitewashed wooden barn almost half as wide as the Wynchesters' sprawling house.

The barn door was visibly ajar. Jacob's heart pounded. He always ensured it remained locked tight when he wasn't there.

He shoved his poetry notebook into the pocket of his leather apron and cupped his hands around his mouth as he sprinted up to the open door.

"How many times must I remind you ne'er-do-wells not to access the barn without me present?" he shouted. "Insecure openings are exactly how we lose a python, and you remember how long it took the last time—"

A trim white man wearing a leather helmet fitted with mismatched goggles poked his head out of the door. "Sorry. I got distracted. Shutting now."

The door closed in Jacob's face.

He sighed and yanked it back open. "I was coming inside. Please remember that everything in this barn is a wild animal, with fangs or claws or venom. It is a privilege and a responsibility—"

And a fire hazard.

He gaped at the absolute chaos his brother-in-law Stephen had installed in Jacob's private barn.

Slippery chutes and knotted ropes and grooved tracks covered every solid surface, and most of the space in between. Each pathway was dotted with random objects: old boots, lined-up dominoes, feathers, wheeled trolleys, glass vials and bottles with varying quantities of colored liquids, hammers, razors, pulleys, trapdoors, and what looked like an entire row of fresh strawberries.

Most baffling of all: the dozens of precarious lit candles.

In a wooden barn.

Here, where a hundred different terrestrial or winged wild animals might bang into them and set the entire neighborhood on fire.

"I know what you're thinking," said Stephen.

"You really do not," murmured Jacob, "or you would be running as fast as your legs could carry you."

"This version is much more pragmatic than the last prototype," Stephen assured him, peering at Jacob with one overly magnified light-gray eye. "The first item of note is the goose-launching station."

Jacob enunciated, "Extinguish the candles."

Stephen beamed at him. "I knew you would say that. I installed them specifically so you could see how quickly the flames can be doused. Watch this."

He pulled a lever.

The entire room came to life. Every pulley in Stephen's contraption dropped or lifted or tugged, sending all the objects crashing into one another, one at a time, until hoses sprang forth from a central cylinder like snakes from Medusa's head. Water gushed forth from each hose, not only extinguishing each flame with enough force to knock the candles over, but also drenching Jacob and Stephen and every other animal or object in a five-yard radius.

Stephen grinned in satisfaction. "What do you think?"

Jacob swiped water from his face. "I think I'll kill you."

"Impressive, isn't it? Elizabeth says—"

"Listen to *me*. Those flames never should have been lit in the first place. This barn is ninety percent wood. And I am one hundred percent opposed to unexpected indoor downpours. Dismantle this abomination at once."

"It's just a draft," Stephen said quickly. "You haven't seen its final form."

"If so much as a single gear remains after nightfall—"

"All right, so you can't see the vision. But there *is* a need for a mongoose launcher, right? You said so yourself."

"I said we frequently utilize avian talent in our missions. Which are ongoing, and the reason I'm in this barn. The animals and I have to work today, Stephen. We've a disaster to quell across town, a freshly forged statue to replace inside a walled garden, a stolen heirloom to recover, and a young mother who badly needs our—"

"*Meow!*" A small calico cat nudged open a square leather flap high overhead. Tiglet squeezed through the opening and dropped lightly to the dirt at Jacob's feet, without banging into any of the newly installed chutes and tubes crisscrossing the barn like a mechanical spiderweb.

"Clever boy!" Jacob scooped the orange-and-black speckled cat into his damp arms, and despite some wriggling, was promptly rewarded by a wet-sandpaper lick to his cheek.

Tiglet had been the first of Jacob's messenger kittens and was now a fully grown, multi-talented part of the Wynchester family.

"Take this, for example." Jacob placed the cat back onto the ground and strode toward the rear of the barn, ducking all the tracks and pulleys. "Tiglet's presence here means Tommy and Philippa need more feline firepower. That cues me to release Dionysus."

Stephen took a step backward. "Is Dionysus a cuddly little messenger kitten?"

"Dionysus is a Highland tiger." Jacob prodded the wildcat to follow Tiglet, who pranced ahead with a self-important sway, his calico tail waving high in the air.

The much-larger wildcat prowled right behind, claws out and teeth bared.

"Only scare the villains, please," Jacob scolded the duo as he pushed open the door to let them out of the barn. "No mauling this time."

Tiglet and Dionysus took off, streaking over the grass and out of sight.

Elizabeth and Kuni didn't even pause their sword fight.

Taking advantage of the opening, a tiny, plump hedgehog waddled into the barn.

Before Jacob could reach for him, the audible clink of swords fencing on the other side of the walls ceased abruptly. He stepped out of the way just as the barn door flew open and his sister Elizabeth barreled inside, sword strapped to her hip.

"Tickletums!" she squealed. "My baby! My heart!"

She scooped up the hedgehog, pressed him to her ample bosom, and swirled around the barn's interior in wide circles, the blade of her sword bumping into absolutely everything she passed.

"My love," Stephen chastised his new bride gently. "Please have a care for my craftsmanship, or I shall be forced to launch the integrated self-defense sequence. You won't like it."

"But my little Tickletums made it all the way back from Regent's

Park," Elizabeth cooed, still waltzing. "That's his farthest distance yet. A personal record. Our sweet Tickletums has now graduated into a full homing hedgehog."

Kuni poked her head into the barn, her black eyes sparkling in her pretty brown face. "Beth, if we're done fencing, then we have to get back to our cases. My client will return in an hour, and I—" She caught sight of Jacob and made a sympathetic expression. "I'm sorry you're always stuck in the barn with the animals."

"I like the animals," he said. "And I'm the only one able to train them."

"I could build—" began Stephen.

"No," Jacob said flatly.

"But you never even leave the property," Kuni insisted. "Just because you're the only one who can do a thing doesn't mean you don't deserve a respite once in a while."

"I respite," Jacob said.

Elizabeth nodded. "Once a week, at your poets meeting."

"Just like you and Kuni only spare an hour a week for sword and dagger training."

Stephen took off his goggles. "I could go to a poetry meeting with you, if you want company."

"No," Jacob replied.

"If you'd like to hear Jacob's work, forget it," said Elizabeth. "Even his poetry group probably hasn't heard any of his poems yet, and he's attended their sessions for ten years."

Twelve years. Jacob was a founding member of the Dreamers Guild. And no, he did not share his poetry there, either. No matter how much his friends prodded him.

"It's not good to be stretched so thin all the time," Kuni insisted. One of her hands rested on her own stomach, just below the row of hidden blades stitched beneath her bodice.

Jacob knew she and her husband, Graham, were hoping for children of their own. He also knew better than to ask about it. If there were any news, he would be the first to hear. Some things took time—and luck. He understood how uniquely frustrating it was to be hounded about when he planned to achieve something that was ultimately outside his control.

"We're all stretched thin. So if you'll excuse me—" His head jerked toward Elizabeth, who had taken a step backward to whisper to her husband. "What did you just say?"

"It's this fellow Sir Gareth Jallow," Stephen said helpfully. "Elizabeth is obsessed with—"

Elizabeth elbowed him in the ribs. "I said *not* to mention him out loud."

Jacob's entire body tensed. "I thought you didn't read poetry. Balderdash for romantics, you said."

She coughed into her fist. "I don't. That is, not usually. But everyone reads Sir Gar...who must not be named."

He sighed. "I can hear the man's name."

"You really can't," said Kuni. "You explicitly warned us never to say those syllables in your presence."

Jacob crossed his arms. Was he jealous of Sir Gareth Jallow? Absolutely. Bone deep. But did he *hate* Jallow? Yes. Maybe. Sometimes. With self-loathing. And anger. This was not who he wanted to be.

In other words, it was complicated. Which was why Jacob would rather not discuss his feelings. There was no telling what unedited words might burst from his mouth.

He glanced at his pocket watch. Blast the interruption! It was time for the next mission already. "Stand clear of the exit, please."

The others scrambled aside.

Jacob pushed the barn doors open wide and gave the whistle.

Ferrets began to stream down the barn's walls and across the dirt floor from every shadowy nook. They arranged themselves in rectangular formation behind Jacob as he marched from the barn like the Pied Piper of Hamelin.

"Close the door when you're done cleaning up!" he called out without looking back. There was no time to delay.

He and his scampering furry army had a legal trial to disrupt.

3

The next morning, with Rufus underfoot, Viv cooked breakfast while straining to read snippets of the new novel she was enjoying. The book was propped up against a water pitcher and held open with a rolling pin. Between cracking eggs and flipping fried potatoes, the scene she was reading was rising to an exciting apex—when it cut off mid-word because the rest of the paragraph was hidden behind the wooden rolling pin.

She reached out with her elbow to nudge the rolling pin out of the way when the front door flew open. Quentin strode inside, the morning newspaper beneath his arm and a new mountain of letters piled in his hands.

Viv served breakfast for herself and her cousin but picked up a handful of correspondence rather than her fork. She broke the wax seals with a knife. "Question for the advice column...Question for the advice column...Another question for the advice column...And new letters from my colleagues!"

Using the word *colleague* was the opposite of brutal honesty. "Colleague" was a big fat fib. Viv's playwright friends were paid professionals, who'd all had at least one play performed in a major theater.

Viv had never received so much as a flicker of interest from a minor theater.

Or even successfully tempted the amateurs who acted out scenes at parties or in parks for a lark.

But these talented playwrights were the best friends she had. They were *going* to be her colleagues. She just had to work harder. Be better than everyone else. And eventually, by God, someone, somewhere, would have no choice but to give her a chance.

It was hard enough to convince the male-dominated world to take a female seriously. Much less an immigrant. Much less a Black woman. Much less a would-be playwright. There were unspoken rules about whose stories deserved to be told, and people like her did not qualify. No matter how fine the writing might be.

She tried to concentrate on sifting through her post. The next three missives in a row were rejections from various theaters for her play about suffrage. She had so hoped the manager of the Olympic might at least have *considered*...Well, it was their loss.

If Viv could write her own future, it might read like:

Olympic Theater: Please allow us to perform your magnificent play, Miss Henry.

Vivian: I'm sorry, but the Opera House has already paid handsomely for the exclusive rights for the next full year.

Olympic Theater: Then let us have something else you've written. Anything at all.

Vivian: Well...I do have a play about Black suffragists. And another about the atrocities committed by British and European plantation owners on their slaves. And another about the evils perpetuated in South Asia by the East India Company. And another about the irreparable harm done by the British monarchy in its relentless attempts to colonize and subjugate existing communities throughout the world.

Olympic Theater: Yes! Splendid! We'll take them all! It is past time that such truths be told, and your voice is just the one to speak out.

Unfortunately, it was just a fantasy. Particularly the scripts about suffrage. To even speak the words *equal voting rights* publicly risked being beheaded in the street.

Viv rose from the table to toss the letters into their specifically designated baskets in the corner.

Quentin watched her. "If you already know everyone is going to say no, then why do you keep trying?"

"They don't all say no. Most don't bother to respond at all. A small percentage reply with a variety of 'I'm sure you're a nice lady, but we receive hundreds of submissions from proven professionals and don't have time to read the inferior first drafts from amateurs like you.'"

Quentin looked at the overflowing basket. "That's a small percentage? How many times do you plan on asking?"

"As many as it takes. I can achieve *anything* if I'm good enough. The key to success is not giving up. I will succeed, and I'll do it on my own."

"You do everything on your own," said Quentin. "Except eat. Your eggs are getting cold."

Viv shoved a forkful into her mouth. He was right. Her carefully cooked eggs were now ghastly.

"I'd have more time," she said carefully, "if I weren't the only one managing the household chores."

She hated how awkward it was to broach this topic. On the one hand, it was unreasonable to expect her to accomplish twice as many tasks as could fit into a day. On the other hand, Quentin wasn't obliged to offer a roof over her head at all. His meager trust was meant for him, not him and a hanger-on.

"Sorry, can't help you," he said with his mouth full. "Our secret society—"

"Quentin—"

"I mean 'innocent group of non-seditious friends,'" he corrected himself. "In order to become the new wave of Wynchesters, we're widening the region in which we operate—"

"You don't have a region, and you don't *operate*. No one with half a brain has mistaken you or any of your friends for an actual—"

"Yes, they have! They *do*. Every day!" he insisted. "No one knows how many Wynchesters there are, so it's easy to pretend to be Nancy or Phineas or anyone else we make up."

"I know exactly how many there are."

True, but not the point. Viv was letting herself get swept into an old argument rather than insist they stay on a difficult topic.

Perhaps she never forced a reckoning about the uneven responsibilities in their household because some of the possible solutions would be worse than the problem.

"*You're* trying to change the world," he said hotly. "Why shouldn't I?"

Though she feared for her cousin every day, Viv didn't want to stifle his spirit. They weren't living in the dangerous environment where she'd been raised. Quentin's biggest fear was spending his quarterly trust money too quickly, not the sting of a whip.

"And we do operate," he insisted. "The Wynchesters are like Bow Street Runners, but better. Instead of helping only wealthy clients, they help anyone who needs them. That's what my friends and I are doing. Whatever we can, for whoever needs it. We might not have much impact now, but Newt and I have plans to—" His mouth shut tight with an audible click of the teeth.

Viv narrowed her eyes. She'd never heard of any Newt but already didn't like him. "You'd better not have plans to do anything dangerous or stupid. Swear to me none of you are foolish enough to commit actual crimes."

He glared at her stonily, then gave a single short nod.

It wasn't a particularly convincing vow.

"I mean it," she warned him. "Let your friends throw their lives away as they wish, but promise me *you* are clever enough never to even appear as though you might have been involved in something punishable by law."

He lifted his chin.

She ground her teeth. *This* was why she hated the Wynchesters. Aspiring to be like them was going to get her cousin killed. At eighteen, Quentin was still young enough to believe himself invincible. At eight-and-twenty, Viv was old enough to have seen firsthand how tragically mortal her loved ones really were.

She tried again. "The Seditious Meetings Act alone—"

"No one knows our secret society exists but you, and I'm sorry I ever told you," Quentin burst out. "I said we're being careful. But if it makes you feel better, I'll suggest we move our meetings. No one will overhear us if we convene in the cellars of a sympathetic church, or deep in the canal tunnels, or if we're outside the city in the mining caves."

"Canal tunnels?" she choked out. "They'd find you when your body floats up because you can't swim! Either let me teach you how or stay away from the river."

"No matter what I say or do, you always manage to find fault with it," he said with disgust. "When will you stop treating me like a child?"

Was that what she was doing? Viv's fears were well founded,

but did that supersede his autonomy? She wondered if this was how mothers felt whose sons Quentin's age eagerly joined the army, knowing the next time they saw their child, he might be in a casket.

If they could find the body at all.

"All right," she forced herself to say. "I can script plays, but not your life. That's for you to write. But as someone who loves you with all my heart, I can't promise to stay silent if I think you're making a terrible mistake."

He snorted. "The only time you're silent is when you're sleeping, and probably not then, either."

They exchanged tentative smiles, but the tension was still thick between them. At least today he'd left his fresh twists alone and looked mostly like himself. If a bit overdressed for eight o'clock in the morning.

She raised her brows. "Who are you supposed to be this time?"

"Baron Vanderbean," he said proudly.

Viv frowned. "Didn't he die a few years ago? As an old man?"

"The Wynchesters' estranged adoptive brother inherited his father's title." Quentin smoothed his hands down the lapels of his finest dark-blue frock coat. A coordinating pale-blue waistcoat peeked beneath his extravagantly folded cravat. "Today, that's me."

Viv didn't have the heart to tell him his clothes were handsome, but not aristocratic quality. A more pertinent detail would give up the ruse at first glance.

"Wouldn't that be...a white man?"

"He doesn't have to be. The Vanderbean barony is from Balcovia. That's an abolitionist nation. Which means the baron could look like anyone, including me."

"Still improbable," she murmured.

"Is it? *My* natural father was a white British lord. If he'd married my mother, I would have an aristocratic title right now."

"But he didn't and you don't. And you wouldn't have anything to do with the Wynchesters if you were titled, either."

"You don't know that. In fact..." His eyes lit up. "You can do anything you put your mind to. Find a way for me to have an audience with the Wynchesters!"

"Over my dead body."

His face fell, anger replacing his hopefulness. "Then I wish *you* would meet them all. I'm sure they'd change your mind if you got to know them."

"No one has ever changed my mind," she snapped, "and the first to do so certainly won't be the dangerously irresponsible Wynchesters. Speaking of dangerously irresponsible, do you know how illegal it is to impersonate a peer of the realm?"

"Balcovian peer," he reminded her. "Not British. It's not this jurisdiction, not that England respects Balcovia anyway. Their royalty hasn't been invited back since the day the Queen of Balcovia and her retinue argued for abolition of slavery throughout all the British territories."

"Well, I don't want you *deported*, either," Viv said dryly.

"My club suspects Baron Vanderbean isn't even real," Quentin protested. "I can't be prosecuted for impersonating a peer that doesn't exist."

"I'm not so certain." Viv sighed. "For heaven's sake, why are you so taken by that family?"

"Because they're wonderful. You don't have to be born into their ranks, like the aristocracy. Parentage doesn't matter. The Wynchesters aren't blood related. They're a family because they decided to be."

"I appreciate their diverse backgrounds and their varied appearances and capabilities," Viv allowed. "But that doesn't make it safe for ordinary people to emulate them. Their privileged status isn't replicable by the masses. They got lucky. They were adopted by the right aristocrat. People like us, on the other hand..."

"People like us," Quentin repeated dreamily, his eggs forgotten. "Can you imagine? You and I might not have influence or power today, but if we were Wynchesters..."

"You and I?" She set down her fork. "Quentin, look in a mirror. We are not the same. You are a man, and I am a woman. Your light skin grants you access to most environments, whereas my Black skin is the first thing anyone notices about me. That is, until I open my mouth and they hear my accent. You were born here in England—"

"But, Viv, don't you see that all those qualities would make you a perfect Wynchester?"

"You must be joking. They're self-important miscreants who flout society and break laws whenever it suits them, and they have the money to get away with it. Their hypocritical self-righteousness makes it even worse."

"You're just jealous—"

"I don't begrudge them their privilege," Viv snapped. "I think we should *all* have the same rights."

"Well, we don't. And I'm not going to sit around waiting for it." Quentin shoved back his chair.

"Equality isn't something you're going to find under a rock. Some people are born into wealth or the aristocracy. The Wynchesters were fortunate enough to be adopted into it. Whereas we—"

"Speak for yourself." He shot up from the table. "*I* was born to an aristocrat, and all it got me was a quarterly pittance from a man who never bothered to meet me face-to-face. Forgive me if I prefer to follow the example of the people daring to challenge the status quo."

"You're going to follow their example right into a death sentence," she said desperately.

His eyes flashed. "You're being dramatic. I'd say it's because you're a dramatist, but that looks like it's just a dream. Maybe you're holding *me* back because *you* can't get ahead."

She gasped at the vicious words—but couldn't deny a grain of truth might hide within them. She was aware that she sometimes still treated him as though he were in short pants. Was that in part because once Quentin fully became an adult, he'd take a wife and Viv would be shown out?

"I'm just asking you to consider potential consequences," she said quietly. "The Wynchesters do what they want because they *can*. The law is lethal to those without their advantages."

"Well, I have advantages, too. You told me to stop wasting my trust funds by changing tutors and hobbies every month. If I now have a purpose in life I want to spend my time and money on—"

"Oh, I agree, time and money certainly *are* advantages not everyone has. Look at me, for example! Whilst you're out running around, I don't have time to leave this kitchen, much less the house."

"You're not the one paying for it, are you? I'm the one keeping a roof over our heads."

"And I'm the one who constantly has to patch it! If one of your hobbies could be 'helping with dishes' or you took some tutoring on 'cleaning up after yourself'—"

"You know what, Miss Know-All? Why don't you save your sack of endless know-all opinions for the misguided fools who explicitly ask you for them?"

He stalked from the kitchen and through the front door.

She hurried after him. "Quentin, wait!"

He didn't wait.

She sprinted to his side. When she tried to kiss his cheek, Quentin ducked out of range and jogged away from her down the busy street without looking back.

"Be back home by suppertime," she called out.

He didn't answer.

"You might beat me at cards this time!"

He didn't slow. Soon, he was around the corner and out of sight.

She reentered the house, then slumped against the front door with a sigh. He *would* be home by supper. He always was. They would play cards. She might even let him win.

Quentin was ignoring her out of spite, just to hurt her—and it was working.

She felt awful.

But not nearly as bad as Viv felt ten hours later, when Quentin's dinner congealed on his untouched plate. Her hurt feelings bubbled into irritation. Expecting her to cook for him and then not even showing up to eat it was incredibly inconsiderate.

She cleaned the dishes and the kitchen, then retook her seat with a deck of cards. Although Viv was dying to finish the book she'd started, she didn't want Quentin's arrival home to interrupt a pivotal plot moment, and risk him seeing even the tiniest flash of frustration in her face. She wanted to make up with her cousin, not make the situation worse.

What she needed was a distraction. Work was always the solution, and there was an unanswered pile of correspondence waiting for her.

She strode to the waist-high cabinet lining one wall of the kitchen. The narrow sideboard on top was never used to hold food, but rather as a repository for Viv's endless stacks of paper.

There were piles for everything: advice column letters to be answered, replies to be posted, plays to be sent to theater managers, drafts in progress, silly scenes she'd dashed out using the wilder anonymous advice questions as inspiration, letters from her playwright friends, and retired scripts that hadn't found a home anywhere and now lived in a dusty corner of the sideboard.

She carried her pen and ink to the kitchen table and set about crafting replies to her correspondence.

A yipping dog...a bothersome sister-in-law...a quarrel over an inheritance...a husband who'd placed an embargo on new bonnets... a wife who had suffered several difficult pregnancies and did not wish to keep bearing children...a valet who butted heads with the butler... a governess whose unruly charges wouldn't sit still for lessons...a petulant individual who wished to know the best way to incapacitate his enemies without being caught...

"Not this oatcake again," Viv muttered, shaking her head.

It sounded like the same man or woman who kept asking for advice on blackmail and kidnapping and robbery. Though Viv turned the outlandish scenarios into scripts, she'd never responded to the letter-writer himself. The farthing she lost out on by not answering was worth the peace of mind of not becoming involved. She couldn't even imagine why the enthusiast kept sending such scenarios. Soon, she supposed, they would tire of being ignored and move on to pester someone else.

Viv forced herself not to watch the time until she composed answers to all the legitimate questions. There—twenty-three responses. One answer shy of earning two full shillings.

She eyed the vanquish-my-enemies letter. No, absolutely not. Engaging with an unstable individual would be irresponsible. She'd turn the missed opportunity into a comedic script. Much better than encouraging the fan to send in even more of his disturbing scenarios.

After tying a string on the pile of responses to be sent to the newsletter office, Viv carried the enemy-quashing letter over to the sideboard to join the other unanswered letters and their respective scripts.

Naturally, she couldn't find the proper pile. Quentin had clearly been meddling in her paperwork again. One more argument to look forward to. Her stomach twisted at the thought.

All right, the work was done. She could check the clock.

Midnight. And still no sign of Quentin.

Her heart sank. It wasn't unusual for him to disappear all day long with his friends. But this *was* the first time he'd missed supper and their standing evening game of cards.

He was clearly doing this for attention. To prove some kind of point. Hours ago, Viv had been ready to beg forgiveness. But now it was Quentin who would need to atone for making her worry on purpose.

It *was* a tantrum, wasn't it?

As the minutes ticked into hours, it became increasingly unlikely that Viv would be able to keep the anger from her face when her cousin finally deigned to return home from his precious club that mattered more than his cousin.

Except that didn't sound like Quentin at all.

The few bites of supper she'd managed to swallow were now burbling with acid in her gut. Was he all right? Horrific scenarios crossed her mind with lightning speed. *Anything* could happen to an idealistic lad like him.

Quentin was fine, she reassured herself. This was nothing more than her overactive imagination at play.

So she shuffled the deck and played yet another solitary hand of patience while she waited.

And waited.

When Quentin finally showed his face, she would give him an earful—and then cross her arms and await a much-deserved apology for worrying her. And then they would have a long chat about how they could both be better cousins to the other.

But when she woke up bleary-eyed at dawn, with a bent jack of spades stuck to her cheek...

Quentin was still gone.

4

In honor of their brother Graham's birthday, Jacob's sister Chloe and her husband, the Duke of Faircliffe, had brought their baby Dorian for a visit. While the kitchen prepared cakes and pies, the others gathered in the sibling sitting room.

Jacob and Chloe were enjoying a rare moment alone in one of the parlors.

Almost alone. Chloe's baby, Dorian, balanced on her hip, flapping his chubby white arms, beamed at Jacob with a delighted grin.

"What's wrong?" Chloe asked.

With anyone outside of the family, Jacob would have answered *nothing*.

He admitted, "When you first married Faircliffe, there was an empty space left behind. We felt as though we'd lost you."

Her face filled with sympathy. "The six of us lived under the same roof for so long. It was hard for me, too."

"But then the others also found someone new," he continued. "Like you, Elizabeth married and moved across town, but Tommy, Graham, and Marjorie each brought their spouses home. Our house now holds more Wynchesters than ever."

Chloe's eyes softened with sudden understanding. "And yet, as the only sibling not to have found love, you feel more isolated than ever?"

He sighed. "It's silly, isn't it."

"I'd say completely understandable. Especially since the only time any of us get together lately is to discuss a new case, not chat with each other. But we love you, even if we rarely have time to say it anymore."

"I know." He gave Chloe and the baby a hug. "I love you all, too."

Dorian squeezed Jacob's cheek. Chloe grinned and passed Jacob the baby.

"How are you?" he asked as he cuddled his nephew.

"Exhausted," she admitted. "Despite my husband's ongoing efforts in the House of Lords, we've made no progress on equal voting rights. Parliament is presenting a new militia act later tonight. Supposedly just administrative changes to make matters more efficient, but some fear it's yet another show of force against commoners. You should hear the things some of the lords say in their arguments."

"I'd rather keep my sanity," Jacob said wryly.

"A wise choice. You need a clear mind for your poetry. If you don't make time for your dream—"

"I've made enough time for it," he said vaguely.

She smiled. "Perhaps one day you'll be rich and famous."

"We're already rich and famous," he reminded her.

In Jacob's case, wealthier than his wildest dreams. Years back, he'd stopped checking his bank balance because the number was nonsensical.

"A gift like yours shouldn't be wasted," Chloe insisted.

He blew raspberries on the baby's plump cheeks rather than respond.

His sister elbowed him in the side. "Who knows...You could be the next Sir Gareth Jallow!"

Jacob rolled his eyes. "England isn't ready for *that* much change."

Famed poet Sir Gareth Jallow was a white knight—or perhaps a baronet, no one was quite sure.

Jacob was an untitled Black man. Because Black men couldn't have titles. Or, apparently, enjoy lucrative poetry careers. It was white men who were published all over England and invited to recite their works at all the most prestigious events.

"I don't need to see my name on the cover of a book," Jacob informed her, keeping his voice calm and firm, the same way he spoke to his Highland tiger.

Chloe didn't look convinced. "You don't think it would be marvelous?"

"No," he answered honestly. "How do *you* think the public would react to books bearing my name?"

"I'd say I don't give a fig about the opinions of anyone who would object to your well-earned success, but my feelings don't matter. You should do as *you* want."

Should he? Could he?

It wasn't as though he hadn't fantasized about it a thousand times. But if Jacob Wynchester were a household name, everyone would look at him differently. Not just the people on the street, but his own family. Who loved him just as he was. So why would he change that?

He already had a life he adored. How many people of any color or class had a barn full of clever animals and a family who fought for justice wherever it was needed?

This home was Jacob's place. Being a Wynchester was how he fit into his family, and into society, and into the world. It was fine. He knew how lucky he was. He was fortunate enough to help *other* people, every single day. Only a self-important prick would aspire for more.

Which...didn't bode well, because Jacob secretly did long to see his name embossed on leather tomes all over the country:

JACOB WYNCHESTER, CELEBRATED POET

He wanted to be known for accomplishments in his own right, and not just as a nameless, faceless, behind-the-curtains animal trainer for the Wild Wynchesters.

But some dreams were just that: a happy fiction.

"If you're not going to be a famous poet," Chloe began slyly, "you could consider being a suitor."

"Not you, too." Jacob groaned. "Did Elizabeth and Marjorie put you up to this?"

"They love you. We all want you to be happy."

"Do I have to marry to be happy?" He looked down at the smiling baby on his lap. "Maybe I don't want a wife."

Her eyes widened with interest. "Do you want a husband?"

"Maybe I'm happy caring for my animals."

She gave him a long look, then smiled gently. "You're right. We shouldn't push. If it's meant to be, it'll happen."

Footsteps sounded in the hallway. Jacob glanced up, expecting to find one of his impatient siblings shooing them into the main room for cakes.

Instead, it was Mr. Randall, their butler. "Pardon the interruption. Do you want the mail, or shall I take it to the others?"

"Are those missives from Graham's informants?" Chloe asked.

"No, I'm afraid it's just a regular post delivery."

"I'll take it." Jacob handed Chloe her baby so he could collect the pile of mail.

"What's that?" She peered over his shoulder. "It looks like it's from a publisher."

It was indeed. The usual *Dear Mr. Wynchester* rejection that all of Jacob's authorial intents engendered.

He crumpled it up and tossed it in the fireplace.

A move that would have been exponentially more satisfying if warm spring afternoons required a lit fire. The current rejection simply sat in a ball of white paper between two logs, along with several more of its brethren. This was the last of several publishers to reject Jacob's latest compilation of poetry without even reading it.

"Keep trying," Chloe said with sympathy. "Some things are difficult to achieve, but worth it in the end."

"Mm-hm," he murmured noncommittally.

"I'm sure you're not the only one whose work has been rejected," she added. "Probably even famous poets like Sir Gareth didn't become country-wide sensations on their first try."

"Jallow landed the first publisher he spoke to," Jacob said sourly.

"Well..." Chloe bit her lip. "There's no reason to be jealous of him."

"I never said I was jealous."

Why would anyone be jealous of the way Jallow's books were on every shelf in every shop and home in London? Or the legions of fans who memorized every word he'd ever written, in order to drop a line or two into casual conversation to appear cultured and worldly? The way Sir Gareth Jallow's name was spoken with awe and respect?

"I just think..." Chloe began.

"Can we please change the subject?" he begged.

Sir Gareth's success and Jacob Wynchester's lack thereof was as complicated as his feelings on the matter. Any attempt at entertaining the conversation without divulging things he'd rather keep to himself was awkward at best, and excruciating at worst. And he feared what words might blurt out of his mouth if he were backed into a corner.

"Gah!" gurgled Dorian.

"You're right," Chloe cooed. "That other letter does look different. Perhaps Uncle Jacob will read that to us instead."

He glanced down but didn't recognize the handwriting. "It's addressed to 'Wynchester Family.'"

"Well, we're the Wynchester family," she said with a smile. "Open it whilst I attempt to mop up some of Dorian's drool."

Jacob scanned the contents, then rolled his eyes. "Another day, another jester."

"What is it this time?" she asked.

He snorted. "Whoever sent this expects us to believe they've kidnapped Horace Wynchester."

Chloe burst out laughing. "How exactly does one kidnap a figment of our imagination?"

Before their adoptive father died, Bean created a fictitious "heir" that any of the siblings could impersonate if they needed the support of a Balcovian baron to achieve a goal. Horace Wynchester would be the new Baron Vanderbean...*if* he existed, which he did not. Their fictitious sibling certainly hadn't been kidnapped.

"Such nonsense," said Chloe. "The last time anyone used the baron identity was years ago, when Tommy was courting Philippa."

Jacob grinned at the memory. "As far as anyone recalls, Horace is a skinny white lad whose tender heart was absolutely crushed by Philippa's eventual indifference."

After Tommy stopped being the baron, the family let slip that the new heir had returned to Balcovia for an indeterminate amount of time. They hadn't thought about old Horace since.

Chloe dabbed at Dorian's cheeks. "And now someone's trying to ransom our make-believe relative for money?"

Jacob skimmed the rest of the letter. "Even more peculiar: We're to 'cease all investigations' if we ever wish to see poor imaginary Horace again."

"Even if such a person existed, why would anyone fall for this balderdash?"

"Such an amateurish extortion attempt. They've included no proof of their claim—"

"Because Horace Wynchester isn't real," Chloe interjected with a laugh.

"—nor does the kidnapper indicate any method for us to contact them for further steps." He crumpled the silly hoax into a satisfying ball and tossed it into the fireplace with the other rejections. "We receive preposterous letters from chuckleheads like this at least once a month, and it never amounts to anything."

"Marjorie thinks we should collect the zaniest letters and save them in an album we can look through whenever we need a laugh," Chloe reminded him.

They both looked at the unlit fireplace. It was impossible to tell at a glance which of the many paper balls behind the grate was the kidnapping note, and which belonged to an entire month's worth of rejections.

"Bah," said Jacob. "That one isn't worth the effort. By the time we've finished our cakes, we'll have forgotten all about it."

5

Viv did her best not to panic.

At eighteen years of age, Quentin was an adult man, whether she liked to admit it or not. He could not be expected to plan his life around the whims of his twenty-eight-year-old spinster cousin.

Nonetheless, if he *had* spent the night with one of his friends, the least he could have done was let her know he would not be coming home. He knew she would have supper on the stove and playing cards ready on the table, watching the clock as she awaited his return.

Quentin wasn't that cruel. Was he?

They'd also never argued like they had the previous morning. Some hurtful things had been said, on both sides. She would have thought their bond was strong enough to weather worse than that. But if so, then where was he?

"Deep breaths," Viv commanded herself aloud, her voice unrecognizably high and shaky. "Think it through."

It was inevitable that at some point her baby cousin was going to grow up. He'd have activities and interests other than the orphan spinster who had been his nursemaid, guardian, and confidante since he was eight years old.

She supposed him being out past dawn was the natural progression of a boy becoming a man and stretching his wings. At some point, Quentin would stay out all night for other reasons. Clubs, drink, women. He would soon fall in love and wish to marry, and thus need *Viv* to find somewhere else to stay.

Was that the answer? He'd spent the night with a secret paramour? Someone whose existence he had not yet divulged, because of the catastrophic effect it would have on Viv's own future?

She hoped that wasn't the case and despised herself for it. Maybe Quentin was right. She *was* holding him back, because it was better for her if he didn't grow up. A serious character flaw, if she'd ever seen one.

Her advice column paid a pittance, and she was contractually prohibited from performing as Ask Vivian outside of the newspaper. The best she'd been able to negotiate was for the paper to offer a guaranteed private response in exchange for a small fee, half of which was shared with Viv. She was popular enough now that almost every letter earned an extra half-penny.

It was better than nothing, but still far from enough. To afford rooms of her own, she needed theater managers to take her and her work seriously.

Or you need a partner, she could hear her mother say. *A husband*.

Out of the question. Viv could not consider courtship until she'd made something of herself on her own. Before opening a door to potential suitors, she had to prove herself first. Her future husband would discover his wife to be competent, and self-sufficient, and successful.

Viv never wanted to feel disadvantaged—or enslaved—ever again.

Nor could she stand feeling this alone.

For Quentin to live a long, happy life had been her sole priority from the moment her toes touched British soil. She might have had a different career by now if she'd spent half as much time pursuing her own dreams as she did ensuring that all of Quentin's came true.

He'd been acting oddly the past few days. She'd suspected him of hiding something from her on more than one occasion. But even if she entertained the notion of love at first sight, when would Quentin have met this mystery woman? While he was out performing ill-advised acts of skullduggery with chalk in his hair?

Maybe, she was forced to admit. The fact that his secret society needed false names and disguises for their missions necessarily implied that there was a client to please. Perhaps a pretty one Quentin's age, who had long prayed to be rescued by a strapping young lad with the high spirit of a pony and the fashion sense of a rag bin.

"Blast it all, where are you?" she asked the empty house.

What would Quentin do? What would he want *her* to do? The answer to both questions was the same: call in the Wynchesters.

Pfft. That was a low she would never bring herself to. She could not be manipulated in such a way. Viv hurried to the sideboard and extracted the journal she'd been keeping about Quentin since he was small.

It had begun as a practical repository of knowledge. Favorite foods, and which ones made him sneeze. Dates of illnesses, along with associated symptoms, and which remedies actually worked.

As he grew, so did her notes. Funny things he said, recurring nightmares, friends, obsessions, hobbies, education, activities, places frequented. He would be embarrassed to know just how thoroughly she had chronicled his life.

But this fat little book was going to help her find him.

After feeding Rufus and checking on Sally one last time, Viv wedged a small green leaf in the crack of the front door. Upon her return, she would know at once if Quentin had made it back before her.

She started with the likeliest sources of information: the members of his secret society. The lads ranged in age from sixteen to four-and-twenty. Though they winkingly refused to admit any such secret club existed, they each spoke highly and enthusiastically about Quentin.

He was a wonderful chap, a right honorable fellow, steadfast and friendly, always up for anything.

"Like what, precisely?" she asked. "Where was he last night? Where is he today?"

The bubbly responses dried up instantly, each secret society member after the other staring at her with the same bafflement. Quentin was missing? Was she certain? Where did he go?

It was enough to make her lose her mind. Halfway down her list, she remembered the odd name Quentin had mentioned before storming out.

This time, the responses were cagier. Newt? Never heard of him. But if Quentin *were* with such a person, they guaranteed he was off doing normal, non-illegal activities. No disguises or capers or seditious acts. And definitely nothing risky or dangerous.

She might have been desperate enough to believe them, if they'd managed to look her in the eye while making these claims. And if the assurances weren't identical, down to the word.

They all advised her to go home and stop worrying, and genuinely seemed to believe there was no cause for concern.

Despite their assurances, Viv's anxiety ratcheted higher with each failed interview. If Quentin were fine, he would have communicated with her by now. Something was wrong. She knew it.

Viv would stop worrying when she found him.

After there were no more friends to interview, she resorted to acquaintances, then prior haunts. Each stop was less enlightening than the last. When she found herself knocking on the door of the barber who'd helped pull one of Quentin's milk teeth after an infection nine years ago, Viv finally conceded defeat.

Despite how thoroughly she'd *thought* she had chronicled his life, neither her brain nor her book were leading her to Quentin.

At home, the little leaf was right where she'd left it.

Full-on panic set in.

Annoyed or not, Quentin wouldn't do this to her. Viv's affectionate puppy of a cousin was either horribly injured, or in mortal danger...or dead.

The worst part was, she wasn't overreacting. She'd seen firsthand the lethal consequences to rule-breaking and good intentions.

Life on the Demerara sugar plantation had been a living hell. Of *course* all of the enslaved residents wanted to rise up against their supposed masters and fight for independence. They also knew exactly what would happen if a momentary flicker of defiance accidentally flashed across their face.

Viv's mother knew the rules and believed breaking them was a risk worth dying for. At eleven years old, Viv hadn't truly comprehended that such an unthinkable outcome could really come to pass.

Until it did.

Her brave, desperate mother was hopeful until the very end. She whispered, schemed, planned. A coordinated uprising in three weeks at dawn. Yes, the aristocratic landowners and the cruel overseers who controlled their plantations had guns, but there were dozens of slaves and only a handful of guards. Rifles must be reloaded between shots, which meant they couldn't *all* die. Some lucky percentage would get away. Escape to much-deserved freedom.

They never got the chance to try.

The head overseer caught wind of the wrong whisper. He didn't ask questions. He dragged Viv's mother by the hair into a clearing in the sugar field and shot her in front of everyone.

Viv couldn't even say goodbye. One minute, she was working at her mother's side, humming a favorite song in harmony...and the next minute, her mother's blood was splattered over her clothes.

They didn't even let her clean up. *Back to work, all of you, lest you wish to be next to die.*

Part of her *did* want to. Eleven years old, no mother or any hope for a better future. If things went "well," she'd have blistered feet and bleeding hands for decades to come. Mother was right. It was no sort of life to live.

As Viv grew older, the desire for revenge increased within her. Along with an unquenchable yearning for freedom. She kept hoping that one of the adults might pick up her mother's thread, but no one wished to be made an example of. Mother's death had been quick, but the overseer promised the next one would not be. Weeks of slow, merciless torture for as long as the rule-breaker's body still gasped for breath.

When Viv turned eighteen, she was willing to chance it. She'd been born into a life of hell and could not continue. If they all worked together, if they were very, very careful, *this* time the rebellion—

Was likewise cut off at the source. Viv was tied to a tree to be publicly tortured until she named her co-conspirators. There was no sense confessing. Her captors would kill her regardless. The only thing to gain was a marginally quicker death—assuming they could be trusted to show mercy. Viv knew better than to trust her "betters."

If the summons to Lord Ayleswick's English residence had arrived even a few days later, Viv would not be out of her mind today with worry about Quentin.

She'd be in an unmarked grave, just like her mother. That was what happened when the unprivileged dared to break rules.

From that day forth she swore never to lose another family member to the careless whims of those in power ever again, no matter what sacrifices that might entail. When she became Quentin's guardian, she vowed to his dying mother to protect her orphaned cousin at all costs.

And if she couldn't do it on her own, it was time for reinforcements. Bow Street it was.

She donned her best dress, taking extra special care with her hair.

Not out of vanity but because if she wished for an authority figure to take her seriously, she needed every possible advantage.

It didn't help.

The first Bow Street Runner she'd ever seen in her life shut the door in her face before she'd even finished giving her name.

Viv banged on the door with both fists until it reopened, this time revealing two gentlemen. One was the same ill-tempered white man as before. The second at least looked at her with curiosity rather than contempt.

By their posture and expressions, she deduced that the second man held seniority, a situation the first was none too happy about. Given the conspicuous finery of the rude investigator's clothes and the whiff of cheap gin clinging to his person, the first Runner was not dealing well with his wish to appear more important than he was.

The more successful man holding the door open, however, had paper cuts on his ink-stained fingers. His clothes were wrinkled in such a way that indicated long hours behind a desk, and the soles of his shoes were worn thin from constant movement investigating his cases. This was a man who made progress. Exactly what was needed.

"I need your help," Viv said in a rush.

"Of course," said the more pleasant of the two men. "I am Basil Newbury, and this is my colleague John Yarrow. What is your name?"

Thank God. "Vivian Henry."

"And what appears to be the matter?"

"My cousin Quentin. He's missing. It's been two days—"

"How old is he?" Yarrow interrupted.

"Eighteen, but—"

"So, no longer under your thumb, eh? Lads do what lads do. There's no case here."

"He knows I worry," she blurted out. "If he were able to, he would have sent word."

"Not if he's a runaway," said Yarrow. "Maybe he's done having words with you."

This stung, having hit a little too close.

"He's not a runaway," Viv gritted out. "I'm the indigent, and *he's* the one with trust money. Why would he run away from that?"

"Aha," said Yarrow. "It's not your cousin you're after, but his pocketbook."

Viv gave up on him and turned to Newbury. "Quentin is a good lad, but impulsive. Anything could have happened to him."

"Is he an English citizen?"

"Why wouldn't he—" Oh. Her accent. "Yes, he's an English citizen."

"You cannot be taking this seriously," said Yarrow. "*Look* at her. We're wasting our time."

"Look at me?" Viv repeated, her limbs and voice shaking. "What about my appearance wastes your time? That I'm poor? That I'm a woman? That I'm Black? That I'm an immigrant?"

Yarrow made a careless, palms-up gesture as though to say, *You said it, not me.*

Newbury looked chagrined. "My apologies, miss. It pains me not to be able to help, but we investigate crimes, and there's no evidence of one. Good luck, and good day."

This time, when the door closed in her face, Viv knew it was final. No one here would help.

Much as it galled her, if professional investigators charged with protecting the public would not help...Viv would have to resort to the *un*professionals. The rule-flouting, law-breaking, self-appointed Robin Hoods of the lower classes.

The Wynchesters.

6

Her legs stiff and her hands clenched into fists, Viv stalked the two miles from her humble dwellings in Cheapside to Islington, where the infamous caper-committing family of delinquents was supposed to live.

It wasn't so much the bending of the rules she objected to. Viv had once plotted a full-on revolt. It was that reckless, privileged pets like the Wild Wynchesters got away with anything they dreamed up. The smug, do-right family didn't even acknowledge the injustice they themselves were perpetrating. Instead, they were idolized and lauded for their law-breaking, whereas people like Viv were beaten and imprisoned and executed for far lesser crimes.

Celebrated career criminals masquerading as poor-me, down-on-their-luck orphans, as if anyone could have what they had just by wanting it hard enough.

She and Quentin were orphans, too, and their circumstances were far removed from the wealthy, famous Wynchesters, for whom neither laws nor etiquette seemed to apply. As far as Viv was concerned, their legendary status and overblown heroics were nothing more than perfume on a pig.

But she would do anything for Quentin. She loved her cousin and would never forgive herself if her personal distaste prevented him from returning home safely.

The Wynchesters' house was massive. A white-columned monstrosity with three stories, huge windows, and an immaculate front garden. The rear garden was walled from view. Likely to keep undesirables like her in her place.

She straightened her bonnet and marched up to the front door, fist poised to knock.

Before she could do so, the door swung open. An older white man with blue eyes, white hair, and a surprisingly pleasant expression greeted her with, "Good afternoon, madam. How may I be of service?"

Viv blinked at him as her brain struggled to recalculate. Had she *ever* been called madam? By anyone? Even in jest?

"Um..." she managed. What on earth was wrong with her? If there was one thing in her life that had never been in short supply, it was her words.

The butler smiled. "Are you here to see the Wynchesters?"

She nodded.

"Are you or someone you know in immediate danger?"

Viv shook her head, then hesitated. *She* might be safe and sound, but was Quentin?

"I see it's complicated," said the butler. "Well, we can't leave you standing outside. Please, come into the vestibule. Wait here for a moment, away from the weather, whilst I see if any of the family is at home."

With that, he left her alone in a gilded room with a marble floor. Everything sparkled so much, her eyes hurt. Viv was glad she'd worn the best of her dresses but was quickly coming to the conclusion that her best wasn't nearly good enough.

Poor little orphans, indeed.

The butler soon rematerialized inside the vestibule. He'd barely been gone long enough to glance into another room, much less enquire if his masters were receiving guests.

Was it all an elaborate scheme to make her feel as though she'd had a fair chance, before dismissing her?

"If you'll come with me," said the butler.

She followed him in awe. There was marble everywhere. Fancy arches, shiny gilding, paintings on every wall. A dazzling amount of sunlight streaming in through countless open windows. This wasn't a home. It was a mansion. And a museum.

The butler led her into a sitting room larger than her and Quentin's entire dwelling. There was a massive twelve-person table in one corner, a pianoforte in another, and enough armchairs and sofas in a half-circle before the fireplace to comfortably seat two dozen guests.

Presently, the room contained five other people.

"Here we are, then." The butler gave Viv a respectful incline of his head and disappeared down the marble corridor.

The five Wynchesters gazed at her with open curiosity.

Viv stared back.

They smiled.

Viv did not.

A diminutive blond white woman with fresh paint on her earlobe opened her mouth first. "Welcome to our home. We're—"

"I know who you are."

"Yes, obviously we're Wynchesters," said the most attractive man Viv had ever glimpsed in all her life. Tall, broad-shouldered, fit but not too muscular, gorgeous chestnut skin, close-cropped black hair, and eyelashes so thick he must've made a deal with the devil. "But specifically, our names are—"

"I said I know who you are." Viv pointed at each of them in turn.

The vexingly attractive one: "Jacob."

The blond: "Marjorie."

The white man with a possessive arm wrapped around her: "Adrian."

The pretty, plump woman in lace: "Philippa."

The older gentleman so hunched and decrepit he looked as though he'd just crawled out of his own coffin: "And Tommy."

All five of their jaws fell open in unison.

"B-but," Marjorie stammered, her eyes wide as saucers, "how?"

"If she says it's because of my lace..." Philippa murmured through clenched teeth.

"I presume the hedgehog in my apron gave me away," Jacob guessed.

Tommy crossed her ancient arms over her thin chest and scowled at Viv like a disgruntled old man.

"It's fairly obvious, isn't it?" said Viv with a shrug.

"Is it?" Tommy groused.

"Wouldn't you say Marjorie is the one most likely to have been painting a portrait of your brother?"

"*What?*" Marjorie glanced around in alarm. "*Shh.* No one knows what I'm working on."

Jacob blinked at her. "And Tommy?"

"Ah, the easiest identity of all to deduce."

"I am *not*," Tommy burst out. "No one can tell I'm anything other than what I appear to be!"

"Precisely. And since there is no five-hundred-year-old Wynchester vampire in residence, I can only conclude that you are the woman behind the impeccable cosmetics."

"How would you know what Marjorie is painting?" Philippa demanded. "*We* don't even know what she's been painting."

"Then you are not very observant," said Viv, "which bodes poorly for my visit here. I had hoped you would be able to help with my problem, but I fear I have come to the wrong place."

"There's more Wynchesters," said Jacob. "We're the only ones here at the moment, but we're rather a large family. The other two that live here are handling a different case, but the others are in their homes. We can summon them if need be."

"You know what? There's no need." Viv took a step back toward the front door. "Coming here was a mistake."

Jacob's eyes met hers and held them. The intensity in his warm brown gaze pinned her in place. He was the one least mentioned in the scandal sheets, yet the most captivating by far. Viv hadn't been prepared for how handsome he would be. If she'd spotted him under different circumstances, she'd have been tempted to lick her lips.

But right now, the only thing tempting her was the desire to burst into tears and demand they comport themselves like the genius heroes they were supposed to be.

"Please," Jacob said softly. "Sit for a moment. If we cannot resolve your problem, the least we can do is offer you some tea."

Nothing good ever came of little girls far from home accepting sweets from attractive strangers. The Wynchesters would be no exception. Jacob was clearly the most dangerous of all of them. But she was here because of her cousin, for whom she would walk through fire to see again.

Viv rolled back her shoulders and stepped farther into their lair.

7

Jacob gestured for the new client to have her pick of the many comfortable seats. He couldn't take his eyes off her. A woman like that could sit on his lap if she preferred.

Except of course she wouldn't want to stand within a yard of him. The rest of his siblings looked reasonably presentable, but Jacob had just rushed in from the barn—and apparently looked like it. Or worse, *smelled* like it.

Nirah had got loose, thanks to Stephen's latest prototype endeavors. Jacob cupped a protective hand around the hedgehog hiding in the pocket of his leather apron. He didn't want to alarm the new client, but he did need to find Nirah before the surly creature scared Tickletums. Or the client.

Perhaps "client" was too strong a word. She hadn't yet shared so much as her name, much less the reason for her visit.

Jacob gazed at her as surreptitiously as he could, trying his best to repeat the divination trick that she had performed so easily.

Observation #1: Did he mention incredibly beautiful? Her smooth, soft skin, the hue a deep walnut, a few shades darker than his own. Her eyes were a gorgeous brown with amber flecks. Her hair was as black and curly as his own, but parted into geometrical sections, each with a spiral coil of expertly twisted long, thick hair cascading over her shoulders.

She looked younger than his two-and-thirty years. Perhaps

mid-to-late twenties? Her form, voluptuous. Her face...Well. That formidable scowl led him to:

Observation #2: Despite apparently having arrived at their front door of her own volition, the gorgeous woman seated before him patently did not wish to be here. She was glaring as if *they* were the villains in whatever nefarious plot was afoot. Jacob could not fathom her obvious animosity. She had come to *them*. Showing up just to sneer made no sense.

Such conflicting signals were precisely why he preferred the company of animals over humans. He understood animals. They were straightforward, with simple needs that he could easily fulfill. They didn't disparage him or look down their noses at him, as tended to occur when Jacob ventured into the finer parts of town. Or visit his own sitting room, apparently, in today's case. Which led him to:

Observation #3: She wasn't from around here, at least not initially. The faint Caribbean accent had given that much away. Her English was perfect, but she did not develop that musical lilt in London.

Perhaps her obvious dislike of him and his siblings was due to some sort of cultural difference. Or perhaps she was here on holiday and had been treated horridly, leading to a general distrust of all Britons, regardless of name or background.

Then again, if she were here on holiday, would her natural accent have faded so much, so quickly? And given her attire—an absolutely breathtakingly tailored lilac day dress, worn thin in places and faded by the sun—did she really seem the sort of lady who would book a passenger ship and sail across the Atlantic on a lark?

Gah, this divining-of-secrets-in-a-single-glance trick was madness. Jacob had less idea than ever how she'd managed it. He'd been gazing at her openly for a full five minutes straight and still hadn't the least idea who she was or why she was here.

The traditional Wynchester code was to give clients their time and let them proceed at their own pace, but this woman appeared content to sit ramrod straight and glare daggers at them from now until infinity.

"May we please know your name?" he blurted out.

Her amber-flecked brown gaze snapped to his. "Miss Vivian Henry."

There. He'd accomplished something. At least he knew what to call her.

And that she was unmarried.

"Whenever you're ready," Philippa said gently. "We're here for you."

Miss Henry gave this claim a look of such unbridled skepticism, it took one's breath away.

She clearly was not yet ready to trust them with whatever trouble had brought her to their door. Nor had she bolted. Was she waiting for some sort of sign?

"Where do you live?" he asked in a low, soft voice. "Are you a London native?"

"Cheapside," she responded. "And, no. I am from Demerara, in the West Indies. Though London is now my home, and has been so for a decade."

Jacob was doubly pleased with himself: not only had the Wynchester most likely to hide from social interaction in a barn actually verbally engaged with a client, he'd even been a little bit right about what her light accent might mean.

"Do you live alone?" he asked, emboldened.

She sent him a flat look. "Do you mean alone in the literal sense, or the way wealthy people claim to be 'alone' when in fact they are surrounded by butlers and maids and valets and footmen?"

Jacob scooped Tickletums to his chest and pretended he hadn't spoken. Miss Henry was pricklier than a hedgehog. Let someone else have a turn.

"I live with my cousin," she continued, surprising him. "Quentin is ten years younger than me, though technically I am his dependent and not the other way around. He has a small trust, but until he reaches his majority in three years, I am his guardian."

At this last word, she winced and pinched her lips shut tight.

Jacob wondered where the trust money came from and made a mental note to follow up later if its origin proved relevant.

"I'm sure guardian of an adolescent boy is a round-the-clock post," Tommy said.

"You probably would think so," Miss Henry answered. "You probably think governess and housekeeper and cook are also full-time posts."

Tommy nodded. "Because they are."

"And yet I am all those things, and a playwright besides. Some of us must work more than others."

"Playwright?" interrupted Marjorie, sending Jacob a meaningful look. "My brother is a poet. Might we have read some of your work or seen one of your plays?"

Miss Henry visibly deflated, then just as quickly resumed her stiff posture. "My scripts have not yet been performed in a public theater."

Marjorie clapped her hands in glee. "Jacob hasn't been published, either. He's an aspiring writer, just like you. The two of you must have so much in com—"

"Don't move," Jacob commanded. Not only because he wished to put a stop to this excruciatingly mortifying line of conversation, but because he'd just caught sight of Nirah.

Coiled beneath Miss Henry's chair.

He handed the hedgehog to Adrian, then started to slide from his seat. "Please don't make any sudden movements, Miss Henry. I don't wish to alarm you, but there is a snake unfurling a few inches behind your heels. Please allow me to—"

Her torso tumbled forward onto her lap. Her head dropped upside down between her calves, spilling long strands of twisted black hair to the carpet as she hiked her skirts up to her ankles. In one fluid movement, she darted her hand between her legs, grasped the writhing snake just behind its jaws, then thrust Nirah out toward Jacob. "This one?"

"Er," he managed, caught in the act of crawling toward her on hands and knees. "Yes. That would be Nirah."

"Aren't you terrified it'll kill you?" asked Marjorie, recoiling against Adrian.

Philippa was practically cowering in Tommy's lap. "How can you stand to touch it?"

Miss Henry looked at them as though they had sprouted reptilian scales of their own. "Terrified? Why would I be? I saw her reflection in the tea urn. She wasn't going to kill me."

"But it could bite you!" insisted Philippa.

Miss Henry shrugged. "Wouldn't be the first time."

Marjorie and Adrian stared at her with their mouths open.

"For the record," said Jacob as he carefully plucked Nirah from Miss Henry's hands, "we do own venomous snakes as well. You shouldn't assume all pets are harmless."

He made a show of closing Nirah safely in a basket to be returned to the barn later.

"I never assume," Miss Henry retorted. "I observe. The green body with dark markings, the pale belly, the gold-and-black collar... This is obviously an ordinary grass snake. In fact, the only poisonous snake native to England is the adder, which has completely different coloring."

Marjorie and Tommy exchanged glances.

"Are you seeing this?" Marjorie asked in her usual far-too-loud whisper.

I can't look away, Tommy had the wherewithal to sign back, so that her words would not be understood by their client. *Aspiring writer and snake charmer? Is Jacob swooning yet?*

"Jacob is a professional who is on a case," he hissed to his sisters. "Or would be, if I knew what was happening. Miss Henry, I do not mean to push you before you are ready, but if you are going to share with us the reason for your visit...might you do so now?"

A clear internal debate raged across Miss Henry's pretty face as she watched him settle back into his armchair.

"Quentin is missing," she confessed at last. "It's not unusual for him to spend all day out with his friends, but he's always home in time to eat supper with me, without fail. Nor would he miss our evening game of cards."

"He didn't come home last night?" asked Adrian.

"Or all day yesterday. He hasn't been home to eat, or to change his clothes. Something is wrong." She took a deep breath. "We parted on bad terms. An old argument."

Jacob leaned forward. "What were his last known whereabouts?"

"After he left home? I don't know. I do know every place he has ever visited up until now, and I personally checked each and every one of them. No sign of him at any of those locations."

"Is there a friend he might be visiting? Or would harbor him in secret?"

"That was my first thought. Quentin has a..." Her face turned shiny, and she shook her head. "He has spent every waking moment with the same group of idiots for years. They would not cause him any harm. I visited each of them as well. They are all at home and accounted for, and assure me that my cousin is safe and will be home soon."

"But you don't believe them?" Jacob asked.

Miss Henry's lips twisted. "They each recited the same memorized speech: That Quentin was no longer in character or on a mission, but rather relaxing idly at an undisclosed location."

"That means they practiced in advance," Tommy said, "but it doesn't mean it isn't true."

Adrian nodded. "Adolescent boys do enjoy relaxing idly."

"Parroting the same speech is suspicious," Miss Henry said flatly.

"You're right," Jacob agreed, with a quelling look at his sibling. "Can you provide us with a list of those names and addresses?"

"Of course." Miss Henry handed him a folded piece of paper. "Please interview them as soon as possible. I fear he's on a new mission that I know nothing about. Ask them for a list of all recent antics Quentin might have been involved in, and any new disguises he might be wearing. They'll be overjoyed to tell *you* anything you want to know."

Implying what, misogyny? A bunch of lads too self-important to spare a moment to help a woman in need? Miss Henry was right. Her cousin's friends *were* idiots.

"Were you able to search their premises?" Adrian asked.

She shook her head. "I was not."

"We'll handle it," Jacob promised.

"I visited the Bow Street Runners, but…" Miss Henry's voice cracked. "They dismissed me out of hand. Thank you for not doing the same."

Jacob regarded her seriously. "We shall not rest until we've resolved the matter to your satisfaction."

Then it's your case, Marjorie signed surreptitiously. *As well as your beautiful, unwed damsel in distress…*

Jacob ignored her. He was never the lead on cases, and he certainly had no time for matchmaking.

Miss Henry's eyes widened. "One more thing. Quentin did mention the canal tunnels would make a good hiding place. As well as church cellars and chalk caves. In or out of London."

Jacob stared at her in dismay. So…her cousin could conceivably be literally anywhere above, below, or carved into the earth?

Tommy and Philippa both shot him looks of horror, as though to say they already had too much going on at once to properly handle their current cases and could not possibly participate in one as vague as this. Especially without any proof the cousin was actually missing, or in any need of rescue.

Miss Henry wrung her fingers. "I checked gaols and hospitals in the city, but I don't have the means to travel farther afield."

Perhaps she was simply excitable, Jacob prayed, as the list of potential places grew longer. With luck, her cousin had spent a rowdy night at an acquaintance's gentlemen's club and was now sleeping off excess drink in a spare bedroom. Or perhaps an old school friend had whisked Quentin off to a country house party, and in his excitement the lad had forgotten to inform his cousin.

Jacob kicked himself to realize now *his* imagination was adding infinite possibilities to the list. It would take weeks to contact every club, hunting lodge, and country house. Months, if they needed to be present for a physical search. Years, if one added every hospital, prison, church, tunnel, or cave into the mix.

There had to be an easier solution. Something quick and logical.

"The friends weren't at all surprised to learn your cousin was missing?" he asked.

"Actually...yes," Miss Henry answered. "At first, they were shocked. Until I said Quentin had mentioned a lad named Newt."

He held up the folded paper. "Is his information here as well?"

Her features tightened in consternation. "I have never heard of Newt. I presume it's short for Newton, but even that is conjecture. Christian name? Surname? Pet name? Who knows. Quentin clearly regretted saying the name at all. I had meant to press him further, but our argument escalated in a different direction, and the next thing I knew, he was gone."

Tommy stroked her chin. "Was he wearing anything that would stand out in a witness's mind?"

"He occasionally dresses...creatively, but never in a flashy way. Although he sometimes tries to look like an aristocrat, he doesn't own anything suitably fancy. For example, on the morning of Quentin's disappearance, he looked like any other young man of his age and station. Dark-blue frock coat, light-blue waistcoat...He thought it made him look Balcovian. Although that's irrelevant. The club members swear that by that afternoon, Quentin was no longer dressed as a baron, and is back to being an ordinary lad again. But where? Doing what?" She swallowed visibly. "Something sinister is afoot. I know it."

"How can you possibly know?" Philippa asked.

"Because that's how I would have written it."

Tommy and Adrian exchanged skeptical looks.

"I know *Quentin*," Miss Henry explained. "He may be as chaotic as a badger in a parlor, but he's a good person when he's not trying to be like one of you. We have a good rhythm. I cook his favorite meals, and we eat together every morning and night. My cousin might make plans without sharing them with me in advance, but he would never worry me this long on purpose. The fact that he hasn't communicated with me means that he *cannot*. Something has happened to him."

"Yet his friends aren't worried," Jacob reminded her. "They insist he's fine, and is off just being Quentin. Is it possible he's communicated his safety to *them*, and their sense of loyalty is preventing them from sharing those details with you?"

Her lips twisted with annoyance, but her eyes held a glimmer of hope.

"Yes, actually," she said. "Those scamps love to have a secret."

"There you go." Tommy slumped back against the sofa in obvious relief. "Case solved."

"Solved?" Miss Henry repeated in disbelief. "I still don't know *where* he is! I should have known you lot would do nothing."

Jacob jumped in, "Tommy just means that he's grown, and there's a logical explanation, even if it's one you don't like. I said we'd look for him, and we will. But please recognize you've given us a million potential hiding places, and no actual indication anything is wrong."

She rolled back her shoulders. "For his sake, I hope you're right. I'd rather him be deeply thoughtless and irresponsible than hurt or in danger."

"He's probably fine," Jacob agreed. "But in the spirit of thoroughness, we will make the rounds to the best of our ability."

"Do you have a portrait of your cousin?" Marjorie asked. "I can sketch from your descriptions, but an existing likeness will improve accuracy."

Miss Henry handed her a painted miniature. "We sat for this a decade ago, just before his mother died. It's the only family portrait we own, and I'm afraid he's eight years old in it."

"Coloring and bone structure won't have changed that much." Marjorie pulled out a pencil and a sketchbook and moved to crouch next to Miss Henry's armchair. "And you're here. Describe his eyebrows?"

"His..." Miss Henry bit her lip. "Not too thick. Gently arched. Slightly higher on the left side."

Marjorie's pencil flew across the page. "Nose?"

Within ten minutes, she brandished what their new client proclaimed to be a surprisingly accurate likeness of her missing cousin.

"Brilliant." Marjorie handed the sketch to Jacob. "My brother will take it from here. If you need anything at all, just ask for Jacob."

He glared at her. *Stop matchmaking.*

She fluttered her eyes.

He turned back to Miss Henry. "Don't be surprised if word of our search gets back to him and he comes home first on his own."

A wry smile lit her face. "Once you visit his friends, that actually might happen. They idolize your investigative skills, and Quentin would never miss the perfect chance to say 'I told you so.' As for payment, I can't offer you much now, but Quentin can compensate you fairly once you find him. His trust is small, so it might take a while to—"

"It's no problem," Jacob assured her. "We don't need your money. We just want to find your cousin. And we will."

For the first time, Miss Henry looked at him as though he might be a hero after all.

Something unlocked deep within Jacob's chest. Something warm and fluttery. He wanted Miss Henry to keep looking at him like that.

Alas, nothing ever quite goes to plan.

8

The next morning, Jacob broke his fast early. Marjorie and Adrian had spent hours making copies of Quentin's likeness. Jacob was needed on no fewer than five different missions, but he managed to stage one of Graham's dwindling informants at every address Miss Henry had provided, armed with a portrait of Quentin and instructions to report back every detail they witnessed.

Philippa's book club was busy writing to every church, hospital, gaol, and gentlemen's club in a hundred-mile radius. Chloe loaned them her husband's seal to frank the letters, because no administration would ignore an inquiry from the Duke of Faircliffe. Given that no one on his team had a spare moment to breathe, Jacob had the case as much in control as possible.

With Miss Henry, on the other hand, Jacob was at sixes and sevens. He would love to be the victorious warrior of the tale, riding in like a shining knight atop his faithful stallion—or, more likely, prancing in sideways atop Sheepshanks, the trick circus horse he'd rescued a few years ago.

Not because he intended to marry, no matter how much his matchmaking siblings might conspire with Cupid. But because he longed for someone to think of Mr. Jacob Wynchester as a hero, rather than a forgotten footnote lost at the bottom of a page.

In this case, dramatic heroics were unlikely to be necessary. The simplest solution was usually the correct one. Wherever Quentin was, he had meant to go there. With luck, he would return home on his own and they could return their focus to the more pressing cases. There were injuries and embezzlement and a housing crisis. The list went on. Jacob missed lunch and grabbed a pie from a street vendor for supper. He almost skipped his Wednesday evening poetry meeting as well, but with his brain so overworked and he and his animals being pulled in so many different directions, it was a relief to sit in the shadows of the parlor's rear wall for an hour.

At least there, he knew what was expected of him: little to nothing.

Nonetheless, after half an hour of silence, he couldn't stand to listen to his colleagues prattle on any longer. The published ones, lording their status over the unpublished. The aspiring neophytes, convinced they would be discovered any day to possess even greater talent than the great Sir Gareth Jallow.

At this, Jacob shot to his feet and headed for the door.

"Where are you going?" cried the friends who enjoyed his company. "We need your insights. We're all learning together."

"Where the devil do you think *you're* going?" said the poets who barely tolerated his presence. "You won't make it without us."

"He's jealous," pronounced one of the worst braggarts. "We have talent, and he'll never amount to anything."

"No one's jealous of you clowns," snapped one of Jacob's allies. "And we *all* envy Jallow. One cannot compete with England's national treasure."

Lips pressed tight, Jacob climbed into his waiting carriage and left without looking back. Maybe he would return to the Dreamers Guild poetry group once the number of open cases lightened. And then again, maybe he wouldn't.

For the record, he was not the least bit jealous of Sir Gareth Jallow.

Jacob was the national treasure.
Jacob was Jallow.

When the carriage arrived home, Jacob headed straight to the barn rather than cross through the house and greet his siblings. There was too much work to be done to risk any distractions. And for all he knew, the house was empty anyway. He wasn't the only one who needed to be six places at once.

As he pushed open the barn door, he nearly tripped over a large trembling ball of fur.

"Dionysus, you snuck out again?" He crouched to inspect the Highland tiger. "You know your sutures won't heal properly if you insist upon—"

Shite. There were matted patches of blood in the feline's fur. Bits of ruptured thread peeked out from the hairs.

"Come on," he murmured as he scooped up the heavy cat. Jacob carried Dionysus through the barn toward the medical station at the back. He placed the growling feline on a low wooden table, cleaned the wounds, and sighed. "You're going to need three new sutures."

Dionysus hated sutures.

Jacob did not blame him. He kept the wildcat calm by continuing to talk in a low, soothing voice.

On the other side of the barn, the door flung open with a bang.

He recognized Miss Henry's voice at once. "Where the devil have you been? I've been searching for you for hours—"

"Close the door," Jacob commanded. "And keep yourself on the outside. I've many animals in this barn. The wounded wildcat on this table is unpredictable."

Miss Henry shut the door—after stepping fully inside. "I believe I'm owed—"

"*Out*," Jacob repeated. "You are trespassing on private property and liable to be the next creature requiring sutures if you do not take yourself to safety at once."

As if to punctuate this threat, the Highland tiger gave another warning growl.

"I'm not going anywhere until you explain yourself. You promised to keep me abreast of all news, and it's gone twenty-four hours without a peep. Either the all-powerful Wynchesters have accomplished nothing, or else you don't respect me enough to share information—"

Jacob cursed beneath his breath. All his work calming down Dionysus was now undone, because he'd been forced to raise his voice in anger at their client.

"Almost there," Jacob murmured to the wildcat as he snipped another thread. "You're all right now. No need to attack our guest. She'll be going soon."

"Is that what you think? I'm not going anywhere. Not until you tell me why Quentin has been missing for another full night and another full day and none of you can be bothered to inform me what is going on—"

At the sound of her raising voice, Dionysus growled louder. Sharp claws protruded from the wildcat's trembling paws.

Jaw clenched tight, Jacob trapped the wildcat with his arms—for now, at least—and looked over his shoulder to glower at his overstepping client.

She was breathtakingly beautiful, damn her. The clinging day dress of cerulean muslin. That touchably soft skin. Even her disgruntled expression was unfathomably fetching. Her arms were hidden beneath a long-sleeved spencer and her hair mostly covered by a straw-colored bonnet with blue accents.

He wanted to untie the ribbon and toss the bonnet aside. Then unfasten the four buttons keeping the short spencer closed tight around her bodice. Then—

No. None of that. He wanted her to go away. Before things got any worse.

"Miss Henry," he ground out, "if you would *please* wait inside the house—"

She snorted in derision. "I have no intention to keep waiting—"

At the aggressive sound of her rising volume, the Highland tiger sprang free from Jacob's arms. With a loud hiss, the wildcat launched himself at the interloper in order to protect his human from feral Miss Henry.

"No!" Jacob scrambled after him.

Miss Henry smiled and sank to her knees, arms out.

Jacob sprinted toward her. "Get up! Get out! He doesn't want you to pet him, he wants to kill you!"

The wildcat opened his jaw wide and sank his fangs into Miss Henry's delicate wrist. When she jerked her arm free, Dionysus turned his claws to her exposed bodice and belly.

Jacob braced himself for screaming as he disentangled the wildcat from Miss Henry and pulled Dionysus back into his arms to calm the injured animal.

Miss Henry chuckled and rose to her feet. "That was quite a welcome."

His heart was still pounding. "Why aren't you sobbing? Do you need sutures?"

She pulled back the cuff of her spencer. "Lined with leather," she explained. "I was never in danger."

"But your chest and stomach!"

"Protected by a reinforced corset. A thin layer of chain mail with whalebone reinforcements. I didn't feel a thing."

Good God, Elizabeth was going to love this madwoman.

"How did you know you were going to need all that?"

"I didn't. It's a habit I picked up after Quentin starting bringing wild animals home. I don't know if you've ever tried to domesticate a polecat. Ours was quite resistant to the idea."

He stared at her. "You wear polecat-armor beneath your clothes when you pay house calls?"

"I have to do *something*. My cousin faints at the sight of blood." She held out a hand toward Dionysus. "May I try again?"

"If he bites you, I won't stop him," Jacob muttered. "You've been warned."

She touched her fingertips lightly down the back of the wildcat's neck.

Dionysus leaped from Jacob's arms in protest and streaked back to his special carpet in the rear of the barn.

"Oh, well." Miss Henry sighed. "I tend to take a bit of time to grow on people."

Jacob had no doubt. He pulled her hand into his to inspect her wrist. There were indeed tiny holes in the outer sleeve from Dionysus's fangs, but the interior leather was perfectly intact.

"Satisfied?" Miss Henry said archly. "Or will you need to inspect the chain mail at my bosom next?"

Just for that impertinence, Jacob did not let go of her hand. He stroked the tips of his fingers against the smooth brown skin, proving her to be every bit as warm and soft as he'd imagined. The pad of his thumb rubbed lightly against the pulse point at her wrist, which fluttered then sped faster than before.

Very interesting. Miss Henry might pretend to be cold and unaffected, but she was anything but. He now knew the truth.

She snatched her hand out of his and shoved both her wrists behind her back.

"Well?" she demanded. "What do you have to say for yourself?"

Jacob blinked at her. He'd forgotten the question.

"My missing cousin," she burst out impatiently. "Which of us did you forget altogether, him or me?"

Right. She'd demanded to know what Jacob had accomplished. His second-by-second whereabouts were none of her business, but all the same, he couldn't stifle a pang of guilt at having escaped to his poetry meeting, if only for half the hour.

Miss Henry read his expression at once. "You weren't even *working* on it?"

"We have loads of cases," he began.

"—and that's why Quentin has fallen through the cracks?"

"That's not fair or true," he protested. "Our entire team has been working tirelessly to find your cousin. We even receive hourly updates from—"

"You do?" she interrupted breathlessly. Her eyes shone with hope as she pressed her hands to her chest. "What is the latest word?"

Jacob not only didn't know the latest word, he didn't know *any* of the words. He'd been on the move all day long and had returned straight to the barn without even trying to catch up with any of his siblings.

"You don't even know," Miss Henry said dully, the light in her eyes fading. "Your family receives 'hourly updates' about my missing cousin, and you don't bother to read them? Wow, such great and powerful Wynchesters you lot turned out to be. I knew trusting you was a mistake. I *told* Quentin I'd never seen a more self-aggrandizing family, drunk on their own reputation and about as genuine as—"

Fury spread through Jacob's veins. She had *no* idea what it was like to be a Wynchester.

"Perhaps *you* should try keeping your opinions to yourself until somebody asks for them," he shot back.

She took a startled step backward, her lips twisting with self-deprecation. "That's the last thing Quentin said to me. Perhaps you're both right. Very well, I'll see myself out."

With that, she strode from the barn, slamming the door behind her.

9

The next morning, Jacob's conscience awoke him well before dawn. He hadn't acquitted himself well in the barn with Miss Henry. She'd come to him a wounded wildcat, just like Dionysus. In response, Jacob had barked at her instead of easing her pain.

The worst part was that she hadn't been wrong.

Jacob *had* promised to keep her abreast of any developments... and then failed to do so. That he'd been busy all day with countless other cases was the reason, but not an excuse. He was lead investigator on this one. If he wasn't going to follow through on a thread, it was his responsibility to delegate the task to someone who would.

The problem was, the team had run out of people to delegate tasks *to*. Everyone had been assigned more than they were capable of achieving, from the siblings themselves to Philippa's book club to Graham's network of spies and informants.

They'd had no business taking on yet another case to begin with. Yet what was the alternative? Miss Henry had already tried everything. She'd done the exact street work the Wynchesters themselves would have done, and she'd taken her concerns to the authorities, who had laughed in her face. If Jacob's family had spurned her, too, she would have had nowhere else to turn.

Which...was how she was feeling right now. Disrespected. Unimportant. Abandoned.

Jacob scrubbed his face with his hands. If Quentin still hadn't come home, then Jacob owed Miss Henry an apology as well as a thorough explanation. Even *if* her cousin was back home.

He bathed quickly and headed down to the breakfast table. Several of his sisters were already there when he arrived.

"Did you see Olivebury was robbed the other day?" Tommy asked as she reached for fresh toast.

"Olivebury, the speaker of the House of Commons?"

"Not the speaker, but one of the most important voices. A lot of members vote however he does."

"And now he's our latest client?"

"Not exactly," said Elizabeth. "We don't even know what was taken. But apparently the robbery unfolded in such an ostentatious manner that the authorities have decided *we* must have something to do with it."

"Oh, for the love of God." Jacob filled his plate as quickly as he could. "We don't have time to defend ourselves from utter nonsense."

"We'd better find time," said Marjorie. "Before it stops us from being able to handle all of our other cases."

"Speaking of which," said Jacob. "Any news about Quentin?"

"No sign of him." Elizabeth pushed the latest stack of intelligence toward his spot at the table. "You can read through the informants' missives if you want detailed descriptions of the most boring houses in London. Quentin's friends never leave their homes except to visit each other."

Tommy set another stack on top of Elizabeth's. "And here are the latest responses from the churches and gaols and hospitals. Nobody has seen anyone matching Quentin's description, though they've all posted his likeness in a prominent place in case he happens to show."

"Wonderful," Jacob said with a groan. "Miss Henry is going to love to hear it."

"Isn't it an odd coincidence for us to have two missing persons cases in one week?" asked Marjorie.

"Actually, we don't," said Tommy. "Chloe said the other was a kidnapping hoax. This disappearance may not pan out to anything either."

"Quentin *is* missing," Jacob reminded his sister.

She waved her hand. "Chloe and I used to go missing from the orphanage all the time. We always came back eventually. Until we found Bean."

"Quentin isn't an indigent in an orphanage. He has income from his trust and a home to return to."

"Doesn't mean he likes it," said Elizabeth. "I ran away from my previous family in search of a better life and found one when I met you all. Maybe Quentin is searching for something, too."

"Miss Henry *did* seem to gloss over a few details," Jacob mused.

Marjorie lowered her fork. "You noticed that, too?"

"I thought her reticence seemed to be related to whatever clothing he normally wears," said Tommy. "Perhaps he's like me and doesn't always fit in the way society expects. And thus embarrasses his cousin."

"She did make a point to underscore that he'd left the house looking like an ordinary young man," Jacob agreed slowly. "But if that's the case, it's unlikely his attire had anything to do with his disappearance."

"I still say runaway," said Elizabeth. "She herself said they parted on bad terms. *How* bad, I wonder? Bad enough never to come home?"

"Maybe so, if his cousin's embarrassment over his appearance makes him feel she doesn't value him as a person," Tommy said softly.

Jacob put his plate down. "I'll go and find out."

Maybe he and Miss Henry both owed each other an apology.

Although the Wynchesters owned several carriages, Jacob decided to walk to Cheapside. He could cover the two miles in half an hour, which wasn't significantly more time than he would waste ringing for a coach to be readied and brought round.

Besides, the fresh air would help to clear his head. He *did* like Miss Henry, human hedgehog. Prickly on the outside, and secretly soft underneath.

He found her door with ease and rapped the knocker.

There was no response for a long minute. Then the door cracked open, revealing Miss Henry in a russet-colored round dress of moderate width, pleated at the bottom in three layers. Bright sprigs of orange ribbon adorned the faded hems, brightening the earth tones with a dash of color. Perhaps it was the simplicity of the dress that made Miss Henry stand out all the more. She would be radiant in a floor-length burlap sack.

"What do you want?" she said with obvious inattention. Her gaze was on the pencil stub she was sharpening with a dull blade.

"To apologize, and to share what information we've managed to gather. Might I come in?"

She glanced over her shoulder, then opened the door wide. "Make yourself at home. But take off your shoes, first."

"Take off my...shoes?"

Miss Henry gestured to a small carpet just inside the door, the leather half-boots she'd been wearing the day before tucked neatly in one corner.

When he hesitated, she crossed her arms. "I'm the one who has to sweep up after any uninvited visitors."

Whether this was a Caribbean custom or a quirk of Miss Henry's, she was right. He removed his boots at once and lined them up next to hers.

"We're alone?" he asked. "You really don't have anyone who helps you in the house?"

"Oh, did you come to Cheapside expecting to be *chaperoned*? Please excuse me for not being an Almack's princess like the fine young ladies you're used to. As I mentioned, I *am* the maid, and the cook, and the butler. Which means I'm very busy, so if you could get to the point?"

Jacob flashed an uncomfortable smile that was more like a grimace and stood awkwardly in the middle of her kitchen in his stocking feet. Stockings that were a Christmastide gift from Kuni and dyed bright Balcovian pink.

"Have you visited all of Quentin's friends?" Miss Henry asked.

Not Jacob personally, although they'd sent spies to each location on the list. For Miss Henry's sake, he hoped they could resolve this case soon. Ideally before the Wynchesters and their extended network fell apart like a broken machine.

"Every one of their homes is under constant surveillance," he assured her. "At the first sign of your cousin—or anything suspicious at all—you will be the first to know."

She arched a skeptical eyebrow.

"I'm sorry about yesterday," he told her. "Our team regularly checks in with each other, but those briefings don't mean there's been a breakthrough on a case. I should have explained better up front, and I should have kept you up-to-date, even if the only news is that there isn't any."

"I may have reacted poorly, too," she admitted. "You cannot understand how terrible it is to sit and wait and wonder, and not receive the slightest communication from anyone. Not you, not Quentin…"

"I do empathize with you. And though we have taken on more than we can efficiently handle, I swear that we are trying to find your cousin." He handed her a two-page report highlighting efforts they had made thus far, and any responses or intelligence their investigation had gathered.

"Thank you," she said softly as she scanned the long list of completed or ongoing tasks. "This makes me feel some better."

"Might I glance around your home?" he asked. "I might see something that could be of use to the case."

He expected her to balk at this, or at least escort him through the premises under her watchful eye, but she simply held up her palm and returned to whatever she'd been doing at her table.

Revising a previous draft, from the looks of it. Some people hated editing their work, preferring only to create fresh, but Jacob loved the refining process. For him, crafting the perfect poem was like whittling a statue out of marble. Slow and painstaking work that required great attention and care, but if all went well, the result at the end looked like it had always meant to be exactly what it now was.

Miss Henry did not look as though things were going well. She was attacking her manuscript pages with such vigor, the pointed tip of her pencil had scratched through the top sheet in several places.

Jacob knew better than to offer unsolicited opinions while a writer was in the midst of her work. Yet he could not resist the urge to inch a little closer.

A whirl of brown fur darted out from beneath her chair and swiped long white claws at Jacob's bootless feet.

"Yowch!" He hopped from one foot to the other, trying to avoid stepping on or being mauled by the rabid creature with the black-and-white-striped face and sharp fangs.

"That's Rufus," Miss Henry said without looking up from her manuscript.

Jacob sputtered, "You have an *attack* badger?"

"Is his high energy bothering you? At ease, Rufus."

The badger immediately lost all interest in Jacob, its fangs and claws disappearing as it curled into a furry ball next to Jacob's stocking feet and fell asleep.

Shredded pink stockings. And lightly shredded feet.

Miss Henry waved a hand. "Sally's around here somewhere, too. Be advised."

Be *advised*? "Is Sally the polecat?"

Miss Henry shook her head. "Had to return the polecat to the wild. Kept biting the postman."

What the devil was Sally then, the friendly neighborhood rhinoceros?

"Badgers are the natural predator of hedgehogs," Jacob informed Miss Henry.

"Mm-hm," she said without glancing up.

Perhaps she'd acquired Rufus for that precise reason. So he would attack innocent little hedgehogs like Tickletums. Or anyone who smelled hedgehog-friendly.

There could not be a clearer sign that Jacob and Miss Henry did not belong together.

Keeping watch on the allegedly napping beast out of the corner of one eye, Jacob made his way around the Henry home on scratched but silent feet.

There were only four rooms, including the kitchen. The next room was a small parlor, containing a pair of armchairs, an unlit fireplace, and mantel piled with curious artifacts. He made a note of the contents on a blank page of the poetry journal he carried in his pocket:

> *thick wax impression of a cameo*
> *travel cutlery*
> *unicorn-shaped lock plate*
> *loose gears (from old pocket watch?)*

Back when Jacob was still confined to the circus, how he would have longed for lodgings such as these! A parlor in which to place his belongings. *Having* any belongings, to begin with. A private bedchamber of his own? Unthinkable luxury.

Then he'd met Baron Vanderbean, and everything had changed. Instead of sleeping in a tent that smelled of animals, Jacob suddenly lived in a two-wing residence with so many rooms, most were left empty. It often still didn't feel real.

The Henry home was a vast improvement over the poverty of Jacob's youth, but still a far cry from the Wynchester mansion in Islington. It was curious that Quentin should have a trust fund yet only be able to afford cramped rooms in a rather poor section of town.

Normally, enquiring about someone else's finances was none of one's business, but in this case, perhaps there was a pertinent detail the Wynchesters ought to know.

Jacob turned from the parlor and faced the other two rooms. Both bedchamber doors were open. Miss Henry's was barely large enough to fit a narrow bed and a small wardrobe. It was so neat, it almost looked as though no one lived there. From this, Jacob could only conclude that the detritus in the parlor belonged to Quentin and not the missing lad's cousin.

The final room was Quentin's bedchamber. The interior looked like a tempest had blown through, followed by a hurricane, and perhaps a tidal wave. Or wolves.

Jacob wished he were with those wolves now. He was not at all convinced he was the right Wynchester to send on an exploratory investigation. His domain was inside the barn, not out in the field. And he absolutely did not know what to do with Miss Henry.

Nonetheless, he tried to pick his way through Quentin's room as carefully as he could. He jotted down notes of everything he observed, in case it was useful later.

The number and style of waistcoats. The rapier under the bed, next to a dried-out paint set. A pile of chalk, some of which had been crushed to powder. A collection of glass jars filled with random objects: marbles, feathers, tiny wheels. A stack of penny caricatures poking fun at Parliament and polite society.

And...what was this? Jacob flipped through the next stack of clippings with bemusement. A four-inch stack of gossip columns and newspaper articles about the Wynchester family. Everything from cases they'd won to hand-painted illustrations of Chloe's latest bonnets.

Perhaps Tommy was right. Was this what Miss Henry had elided, when she'd stressed that her cousin had gone missing dressed as a normal boy? Did Quentin long for ribbons and ostrich feathers, only to be told by society—and his cousin—that men were not allowed such fripperies?

When he felt he'd amassed a comprehensive list of the disparate props making up the missing lad's life, Jacob made his way back to the kitchen.

He came up behind Miss Henry as silently as he could, not because he wished to startle her, but because he did not wish to wake the sleeping attack badger at her feet.

"All finished?" she asked, again without looking up.

Apparently, he had not been as silent as he'd thought. At least he hadn't awakened the badger.

"For now," he answered, then hesitated. "I came across quite a bit of intelligence gathered in relation to my family."

"He's your biggest admirer," she said in the same tone as one might regard a fondness for bathing in cesspools. "He'd rather be related to you than to me."

A sore spot, clearly. Perhaps there was a reason Quentin wished to separate himself from his family. Was there a nice way to ask if perhaps the sketch Marjorie had made of him didn't quite tell the whole story? No easy way, but out with it.

"If your cousin is off with a lover and you're not giving me the details we need to narrow the search, we're not going to be able to help you."

"To my knowledge, Quentin has never been enamored with

anyone," Miss Henry said in surprise. "Though he has acted uncharacteristically secretive lately, he knows all I care about is his safety and his happiness. I cannot imagine him keeping the identity of a paramour secret for long."

"Can you not? You were careful to mention your cousin left home looking like an ordinary young man. Did he often dress like a woman?"

She blinked at him. "What?"

"If your cousin usually lives as a different sex, or might have gone into hiding because he fell in love with another man and feared your disapproval—"

"For heaven's sake, the last thing on my mind is who or how Quentin loves. He can wear my best dresses any time he wishes, for his own wedding or otherwise. But no, I've never seen him do so. Though..."

He raised his brows. "Yes?"

"Well, you've interviewed his friends, so you know what they're like. Like you all, they're 'better than Bow Street Runners' according to Quentin, though *that's* not much of a challenge. I'm sure the boys bragged about every detail, though they might not have mentioned they call themselves a"—she lowered her voice to a whisper—"secret society."

These last two words were spoken with portent.

"You think this club has something to do with wherever Quentin is?" Jacob guessed.

"Don't you?" she asked. "Those meetings, and them running around trying to be Good Samaritans like the wonderful Wynchesters, and—of course—the mysterious Newt. Have you found Newt?"

"Not yet," he was forced to admit, and made a mental note to double-check that they'd sent someone to find him.

"I've told Quentin time and again not to use that phrase," she muttered.

Jacob stared at her. "'Newt'?"

"*Secret society*," she whispered again. "Quentin would never involve himself in anything illegal, but the fact is that the Seditious Meetings Act made all secret clubs illegal. I warned him that using the wrong phrase could lead to disastrous consequences..."

Jacob nearly laughed out loud. She thought her adolescent cousin would be arrested because he and a few other lads claimed they were a secret club? If the authorities couldn't be bothered to search for a missing person, they certainly weren't going to waste time listening at the keyholes of random adolescent boys to see if they used the words "secret club."

"I wouldn't worry about that," he said with a comforting smile. "The possibility of legal ramifications for playing pretend is so remote as to be nonexistent. Nothing has happened to my family. And as my sister says, we do seditious acts every morning before breakfast."

Miss Henry's expression was flat. "I'm sure that's very gratifying, for *you* all. Unfortunately, people like us don't share your luxuries."

He winced. Once again, he'd managed to say the wrong thing, when all he wanted to do was to help.

Notebook in hand, Jacob approached the kitchen table. From this angle, he could see what she was working on. It was not a manuscript anymore, but correspondence. He could not help but note the curious way every single one of the missives appeared to be addressed. In fact—

"*You're* 'Ask Vivian'?" he blurted out in disbelief. This was the very definition of public adulation and interaction!

"I'm Vivian," she replied. "My readers do the asking."

"I thought that name was a pseudonym," he stammered, realizing he'd walked back into hazardous territory. He'd allowed himself to forget she was a human hedgehog.

Miss Henry pushed the stack of letters away, one black eyebrow cocked higher than the other. "Why would it be a pseudonym?"

"Well...Vivian is a unisex name, is it not? Rather, England has significantly more male Vivians than female ones. It would be the perfect way to disguise the gender of—"

"I don't want to hide that I'm a woman."

"Even from..." Jacob trailed off.

His first concern with Miss Henry using her real name was safety. The Ask Vivian column was infamous for its brutal honesty and searing advice. The clever author was rational and insightful, but also direct to the point of rudeness. One could practically feel the disdain behind every sneered word of her replies.

Indeed, it seemed more logical for Ask Vivian to be the one in danger of some violence being perpetrated against her, rather than any trouble her young cousin might have got himself into.

"What if an unhappy reader shows up at your door?"

"You think I should fear an attack from a disgruntled admirer?"

Jacob didn't wish to alarm her, but the possibility couldn't go unaddressed. "Strangers can be surprisingly possessive."

She gazed at him in silence for a moment, then said quietly, "Is that why you're really here? You think whoever came after my cousin was actually trying to hurt me?"

"We don't know yet that anyone other than Quentin is involved in his disappearance," he reminded her.

"And yet you're looking at me as though you cannot quite fathom why I haven't been murdered."

"You're not at all worried about your own safety?"

"No one has any clue *I'm* that Vivian. The paper wants to keep that secret even more than I do. Besides, I have Rufus, and other defensive measures. And I never respond to the letters written by madmen."

"You receive letters from madmen?"

"Weekly. Names and identifying details redacted, of course. These are the questions that get replies." She gestured toward one pile of correspondence, then pointed at a different stack across the table. "Those are the answers that will be going back to the newspaper clerk in the next batch."

"Might I review them?" he asked.

She crossed her arms. "Is it relevant?"

"I don't know," he answered honestly.

She hesitated, then waved him toward the letters. "They're going to be printed in the newspaper anyway. You're just getting to see them a few days early."

"You don't mind people looking at your unedited work? I just... If it were me..."

"I'm not you, thank God." She gestured at the sideboard behind her. "I *want* people to read what I write. I have duplicates of every play I've ever written. I send a fresh copy to every theater manager in England every time I write a new script. You can read those, too, if you like."

He stared at her. "Really?"

"Then at least someone will. You can memorize each line and put on a one-man play at Vauxhall for all I care, as long as you credit me as the author." Her face brightened. "In fact, I've written several anti-Wynchester plays. It would be the most delicious irony to hear an actual Wynchester perform the monologues."

The very thought of a public performance nauseated him. Or rather, the thought of the audience's inevitable rejection. "I don't perform in front of crowds."

"Well, read the lines in your parlor with your siblings, then, if it amuses you."

"I don't read in front of them, either," he admitted.

"Just the poetry group your siblings mentioned?"

He didn't answer.

"Oh, for God's sake. You're not an 'aspiring' writer if you don't let anyone read your work. What is a publisher supposed to publish, your good intentions?"

His voice hardened. "You don't know anything about me."

Her eyes flashed. "Let's keep it that way, shall we?"

He should have said *yes* and walked away. It was the perfect chance. Abandon this human hedgehog and her attack badger. Flee home to the safety of his barn, where a menagerie of furry friends awaited him.

But he could be stubborn as an ox himself. It was how he'd lived through those early years. How he'd managed to find and rescue and train hundreds of wild animals. Jacob did not take the first growl as the final answer. He never gave up. He kept trying until all that he heard was purrs.

"No," Jacob responded firmly. "We're not done with each other quite yet."

He sank into the seat next to her and settled in.

10

Viv glowered at the dashing, maddening Wynchester making himself at home at her breakfast table. Also known as the nuncheon table, coffee table, tea table, supper table, worktable, ironing board, and escritoire. She had only the one surface, and his presence was taking up all of it—despite him not touching a single thing.

Unlike her habitually correct posture, he slouched casually in one of the hard wooden chairs as though this were his space and not hers.

Not that it was technically Viv's, either.

Given Mr. Wynchester spent his life roaming his vast mansion and its equally sprawling grounds, the rooms she shared with her cousin must look sad, indeed. She hated the thought of him inwardly judging her and finding her lacking.

If only he weren't so infernally handsome, on top of it all! His attractiveness didn't even make logical sense. Not too tall and not too short. Not too bulky and not too scrawny. Neither slovenly nor dandy-ish. All those "mediums" mashed together should combine into mediocrity, not extraordinariness. He wasn't playing fair.

She liked the bright intelligence in his eyes, the full thickness of his lips, the slight shadow at his jaw. She even liked that he—or his valet—had taken the time to craft an extravagantly folded cravat, yet a leather apron was still slung around his narrow hips.

As though Jacob—the vexing man had wormed his way far too deep into her life for her to keep thinking of him as Mr.

Wynchester—had either left home in such a rush that he'd forgotten to remove his apron...or else he cared more about everyday practicality than polite society's fashion sensibilities.

An admirable characteristic that absolutely could not be borne. She was right to distrust the Wynchesters. She definitely wasn't going to start liking *this* one. Maybe her badger would bite him, and he'd never return.

"I suppose you find our humble living arrangements tragic." Viv barely kept the bitterness out of her voice.

He sent her a curious look. "What's wrong with this house?"

"It's not much compared to yours."

"Why compare? There's always better than where we find ourselves, just like there's always far worse. You keep your home beautifully...except for your cousin's bedroom. I regret to inform you that he may not be missing after all, and might simply be lost under one of his heaps of random objects."

Viv pressed her lips together to keep from smiling in agreement. She was *not* going to find Jacob Wynchester charming.

"Since you mentioned the living arrangements, might I ask how the cohabitation with your cousin came about?" he enquired.

Her knee-jerk reaction was that her family's financial situation was none of his business, but the facts were: She'd gone to *him* for help, he was here trying to do just that, and neither of them had any idea which detail would or would not prove decisive in locating Quentin.

She'd braced herself for ridicule when she'd handed over the list of secret society members. Obviously, the moment Jacob and his family visited those moonstruck lads, there'd be no hiding the depths of Quentin's Wynchester fanaticism. His friends would have explained every "secret mission" in minute detail. Had probably begged the Wynchesters to autograph every surface in their house.

To Viv's surprise, Jacob and his family had seemed to take the youthful club's enthusiasm in stride, with nothing more than, "We'll let you know if it leads to any relevant clues."

Perhaps their fanaticism wasn't unusual. Maybe every adolescent boy in England—and a fair number of grown men—did the same. Given the Wynchesters' royalty-like praise in the newspapers and scandal sheets, Viv might be the only person in the entire country not to bow down before them in awestruck sycophancy. She'd sworn never to behave like that again, for any reason.

But her personal reticence didn't matter. If he and his siblings needed to know Quentin's personal history in order to find him, then Viv would have to tell the truth about that, too, no matter how she felt about sharing her cousin's private business with strangers.

She lifted her chin and replied, "My cousin is the illegitimate son of Viscount Ayleswick."

Jacob's forehead lined briefly.

"Correct, the prior one. The current viscount is legitimate—and thirteen months younger than Quentin."

She did not need to explain how different the firstborn son's life might have been if his viscount father had deigned to marry Quentin's mother.

Nor did Viv need to spell out why such a marriage had not happened.

"Upon Quentin's birth, the viscount created a small trust for him. Honestly, the effort was more than I would have expected, given the situation. Of course, Ayleswick *could* have publicly acknowledged his son's existence. Illegitimate sons of lords move much more freely through society than run-of-the-mill bastards of ordinary mistresses. Though I suppose it was too much to hope an aristocrat might acknowledge a Black child."

Jacob inclined his head. "I can only think of one recent occasion that came close. A few decades ago, Miss Dido Belle was born into slavery in the West Indies before being brought here to be raised by her great-uncle, the Earl of Mansfield."

"Raised as a lady?" Viv asked with interest.

He made a face. "As...a free gentlewoman and companion to her same-age white cousin, who was indeed raised as a lady. Miss Belle lived with the family for thirty years. Although the earl left her a significant sum and an annuity in his will, even upon his deathbed, her uncle still did not acknowledge Miss Belle as his niece."

Viv sighed. She had written several plays in which the lives of people like her cousin and his mother had turned out much differently. Those scripts were probably destined to remain fairy tales for centuries to come.

"I miss Quentin," she said quietly. "The house is finally clean and quiet, and I couldn't hate it more. My cousin has driven me mad since the moment I arrived on this shore to take care of both him and his ailing mother. Nonetheless, since that first hug, we've never been apart...until now. It's been three days, but it feels like three decades."

Jacob nodded with obvious empathy. "Family is like that. Every time one of my siblings moves out, it's like I have to learn what 'home' means all over again. But don't worry. This isn't permanent. We'll find Quentin and bring him home where he belongs."

"Please do so swiftly," she said with feeling.

"I shall do my very best." He hesitated. "How did you do that trick yesterday?"

She reached under her chair to scratch Rufus's head. "What trick?"

"When you looked at us and knew everything about us. How could you possibly know Marjorie was specifically painting a portrait of one of her brothers, for example?"

"Ah."

She nodded. Not just any brother. Jacob Wynchester, specifically. Three disparate flecks of paint on Marjorie's clothing and person had led Viv to that conclusion. There was a bit of green the exact color of the Wynchesters' lawn, though that only indicated the painting was likely to be or to contain a landscape scene. The other two smudges were both brown: One, the exact hue of Jacob's gorgeous skin. The other, a perfect match to his beautiful eyes. If Viv were forced to guess, she would daresay the portrait was of Jacob outside, likely with his animals.

But she would not say so. When she'd voiced her initial conclusions, she hadn't known the portrait was meant to be a secret. Perhaps the painting was a surprise, and Viv had almost ruined it. Now that she knew, she would not break Marjorie's confidence, given it hadn't been granted to Viv to begin with.

"I might have been wrong," she said, though anyone who knew her well would know this was a lie. Viv was rarely if ever wrong, and even less likely to admit it.

Jacob didn't particularly look as though he swallowed this explanation, but he did not press further. He glanced over her shoulder at the sideboard against the wall. Then his eyes traveled higher, to the long wooden shelf containing Viv's most prized possessions. "Are those your books?"

"Most of them," she said with pride. "A few are borrowed from a lending library and need to be returned."

"Novels? Poetry?"

"The books I own are novels I enjoy rereading. The items from the lending library tend to be biographies, history tomes, travel guides, or manuals on various fields of study."

His brows raised. "How many fields do you study?"

"As many as necessary to pen whichever play I'm currently writing, with as much verisimilitude as I can reasonably convey." She paused. "Are you disappointed I am a plebeian who does not read poetry?"

He grinned at her. "Relieved, more like. Please tell me you'll be the one person who doesn't constantly opine about what I should do with my poems."

"I can't promise *that*," she said with a smile. "I do love telling people what to do."

He gestured at the letter she'd been writing. "Is that what you're doing now?"

She shook her head. "I was, but this is personal correspondence. I am friends with a handful of playwrights throughout England, and it is my turn to contribute to our monthly meeting."

His forehead creased. "You meet...on paper?"

"We each write a letter, explaining what we've accomplished, and what our plans are, as well as responding to the same from the four others. Once a month, I receive a packet containing the current letters. I replace my old letter with a new one and send all five to the next in the circle. That way, we each only have to write our news once, and we're always the first to know the latest happenings of the person before us in the list."

"You sound like very good friends."

"We are." Her eyes narrowed. "*You* sound surprised. Or skeptical."

"These playwrights have never met you?"

"Impractical. They all live several days' drive away. What is your point?"

"I just wondered if they understand who they're writing to."

"Do you mean respectable British playwrights might not wish to associate with a Black female immigrant?"

"I only note that Vivian is often a man's name. And that most people find it difficult to determine accent and skin color from the shape of one's handwriting."

Viv clenched her fists. She did tend to sign her letters "Yours &c, Vivian," but surely her initial correspondence had clearly stated she was *Miss* Vivian Henry. If her handwriting had been messy that day, or if they'd skimmed her scrawl and assumed that of course she was a mister, well, that was their erroneous conclusion, not Viv's lie.

"I will be certain to sign this letter as MISS VIVIAN, with all capitals," she informed him. "And I will mention my personal connection to the themes in my play about Black female suffrage."

"You may not wish to do that," Jacob said. "What if they exclude you from the circle?"

"Then it is their loss," she said firmly. "I shall never compromise my integrity. Only a coward hides behind a false name."

He did not look appeased by this response. Viv didn't care. No man would ever again tell her what to do.

"If you're finished here, either go and look for my cousin, or worry about your own writing career. I'm sure you have poems to rhyme, or whatever it is you do."

"I work on cases or with my animals," he answered. "My poetry muse does not visit me nearly as often as I might like."

She goggled at him. "Your poetry muse?"

"Inspiration," he clarified. "Not an actual person."

"I understood you the first time," she bit out.

Good God, the Wynchesters were outside of enough. Handsome or not, she could not stand entitled men like Jacob who had never known a true day's work, much less a lifetime of it.

"Only the most privileged of people have muses. The rest of us have to work, regardless of whether the whim strikes. Has your chambermaid ever said 'Dear me, I cannot possibly empty any chamber pots today, I did not awaken inspired enough to bother'?"

He did not rise to her bait. "And the sideboard...Those are your plays?"

She let out her breath and tried to recover her calm. "Some are passion projects. Some were written because a theater manager or aficionado specifically said, 'I wish we had more of this sort of thing.' And a few are just silly, inspired by the less credible queries sent in to my column."

"So you do respond to inspiration," he murmured.

She glared at him.

He grinned back. "Show me one? I'd love to see the difference between an audience-demanded play and a script bringing some featherbrain's letter to life."

"Not as mad as you might think," she said as she crossed to the sideboard. "Just the other day, the newspaper reported a bizarre robbery that had unfolded almost word-for-word the way I'd written it. Not that anyone should have had the pleasure of reading that manuscript."

"Not even Quentin?"

"He doesn't have much time for reading. He does handle all my post, ensuring my answers are sent to the paper, and my scripts shipped to appropriate venues. The silly ones don't go anywhere. Usually. He seems to have misplaced the one about the burglary."

Jacob pushed to his feet and joined her. "It's missing?"

"Quentin occasionally mishandles the post." She made an exasperated expression. "He gets distracted, particularly by his antics with his friends. Or arguments with me. He might even have thought he was being extra efficient, just to please me. When I finish writing each script, I tie it up and tuck the original letter behind the twine to remind me why I'd written it."

"I don't understand. Where would he have sent it?"

"Back to the paper, which is where all my real responses go," Viv answered grimly. "The clerk would have forwarded the pages to the question-writer, along with their original letter."

"Wait. What burglary? You cannot mean the robbery of Mr. Olivebury, the politician?"

She nodded grimly. "None other."

"My siblings were discussing that incident at the breakfast table. Wasn't there something odd about the manner in which it occurred?"

"Only creative use of balloons, shepherd's pie, and a whooper swan. Just like I wrote it."

He snorted. "No wonder they think we did it."

She frowned. "Who thinks that?"

"The local magistrate, apparently. Which means now we've got to solve the Olivebury robbery, on top of everything else, before it derails all of our other cases. You're saying you wrote a similar crime in your play?"

"The same crime. To the letter. The thief performed each stage direction brilliantly. I suppose it could have been worse. At least he only received that play, and not the ones about abduction and blackmail."

Jacob looked startled. "May I see those?"

"I'm looking for them now. They were right here, with the others. I'm sure of it." Heart thumping, Viv leafed through the piles a second time, then a third. Her throat was dry when she glanced back up at Jacob. "They're not here."

"Not here," he repeated.

She shook her head. "Not here."

"And we don't know who you were corresponding with?"

"The system is anonymous," she reminded him. "No one who writes in shares their real names or addresses. Each correspondent is assigned a temporary number, and the query forwarded to me without any identifying characteristics. I send all my replies to the newspaper, who chooses which to publish and disperses the rest, returning the original letters in the process, ensuring complete anonymity."

He appeared to think this over. "Do you think the more concerning queries came from multiple people?"

"I felt like it might be the same person."

"Man or woman?"

"As you pointed out...that's hard to say. If I had to guess, I'd say white, male, and British, but it really would be conjecture." She swallowed. "You think the missing plays have something to do with Quentin's disappearance?"

He shrugged. "We don't know."

"I can guess. That *would* be a good twist. I'd write it that way."

"We don't yet have reason to believe the letter-writer has been in contact with Quentin. It's still more likely that your cousin is out adventuring and has no idea there's been a mix-up with your plays."

Viv desperately wanted Jacob to be right. For Quentin simply to be gallivanting around, sure to walk through the door at any moment.

But she suspected the surprises were just beginning.

Jacob's pencil paused in his notebook, and he turned toward her slowly. "Just so I understand the timeline correctly...Both Quentin *and* the play that inspired a robbery disappeared at the same time?"

She folded her arms over her chest, her hackles rising. "What are you saying?"

"I'm saying the play was in your house, and now it's not. You're saying the thief has the play. Therefore, someone in this household, either purposefully or inadvertently, put the missing play into the thief's hands. You have no servants, which means the culprit can only be you... or Quentin. And only one of you is missing. Do I have the facts right?"

"I don't appreciate your tone or your conclusions. For your information, I don't know *when* the play disappeared. It might have happened weeks ago, not the day Quentin went missing."

"And in that time, was there someone other than you or Quentin who might have had access to it?"

She glared at him. "You know there was not, but that doesn't prove nefarious intent."

He held up his hands. "I'm not claiming anyone in this household had nefarious intent. I'm looking at the facts the way a magistrate might. And we know the case is being investigated seriously."

Viv's blood drained. Jacob was right. Mr. Olivebury was a powerful MP. Rich, white, important to society. Her cousin was none of those things. It would be easy for the magistrate to point a finger at a boy like Quentin.

And the courts could sentence him to death.

Her limbs trembled in fear. Viv would never breathe another word of the play's existence, much less Quentin's proximity to it, but she might not have to. If she was right, and Quentin had accidentally sent the pages to the question-writer via the newspaper, the clerk might remember Ask Vivian giving advice about whooper swans and robbery.

And if Viv was wrong about it being an accident, and Quentin had done something else with her script...Such as share it with some miscreant named Newt...

"I have to go." Jacob snapped his notebook closed. "I need to share the latest developments with my family."

She grabbed his arm before he could turn away.

"I'm coming with you," she informed him grimly. "Until you find my cousin and clear his name, I am your shadow from this moment forward."

11

Jacob and Miss Henry stepped into the siblings' sitting room side by side. Although there were now a dozen members of the Wynchester family, only two were currently present, both hard at work at the long table: Tommy, adding details to her latest cartography, and Marjorie, making copies of who-knows-what for her current mission.

The plush cushions of the relaxing armchairs and sofas on the other side of the room were empty, save for Tickletums, the hedgehog, napping against an embroidered pillow.

Marjorie looked up as they entered. Her eyes sparkled. "Miss Henry! A pleasure to see you...and Jacob are getting on so splendidly."

Jacob glared at his sister. Miss Henry's iron fingers were still locked on to his arm, as though she fully believed that if she weren't latched on to him like a barnacle, he would forget about her and her cousin altogether.

It wasn't a romantic embrace. He was a means to an end.

"What are you working on?" Miss Henry asked.

He tensed. This was a trick question. She wasn't curious about their other cases. The only answer that would be acceptable to her was if every single Wynchester had foregone food and sleep altogether in order to devote twenty-four hours a day to finding the cousin who increasingly looked as though he was missing on purpose, and did not wish to be found.

"What *aren't* we working on?" Tommy answered with a groan. Which, in the scheme of things, was not only true but also a reply difficult to find fault with, even for prickly Miss Henry. "A hundred cases at once, plus one that doesn't even have a client—"

"Olivebury's robbery?" Jacob stepped forward. This would be the perfect segue into the latest Quentin development. The *only* Quentin development.

Miss Henry's free hand tightened on the satchel she'd retrieved from her quarters before they'd left her home. Best guess of its contents: wooden stakes with which to stab the Wynchesters through the heart if they failed to find her cousin before midnight.

"What did I do with the map I drew of Olivebury's street?" Tommy stood over the table to rifle through stacks of parchment. "If we can put an infiltration team together—"

"*We* don't have to break in," Jacob reminded her. "The thief already did."

"It might help to walk through how it was done." Tommy plucked a map from the pile with a flourish. "The account in the paper was woefully scarce on details. We all know where to find pies, but can you acquire a whooper swan for me?"

"We're not going to re-create the robbery," he repeated in exasperation.

"Only because we don't know how!" Tommy shook out her map. "How did the thief even come up with a plan so unlikely?"

Miss Henry's grip on his arm threatened to shatter his bones, though it now felt less like anger and more like embarrassment and worry. Almost as though she were holding on to Jacob for strength.

"The swan sounded believable when I wrote it," she muttered. "I thought it added a certain comic flair."

Tommy and Marjorie stared at her.

"*What?*" came twin voices from the entranceway.

Jacob pulled Miss Henry aside to allow Graham and Kuni to enter the room.

"You may recall Miss Henry is a playwright," Jacob began. "What might surprise you to learn…"

Quickly, he ran through the essentials, from Miss Henry's alternate identity as Ask Vivian, to the letters from the morally questionable advice-seeker, to the burglary play he had inspired.

"You wrote an instruction manual?" Tommy looked thrilled. "Can I read it?"

"She doesn't have it anymore," he reminded her. "Quentin sent it to the burglar."

"We don't know that he…" Miss Henry began, then trailed off unhappily. The delivery of her play into the wrong hands might not have been deliberate, but there was no other explanation. "I admit, none of this appears to be a positive development."

Tommy glanced down at her endless stacks of maps. "Sometimes it feels like we haven't had a positive development in months."

"I don't know about that." Marjorie's calculating gaze snapped to Kuni and Graham. "Someone *might* have good news, if they wished to share it."

Kuni shot her a sharp glance. "Are you using your colors on us?"

Marjorie fluttered her eyelashes. "Did I err?"

Kuni and Graham exchanged soft smiles, then clasped hands.

"I knew it!" squealed Marjorie.

Tommy elbowed her. "Let them say it."

Graham admitted, "There might be one ray of sunshine."

"We're going to have a baby!" blurted Kuni, grinning ear to ear.

Jacob was the first to hug them, followed by Marjorie and Tommy. "Does Chloe know?" he asked.

Kuni shook her head. "We weren't planning to tell anyone for another few weeks. Not until I start to show."

Marjorie bounced in place. "Chloe's going to lose her *mind*. Just think, a cousin for Dory! We really are starting a new generation of Wynchesters."

"Unfortunately," said Graham with a wry expression, "it'll be a while before they can lend us a hand."

"If they want to," Kuni said quickly. "Our children can be anything they choose."

Miss Henry was being surprisingly silent. Either she was vibrating with impatience at this latest distraction from her case, or else she was plotting how to turn the Wynchesters into victims of an unfortunate Kraken accident in her next play.

Or both.

"We'll celebrate as soon as you're ready," Jacob told Graham and Kuni with a smile. He gestured toward Miss Henry. "As for Quentin's disappearance and the Olivebury robbery—"

"Which are now the same case," added Marjorie.

Tommy straddled her seat to face their client. "Do you memorize your plays?"

Miss Henry blinked. "Why would I?"

With anyone else, Jacob would assume that response meant *no*, but with Miss Henry, he leapt to no such conclusion.

"If what you need is a copy of the text, I shall give it to you." Miss Henry pulled a stack of papers tied with twine from her satchel.

"You have a spare copy of the missing script?" Jacob asked in surprise.

"I have a spare copy of all my plays."

"But you couldn't find it with the others—"

"I can only keep one copy of each script on that sideboard, or I'll run out of space for the outgoing correspondence Quentin takes to post. You saw the wardrobe in my bedchamber. That's where I keep my duplicate manuscripts."

Marjorie's face snapped to Jacob with open delight. "You were in her *bedchamber*?"

"No," he said firmly. "I entered Quentin's private quarters to search for clues."

"But my door was open, too, so he looked inside," said Miss Henry. Marjorie grinned at Tommy, who winked back.

Jacob prayed for strength.

"Couldn't you have sent the play home with Jacob?" Kuni asked in confusion. "There was no reason for you to come all this way unnecessarily."

"Oh, it's necessary," answered Miss Henry. "I'm your new shadow. I have never before left an important task up to someone else to perform, and I see I should not break that streak now. Not when Quentin's life may be on the line."

Graham connected the dots at once. "If they can't pin the robbery on us, your cousin is the likeliest scapegoat."

"If he *is* a scapegoat," Tommy murmured. "It sounds like one possibility is that he willfully—"

Jacob cleared his throat. "Perhaps we should adjourn to the Planning Parlor?"

"What's a Planning Parlor?" asked Miss Henry.

"Something private. Just for Wynchesters," answered Tommy. She shot a knowing look at Marjorie, who grinned.

"Except for clients who later become Wynchesters," Marjorie agreed. "Of course you're welcome. Philippa and Adrian might already be in there."

Tickletums waddled up to nudge Jacob's boot. He scooped the hedgehog against his chest and cupped a hand around him protectively.

"Does he bite?" Miss Henry asked in surprise.

"You might," he muttered.

His siblings gazed at them both with open fascination.

"I *tried* to befriend your cat," Miss Henry protested.

"Tiglet?" asked Tommy.

"Dionysus," Jacob said grimly.

Marjorie gasped. "Dionysus doesn't like people. Except for Jacob. Did he growl at you?"

"They both did," Miss Henry said with a shrug. "Dionysus attempted to claw open my ribs and bite off my hand. When that didn't work, he ran away. That's how most of my interactions with strangers tend to go."

"What did Jacob do?" Marjorie asked.

Jacob and Miss Henry stared at each other, both remembering precisely what he had done. He'd taken his client's hand in his, stroked the soft skin, and discovered her unsteady, racing pulse.

If they were alone, he'd be tempted to do it again. He wanted to explore every inch of her warm skin, not just her hand and the pulse point at her wrist. He wanted to taste her skin with his tongue and use his hands to—

"We argued," said Miss Henry without meeting his eyes.

Yes. He should focus on the ways they didn't mesh. And keep his mind on the case.

Marjorie gave a knowing grin.

It means nothing, he warned her in sign language. *As soon as we find her cousin and clear his name, our new client will be gone from our lives for good.*

His sister smirked, then turned to dash from the sitting room and race up the stairs. The others were right on her heels. Leaving Jacob... alone with Miss Henry. Subtle.

Nonetheless, he offered her his free arm.

"I know how to walk," she snapped, and stalked to the stairs without aid of chivalry.

Maybe he should make chain mail for himself and Tickletums. Jacob cuddled his tiny hedgehog closer to his chest for safety. He wondered if her satchel contained a change of clothing.

Now that she'd been invited into their inner sanctum, Miss Henry might not plan on leaving.

12

Viv hated how much she loved the Planning Parlor.

She'd long despised people who floated through life, blissfully exempt from the rules and punishments designed to keep people like Viv in her place—or eradicate people like her completely. Therefore, she'd fully expected to hold everything the Wynchesters had or did in equal contempt.

But she hadn't known about the Planning Parlor. Quentin didn't know such a location existed either, which was the main reason Viv had been unawares. He would absolutely lose his mind to know she had glimpsed their secret lair firsthand.

> **Quentin**: They have a WHAT?
>
> **Vivian**: Planning Parlor. A special room dedicated to strategizing their missions.
>
> **Quentin**: What's so special about it?
>
> **Vivian**: The walls eliminate even the slightest sound from the outside world—
>
> **Quentin**: WHAT

Vivian: Which means even a servant standing on the other side of the door would not be able to overhear what goes on inside.

Quentin: Do their servants eavesdrop?!?

Vivian: [begrudgingly] I doubt it. The staff is unflaggingly respectful and seem improbably content.

Quentin: [slyly] As if perhaps the Wynchesters are nice people?

Vivian: *Rich* people, anyway. The table in the Planning Parlor is the size of our entire kitchen.

Quentin: Well, there are a lot of Wynchesters, and they'd need some sort of stable surface upon which to take notes.

Vivian: Actually, they use the floor for that.

Quentin: WHAT

Vivian: And the walls.

Quentin: WHAT

Vivian: For example, the floor is made of black slate and is full of white chalk outlines and plans for current missions.

Quentin: And the walls?!?

Vivian: Covered in bookshelves, maps, lists, sketches...

Quentin: None of them keep an ordinary logbook?

Vivian: Graham keeps extraordinary ones. Half of the overstuffed shelves contain journals of intelligence he's gathered on everyone he deems important enough to surveil. And Jacob always carries a journal, though he never lets his out of sight. It's as likely to contain unpublished poetry as mission notes.

Quentin: *You* don't know what's in his book? You hate not knowing things. His secrets must be killing you!

Vivian: I don't give two figs about Jacob Wynchester.

Viv would actually give her left boot for a single peek inside that journal, and these were her favorite shoes.

Her only shoes.

But limping along with one bare foot for the next year would be worth the pain if it meant having answers to her questions.

What *did* Jacob pen in that journal? Case notes, revealing a mind far more clever than the "I live in a barn" external persona he attempted to portray? Poetry so poorly written it had made every publisher's eyes bleed from here to Scotland? Or poems so hauntingly beautiful the greatest crime this Wynchester committed against the world was refusing to share his brilliance with others?

"Over here." Jacob motioned to Viv. "You can sit next to me, if you like."

The armchair he patted was on the opposite side to the pocket where he kept his journal. Not that Viv had experienced many opportunities to practice pickpocketing skills. White women like Chloe Wynchester—even before she became a duchess—could get away with a giggled "oh dear, how clumsy of me" if caught in the act.

Whereas someone like Viv only had to be in eyesight of the upper class to receive suspicious looks, as though she were permanently on the cusp of committing a horrendous crime.

"You may wish to remain silent and observe," Jacob murmured as she settled into the chair beside his. "Our methods can be...chaotic."

She scowled at him. The only thing she hated worse than not knowing was not *talking*. It was why she was a writer. The only way to unclutter her constantly busy mind was by sharing with others. So she wrote plays and lists and correspondence and diary entries and answered the letters sent to her advice column, no matter how corkbrained the question.

Viv loved to be useful. To be *clever*. She would never forgive Jacob for presuming her presence worthless, her mind incapable of adding any value to the discussion.

She also declined to forgive him for wearing whatever subtle cologne currently wafted to her nostrils while she was seated right next to him. He smelled like holiday spices and deep forest. Dark and inviting, all at once. A barely there scent designed to tempt innocent women into crawling onto his lap and wrapping their limbs about his hard, muscular body in an attempt to get closer to that divine perfume.

Or maybe that was how Jacob naturally smelled. Viv wouldn't put it past him. Wynchesters were devious like that.

Marjorie clapped her hands loudly. "Before we begin, Adrian and I have a ray of sunshine of our own."

Kuni gasped. "Are you also—"

"No! Not yet, at least." Marjorie's face flushed bright red.

"Our news is about our other baby," Adrian explained. "The art studio. Our second annual exposition showcasing the works of past students."

Marjorie nodded. "It won't take place for another month, but we're starting to plan the festivities now. If any of you would like to help—"

"Who has time to help?" murmured Tommy. "We can't go five minutes anymore without something else looming over us." She clapped a hand over her mouth and paled. "Kuni and Graham, I don't mean your baby! That's marvelous news! And so are your and Adrian's achievements, Marjorie. I meant…I was only…"

Against her will, Viv felt a pang of sympathy for Tommy. Loved ones growing up and doing positive adult things sometimes did feel like a disaster for those around them. Especially when one's time and mental fortitude were already stretched well past the breaking point.

"Maybe it was the wrong time to bring up the exposition." Marjorie exchanged a nervous glance with her husband. "It's just that… Jacob, I would *love* if you would say a few words and give the official toast."

He stared at her in disbelief.

"It doesn't have to rhyme," she said quickly. "But if you'd like to throw in a poem or two for good measure—"

"No." He shook his head. "Absolutely not."

She tilted her head. "No to which part? The toast, or the rhyming?"

"All of it. Give your own speech. It's your party."

"But this would give you a public platform to—"

"Being privately rejected by some publisher's secretary stings quite enough. I don't need to be mocked or judged by a hundred artistes."

"Two hundred," Adrian murmured. "It's a big party."

"Jacob—" began Marjorie.

"He said no," Kuni said firmly. "Which you should respect. After all, don't *you* have a secret project you don't want anyone looking at until you're ready?"

Marjorie bit her lip.

"She does indeed," agreed Graham. "There's an entire wall of easels whose canvases she keeps covered in burlap to prevent us from peeking."

"All right, all right," Marjorie muttered. "Jacob, if you change your mind, the master of ceremonies position is yours."

"It's already gone from 'make a brief toast' to 'master of ceremonies'?" Jacob's entire form radiated tenseness. "Should I flee now before you start expecting me to run for speaker of the House of Commons?"

"Olivebury is the most likely contender for that role," said Graham. "Which brings us back to…"

As he talked, Jacob made several strange hand gestures across the room.

Viv blinked at him. "Is that supposed to mean something?"

"Arguing with my sisters," he muttered.

Belatedly, Viv remembered Marjorie was deaf in one ear. "Sign language," she said in sudden understanding.

He nodded distractedly. "We can teach you later."

Viv was too embarrassed to admit it hadn't occurred to her that *he* would speak it. Yet the impulse to communicate silently had been second nature to him.

Of course she'd known Marjorie Wynchester was hard of hearing, but in Viv's experience, the needs of one person did not generally inspire those around them to go out of their way to provide accommodations.

If she'd been forced to guess, Viv would have predicted the onus would be on Marjorie to learn to read lips, or to say *Could you repeat that a little louder?* a thousand times a day. Or just to live her life in constant confusion.

The discovery that the entire Wynchester family had learned sign language in order to communicate with their sister meant Viv was forced to reevaluate her opinion of them. Again.

Maybe the line between Good People and Bad People wasn't always as clear as she'd believed.

"Think back to Quentin's state of mind the day he didn't come home," Graham said. "Did he voice any particular goals?"

Viv stared at him. How could these geniuses interview even a fraction of Quentin's friends without realizing their one and only goal was to become a Wynchester? Did he just want to force her to say it aloud for his own amusement?

"Besides training to join the world's greatest investigative philanthropists?" she replied icily, then realized of course Graham must be asking about hints of any conflict *outside* of the obvious. "Oh, you mean our argument. I'd told you Quentin and I parted on bad terms."

Tommy nodded. "Jacob said your cousin and his friends were Good Samaritans. I think it's noble."

Of course she would. Wealthy white women didn't die for being noble. Especially ones who could pass for wealthy white *men.*

People like Viv's mother on the other hand...People like Viv and her young cousin...

The Wynchesters either didn't understand or didn't remember what life was like for ordinary people.

Worse, Quentin already had a family. *Viv* was family. She kept him fed and clothed and comfortable. He didn't realize how much it hurt for her not to be enough. Even at home, in the house she maintained no matter the ache in her back or the toll of never getting sufficient sleep.

No matter how hard Viv tried, she was never good enough for the world around her. Including the cousin who was her only other family alive. He shared a surname with her and wished he didn't.

Marjorie leaned forward. "Did your row have anything to do with your plays?"

"Or him dressing in a way you didn't approve of?" added Tommy.

"Or falling in love with the wrong person?"

"No," Viv answered. "Though you've got the wrong idea about what sort of love affair would most disrupt my life. I've spent a decade being Quentin's caretaker. Once he reaches his majority, he won't need me anymore."

"Won't that give you more time to work on your plays?"

"It would, if I had a table to write on. My newspaper money barely covers stationery. It's not enough for food and rent."

"Quentin would kick you out?" Kuni said in surprise.

"If he marries, he'll want and deserve privacy. Even if he's willing to house a spinster cousin post-wedding, if Quentin takes a childbearing wife, the only place for a nursery is my small bedchamber. Before, he needed me. Soon, he'll need me gone. I'm caught in-between. But I would happily move out tomorrow if it meant Quentin could come home today."

Tommy nodded her understanding. "Your fears are about what *you* are going to do with your life, not how Quentin wants to live his."

"As long as he's happy and safe," Viv confirmed. "On my Aunt Kamia's deathbed, I swore to protect Quentin from harm. Which includes out of gaol and out of the hospital, but also to protect him from his own poor decision-making. He has neither deep pockets nor lofty connections, and therefore should not comport himself as though he were invincible. And he ought to remember once in a while that I am only human, too. These are old arguments. But the words we threw at each other this time cut a little deeper."

"We'll find him," Jacob promised, his brown eyes full of empathy. "We're doing everything we can."

"Are you?" she asked softly. She wanted to believe him. But if his claims were true, then why was Quentin still missing?

"Based on the intelligence we've been able to gather," Graham began.

Viv listened as he summarized the facts of Quentin's disappearance, and the steps the collective had taken to uncover his whereabouts. As the Wynchesters talked, Viv jotted notes in her latest writing journal. She always carried around a script in progress, so she could scratch out a few lines of dialogue while waiting for water to boil, or while waiting for it to be her turn at the market. Everything around her was potential fodder for a future play.

This was no exception. The Wynchesters were practically a Drury Lane production in their own right. The lengths they had gone to in the hunt for Quentin were astonishing. They'd actually paid boatmen to search the canal tunnels and sent several scouts all the way to the Chislehurst chalk caves!

London's finest Bow Street Runners *wished* they had half the influence and reach of the motley family in this room.

Viv was forced to admit she might once again have underestimated them.

"I spent his entire life showing by example that if you want something bad enough, you must put in any time, effort, or sacrifice necessary. So I suppose I have only myself to blame for his good-hearted, wrongheaded behavior. Quentin would rather prove himself dangerously than let me ruin his dreams."

"Could he defend himself against violence?" Kuni asked.

"He...has had a few fencing lessons," was the most charitable way Viv could answer that question. "Quentin has had tutors in every topic or skill imaginable. Which is only possible because he grows bored by the third or fourth attempt and thus moves on to the next item on the list."

Which was what Viv had previously been afraid of. That Quentin, in his desperation, would attempt brave acts of heroics so far outside his capabilities that he would injure himself irrevocably—or worse. The mysterious Newt, and Quentin's possible connection to the Olivebury robbery, were pieces she could not yet fit into the puzzle.

Jacob seemed to sense the fear and frustration warring within her. "Please don't panic unless there is reason to. I'm sure your cousin is unhurt."

"You can't know that."

"You're right," he agreed. "I can't know that. It's what I'm choosing to believe until facts indicate otherwise. There's been no sign of him at any hospital, morgue, or prison. I've learned one's attitude can help keep unproductive worries at bay. I suggest you practice some optimism as well."

"I didn't ask for your advice," she snapped.

He looked at her.

Her face heated. All right, that was rich, coming from her. Viv spent 90 percent of her day doling out advice to others. She ought to be able to take a little in return.

The truth was, the worry *had* abated. Everything was topsy-turvy not because Jacob and his family were overbearing and intolerable, but because they were kind and made her feel safe, despite the unanswered questions.

Viv hadn't been able to rely on anyone but herself for so long that life felt like crossing the ocean in a rowboat without oars. She'd spent her days paddling her bare hands as hard as she could without getting anywhere. Now that a larger vessel of friendly forces had tossed out a life buoy, she wasn't sure she knew how to float in these waters.

"With no evidence of injury or arrest, and with no public sightings in several days, we must consider the possibility that Quentin has gone into hiding for his own reasons."

"Such as to punish me because he was angry with me." Viv's shoulders were tight and her stomach sour. "He'd had enough."

"Actually," Tommy said, "Jacob's referring to Olivebury's robbery. We don't know why Quentin would have masterminded such an escapade—"

"My cousin did no such thing!"

"We have to consider every possibility."

"He accidentally returned the script to the question-writer—"

"—who could have been Quentin in the first place. He might have sent those letters himself, to disguise the fact that he was the one in need of such stratagems."

"Quentin would never manipulate me like that."

"He's manipulated you into doing everything else for him."

"No," Viv said frostily. "He's family, and family helps each other. I would think a Wynchester could understand that, of all people."

"An exciting caper would be an adventure," Jacob pointed out. "You said he liked those. Plus, if he's the mastermind behind the Olivebury burglary—"

"I would be the mastermind," Viv muttered. "They're my scripts."

"—then that means he's *fine*. And he's hiding from you because he knows by now you've figured out what happened to your missing plays."

Viv's fingers curled into fists. She wanted to believe her cousin was safe almost as much as she wanted to slap Jacob for doubting her cousin's integrity.

"It wasn't Quentin's handwriting," she said triumphantly. "I was his first and only governess and have had many occasions to glimpse his penmanship since."

"Quentin's, maybe," he agreed. "But what about his secret club? By your own description, he has a lot of young, impressionable, risk-taking friends. Am I leaping to conclusions by assuming you to be unfamiliar with their handwriting? Or his co-conspirator Newt, whom you don't know anything about at all?"

An excellent point. Viv hated him for it. She increased her scowl.

"If one of his friends is behind the robbery, it was without my cousin's knowledge. Not only wouldn't he risk the hangman for something so stupid, Quentin would never use my fiction as an instruction manual, and implicate us both. He knows the risks."

"But we'll still have to rule it out empirically," said Tommy.

The problem was, Viv was warring with herself as much as with the Wynchesters. Given the rebellions in her own youth, charging full steam ahead in pursuit of adventure was unquestionably in Quentin's blood.

As much as she didn't wish to believe him or his secret society foolish enough to rob an aristocrat, she wouldn't put it past him if her cousin believed he was doing a bad thing for good reasons—just like his infamous, lawbreaking idols.

And Quentin would know better than to come home after pulling a stunt like that.

"Maybe he did fall in love and elope to Scotland," Viv muttered. "Or tag along on some harebrained holiday to Antwerp."

She'd still kill him, but these were much better options than him being in danger—or gaol.

"Enough speculating," Elizabeth said. "Let's solve the robbery. That should lead us to Quentin."

"Do we know what was taken from Olivebury yet?" Marjorie asked.

Graham shook his head. "By all accounts, he refuses to disclose the missing item or items."

"Have you considered interviewing one of the servants?" Viv suggested.

The entire family looked amused. She bristled.

"It's not a bad idea," Jacob said quickly. "But believe me, it has occurred to Graham to interview everyone Olivebury has ever come in contact with. Graham has journals containing detailed accounts of the private lives of half the population of London."

"I have notes on everyone of note," his brother agreed with a laugh.

Teeth clenched, she arched a brow. "Everyone who matters, eh? Do you keep a book about my cousin?"

Graham had the grace to look chagrined.

"No? Well, I do. Allow me to help flesh out your library." Viv fished in her satchel, then slapped her Quentin journal into Graham's hand.

"He didn't mean..." Jacob said quietly.

"I know exactly what you all meant," she replied bitterly.

Kuni cleared her throat. "If the stolen object isn't visibly apparent to staff, that means the thief took something Olivebury hoped to keep hidden."

Graham nodded. "Whatever the item, it hasn't turned up yet, openly or underground. The moment it does, I'll be the first to know."

"That's only one possibility," Viv said. "Maybe whatever was stolen is not for sale. Perhaps the thief wishes to keep the object for himself."

"Or use it for blackmail," Jacob suggested.

"Quentin would never stoop to blackmail," said Viv with satisfaction. "I told you he had nothing to do with the burglary."

Tommy arched her brows. "A lad who *would* have otherwise been born a wealthy, respected viscount...and who instead receives a pittance so small, he cannot even afford to hire the cheapest maid-of-all-work to share some of the load dumped upon his already busy-with-two-careers-of-her-own cousin...You're saying a lad like that couldn't use an extra shilling or two?"

"I didn't say he couldn't use the shilling," Viv said tightly. "I said he wouldn't steal it."

Not because she or Quentin held any particular respect for British property law. To their eternal rage, Viv and both of their mothers had *been* British aristocrats' "property." Hers had died because of it.

To this day, tens of thousands of other men, women, and children like them were still enslaved on rich English lords' offshore properties and plantations. To the devil with the British, and all their self-serving conscienceless behavior!

The reason her cousin would never steal from an aristocrat, regardless of his feelings on who was allowed to own what, was because Quentin knew exactly how and why Viv's mother had been murdered. That Viv herself had almost suffered the same fate. How close they'd both come to never meeting each other, much less being a source of daily happiness in each other's lives.

Quentin also well knew that here in England, the poverty-stricken were regularly prosecuted on theft charges. The indigent could be hung for pickpocketing so much as a penny. Quentin would *never* risk his life in such a foolish way. Or force Viv to relive her grief at the loss of her last living family member.

Her lungs seized and her throat closed up just thinking about it.

"I agree with Miss Henry," Jacob said. "At least with regard to Olivebury. Given that Quentin would *be* the current Viscount Ayleswick, if the lord had married Quentin's mother, it would make more sense for Quentin to rob the half-brother who took his place in the aristocracy, rather than a total stranger."

"Then who did it?" asked Elizabeth. "This would be far easier if Olivebury would just tell us what the thief stole."

"Offering our services was the first thing I tried," said Graham.

"Olivebury refuses to speak to me. He hasn't answered a single call or letter."

Viv gave him a considering look. "Maybe that's because you're... you?"

Graham raised his brows. "Are you referring to my skin color, or the fact that I'm a Wynchester?"

"Both," she admitted.

Though from her perspective, the Wynchesters as a whole lived a life of privilege...for some of them, life was still sometimes cruel and arbitrary and unfair.

Elizabeth leaned on her sword stick. "Mr. Olivebury may not be an aristocrat, but now that Philippa's father has retired, Olivebury is one of the most important voices in the House of Commons. What he says, others believe. Where he goes, others follow."

"Didn't he work with Faircliffe on the factory reform bill?" asked Jacob.

Graham nodded. "Yes. He's been one of the duke's best allies for years. Their progressive politics is why neither has been elected speaker of their respective houses."

"With so much in common, perhaps Olivebury would open up about the robbery at his gentleman's club, over a brandy or two," Viv suggested.

"Superficial confidants might not be enough," Jacob. "The plan ought to include a firsthand look at the scene of the crime."

Viv nodded slowly. "If that were possible, you ought to be the one to lead the search."

They all stared at her, uncomprehending.

"Did you say...Jacob?" Elizabeth repeated.

"He's the reason anyone drew a connection between Quentin's disappearance and my missing plays in the first place," Viv reminded her. "Sometimes we don't know what we're looking for until we stumble across it."

Jacob suddenly became very interested in picking invisible lint off his waistcoat.

Graham closed his notebook. "We can send a team to sneak in while Faircliffe attempts to charm Olivebury at a club."

"I never say no to a good infiltration," said Tommy. "Let's do it."

"I don't have *time* to do it." Marjorie groaned. "I can barely spare a minute to forge a set of keys, much less pick locks in person."

"I didn't say we should break laws ourselves," said Viv. "It's irresponsible and an unnecessary risk to behave like a villain."

"Take that back," Elizabeth protested. "We're not the villains."

Viv snorted. "You're not morally different, if you think it's fine for you to break rules when they get in your way, but you nonetheless expect others to adhere to them."

Marjorie gasped. "Not morally different!"

"Even if you've never blackmailed anyone," Viv began.

The family exchanged glances.

"—or kidnapped someone—"

The Wynchesters smirked.

"—or stabbed someone—"

Elizabeth whistled innocently.

Viv couldn't believe them. "How can you believe yourselves ethically superior to anyone? Do you even register the hypocrisy of your actions?"

"Listen," said Elizabeth. "Do you want to find your cousin or not?"

Viv clicked her teeth together and crossed her arms. She needed the Wynchesters' help to find and exonerate Quentin. And she'd be damned if she let them bollocks that up without her oversight.

Besides, Quentin wasn't the only one who enjoyed a good *I told you so*. He'd begged her to spend time with the Wynchesters, believing she'd come to love them in the process. If they proved themselves to be even worse role models than she'd feared, he would have to admit she was right about them all along.

> **Vivian**: All right, Quentin. You win. Until I find you and exonerate your name, I will spend every waking moment with your Wynchesters and do my best to take their measure with an open mind. You have my word.
>
> **Quentin**: Huzzah! If I'd known this would work, I would've disappeared ages ago!
>
> **Vivian**: Addendum. If you've put me through this panic on purpose, in some harebrained scheme to soften me toward this family, then when I lay eyes on you, so help me God…

"Very well. I'll help you," she forced herself to say aloud. "Solving the robbery will clear Quentin's name, and then we must find him posthaste."

"We could follow your script," Tommy suggested. "It worked before. No one would be expecting a *second* whooper swan invasion."

Jacob shook his head. "The Olivebury household is unlikely to be fooled by the same thing twice."

"If you two sneak in through a window on a moonless night—" began Elizabeth.

"I shall not participate in breaking the law," Viv interrupted.

The Wynchesters might take for granted that their deep pocketbooks and aristocratic connections provided *them* with impenetrable armor, but Viv's reinforced sleeves could barely protect her from a disgruntled badger.

She straightened her spine. "However, I do have an idea on how we might be invited inside…"

13

In less than three short hours, Viv found herself living her cousin's wildest dream.

She was in costume. Accompanying the *Wynchesters*. About to enter an upper-class town home on false pretenses.

And she'd helped plan the whole thing.

She tried to steady her trembling hands by pretending she was a character in one of her plays. "You're sure his wife is at home?"

"Graham's sure," Jacob confirmed.

Viv's strategy hinged on Mrs. Olivebury's presence. Her husband's influence was in the House of Commons, but a woman's power depended on her place in society. As wife of the Duke of Faircliffe, Chloe Wynchester would be a valuable connection for both political and aristocratic aspirations. With luck, the wife would confide to the duchess everything they needed to know.

And without luck…the team had Viv's contingency plan.

"Ready?" Jacob asked her quietly.

"She's ready," Tommy interjected. "I dressed her myself."

"As ready as I'll ever be." Viv touched her reticule lightly. She hoped not to have to use her secret weapon, but she hadn't come this far to give up now.

The Wynchester carriage slowed to a stop in front of the long brick terrace where the shepherd's-pie-and-whooper-swan incident had taken place. Er, one of the Wynchesters' *multiple* carriages. Viv suspected they lived out in Islington rather than fashionable Mayfair by choice, not because their coffers wouldn't cover the high rents.

Then again, maybe it wasn't money that kept them on the fringes of society. More than half of the Wynchesters were white as a lord, but almost all had been born poor, or on the wrong side of the blanket, or other such unforgivable offenses amongst the beau monde.

"So far, so good," said Jacob. "It looks like Faircliffe's ducal coach-and-four arrived seconds before us. He's helping Chloe down now."

"Then what are we waiting for?" Tommy flung open the carriage door and bounded out onto the cobblestones. She motioned to them impatiently. "Come on, come on. Don't worry, I memorized the interior distribution of the house."

Of course she had. That's why she was leading the reconnaissance squad.

Jacob gestured for Viv to exit the carriage next. His voice was chagrined. "I'd give you my arm, but you're supposed to be a chambermaid, not my client."

Did all clients receive such gallant attention?

"I wouldn't want your arm anyway," she lied. Viv thought way too often about Jacob Wynchester's arms. And the rest of his body. The sight of him alone could make her purr.

Viv joined Tommy on the pavement, followed by Jacob.

"Look humble," Tommy warned.

"Trust me," Viv muttered. "I know what people like this expect from people like me."

When she'd escaped the plantation on Demerara, she'd vowed never to behave as though she was worth less than anyone else ever again. Viv tried to tell herself that this time, she was just pretending. But the prickly, unwelcome sensation felt far too close to her early life for comfort.

As the two teams united on the walkway, the trio exchanged secret glances with Chloe and Faircliffe before falling behind the regal duke and duchess in faux subservience.

The butler welcomed them in at once. If he was surprised that his aristocratic visitors paid morning calls flanked by multiple servants, he gave no sign. Perhaps this was normal behavior in the world of the nobility.

More likely, servants were simply invisible.

"Please," said the butler. "Come this way. My master and mistress are expecting you."

Chloe straightened the most hideous bonnet Viv had ever seen in her life. The duchess looped her arm through the duke's and sashayed importantly down the corridor.

Viv would have sworn a headpiece so garish must be part of a costume, but apparently Chloe always strolled about town with two dozen ugly silk flowers and five yards of mismatched ribbons glued to her head.

"The parlor is just ahead," said the butler.

Mr. Olivebury's respected position as the most influential man in the House of Commons was clear at a glance. Although not a titled aristocrat himself, he lived amongst the haut ton. His house was as full of marble and gilding as the Wynchester residence.

Was that related to why he'd been targeted by the thief?

"The Duke and Duchess of Faircliffe," the butler intoned as they reached the parlor.

Mr. and Mrs. Olivebury scrambled to their feet. The ladies bussed each other's cheeks, while the gentlemen merely inclined their heads rather than bow.

No one remarked upon Viv, Jacob, and Tommy's presence, much less glanced in their direction.

Chloe engaged Mrs. Olivebury in bright chatter about fashion and theater. Faircliffe and Mr. Olivebury launched straight into talk of politics, and the prevalent issues with each of their respective houses of Parliament.

Viv could practically hear Jacob in her head: *Everything is going to plan.*

The Faircliffes had long been political allies of the Oliveburys, but today they hoped to gain their personal confidence. Perhaps in an unguarded moment, they could learn directly from the source what had been stolen. As a contingency, Viv, Jacob, and Tommy were to nose about where they didn't belong.

Assuming the trio could *get* where they didn't belong.

Viv had written Chloe's next line herself and was itching with impatience for the duchess to get on with the show.

Or maybe her anxiousness had nothing to do with the Oliveburys at all, and Viv simply was eager to hear someone, anyone, perform something she had written. Even if it was just one line of dialogue.

On cue, Chloe glanced over her shoulder and made an exaggerated expression of shock to see her three "servants" hovering against the wainscoting.

"This isn't *your* holiday," she said coldly, just as Viv had scripted. "I suggest you make yourselves useful if you wish to remain employed."

Viv, Jacob, and Tommy bobbed in chastisement and scurried from the parlor before anyone recalled that this wasn't their place of employment, so of course there were no tasks they ought to be performing.

As she filed out last in line, Viv overheard Mrs. Olivebury scold Chloe.

"Now, was that necessary, Your Grace? I'm sure every member of your loyal staff works very hard. A few moments of idleness whilst the four of us have a chat wouldn't hurt anything. In fact, my husband has been drafting a reform bill in which protections for residential employees would be—"

Viv nearly tripped over her own feet. A plain old ordinary Mrs! Criticizing a duchess to her face! Over perceived rudeness to paid servants!

Jacob made several strange hand gestures.

She made a face and whispered, "I haven't finished learning sign language yet."

"I said, Faircliffe *told* you Olivebury's politics are on our side," he whispered back.

Viv could still hardly credit that a wealthy white stranger would leap to her defense without hesitation.

"Oy!" A hall boy rounded the corner up ahead of them and stopped in his tracks. "What are you doing back here?"

"I'm assistant housekeeper to the Duke and Duchess of Faircliffe," Tommy announced grandly, patting her white wig. She lowered her voice. "But I used to be maid-staff for Mr. and Mrs. Olivebury out at the Yorkshire cottage. Now *that's* how a household should run, am I right?"

This was a calculated risk. Graham had provided them with a list of names and dates of service for every servant who had ever worked in the Oliveburys' country residence, so that Tommy could pretend to have been briefly employed there in whichever era proved most convenient. But that didn't mean the London staff weren't equally aware of the list of names and would realize Tommy wasn't who she claimed to be.

The hall boy's eyes widened. "I wouldn't know, ma'am. I've never been to Yorkshire."

Perfect.

"And why would you need to?" Tommy beamed at him. "The ones who do their jobs best are based in London. Which is why we're here today—we've been instructed to have a look around, so that these two new hires can see how things ought to be done."

This was almost, but not quite, the dialogue Viv had written. She did not fault Tommy for embellishing at will, however. Chloe had followed Viv's script to the letter, and it had nearly ruined everything. If the trio hadn't left so swiftly, Mrs. Olivebury might have insisted the duchess's servants spend the entire visit right there in the parlor with them, relaxing on cushioned chairs.

"Um," said the boy, clearly at a loss how to proceed next.

"Now then." Tommy turned to Viv and Jacob, raising one finger in a stern gesture. "You're to stay behind me and not touch anything. Up ahead, we have..."

She kept up a steady patter, regurgitating rules their own housekeeper had provided about how often floors should be swept and mopped, and shelves checked for dust.

Nonplussed, the hall boy watched them disappear around the corner, but did not try to stop them.

"He's gone," Tommy whispered after a moment. "*Hurry.*"

They sprinted after her to a closed door at the end of the corridor. Mr. Olivebury's personal study, from which some unknown object had been purloined. Tommy jiggled the handle.

It was locked.

Viv tried to remember which contingency plan this corresponded with. Five? Three?

Tommy held up a ring of keys and grinned. "Thank you, Marjorie."

The trio hurried inside the room and shut the door behind them.

"Should we lock it?" Viv asked.

Tommy shook her head. "Too suspicious. This way, if we're caught inside, we can claim the door was unlocked and we wandered in by mistake."

Viv glanced around the room. Though she'd never before been in the private study of a representative of Parliament, it looked exactly as she would have written it. Thrice the size of her parlor at home, with large furniture and large windows and a large fireplace, and more shelf space dedicated to bottles of Madeira than to anything resembling paperwork.

If anything looked out of place, it was the three of them.

"I'll check behind the paintings," said Tommy.

"Check for what?" asked Viv.

"No idea," Tommy answered cheerfully. "I'm counting on you two to let me know when we've found what we came for."

"I'll take the desk," said Viv.

She settled into the tall, well-cushioned armchair. It felt like floating on a cloud. Good God, how did Mr. Olivebury get any work done? She could sleep in this thing.

Tommy tossed her the ring of keys. "If any of the drawers are locked, one of these might work."

"Thank you."

Viv peeked under her eyelashes at Jacob. He was on his knees before the bookshelf, releasing a quartet of mice from his coat pockets.

"What are they trained to sniff again?" Viv asked. She knew the answer but liked the warm rumble of Jacob's voice.

He pointed at each mouse in turn. "Opium. Gunpowder. Pound-note ink. Refined sugar."

Viv had her doubts that the answer to the mystery lay in a missing box of chocolates, but then again, if someone had broken into her house and stolen her emergency candy supply, she might not have wished to tell the newspapers about her secret addiction, either.

Just like she didn't wish to admit her fascination with a certain Wynchester.

Despite herself, Viv could not help but be charmed by the handsome poet. Jacob was an unpublished writer like herself, and a sweetheart of a man around whom animals flocked like mystical fairy tales. If he'd told her his trained mice could lead them to gold, silver, uncut diamonds, and whooper swans, she absolutely would have believed it.

Jacob stroked the short fur behind the ears of the currency-sniffing mouse, which wiggled in obvious pleasure.

Viv couldn't blame the creature. She'd reacted in much the same way when Jacob had caressed her wrist. Which was why she'd run from the barn rather than acknowledge her obvious attraction.

Ever since that day, Viv had wished she'd stayed a little longer. Experienced a few more strokes of his finger. Perhaps even—

The door to the study flew open.

Shite! Viv leaped up from the chair and shoved the ring of keys into her pocket. She hadn't even had a chance to try them yet, and already they'd been caught in the act.

The hall boy stood in the open doorway, this time flanked by two young maids.

Reinforcements. Not a good sign.

"What do you think you're doing in here?" demanded the elder of the two maids.

Jacob's turn to deflect suspicion.

He'd made a nearly inaudible whistle, and now all four trained mice scrambled back and forth across the expensive carpet as if the politician's study doubled as a playground for rodents.

"Chased these creatures in," Jacob replied briskly. "If you'd like to wait out in the corridor, I'm sure I'll have them rounded up in no time."

To Viv's surprise, the maids did not cringe back in alarm. If anything, they looked relieved that there was such a simple explanation for the trespassing.

"I told you that mouser isn't worth a boiled bean," the younger maid said to the older one. "We ought to acquire a new one, if you ask me."

"Pah," said the hall boy. "Who needs cats when you have me? I'll catch these mice and wring their necks quick as you can say 'squeak.'"

He dashed forward, arms outstretched, a mean smile stretching his lips.

Jacob brought his fist to his lips as if covering a cough—though in fact he was hiding another barely audible whistle.

All four mice immediately ceased crisscrossing the carpet and vanished into the shadows instead.

The hall boy stumbled, glancing around the study in confusion.

"You can wring the rodents' necks later," said the older maid. "I'll have the mouser sent in. But all humans must exit. No one is to be in the master's study without him present."

Tommy clutched her chest, mere seconds away from feigning an apoplexy in order to give Viv and Jacob a few more moments in the study before they were all evicted.

Apoplexy was a terrible plan. Viv had *told* Tommy it should be much further down the contingency list. A medical emergency meant every servant in earshot would come running. Doctors would be summoned, and soon the entire household would be crammed into the study, making it impossible to search for anything.

Jacob had the right idea with his mice. There'd been no way to predict that the maids would simply shrug rather than be scared off.

But that was why Viv had brought Sally.

Jacob noticed first. His eyes widened and he took an instinctive step toward Viv before cautiously freezing in place.

"Er..." He cleared his throat. "I don't mean to alarm you..."

A string of garbled syllables tangled in Tommy's throat. "I really am going to suffer an apoplexy, if someone doesn't get that thing out of here!"

Most likely because Viv had failed to mention she'd brought Sally along for the ride.

If the contingency became necessary, she'd need everyone's reactions to be genuine.

The youngest maid gasped and stumbled backward toward the door. "What *is* that thing?"

"It's crawling up her bodice," the older maid whispered in obvious horror. She scrabbled to join the other maid in the relative safety of the corridor.

The hall boy's face drained of color. "It's...a furry...spider? The size of my fist!"

Small fists that were currently pale and trembling.

"Kill it!" called one of the maids from just out of sight.

"I can't look," moaned the other. "I'm going to have nightmares for years!"

The hall boy was still frozen in place.

Viv could fix that.

She feigned a panicked cry, bringing her arm up to her chest and flinging the enormous tarantula directly toward the hall boy's shocked face.

He shrieked and dashed from the room before Sally even landed, slamming the study door shut behind him.

Viv leaped over her spider and bent her mouth to the keyhole. "Stay far away until we find it," she called. "Save yourselves!"

"We will," came the muffled reply.

Viv turned around and curtsied at Jacob and Tommy.

"What," whispered Tommy, "was that?"

"Wolf spider," Jacob answered. "*Lycosa tarantula*, native to southern Europe. Because of the madness its venom is said to cause, Italians invented a dance called the tarantella, designed to represent—"

"Let me interrupt this fascinating lecture to rephrase my question," said Tommy. "What the devil was that eight-legged beast doing on Miss Henry's bodice, and how do we keep it from killing us?"

Viv dropped to the floor, palm up on the carpet.

"Sally wouldn't hurt a fly, would you, Sally?" she cooed. "Well, maybe a fly. You'd inject it with poison to dissolve its innards and swallow the remaining glop whole."

Tommy gurgled wordlessly.

"Come on, sweetling," coaxed Viv. "I'm sorry I tossed you at that nasty human, but you did the very right thing and scared him away. He doesn't know that your venom is only capable of murdering small mammals, and that you rarely bite humans at all."

"Rarely," Tommy choked out. "Comforting."

Sally scurried across the carpet and into Viv's outstretched palm. Viv tucked the tarantula back into its protective sugar shaker in her reticule, then tied the string closed for safety. *Sally's* safety. Viv would be very upset if any injury were to befall a beloved pet.

"I thought Sally was a rhinoceros," muttered Jacob. "Or another attack badger."

Tommy's eyes widened. "I won't even ask."

"She's a distraction," Viv said firmly. "And it's working, at least for now. We should still hurry. The maids might summon a stableboy with an affinity for stomping spiders."

Jacob took her fingers in his larger hand. "I'm glad you're all right. When I first saw that tarantula, I feared it would bite you."

"She has, many times." Viv couldn't concentrate on her words, not with her suddenly trembling hand back in the warmth of Jacob's. "Never hurts more than a bee sting."

"I wouldn't want you to suffer even that." His voice was low as he rubbed the pad of his thumb over the sensitive flesh of her hand. "I wish you only pleasure, not pain."

"I like pleasure," Viv said inanely. She imagined it would be nothing but pleasure if he kissed her. In fact, she often imagined a lot more than that.

"Yes," said Tommy. "You're both clearly in a big hurry to solve this robbery and exit the study."

Viv's face heated. Jolted out of her trance, she jerked her fingers out of Jacob's hands and threw herself back into the armchair behind Mr. Olivebury's desk, refusing to meet either Wynchester sibling's eyes.

Tommy was right. They might not have much time.

As his sister peeked behind portraits, Jacob whistled for his mice to resume their original missions.

Viv tried all the drawers in the desk, and discovered only one of them was locked. She decided to ignore the rest and start there. Whatever Mr. Olivebury didn't want the world to see wouldn't be kept somewhere easily accessible.

It took until the thirteenth key, but Marjorie's ring of skeleton keys worked as advertised. Viv slid the drawer open all the way, torn between sifting through in a rush before another interruption came, or taking her time so as not to miss something important.

"No opium," Jacob called out quietly. "Gunpowder residue on the carpet, but nowhere else. Probably tracked in on hunting boots, either Olivebury's or a visitor's."

"What about the other two mice?" asked Tommy.

"Still working."

"I've got something," said Viv. "I think. Maybe."

Jacob and Tommy hurried to her side.

"What did you find?" Jacob asked.

"A diary." Viv opened the journal and pointed at a random page. "It goes back years. Every few lines is a new date, and notes like 'Meet the lads at the club at seven' or 'Don't forget to accompany Mrs. O to the theater.'"

"That sounds innocuous enough," said Tommy. "Does it mention insurmountable gambling debts or a secret love child?"

"No," Viv admitted. "But every Wednesday and Saturday, it says 'Fs 4 in' or 'Jy 4 in' or 'Ch 4 in.' The same three phrases are listed for this week and the next."

"'In'?" repeated Tommy. "In what?"

Viv pulled out her writing journal and started scribbling notes. "I don't know yet."

"It's a code," said Jacob. "For...something."

Tommy's brow creased in thought. "Maybe something legislative? What days does Parliament meet?"

"Monday, Tuesday, Thursday, and Friday," he replied.

"How do you remember that?" she groused.

"How *don't* you remember?" He gave a dramatic shudder. "If I'm not safe in the barn on those days, Chloe ropes me into attending the sessions."

Tommy groaned. "That's how she traps me. My bad sense of calendar."

"I don't know if Mr. Olivebury kept more diaries before this one," Viv said, "but for the past three years, similar entries appear biweekly—and only when he's in London."

"So, matching the social season?" Jacob asked. "As in, it might be related to parliamentary sessions after all?"

She rifled through the pages. "Yes. No. Here, I found a visit to London when the House of Commons was adjourned, and the cryptic entries are still present."

"At least you found something," said Tommy. "There's nothing behind these portraits but—"

Viv and Jacob looked at her.

Frowning, Tommy gripped the final framed painting. "It's stuck to the wall."

"Stuck?" Viv repeated.

"It can't be." Jacob crossed the room. "I'll help."

He tugged on the gilded frame.

It didn't budge.

He narrowed his eyes, then pushed the painting toward the left.

Nothing moved.

He shoved the painting toward the right. A six-foot section of wall moved with it.

Viv gasped and leapt to her feet, then remembered to lock the diary back in the drawer where she'd found it.

"It's a secret panel," Tommy said with respect. "But it doesn't appear to go anywhere."

The movable wall hid an eight-inch-deep recess, stretching from floor to ceiling, and as wide as Jacob's outstretched arms, from fingertip to fingertip.

There was nothing inside but dust.

"Wait," said Viv. "I see something."

"I can see that it's empty," said Tommy.

"Empty now," Viv agreed. "But look close."

She traced a barely discernible rectangle, in which the wallpaper's floral pattern was ever so slightly brighter than the rest.

"Something hung here," said Jacob.

Viv tilted her head. "Mr. Olivebury must leave the secret panel open when he's alone in his study. Light from the window fades the bits of wall covering exposed to the sun, but the part behind the object stays protected."

"Until it was stolen," said Tommy. "This has to be what the thief took."

"Another watercolor, like the ones decorating the rest of the house?" Jacob guessed. "But why would anyone steal that? Or hide it in the first place?"

"A treasure map," Tommy said confidently. "That's what the letter-writer to Ask Vivian wanted to find, remember? And did so successfully, from the looks of it."

Jacob appeared skeptical. "What kind of treasure? You really think there are chests of gold buried here in London?"

"Maybe in America," Tommy suggested. "No one said the treasure had to be located in London. Gold could be anywhere."

"The missing rectangle could be anything," Viv said in frustration. She straightened. Not knowing gave her an idea. She turned to a blank page of her journal and fumbled for a pencil.

"I've got the mouser!" came the hall boy's voice from the other side of the study door. "I'm coming in!"

Blast. Viv ripped out the sheet she'd been scribbling on. She folded the page in half, then hurriedly affixed it to the wall covering using a pin.

"Close it, close it!" she hissed, motioning frantically to Jacob.

He hauled the panel shut just as the study door banged open, revealing the pasty hall boy, a hissing cat, and no sign of the two maids.

"Good man," Jacob said grandly. "But there's no need for your assistance. We've killed the spider and caught the other beasts." He scooped up the last two mice.

The hall boy did not look impressed. "Those are still alive. Want me to kill them for you?"

"I'll handle the rodents," Jacob assured him. He raised his brows at Viv and Tommy. "Ladies, if you've had enough excitement for one day?"

"Oh, yes." Viv fluttered her hand at her throat and tried to look properly traumatized. "I hope never to set foot into a house like this ever again. My poor nerves. Maid service doesn't suit me in the least."

"I tell you, lad. Aren't young girls missish?" Tommy murmured to the wide-eyed hall boy as the trio sailed past. "Good help these days is so hard to find."

14

The next morning, Jacob was unsurprised when Miss Henry arrived to interrupt him. He was in the barn, unwrapping the front paw of an injured fox he hoped to release back into the wild.

Jacob *was* surprised that his beautiful client had knocked, rather than barrel into the barn as though she'd been launched from a cannon.

The paw had healed beautifully, so he placed the fox in a temporary carrier and opened the door.

Miss Henry looked as unsettled as the injured fox had done upon losing a battle with a wild boar. Jacob found it unlikely his client had been brawling with wildlife in the forest. Then again, Miss Henry was the sort of woman to charge in absolutely anywhere...while secretly wearing leather-reinforced sleeves for safety, and a corset lined with chain mail.

Which meant she was brave *and* scared, he realized. She tried to do it all. To control everything around her but knowing she could not. So she shored up her defenses as best she could, and hid her interminable worrying behind a mask of total competency and fierce independence.

Coming here and asking for help must have nearly felled her.

Jacob gave her his gentlest smile. "Good morning. And congratulations on completing your first mission."

"It's far from complete. We haven't found Quentin or cleared his name."

"But we do have clues we wouldn't have known about if it weren't for your help. I'm glad you were with us."

Miss Henry glanced away, as if unsure what to do with such a compliment. Her darting gaze locked on the basket at his hip instead.

"Packing a picnic?"

He shook his head. "*Vulpes vulpes.*"

"A red fox?" She looked intrigued.

So was Jacob. This wasn't the first time she'd demonstrated uncommon knowledge of the animal world. Usually, his siblings' eyes glazed over whenever a Latin genus escaped his mouth. Miss Henry hadn't even blinked.

"How do you come by your passion for zoology?" he asked. "Have you always loved unusual animals?"

She looked embarrassed. "Secondary effect from proximity to Quentin, I'm afraid. What are you going to do with this creature?"

"Release him."

"Might I go along, too?"

He surprised himself by considering the offer before shaking his head. "It's better if you don't. Not because I wish to exclude you, but because the fewer distractions for our friend the fox, the better. He needs to return to his home."

As he spoke, Miss Henry flinched, then nodded.

Jacob wondered at her initial wince. Had he offended her by not accepting her company? Or was Miss Henry's mind with her cousin, whom she also hoped would return home? Perhaps Jacob's words had even made her think of her prior home in the West Indies. She must have left it for a reason. He well knew from experience that not all homes were the sort one ever wished to return to.

"I'll be back within the hour, if you'd like to wait inside the house with my family," he offered.

She glanced over her shoulder. "I suppose I shouldn't waste an opportunity to study the character of each of your siblings."

"Planning a future play?"

She'd already admitted to having penned several anti-Wynchester scripts. He hoped her opinion of them was starting to mellow. Even if it hadn't, his siblings would still thrill at the notoriety, the rogues.

Miss Henry widened her eyes with exaggerated innocence. "I can only go where my muse leads me."

He snorted. "You don't believe in muses."

"And you have a fox to release. Don't worry about me. Your family and I cannot get into *that* much trouble while you're gone."

Had a more ominous phrase ever been spoken?

Jacob did his best to hurry. He was back in less than forty minutes and wasted no time dropping off the empty basket and hunting down his family members and client.

He found Miss Henry in the siblings' sitting room, discussing tenement mismanagement with Philippa in between exchanging insightful commentary with Graham as he read lines aloud from the daily newspapers.

"What did you burn down while I was gone?" Jacob asked suspiciously.

"The patriarchy," Philippa answered without looking up from her book.

That sounded like a normal afternoon, but Miss Henry looked unusually...*bubbly*.

"Did you *outlaw* men in my brief absence?" he asked.

"No, but we found one," she replied with a joyous smile. "Or are soon to, anyway. Graham has a lead on—oh, my apologies, I shouldn't use your Christian names without permission."

Jacob waved a hand. "By all means, Miss Henry. No one's ever accused this family of standing on propriety. I beg you to call me Jacob."

"I...Vivian." Their gazes locked for a brief moment. She looked flustered, then continued, "Your brother believes he'll have located and interviewed Newt by this time tomorrow."

"Then so it shall be. Graham's network is remarkably industrious." She pressed her clasped hands to her chest as if praying. "Hopefully that means Quentin will be home tomorrow, too. Thank God. I can't decide whether to box his ears, or give him an earful, or both."

"Possibly why he hasn't returned home," Jacob said with a small smile.

She sighed. "I know it's normal for lads his age to push at boundaries and spread their wings. I'm just not certain Quentin was ready to be released into the wild quite yet."

"If it helps," Philippa began. "On average, most adolescents—"

Before she could give whatever insight she'd been about to impart, Mr. Randall strode into the sitting room with a bemused expression. There was no calling card in his hand.

"Pardon the interruption. A 'Mr. Smith' urgently requests an audience." The butler lowered his voice. "Whoever he is, he's patently not Mr. Smith. He's a man disguised as...something. His ruse couldn't be more obvious if he were wearing elephant ears."

"Quentin!" Vivian exclaimed in delight. Her shoulders relaxed in obvious relief. "Of course he would come here rather than go home first, the scamp. Is our caller tall and lean, with light brown skin and short black hair styled in raffish twists? Possibly covered in chalk?"

The butler blinked at her. "No."

She visibly deflated, her shoulders sinking and her spine wilting.

"Does your cousin often wear...chalk?" Jacob enquired.

"Didn't his club provide a full list of their games?" she replied with a roll of her eyes. "Please, show in your guest."

Jacob inclined his head to Mr. Randall, who returned to the sitting room in short order, this time accompanied by a stocky white man wearing a footman's white wig pulled low over his eyes, and threadbare coattails at least three sizes too small.

Their guest's pristine champagne-polished black leather boots had been shoved into a pair of worn wooden pattens. The sort servants sometimes used to keep their shoes free of muck. This man teetered on the five-inch platforms as though a light sneeze would topple him over.

"Thank you for seeing me," the alleged Mr. Smith said without preamble. His accent was aristocratic, and his voice familiar. "I am the valet to a very important man who finds himself facing an unpleasant dilemma of extreme—now, you wait just a bloody minute. Are you two servants or Wynchesters?"

"I'm neither," said Vivian, clearly shocked at being recognized and remembered. She rose to her feet. "Why don't you have a seat, Mr. Olivebury?"

The man's mouth fell open.

"All the rest of us are Wynchesters," Philippa said quickly. "You may not remember me, but I recall you visiting my father, Mr. York, to discuss matters for the House of Commons before he retired."

Mr. Olivebury blinked. "Your father was my mentor. He's the reason I enjoy the powerful position I have today."

Philippa held out her palm. "Do take off your pattens. They look as uncomfortable as that wig. Shall I ring for tea?"

With a sigh, Mr. Olivebury sat down heavily in the closest armchair. "Madeira, if you have it."

Graham summoned a footman.

Jacob joined Vivian on the sofa across from their newest guest. Philippa took the armchair next to Graham.

"What seems to be the problem?" she asked politely.

Mr. Olivebury gave Jacob and Vivian another mystified look before bursting out, "I've been burgled, blackmailed, and harassed. Make it stop. This cannot be borne."

Graham withdrew a notebook. "Do you mind if I take notes?"

Vivian was already scribbling in her journal.

"Do anything you please, as long as you put an end to this," said Mr. Olivebury. He rubbed his face with his hands. "You must have seen in the papers that I was robbed some days previously?"

Graham nodded. "We're aware of the incident, but not the nature of the item stolen."

"That is by design. The malefactor who stole from me intends to use his spoils as leverage against me. Whatever mischief he's planning, he intends for it to unfold soon."

"How do you know?" asked Philippa.

Mr. Olivebury pulled a square of parchment from his waistcoat and shook it out angrily. The torn page bore only one word, written in all capitals in the very center:

SOON.

"Your handwriting, I presume?" Jacob whispered to Vivian.

A satisfied expression filled her face. "It worked!"

"You terrorized our client," he pointed out.

She nodded. "I said it worked."

Face pale, Mr. Olivebury shoved the paper back into his pocket. "The first letter forbade me from coming to you for help, but I see no other choice. What do we do?"

"You haven't fully explained what's happening," Graham pointed out gently. "What was stolen? What blackmail is the thief requesting?"

"This is ruining my life," Mr. Olivebury said in despair. "The thief wants me to argue as instructed for an act that's already been delayed three times. How am I to live in the meantime, when this villain possesses..." Mr. Olivebury dropped his face into his hands and let out a sound not unlike the cry of an injured loon.

"We should unmask him quickly," said Graham. "We tend to be quite efficient...when we have all the facts."

"Here's a fact," said Mr. Olivebury. "The Duke of Faircliffe came to visit me yesterday, as you apparently well know. Although neither of us are the official heads of our respective houses, I am generally regarded as the leading voice in the House of Commons in the same way that Faircliffe is the leading voice of the House of Lords. If I *were* to agitate against my own best wishes, others would follow."

Jacob leaned forward. "What does the blackmailer want you to influence?"

"Voting reform." Mr. Olivebury's face was grim. "My personal strife pales compared to the unconscionable tragedy that felled so many peaceful protesters in Manchester. Unfortunately, in both houses, most members of Parliament prefer the status quo. No one enjoys giving up power, no matter how unequal it may be."

"Yet you would do so, willingly?" Vivian guessed.

She looked thrilled at the possibility that her latest play might soon cease to be fiction. Jacob didn't blame her. The idea was seductive.

"I have argued in favor of the common people for years," Mr. Olivebury confirmed. "Equal suffrage rights are the least we can provide, to ensure the voices of the citizens we represent are actually heard."

"Which narrows the list of suspects to...everyone else in Parliament?" Vivian said dryly.

"Fifty percent," Graham corrected. "If the thief believed the measure would be defeated in a landslide, he would not resort to robbery and blackmail. Acts pass by majority, which means even one vote over half is enough to tip the scales."

"Just think," Vivian breathed. "All men and women, voting!"

Jacob exchanged a grin with her.

Mr. Olivebury had the grace to look embarrassed. "All men, as a first step."

Jacob could feel Vivian's disappointment rising like smoke from an extinguished fire. He wished he could squeeze her hand and swear things would change soon, but he could make no such promise. "Even that much shan't be easy to pass, I imagine."

Mr. Olivebury nodded. "Should I manage to convince the House of Commons, the House of Lords could still stop it cold. Most aristocrats would rather keep untitled landowners like me in our places, rather than open the floor to even more commoners."

Philippa nodded. "The Marquess of Leisterdale has been especially vocal in his opposition to suffrage of any sort. He and my father have never seen eye to eye."

Graham consulted his notes. "Leisterdale is far from alone. I could name at least a hundred other lords who share his sentiments."

"But would disgruntled noblemen actually slink through the night with shepherd's pie and a whooper swan, and burgle the most important voice in the House of Commons?" Jacob asked doubtfully.

"Someone did," said Mr. Olivebury.

"Probably not the Marquess of Leisterdale, though," admitted Graham. "He's sixty-five years old."

Mr. Olivebury raised his brows. "I'm sixty-three and hardly decrepit."

"Neither is Leisterdale," Philippa said. "Though he does limp from gout. Perhaps I'm biased against him. After years of watching him obstruct my father, I can vouch that Leisterdale is not a good man. What about his heir? The son he's been out carousing with?"

"Lord Uppington?" Graham consulted his journal, then shook his head. "The timing makes it unlikely. Our thief was writing his anonymous letters a full month before the papers reported Uppington's arrival back home. More importantly, that's only a courtesy title. Uppington is not a member of Parliament. The blackmailer sounds like someone with the ability to claim 'privilege of peers' to escape being judged by a jury of commoners."

Vivian said bitterly, "How lucky we are to have a Parliament full of thieves and blackmailers 'protecting' our rights by silencing us."

Jacob wished he could fix it for her. For all of them. "What else did the thief say?"

Mr. Olivebury rubbed his side whiskers. "I'm instructed to convince my followers to reject any measure of voting reform, or suffer the consequences."

"Have you followed instructions so far?" asked Philippa.

"Not yet," Mr. Olivebury admitted. "My scheduled speech is next week. If it goes forward as planned, I *will* have to make my arguments publicly. As to what I will possibly say..."

"We'll unmask the villain before that happens," Jacob promised him. "We won't let him get away with attempting to take the law into his own hands."

"Rich, coming from you," Vivian murmured.

He shot her a pointed look. "You object to my stance on this issue?"

"I point out the hypocrisy of your stance," she clarified, uncowed. "This mystery thief is a villain because they've broken the laws in a way you dislike, so in retaliation, your plan is to...break the laws in a way that you do like?"

Jacob glared at her.

She gazed back, unblinking.

"Um," said Mr. Olivebury. "Could you lot wait to turn over a moral new leaf until after you've extricated me from the blackmail situation?"

"We would love to," Graham assured him. "The first step—"

"—is to steal back what's been stolen," blurted Mr. Olivebury. "*Please.* Before anyone else sees it."

Vivian tilted forward. "Is it really a treasure map?"

Mr. Olivebury stared at her. "A what? No. They took a portrait."

"A...portrait," Philippa repeated. "Might I ask of whom?"

"My mistress," Mr. Olivebury hedged.

"That's the 'in,'" said Vivian with excitement. "You bring her flowers or jewelry or chocolates on Wednesdays and Saturdays."

Mr. Olivebury gaped at her. "How could you possibly know—"

"Not 'in,'" Vivian corrected herself. "*I.N.*"

It was possible Jacob found her brains even more alluring than her beauty.

"Lots of men have mistresses," Philippa said with skepticism. "Is yours even a secret? Practically the entire male segment of the ton keeps one, according to my mother. Is owning a portrait of yours really such a scandal?"

"She might not be alone in the portrait," Mr. Olivebury mumbled. "I might also be in it. Without any clothing. Performing acts that would destroy me socially and eradicate any remaining influence I have in Parliament."

"Good Lord." Vivian groaned. "You kept something like that on your wall?"

"We don't judge our clients," Jacob said firmly. "We simply retrieve what's been stolen."

"Please hurry," begged Mr. Olivebury. "My marriage and the fate of England hang in the balance."

15

The next morning, Viv sat alone in her silent, empty kitchen in her equally silent, empty house, slowly—make that rapidly—spiraling into a vortex of panic and preemptive grief.

Quentin still hadn't come home. What if he were never found? Or turned up dead? What if the last words they ever exchanged weren't their usual *I love you*s, but a stupid argument for which she would never be able to beg forgiveness?

When the knock came at her door, she flew out of her seat and across the kitchen in hope and eagerness, before remembering that Quentin would have no reason to knock at his own door. A knock meant bad news, not good. An administrator from a hospital. A mortician.

The door opened to reveal...Jacob Wynchester.

She nearly tumbled boneless into his warm chest in relief. Only by sheer will did she remain standing on her own two feet.

"No word?" she said dully.

"I do bring word," he said with a smile. "Wonderful words."

Scratch that. She was absolutely going to be a sobbing mess. But into Quentin's cravat, not Jacob's.

She pushed him aside in order to lay starving eyes on her cousin.

No one was there.

"Where is he?" she demanded. "Take me to him!"

"Moderately positive words," Jacob amended, cupping her shoulders gently. "I don't have your cousin's precise location quite yet, but we do have proof of his safety."

Disappointment clawed at her throat. "You mean, someone claims Quentin is safe and sound. Just whose word are you so confident about taking at face value?"

Jacob smiled. "Quentin's."

He placed a folded letter into her hands.

She blinked at it in confusion.

"We found Newt," Jacob explained. "Graham wanted to conduct the interview himself, but we've been spread so thin...It doesn't matter. We have our answer. Newt is actually a lad called Isaac Newton Blythe, named after a distant relative."

"*The* Isaac Newton?"

"The very one. The family does their best to capitalize on this tenuous connection, which is how Graham's network was able to follow it to the lad. During the interview, Newt reluctantly divulged that Quentin has been gathering secret intelligence."

"There's no cause for alarm, because my cousin is off...acting as a spy?"

"Let's go inside," Jacob coaxed. "Why don't you sit down and read his words for yourself?"

She allowed him to lead her back into her silent, empty kitchen. It felt better now that Jacob was here. Warmer. Safer.

Viv settled in her usual chair. Rufus nudged at her skirts, and she absently reached down to scratch behind his ears. The house hadn't truly been empty all this time, she realized. It simply felt that way without Quentin. Like she was missing one of her lungs, and the biggest part of her heart.

She unfolded the letter.

N—

I'm gone to gather evidence on Lord S. Although we're not to write down any details of our missions, my cousin will be terrified if I'm gone for more than one night. Since I don't know whether I'll be able to send word from the Isle, or how long I might be gone, please contact Viv if you don't hear from me within twenty-four hours, so that she doesn't worry.

Tell her I'll be home in a fortnight or so, that I love her very much, and that I'm in no danger. Say I swear on our mothers.

If she still looks worried, tell her I bragged to everyone we know that I'd beat her at cards when I return. That'll tweak her ear. Viv never remembers to be scared when she's feeling angry or righteous.

Also, don't you dare touch my tobacco. I expect my snuffbox to be just as full when I return to headquarters!

Yours &tc,
Q

Viv's mouth fell open. "The unbelievable gall of that bounder!"

"It's definitely his handwriting?"

"His handwriting, his voice, his shameless admission of snorting tobacco! He *promised* me he would never take up such a disgusting habit."

Jacob stared at her, then burst out laughing.

She glared at him. "What?"

"Quentin was right," he said, still chuckling. "You do forget to be scared when you're feeling angry or righteous."

Her cheeks warmed, and she rolled her eyes—at herself, as much as at Quentin.

"He knows me too well, the rascal. Who's the 'Lord S' he's spying on?"

"No idea," Jacob admitted. "Some sort of code to avoid writing a subject's true name, obviously, but Newt couldn't recall what it stood for in this case."

"What 'isle' did Quentin go off to?" Viv asked, then answered her own question. "The Isle of Wight, I presume, since it's only a hundred miles from London."

"Newt couldn't remember that, either, I'm afraid. First he thought the Isle of Skye, then the Isle of Man. Then he remembered someone mentioning the Isle of Bute, or was it the Isle of Mull?"

"How old is this Newt?" she asked suspiciously.

"Sixteen."

"Obviously," she muttered.

Jacob's expression was sympathetic. "There's also a possibility that the reference isn't to an actual isle, but rather another code for an unnamed location."

"So, Quentin could be...literally anywhere?" Viv expected to feel the yawning emptiness return in a tidal wave, but the familiar handwriting in her hand kept the panic at bay.

Tell her I love her very much, and that I'm in no danger.

She would box his ears for this *because* she loved him, but she knew Quentin as well as she knew herself. As well as he knew her. Which meant, whatever and wherever this so-called mission was, he absolutely would stay safe. Perhaps he wasn't mature enough to confess his actions to her face—or, being charitable, he didn't trust her reaction enough to confide in advance—but he loved her enough not to risk getting himself killed.

Tell her I swear on our mothers.

There could be no stronger vow.

She read the letter again, then frowned at Jacob. "It's been well over twenty-four hours, and this Newt didn't tell me a bloody thing. Don't tell me he forgot about that request, too?"

Jacob grimaced. "He forgot to read the letter. Our informant said it was mixed in a pile of other unread correspondence. Newt broke the seal right in front of him."

Viv narrowed her eyes. "Newt 'forgot' to read Quentin's instructions...or he suspected the contents prohibited him from taking Quentin's snuff?"

Jacob grinned and placed an empty snuffbox on the table. "You are terrifyingly good at reading people."

"I have to be." She sent a despairing glance at her own pile of unread correspondence. "It's the only way I have to earn money."

"Until you sell a play. Which *will* happen."

"I know." She rubbed her face. "If only I could make Fate faster. Speaking of speed, how quickly do you think—"

"As soon as we can," he replied. "Graham doesn't have local spies on the British Isles, but he's sent word to everyone in the vicinities. He's also sent sketches to any coastal towns with an aristocrat in residence." He reached for her hand and squeezed it. "We'll find your cousin and bring him home. I promise."

She returned the tender squeeze reflexively, then stared in disbelief at their enjoined hands as a new suspicion formed in her gut.

Quentin had asked his friend to allay her fears if he hadn't returned home in twenty-four hours...but the brat well knew she'd be worried sick the moment he failed to show up at the dinner table in time for supper.

Had the rascal been hoping to send her straight to the Wynchesters all along? Had she played right into her cousin's hands? Was he back from the Isle and biding his time somewhere in London, refusing to return home until he was certain she'd given the Wynchesters a fair chance?

No. Quentin wouldn't stop there.

He'd refuse to show his face until he was certain she adored this family of do-good scoundrels as much as he did.

Her besotted cousin would voluntarily dangle from the side of a cliff by his fingertips for days on end if it meant Viv warming up to the family she'd vowed to hate. If he was nearby—or had a confederate passing him intelligence—Quentin would be over the moon to know Viv's fingers currently rested inside Jacob Wynchester's warm hands.

Jacob's fingers tightened. "What is it?"

"Me, hating my talent for reading people," she muttered, and pulled her hands back to her lap.

They felt cold without the warmth of his flesh. Bereft.

Damn you, Quentin.

"Are you all right?" Jacob asked with concern.

Was she? Viv rubbed her aching temples. "I won't be well until Quentin is back home. He may be having the time of his life, but I need to confirm his well-being with my own eyes."

Although her manipulative cousin was fine—for now—she needed to find him and shake some sense into him for his own safety.

Perhaps Quentin didn't fully comprehend that Viv's objection to the Wynchesters wasn't their rule-breaking per se. She herself had blatantly attempted to circumvent cruel and unethical property laws. The problem was that her mother died for her bravery, and Viv would have been killed, too.

She couldn't let Quentin suffer the same fate.

It wasn't safe for ordinary people to act outside the law. The impervious, carefree Wynchesters made impressionable young people like Quentin believe consequences weren't real. He and his friends thought that because these orphans had achieved the impossible, fame and fortune and privilege and power were as easy as wanting them hard enough. That society would accept everyone. That the authorities would react with good humor to discover an eighteen-year-old spying on an aristocrat, no prison sentence necessary.

"We'll find your cousin before you know it." Jacob took her hands in his. "I want to be clear that your cousin absolutely is a person of worth. When Graham said he keeps journals on people of note, he did not mean to imply that Quentin matters any less. It's simply not possible to collect a detailed biography about every human in England, no matter how worthy."

That was true. A book on every living person in the city would fill the Tower of London. And yet, there was no denying the celebrated class system that permeated every aspect of life. Had Viv been a wealthy white marchioness calling upon the Bow Street Runners, they would have fallen all over themselves to solve the mystery of her runaway poodle.

"To be honest," Jacob continued, "Graham hasn't added intelligence on anyone not directly related to an open case in over a year, because there hasn't been time for anything but work. Stephen keeps trying to make machines to ease the load, but short of the Wynchesters replicating ourselves like bunnies—and even that takes years—we don't allow ourselves a full night's sleep, much less have enough time to solve everyone else's problems. We take on far more than we can competently manage, and even then, it's never enough."

"I know none of you meant any offense," she replied. "It's just hard not to take one's personal life...well, personally."

Nonetheless, she understood Jacob's perspective. While Quentin was not and could not reasonably be their sole priority, he *was* Viv's. She'd spent days trying to find him and failed. Of course, she was no professional investigator, and had thus been acting alone.

Then again, despite their numbers and resources, it sounded like the Wynchesters themselves also often acted alone. Not assigned to a single individual case, but juggling dozens of urgent mysteries to solve at the same time. Each of which might have desperate clients just like Viv, for whom their open case was their sole and all-consuming priority.

"I do understand," she said at last. "If I know anything, it's what it is like to have more work and responsibilities than any human could possibly accomplish."

But though she might sympathize, it did not ease her anxiety. Viv might be used to falling through the cracks, but she'd be damned if she let it happen to Quentin.

"Will you be all right here, by yourself?" Jacob asked.

Just the simple question was enough to bring the suffocating emptiness crashing back down around her. The house wasn't a home without Quentin. It was an empty shell. A failure. The constant reminder that she'd driven her own cousin to lash back at her like this.

She wanted to make up, more than anything. Wanted to hug him, and slap him, and cry buckets of tears, and fix his hair, and let him win at cards.

Instead, all she had was a silent, empty house.

"I can take care of myself," she managed, without meeting Jacob's eyes.

"I know you can," he replied. "I also know that if I had to spend night after night in my house without a single one of my siblings present, I would go batty as a banshee before the first sunrise."

Her gaze flew up to meet his in surprise. He *did* understand.

"I'm already there," she admitted. "One hundred percent banshee. When you knocked on the door, I was seconds away from screaming loud enough to break the glass of every window in Cheapside."

"Stay with us," he offered without hesitation. "I don't even need to ask my siblings. They like you, and we have dozens of empty rooms."

Of course he did. Whereas Viv and Quentin's entire home consisted of exactly four small rooms.

"I can't leave," she said reluctantly. "There's Sally and Rufus to care for...and what if Quentin returns home, only to find me gone?"

A niggling voice in the back of her mind whispered that Jacob's kind offer was exactly what Quentin wanted. Her cousin would roll naked through a briar patch if it put Viv in closer contact with the Wynchesters.

"Then come during the day," Jacob coaxed. "Once you've fed the animals and the house starts to feel lonely. Didn't you say you were our shadow? Graham can keep your house under surveillance and have a messenger boy send immediate word of any visitors—Quentin or otherwise."

She bit her lower lip. It...wasn't a bad plan.

Jacob bent down to pet Rufus. "Plus, you'll be right there in the room with us, as we're planning whatever cases we're working on." He added quickly, "Not that I'm asking you to come work for my family, of course."

Of course not.

"Because all I contribute is the word 'no'?" she asked dryly.

"Are you jesting?" He held her shoulders, his open expression sincere. "We've got forgers and acrobats and warriors, but are desperately in need of a clear head in the room. We sent Elizabeth to resolve an inheritance dispute with a box of swords and no plan. Just because we rush in headlong whenever someone's in trouble doesn't mean it's always the right tack. We'd be foolish not to Ask Vivian while she's sitting there next to us."

She gaped at him, unable to believe what she was hearing.

"I'm not swearing we'd take every word of your advice as gospel," he admitted with a self-deprecating grin. "But we'd listen to your suggestions and consider your viewpoint carefully."

"Your entire family would welcome my opinions in your Planning Parlor?"

"Without question," he replied. "Not only does your practicality balance our impulsivity, but also quite frankly, we could use all the help we can get. You wouldn't be a hindrance, Vivian. You'd be a godsend."

Her heart pounded and her skin flushed. Who could say no to that?

She dashed a note for her cousin—though she suspected he well knew where to find her—then packed her correspondence and writing implements into a traveling satchel.

If spending every waking minute with the Wynchesters was what it took to convince Quentin to come back home faster, then so be it. She could spend a day or two in a comfortable chair at a larger table, participating in strategy sessions that would undoubtedly be far more interesting than replying to the usual letters about unfaithful fiancés and overbearing mothers-in-law.

Viv hoped it would be enough. Her throat grew thick, and she swallowed hard. She wouldn't put it past Quentin not to return for anything short of full and complete acceptance of his beloved idols.

If she didn't embrace the Wynchesters to Quentin's satisfaction, he might choose them over her...permanently. Spending sufficient time with each of them was her new mission. If she failed, Quentin could return home only to send Viv packing. He was grown now. He didn't need her.

The letter he'd written to Newt proved Quentin was perfectly capable of sending word to Viv—but chose not to. A discourtesy that was unprecedented, hurtful, and clearly as serious as an aristocrat disowning one of his heirs.

If she didn't play her hand right, she would lose Quentin forever.

16

Together, Viv and Jacob moved her working quarters from her tiny kitchen table to a significantly larger corner of the Wynchesters' oversize sitting room table, ostensibly to help them with their planning. The "small" space allotted to her here was bigger than the entire table back home. She could move her elbows without knocking things off walls, and stretch her legs without banging her feet against her cousin—or taking out poor Rufus.

Who was currently at home, awaiting Viv's return. Her temporary relocation was only for the middle daylight hours. She spent time every morning and early evening playing with Rufus, as was their routine. He slept curled at the foot of her bed every night.

"You're sure I can't bring Rufus here?" she asked.

"No attack badgers allowed," said Jacob. "It's a house rule, and a hazard to hedgehogs."

She made a note in her journal. What had started as one page on Jacob Wynchester had turned into a dozen. There were now pages for every member of his family, as well as the creatures in his barn. Quentin *had* to accept this evidence as proof of her good-faith effort to get to know them.

Her studiousness certainly wasn't because *Viv* was at all fascinated by anyone in this family.

"What?" Jacob asked.

"W-what?" Viv stammered.

"You're staring at me."

"I'm not." She definitely was.

Was it her fault this man looked as thirst-quenching as a cold glass of lemonade on a hot summer's day?

She could sense his warmth and his masculine scent from yards away. It was as if every particle in her body became aware of him even before he came into view. And whenever he was right there before her very eyes, her traitorous fingers longed to pull him to her by the lapel and taste his kisses for herself.

Jacob stood and turned to stride from the room.

Viv pushed to her feet. "Where are you going?"

"To drill Hippogriff on his new tricks. You can watch if you like."

She hurried to keep up as Jacob headed outside.

Hippogriff was a hawk. *Accipiter gentilis*, to be exact: a large goshawk with red eyes and black wings and white eyebrows and a black-and-white patterned belly above yellow clawed feet with sharp black talons.

The moment the raptor appeared in the sky, Jacob lifted his leather-gloved forearm up high, signaling for Hippogriff to land on his massive wrist.

Viv was faster. Or perhaps, more persuasive.

Hippogriff swooped down, cutting across the wide blue sky with a speed so swift the air whistled past his wings.

His hurry wasn't to reunite with Jacob. Hippogriff's singular focus was Viv.

When Jacob realized the deadly hawk intended to ignore his master's outstretched arm, he spun around in alarm—

Just in time to see Hippogriff alight on Viv's reinforced wrist light as a feather, as she fed him a treat with her other hand.

Viv smiled. Cute creature. Docile as a lamb.

"You carry around dead mice in your pockets?" Jacob demanded in disbelief.

She shook her head. "It wasn't dead until I gave it to him."

He stared at her. "You are a deeply peculiar woman. I like you much more than I anticipated."

Her cheeks heated. Possibly because she'd never before been complimented for sacrificing an innocent wood mouse to a bird of prey.

Or possibly because she herself liked Jacob Wynchester significantly more than she'd bargained for.

Hippogriff gulped down the last of his meal and took to the sky.

Jacob didn't try to stop him.

"Weren't you going to teach him a new trick?" Viv asked in surprise.

The corners of Jacob's mouth twitched. "I think you just did."

She bit her lip. "You're not upset with me?"

"No." He took her hands in his. "Do you want me to dislike you?"

"No," she whispered.

"Good. That would be impossible." His voice was low, and rich as spiced rum. The toes of their shoes were barely far enough apart for a blade of grass to poke through.

If he tilted his head down an inch or two…If she raised her chin, just a little…

Belatedly, Viv began to suspect she'd brought the mouse along not to tempt Hippogriff, but so that Jacob would look at her exactly as he was doing now.

Don't do it, she told herself desperately. *Don't you dare kiss this gorgeous specimen of a man. No matter how much you desire him.*

She forced herself to turn away before they committed an irreversible mistake. He was wrong for her in every way. This family was dangerous. The sort of role models that would send her cousin to the gallows. She couldn't throw herself into a Wynchester's arms now.

And absolutely no kissing, blast it.

In the interest of making good use of her brain, she could aid them in their cases, but nothing more. Definitely no reason to involve hands and lips and tongues. Not until she found Quentin and cleared his name.

"We should find out who the mistress is," she blurted, as though she'd been thinking about Mr. Olivebury all along.

"We know who the mistress is," Jacob answered. "Miss Ines Nixon. After you realized the diary entries were initials, Graham had her address in less than an hour."

"Then we should visit her," Viv suggested. "Find out what she knows."

"I did, this morning," he replied.

Humph. Anticlimactic. Perhaps the Wynchesters didn't require Viv's advice-giving skills after all. Their competency rankled.

"Well?" she said, peevish. "Did she seem like she might be working with the villain?"

"Not at all. She was very sweet and utterly perplexed as to why I was there."

"I'm sure she threw herself into your arms," Viv said acidly.

"Miss Nixon said she enjoyed her current arrangement, and hoped very much that Mr. Olivebury had no intentions of throwing her over. She didn't seem to have any notion the portrait had been stolen."

"What did she say when you told her it was gone?"

"That maybe the wife took it. Miss Nixon is of the opinion that no household keeps secrets from its servants for long. Perhaps the Oliveburys' housekeeper is ally to her mistress."

"Or a servant who accidentally found it, took it?" Viv mused. "Or perhaps Miss Nixon is trying to throw us off her trail. What could be better advertising to new clientele than having no less than the leader of the House of Commons at her feet?"

Jacob shook his head. "She could have divulged that connection at any time but has kept silent all these years instead. She seems to truly care for him. And she would very much like the portrait to be found."

"What about the portrait artist? Now, there's a chap in a fine position to blackmail."

"The artist is the mistress's sister," Jacob answered dryly. "One who apparently also figures prominently in the stolen portrait, along with..." He pulled out a notebook, hesitated, then shoved it back into his pocket unopened. "Perhaps some details are best left to the imagination."

No pronouncement could make Viv salivate more. She possessed a prodigiously overactive imagination. It was now her life's mission to see that painting with her own eyes.

"We can reinterview the Nixon women later if necessary," he said. "But regardless of political leanings, the portrait artist is unlikely to harm a beloved sister."

"You can't be certain," Viv insisted. "You only have her word."

Jacob sighed. "You're right. Happy now? Fine, perhaps the sisters had a row. Or maybe the housekeeper found the portrait and told the butler who told a chambermaid who told the cook who told a stableboy, and now we have eighty-nine additional suspects. All of whom could have inadvertently spread the gossip to the wrong person. Maybe the butcher's mother's cobbler's sister-in-law is the blackmailer and we'll *never* solve the case."

"It would be a good twist," Viv muttered.

He was right to be vexed with her. Jacob wanted to solve this case as much as she did, even if their motives were different. Viv wanted Quentin home, and Jacob's overwhelmed family wanted at least one fewer mystery taking up precious seconds.

"All right," she said. "I'll grant you the point. Literally anything *might* have happened, but our time and resources are finite, so it would be prudent to concentrate on the likeliest solutions."

"These days, Wynchester resources are worse than finite. They're nonexistent."

"I hope that's not true. Once in a while, you ought to take at least a short break for yourself." She gestured toward Jacob's pocket. "Is that your casebook or your poetry journal?"

He narrowed his eyes. "Either way, it's private."

At least here, she could offer solid advice!

"Your poetry need not be private," she told him. "You could do something with your poems. At least try to sell them."

"I have tried," he said tightly. "More than you know."

"Have you considered—"

"Yes. Exhaustively. The only chance my words have of being published is if I were to do so anonymously."

She scoffed. "Only cowards hide behind anonymity. It is nobler to fail as oneself than to win as someone else."

He was unmoved. "What do you know about my personal situation?"

"Do you think I've never received a rejection before? That's all I've ever been sent, if I receive a response at all. But I won't let them keep me down. I shall keep popping up, again and again, until someone, somewhere, is forced to behold me."

"Congratulations," he drawled. "You're a perennial weed in want of a scythe."

"Oh, be honest. Don't you want to look in the mirror with pride? To feel proud of how far you've come?"

He crossed his muscular arms. "I do and I am, every day."

"Then why do you look so haunted, any time someone asks you to share your talent with the world?"

"Maybe," he said tersely, "it's none of your business. When I want your publishing advice, I'll be certain to 'Ask Vivian' in writing."

She propped her fists on her hips. "I'm sure you don't think I am your equal in any form—"

He arched his brows. "Is this about my poetry or about you?"

"Everything we experience is about ourselves in some way. We can't help but see the world through our own eyes. Just because you've never known a single sleepless night—"

"You don't know the first thing about me. You can try to size me up in one glance as you please, but all you know is what you see. It's dangerous to fill in the blanks with unfounded conjecture."

"Oh, yes, good sir, please explain danger to me. I am but an impoverished unmarried immigrant Black woman currently living all alone in a not particularly affluent part of town. I *love* lying awake at night, jumping at every sound. Obviously I don't know the first thing about danger, what with all my privilege." She jabbed a finger at his chest. "What sob story do you think *you've* suffered?"

He stepped back. "Of all the insufferable, presumptuous—"

"Am I presuming? You've seen my home, and how I live. Now we're standing here in yours. Can you really look around at all your servants and comforts, and tell me with a straight face—"

"I didn't always live in this house!" His brown eyes flashed. "I didn't always have a house at all. You know nothing about me, Miss Henry. Perhaps we should keep it that way."

He spun on his heel and marched toward his barn.

Miss Henry. Not Vivian anymore.

She hurried after him in dismay. "Jacob—"

"No," he said without turning around. "I've had more than enough of your opinions for one day. Go and meddle in someone else's life."

She stopped walking, stung.

He didn't slow.

Viv had no one to blame but herself.

17

Viv considered attending to her unread correspondence in the Wynchesters' sitting room but decided Jacob deserved more space than that. After the heated words they'd exchanged, she didn't want him to feel as though he couldn't reenter his own home out of fear she'd be there ready to pounce.

Especially since her hope had been to lure him out of the loneliness of his barn, not force him deeper into solitude.

She, too, spent most of her time alone with her projects. While she wouldn't trade her passions for anything, she sometimes longed for someone who understood her. Quentin could barely manage to post parcels properly and wasn't at all interested in Viv's writing process or her thoughts about the publishing industry.

Perhaps the Wynchester siblings were different.

Or perhaps they were just as indifferent to Jacob's passions in their own way. Too busy to have time for their own brother. Maybe he was just as exotic and incomprehensible to them as a Highland tiger or an antbear.

Which…was apparently how Quentin felt with Viv. That she didn't understand him. That she didn't take him seriously. That he would have to disappear off the face of the earth for her to pause and question her assumptions.

Viv's future relationship with her cousin depended on how well she took advantage of the opportunity to get to know all of the

Wynchesters, not just Jacob. Time was running out. She had to make the most of it.

If she failed, she might never see them or Quentin ever again.

"Begin with the one whose own siblings admit she's been hiding secrets," Viv murmured aloud. She would check each Wynchester off her list one by one, and comply with Quentin's wishes this very day.

She made her way to Charlotte Street, where Marjorie and Adrian's art studio was located.

When Viv arrived on the premises without an appointment, she expected to be barred at the door. She was pleasantly surprised to be greeted by a friendly sign inviting visitors to come upstairs to observe art in the making.

Annoyance rankled beneath her skin. They couldn't find Quentin—whom Viv suspected was right here in London—but these two had time to flit about with their little art projects? Perhaps the wonderful Wynchesters weren't as benevolent and all-powerful as the adoring public believed.

Even as she had the thought, a small part of Viv railed against it. She wanted to be wrong. She wanted to keep Quentin safe. And she needed him to come home. The Wynchesters were the best chance she had.

Ascending the stairs to the art studio took longer than anticipated. Every inch of the wall was covered in framed canvases. The variety of styles, signatures, and skill levels indicated these works were likely created by Marjorie and Adrian's students. All were intriguing in their own way, with raw talent emerging from the brushstrokes.

Up in the main hall, however, there was no oil paint being spread onto linen canvases.

Viv's jaw fell open. Marjorie and Adrian strolled between rows of nine- and ten-year-old pupils, studiously making illegal copies of the key to some poor sap's home. Good God. The Wynchesters might get away with such brazen antics, but the average child most certainly could not! There was no minimum age for gaol—or worse.

"Forgeries?" she spat in disgust. "I cannot believe you're teaching children to break the law. I should have known scoundrels like you lot would encourage the most impressionable youth to rob their neighbors."

The entire room stared at her as though she had sprouted a beak and feathers.

Marjorie spoke first. "Er...*Is* it forgery if they're copying their own keys for personal use?"

The back of Viv's neck heated. "They're duplicating their own keys?"

Twenty little faces nodded, wide-eyed.

"Have you never in your life misplaced an important item?" Adrian asked.

"Um," said Viv.

"Many of these girls live in families that cannot afford the expense of a locksmith, or the time it would take to find a suitable professional and wait their turn for something so simple," Marjorie explained. "Not only are using molds and filing down blanks practical life skills, these girls are helping out their parents, who often must juggle a single house key amongst multiple family members."

Several students nodded.

Viv and Quentin had run into the same problem when she'd first moved in. She'd used the entirety of her first month's pin money to make herself a spare copy of the house key, only for him to continually lose his own amongst the abandoned projects he left piled in every room. She would have killed for multiple spare copies.

"Back to work, girls," said Adrian. "You're doing splendidly."

"Marvelous job, all," Viv said weakly. She wondered if anyone would notice if she melted down the stairs.

Before she could attempt a strategic retreat, however, Marjorie cut her off at the pass. "I can show you forgeries, if you want to see forgeries."

"No," Viv mumbled. "That's all right."

"Extremely illegal forgeries," Marjorie said dryly. "If you'll wait here for a moment, I'll rob the Prince Regent myself. Oh, wait, that was our last student trip. We have copies of his crown. Mine is the real one; His Majesty's is the forgery."

"I shouldn't have accused you of corrupting minors," Viv said. "Particularly in front of the minors. At least not without evidence."

"Well, that's gracious of you. I hope you come to like us a little bit better before you marry my brother."

Viv choked on her own spit. "Before I what?"

"You care for Jacob, Jacob cares for you." Marjorie shrugged. "Doesn't seem confusing to me."

"Listen," said Viv, then wondered if it was the wrong thing to say. Marjorie was hard of hearing. Viv hadn't meant to add insult to insult. "I'm not going to marry your brother. I don't even like your brother."

"Hmm," said Marjorie.

"He doesn't like me either," Viv insisted, raising her voice. "Go and ask him."

"Hmm," Marjorie said again.

"I don't like any Wynchesters," Viv said desperately. "That's why I walked in here insulting you without a second thought. I hold your entire family's breathtaking hypocrisy in utter contempt, and I fear for every child your good-hearted obliviousness corrupts."

The room was staring at her again.

Marjorie and Adrian exchanged a brief flurry of hand gestures. Probably plotting how best to murder Viv and where to hide the body.

"No offense," Viv added quickly.

Marjorie's expression was amused. "How can I take offense when even you don't believe your own words?"

"I definitely do," Viv assured her. "I don't lie."

"Neither do your colors," Marjorie said cryptically, then gestured toward an empty table and chair. "Sit down, stay awhile, copy a key. Perhaps it'll unlock your future."

"Er, no thank you," Viv stammered. "I'm rubbish at art."

Marjorie raised her brows. "Have you ever tried?"

"Exhaustively. Quentin and I took a week of cosmetics lessons at the Royal Theatre; I've seen clowns more fetching than the looks we designed. Later, we shared an art tutor for a full month. He left in tears. We were more likely to break the frame than to stretch a canvas properly, and when it came to mixing powders into paint..." Viv shuddered. "Some people are born artistic souls. And some people are me and Quentin."

Marjorie hugged her.

Viv stood there and took it, frozen in place. "What on earth are you doing?"

"Comforting you. Not everything will come easy. You've got to keep trying."

Viv snorted. "I gave up art a long time ago, and the world is better for it. If you'd seen those canvases—"

"Not the paintings. Don't give up on Jacob." Marjorie pulled back and gave Viv several pats on the shoulders. "Whatever you did—"

"Who says I'm the one in the wrong? Or that there's a problem I'm avoiding at all?"

Marjorie looked at her in silence.

Viv swallowed. "You know what? A grumpy man recently told me to go and meddle in someone else's life. I think I'll do that now. Enjoy your forgeries. Good day!"

She raced down the stairs, fully cognizant that two dozen pairs of eyes were watching her flee in haste from a diminutive Wynchester in a paint-flecked apron. Who'd got the better of Viv by hugging her when she wasn't expecting it.

This family was devious indeed.

After checking Marjorie off the list, Viv arrived in Islington in time to see Graham and Kuni race each other around the garden, up the high stone walls, then leap from tree to tree.

They moved so quickly, Viv could barely jot down their current position in her log before they sprang to another spot. Both athletes kept up competitive chatter, teasing each other as they jumped and climbed and ran, as if doing so were no more strenuous than lifting a lemon cake to one's mouth at teatime. Viv was out of breath just watching them.

This time, she knew better than to presume mischief was afoot. Even without considering her experience with Marjorie and Adrian, Viv could clearly recognize that Graham and Kuni were executing some sort of training routine.

At last, the duo collapsed onto the grass. Or at least, Viv would have collapsed. Fainted. Slept.

Kuni and Graham, on the other hand, rolled onto their stomachs for the barest of seconds before rising on their hands and toes, keeping their spines and legs straight as they pushed their chests up from the grass, shouting out numbers from one to ten…to fifty…

Only after one hundred press-ups did they flop onto their backs, side by side, their fingers entwined.

"Not going to join us?" Graham called out, eyes closed, his face tilted up to the sun.

"Um," said Viv. "Good afternoon. I didn't mean to interrupt."

"You absolutely meant to interrupt," said Kuni, flipping a handful of long black braids out of her face. "You're doing splendidly at it."

"I meant to observe," clarified Viv.

"Did you get what you came for?"

"Not really. I write stage directions for a living, and I don't have enough words to describe what the two of you were just doing."

"I thought you wrote letters for a living," said Graham. "Do many people write in asking how best to scale walls and navigate rooftops?"

"I didn't think you really did the roof bit," Viv said. "I thought that rumor might have been greatly exaggerated."

"*Un*-xaggerated," said Kuni. "Graham can do tricks you cannot imagine."

"*Un-xaggerated* isn't a word," her husband whispered.

"It should be," she grumbled. "Your language is woefully incomplete."

"Minimized," Viv suggested. "Understated. Underreported. Misconstrued. Underestimated. Miscalculated." She remembered Kuni was Balcovian and switched to Dutch for the next dozen synonyms, since the two languages were close enough to be mutually intelligible.

Kuni and Graham both opened their eyes to stare at her.

"Writer," she mumbled. "I like words."

"Apparently." Graham pushed himself up on his elbows. "Do you know who else likes words?"

"So help me, if you attempt to match-make me to your brother—"

"Sir Gareth Jallow," Graham finished with satisfaction. "Now, there's a poet's poet. I cannot wait for his new book next week."

"Jacob hates Jallow," whispered Kuni. "We're not to mention his name."

"Not in front of Jacob," Graham agreed. "But we are allowed to say 'Sir Gareth Jallow' in front of Miss Henry."

"Vivian," Viv said. "We did the first-name thing yesterday."

"Do you know what the biggest problem with Jallow is?" asked Graham.

Kuni covered her face with her hands. "Here he goes. If you have any ability at all for running away over rooftops...this is your cue to deploy your emergency evacuation skills."

Graham threw his arms out wide. "Jallow isn't a prince! He's a mere *sir*."

"Knights are respectable," said Kuni. "Baronets are respectable."

"They're not royalty," Graham said. "Just think how much better that poetry would be if it had been written by a king."

"It would be the same poetry," Kuni said. "Literally the exact same words in the exact same order. Just by a man with a different name."

"Precisely," Graham said dreamily. "So much better."

"Words should be written by whomever they're written by," said Viv. "Man, woman, Black, white. It shouldn't matter."

"You're new here," said Graham. "Gender and racial equality is definitely not how England works."

"Or anywhere," Viv muttered.

"Actually," began Kuni, her eyes lighting up.

"Now you did it." Graham pulled his wife to her feet. "You got *her* started. Prepare for waves of vomit-inducing jealousy."

"We can all move to Balcovia at any time you want," Kuni scolded him. "Winter at the Summer Palace, then move back here in time for spring."

"Winter...in the Summer...Palace?" Viv echoed blankly.

"That's when the royal family isn't using it," Kuni explained, leaving Viv even more confused than before. "I suppose we could take summers in the Winter Palace, but honestly, if you force me to choose—"

"No more choosing," said Graham. "You already chose the exquisite fairy tale that is England."

Kuni sent Viv a speaking look. "Something is definitely lost in translation."

"My cousin would love to winter in the Summer Palace," Viv said. "He would wear his all-blue 'Baron Vanderbean' outfit—"

"Blue?" Kuni recoiled in mock horror. "Any respectable Balcovian aristocrat would never be seen in anything but our national pink."

"My wife would be happy to loan him a more appropriate frock coat," Graham told Viv with a grin. "Why aren't you off with Jacob?"

"Why should I be with Jacob?" she countered, defensive.

"Didn't you say something along the lines of, 'I shall be your second shadow until my cousin returns home'?" Graham asked mildly.

Oh. That.

"I perceive how you might draw the conclusion that a shadow would be near its object," she mumbled. "I tried that. It didn't go well."

"Jacob was unfriendly to you?" Graham said in surprise.

"I...might have been unfriendly to him," she admitted. "I provoked him, and he got upset. Out of sorts enough to allude to something dark in his past, which he refused to elaborate on."

"Well," said Graham. "You're the advice column writer, but if you ask me—"

"I did not ask you."

"He's about to tell you anyway," said Kuni.

Viv tightened her jaw. That was *her* unwelcome trick. She was starting to see how annoying it could be.

"Whether you ask me or not," said Graham, "the truth is this: You can't demand to be in someone's confidence. You have to deserve it."

Ouch. Sharp blade, right through the chain mail. Touché.

"You know what?" said Viv. "I think I'll go and meddle in someone else's life now."

Halfway through the list. Things were going...well, perhaps not swimmingly, but things were certainly going.

Elizabeth and Stephen's London residence *looked* safe enough to the naked eye. However, the moment Viv lifted the ordinary brass knocker, something metallic clicked three times and the doorjamb shattered into pieces.

She jumped backward, only for the wooden pieces to be swept away down a previously hidden channel. The door itself flew upward, as if inhaled to a higher story. Behind it now hung a wall of ceiling-to-floor fringe made of yellow yarn glistening with…oil?

As the dripping liquid pooled onto the floor, Viv gingerly smudged it with the tip of one shoe. Definitely oil. The growing puddle covered the marble entryway three feet wide, inviting anyone who dared cross to slip and break every bone in their body.

"Have you considered simply hiring a butler?" she called into the void.

No one answered.

Were they not at home? Or were they ignoring her?

Viv knew they had other cases. She'd helped plan half a dozen of them. The mother had been reunited with her child, the gambled dowry had been restored to the distraught daughter in time for the wedding, and the church's landlord had been forced to repatch the roof.

She glared at the yawning darkness. Either Elizabeth and Stephen weren't home, or the bizarre blanket of oily fringe had muffled Viv's words. Lord help her. She hadn't planned to ruin her best bonnet today, but there was no way through except forward.

She found a stick to push the wet fringe aside, and placed a tentative boot onto the slick marble.

Two things happened at once: The fringe jerked to one side, disappearing as though a team of invisible stagehands had yanked the curtain away for the final show. More concerning, however, was that the floor beneath her foot did not stay put. The marble heaved, as though giving a great belch.

Viv windmilled her arms to keep her balance. She barely managed not to tumble arse over teakettle. What had previously seemed solid marble was now a thin checkerboard pattern of tiles, with every other square half an inch shorter than its neighbor. The result was that the oil drained away.

A pulley to her left clacked, drawing Viv's attention and alarm. An object that looked like a gigantic fireplace bellows emerged from a panel above the baseboard and gave a great heave, depositing not air but a thin layer of sand over the floor. Making it as safe to transverse as Viv supposed it was ever going to be.

She crossed with care, narrowly avoiding a gossamer thread poised to launch a chute of overripe plums atop the unsuspecting visitor.

At the other end of the six-foot entryway was an innocuous-looking wooden door. Viv wasn't certain whether to attempt to knock on this one or simply to fling it open and take her chances.

She settled on flinging it open.

Though she tensed in anticipation of a falling ceiling or the floor vanishing beneath her feet, nothing prevented her from crossing the threshold farther into the house.

There, on the other side, she glimpsed what might have been a huge parlor. Difficult to tell, what with cords and chains and wheels and gears and pulleys covering every inch of the walls and most of the ceiling.

A blank spot in the middle contained a man hanging upside down from his knees on a short trapeze, with a hammer in one hand and a wrench in the other. A leather helmet covered his head. One eye was hidden behind some sort of telescoping lens, whereas the other was magnified fivefold behind an inch-thick circle of glass.

He grunted toward the ceiling. "This will be ready for deployment within the hour."

Beneath him on the ground stood a woman free of helmets but wielding a sword in each hand. She danced erratically amongst the disparate items of furniture, fencing wildly against an attacking army of invisible foes.

"Took you long enough," Elizabeth Wynchester said. Not to her husband. To the unexpected visitor.

Viv blinked. "You didn't know I was coming."

Elizabeth jabbed a sword above the sofa, then swung the other blade over her own head, narrowly missing her husband—who carried on with his tinkering without flinching.

"I knew it was you the moment the fringe of death didn't frighten you off." Elizabeth hurled a sword toward Viv.

Viv caught the handle reflexively, dropping into a defensive position just in time to parry a dizzying flurry of Elizabeth's expert thrusts.

The fight, if one could call it that, was over in under thirty seconds. Viv's hands were palm-up in the air, her temporary rapier lying useless at her oil-stained feet.

"Impressive." Elizabeth sheathed her sword. "Most people don't last ten seconds against me."

"Not even five," said Stephen from his upside-down perch on the ceiling.

Elizabeth motioned Viv to the sofa, which might or might not have been rigged to murder anyone whose derrière touched the cushion. "Biscuit? Today we have oat, cinnamon raisin, and shortbread."

Viv decided to risk the sofa. "I'll take one of each, if you've enough to go around."

"Exactly the combination I would have chosen myself," Elizabeth said in approval. She piled a plate high with biscuits and passed it to Viv. "How did you enjoy our mechanical butler system?"

"That was a mechanical…butler?"

"The murder room is at the rear door," Elizabeth answered, as though that explained anything. "The front door is merely designed to test the mettle of those who come to call. Anyone who makes it through the entryway deserves an audience—and a biscuit. I couldn't resist adding a sword fight. I'm sorry I put you at a disadvantage."

"Oh, I was never at a disadvantage," Viv assured her. "I could have murdered you at any time."

"You could not have done," Elizabeth said hotly. "I had you disarmed in seconds without even trying!"

"I don't need a sword. I have Sally." Viv licked her fingers.

Elizabeth glanced around. "Who is Sall—"

Viv opened the sugar shaker in her reticule and flung her furry pet into the air.

The tarantula landed in the middle of Elizabeth's plate of biscuits.

"Aaugh," she screamed, tossing the plate aside and springing to her feet. "What *is* that?"

"Wolf spider," said her husband as he dropped down from the ceiling. Not to rescue his wife, but to perform several press-ups before tossing the leather helmet from his head and helping himself to the remaining biscuits.

"Sally is my personal defense tarantula," Viv explained, crossing her legs at the ankles.

"Your personal defense tarantula," Elizabeth repeated. "What is it trained to do?"

"Oh, I haven't trained her to do anything. All I need is for Sally to do whatever a wild tarantula wants to do."

"Chaotic." Elizabeth's tone was impressed. "I like it."

"You threw your plate of biscuits across the room," Viv pointed out.

"Everything in this house gets thrown across the room," Elizabeth said. "I was responding in keeping with the theme. Besides, we have more biscuits. Is your tarantula hungry?"

"She ate this morning." Viv held out her hand for Sally. "I'm guessing your nephew rarely comes to visit. This house doesn't seem particularly safe for children."

"Dorian can't even cross the threshold," Elizabeth said with pride. "Our home is designed to be one thousand percent impervious to babies."

"You don't want children?" Viv asked in surprise.

"I would rather eat your personal defense tarantula alive," Elizabeth answered cheerfully. "Stephen feels the same way."

"I'm not eating a wolf spider," said Stephen.

His wife smiled. "Not even if doing so would magically ward us from now until eternity against any possibility of spawning offspring?"

Stephen turned to Viv. "Can I borrow your spider?"

Viv tucked her reticule away protectively. "Not on your life."

"Do *you* want children?" Elizabeth asked with curiosity. "Have you discussed how many to expect with Jacob?"

Viv set down her empty plate in haste. "I haven't even kissed Jacob!"

"*Yet*," came Jacob's voice from the sofa behind her.

Viv spun around in mortification, her heart pounding.

No one was there.

Elizabeth cackled. "You were about to kiss him right then, weren't you?"

"My wife loves to throw her voice," Stephen said apologetically. "I can't stop her."

"Nothing and no one can stop me from anything," said Elizabeth. "Except sometimes my hip. And my back."

Stephen raised his brows. "You only ever admit that in front of family."

Elizabeth waved a hand. "Miss Henry is clearly destined to—"

"Vivian," Viv corrected as she sprang to her feet. "And if this is the way the conversation is headed, then I am going in the opposite direction."

"Come here and kiss me," called Jacob's eerily accurate voice from behind the sofa. "If we make babies, you'll never have to visit Elizabeth and Stephen's home ever again."

Viv didn't look back.

Elizabeth's delighted chortles followed her all the way out the door.

Only one more stop remained so that no one could claim Viv hadn't given every single Wynchester a fair chance to display their true character.

"This is for you, Quentin," she muttered under her breath.

As Viv approached the Duke of Faircliffe's Mayfair terrace, a human butler opened the front door. She expected that her calling card—VIVIAN HENRY, PLAYWRIGHT—would not be enough, and had mentally prepared several arguments to convince the butler to at least inform his mistress of her presence.

The butler didn't even glance at her card. To her surprise, he smiled the moment she spoke her name and immediately welcomed her into the terraced home without even dashing inside to enquire whether his employers were receiving guests.

He led her into a dining room the size of her and Quentin's entire home. In the center of the vast room was an equally oversize table, upon which cluttered a cornucopia of bits and bobs. There were flowers and ribbons and lace and pearls and feathers and odd fruits dipped in wax.

There were also the duke and the duchess themselves, casually sewing the colorful items onto bonnets. Their baby, Dorian, sat between them, stray bits of ribbon pasted to random spots on his sticky arms and head.

"I didn't mean to interrupt," said Viv.

"Sit, sit," said Chloe. "Do you want to make yourself a bonnet?"

"I..." Viv considered the oily mess Elizabeth's automated butler had made of what had previously been Viv's best bonnet. "Maybe? I don't really know how."

"Have Lawrence do it, he's good at it," the duchess suggested.

Viv stared at her, bewildered. Had she just been invited to give instructions to a duke?

"Er," she managed.

The truth was, Chloe's bonnets were legendarily hideous. A duchess might be able to wear an entire millinery shop glued to her coiffure, but Viv would rather exhibit at least some sense of style.

The Duke of Faircliffe lifted the bonnet in his lap. "I'm almost done with this one, if you'd like it."

Viv's mouth fell open. It was beautiful. More elegant than anything she'd ever worn. The sort of bonnet whose price was so far outside her means, it would've hurt her eyes to behold it in a shop window.

"Take it now," Chloe whispered. "Before Dory gets his paws on it. Unless you *want* to copy my appearance."

Viv looked at the duchess, looked at Dorian, then took the bonnet from the duke. "Thank you. I don't have enough coin with me at the moment to repay—"

"It's a gift," Chloe interrupted. "We're making a new batch for the women's refuge. As each season turns, I drop off my used clothing and try to add at least a few decent bonnets to the mix."

"You donate your entire wardrobe four times a year?" Viv asked in surprise.

"Not me," said the Duke of Faircliffe, leaning back in his seat to hook his thumbs into his waistband. "I've been wearing this coat and trousers for the past five years and I don't intend to break my streak now."

"Not the *same* coat and trousers," Chloe whispered to Viv. "He has half a dozen identical pairs he cycles through."

Viv wasn't sure which stunned her more: the duchess giving away all of her fashionable garments every three months, or that the duke didn't bother attempting to be fashionable at all.

"Dory acquires more than enough new clothing for all of us," said Faircliffe. "I will never understand how someone so small can outgrow dozens of play clothes overnight."

"We donate those, too," Chloe assured Viv. "All of Dory's outgrown items go straight to the orphanage where I grew up."

"You don't want to save Dorian's baby clothes in case he acquires a brother or sister?" Viv regretted the question as soon as it came from her mouth. Obviously, a duke and duchess wouldn't fret over every farthing the way Viv did. They could probably afford to replace the wardrobe of every person in the household nightly if they so wished.

"I don't know that I will have another baby," Chloe answered with astonishing honesty. "Oh, I know it's expected of me. First the heir, then the spare, et cetera. But we adore spoiling Dory with our full attention—when we're not crafting speeches for Parliament. Fifteen months is a little too young to join in on that."

"*You* craft speeches for Parliament?"

"Just Lawrence's," Chloe said quickly. "He's the one who gives them, not me. Come to think of it, you're a writer. A playwright must know how to pen convincing dialogue. You ought to come join our planning sessions. If we were faster at it, maybe we *could* offer speeches for our allies as well. I'm sure you have pet topics you'd like the lads to discuss, am I right?"

"Um," said Viv, showcasing her stunning ability to generate riveting dialogue.

Had she really just been invited to literally help script the next session of Parliament?

A hair-raising wail rent the air.

"Ah," said Chloe. "Those dulcet tones indicate Dory is ready for teatime."

"Milk time," said Faircliffe. "After which he falls asleep, giving us a solid thirty minutes for adult conversation."

"Or a much-needed nap." Chloe pantomimed falling asleep right there in her chair.

Viv pressed her new bonnet to her chest and rose to her feet. "I won't interrupt you further then. Enjoy your nap."

Chloe pretended to let out a loud snore.

Dorian giggled and did the same. Although his came out sounding more like baby pig noises.

"Here." Viv put her old bonnet on the table. It had oil smudges, but it wasn't unwearable. "Please donate my hat when you go."

"With pleasure," said Faircliffe.

"Come back on Monday," Chloe called over her shoulder as she scooped up the baby for his mealtime. "We can chat more once we've hammered out fresh arguments for women's suffrage."

Viv left the house feeling more disoriented than when she'd battled her way through Elizabeth's entryway.

Had she just been *invited* to meddle in the aristocracy's lives? An hour ago, not a single line Viv had written had ever been used in a play. And now her unlikeliest political dialogue might be performed by the highest-ranking lords in Parliament?

These Wynchesters were wild, indeed.

Viv returned to Islington wearing her new bonnet. She headed straight to the sitting room, where today's unopened advice letters still awaited her.

Tommy and Philippa were already seated at the table. Lace-draped Philippa sat behind a stack of books taller than her head. Cravat-less Tommy, in men's shirtsleeves, bent over a new map she was sketching out. At Viv's arrival, Tommy glanced up. A grin spread across her face.

"You're wearing a Faircliffe special!" she crowed. "That duke is my favorite milliner in all of London."

Viv couldn't help but grin back. "His grace is a surprisingly handy craftsman. I can't wait to tell Quentin. Maybe he'll start sewing his own costumes."

"What kinds of costumes?" Tommy asked. "Does he often require fancy bonnets?"

"Not that I've seen. Ask Graham for a full list of the club's false identities." Viv gave a fond shake of her head. "Even when Quentin is supposedly dressed as a cobbler or a parson or a Wynchester like you, his 'disguises' are usually just his ordinary clothes. He probably would appreciate a good hat, though."

Philippa turned to Tommy. "Do you think I should learn millinery?"

Tommy snorted. "I don't see how you can fit anything else in your brain. Didn't you just learn Turkish, for fun?"

"Not for fun," Philippa protested. "To understand local texts describing traditional methods of preparing Turkish coffee."

"Which you drink for fun," Tommy said. "I rest my case. If a random document exists anywhere, written in a language you don't speak, you'll rectify the situation within a month. Whereas those of us ordinary folk who are *not* bluestockings...How many languages do you speak, Vivian?"

"Um," said Viv. "Five?"

"Good God." Tommy set down her pencil and threw her hands into the air. "Am I the last non-bluestocking on earth?"

"You know three," Philippa comforted her. "That's decent."

"My French is the worst of anyone in the family," grumbled Tommy. "And the other two languages, I'd have no excuse not to speak, since we use both English and sign language every day at home. What's your story, Vivian?"

"Dutch, French, and English, because they're spoken on Demerara. Latin and Greek because I helped tutor my cousin during the entirety of his school years."

Tommy ran a hand over her short brown hair as she shook her head. "You should come back on Thursday. You'd fit right in with Philippa's weekly reading circle."

"She didn't say she liked to read," Philippa whispered.

"She's a playwright who speaks five languages," Tommy whispered back. "She can read."

Viv's heart pounded. This was the second time in as many hours in which a Wynchester casually referenced Viv's career as that of a playwright, despite her not having sold a single word. It was as though they could see a successful future in store for her, and found no reason to wait to bestow her proper title.

Philippa smiled at her. "If you're at all interested in biscuits, wine, or Turkish coffee, then by all means, please join us on Thursday afternoon."

"There's also books involved," warned Tommy. "Don't let her fool you."

Viv hadn't expected to be invited to something unrelated to their cases. "I could stomach reading a paragraph or two in exchange for wine and biscuits."

"Mm-hm, that's how it starts." Tommy clucked her tongue. "You'll be crafting military ciphers and performing natural philosophy experiments in no time."

"Don't be a spoilsport," Philippa chided her, softening her words with a kiss to Tommy's cheek.

Tommy swiveled her head at the last second, intercepting the chaste buss and turning it into a proper kiss.

Philippa blushed scarlet, though it was clear she didn't mind at all.

Viv grinned at the now-familiar sight and settled into her seat at the table. Begrudgingly, she was forced to admit she'd begun to understand what Quentin saw in the Wynchesters. Rather than a morally gray, hypocritical monolith, each of them was refreshingly unique and unapologetically themselves in every way.

Complete disregard of society's impossible-to-achieve demands was a lifestyle Viv couldn't help but respect. She herself dedicated her days to bucking expectations and making her own way despite the world she lived in, rather than conforming to it.

She wished Quentin understood that she didn't think he was *wrong* for wanting to help others. She simply feared for his freedom and his life.

Even if Viv wanted to break rules—and she did! She'd tried to break the biggest one of all!—in doing so, she'd risked torture and death. That was not a fate she wished to fall on Quentin. He was a good lad, and deserved to live a long, happy, safe life.

The Wynchesters were unquestionably and mind-bogglingly privileged...but they were conscious of the discrepancy. Each of them did their best to spread that privilege around to those who weren't in the same enviable position.

Quentin needed to comprehend that rule-breaking wasn't the problem.

Retaliation was the problem.

The Wynchesters were powerful enough to shoulder that risk for their clients. Putting themselves on the line without hesitation didn't erase the unfairness, but Viv acknowledged that they were doing their best to restore as much balance as they could.

She opened her journal and jotted a few notes to prove to Quentin she'd truly come to know each of them.

Viv fully supported Chloe ceasing her childbearing after one birth, if that's what she wanted to do. Or Elizabeth, choosing not to have any babies at all. Willfully barren was a stance rarely seen in England, as childlessness was often considered unnatural or a personal failing. It was even legal for husbands to impregnate their wives against their will.

And then there was Tommy and Philippa, who were each other's wives…partners…whatever. Viv didn't have the words to describe their relationship, or to explain Tommy's equal ease in the role of man or woman. The obvious truth was that the two were deeply in love. And honestly, did anything else matter beyond that?

Viv had misjudged Marjorie and Adrian when she'd thought them capable of pushing children toward a life of crime. Graham and Kuni also seemed to be unusual, but genuinely kindhearted people. And no one could deny their methods were effective. They wouldn't be stretched to the limits if they didn't keep their word.

Quentin would be thrilled at her conclusions.

Viv closed her journal and sifted through her correspondence instead. Helping the Wynchesters with their cases was gratifying, but the newspaper was her only source of income, without her pin money. And there was no way to know when Quentin would tire of playing adventurer and judge Viv worthy enough to come home.

Which *had* to be soon, didn't it? Rent would be due in a fortnight, and her Ask Vivian earnings wouldn't come close to the sum. No matter what point he was trying to make or how angry he had been, Quentin would never leave her in such a position…would he?

Viv swiftly sorted through her newest batch of letters, in hopes of receiving another query from the burglar. Nothing today, damn it. Ironically, she had once prayed never to hear from a madman again, and now she was eagerly awaiting his next missive, in the hopes that some clue in his letter would lead them to his identity.

Better yet, Viv might be able to craft a response whose instructions would lead the villain to be caught red-handed.

"Do you think Kuni prefers whipstitch or French hems?" Tommy asked suddenly.

Philippa jumped, causing her magnifying glass to tumble to the floor. "What?"

"I'm sorry." Tommy bent to retrieve the glass. "You were concentrating, and I interrupted. I just wanted to make her Adrienne gown perfect without her knowing I'm working on a dress for her. If I ask, she'll know I'm up to something."

"Give me an hour or two, and I'll ask. I need to finish this," Philippa murmured, bending back over her research.

"Kuni will be gone by then. She's leaving for the Kensington case in thirty minutes. That one won't be over until morning, at which point she and Graham head to Oxford for—"

"I'll go." Viv leapt to her feet, without responding to the ordinary advice letter in her hand. "She's in the rear garden?"

Tommy nodded gratefully. "Remember, you can't tell her what it's for."

Viv smiled. "Kuni won't suspect a thing."

18

Jacob stood in the open doorway of the barn, deep in conversation with Marjorie. Now that she and Adrian were home from their art studio, they'd promised to look after his water shrews while Jacob attended his poetry meeting. He'd been training the baby shrews to respond to different whistled tones, which Adrian could replicate almost perfectly.

"All right," said Jacob as he deposited two shrews into each of their arms. "They're unlikely to bite, and don't worry if they lick you. Their venomous saliva only kills small mammals."

Marjorie looked at the baby shrews in her arms doubtfully. "I'm small."

"You'll be fine," Jacob assured her. "The important thing to remember is—"

"Ha!" shouted Kuni, followed by a resounding *thwack*.

Jacob glanced out toward the garden to see his sister-in-law engaged in one of her dagger-throwing sessions. Occasionally Graham joined her, when he felt like looking comically incompetent. Kuni's daggers could hit the bull's-eye of a target from a dizzying distance. None of the other siblings bothered to try.

"About the robbery," Marjorie said. "The mistress has a point. We cannot rule out Mrs. Olivebury. An elaborate revenge plot does show a certain sense of style."

"She had means, motive, and opportunity," agreed Adrian. "If she stumbled across that portrait unexpectedly...Hell hath no fury, et cetera."

"Look!" Kuni yelled. "I can hit the middle throwing backward over my shoulder!"

They looked.

Which was how Jacob saw the rear door to the house swing open and Vivian step out, just as Kuni was letting fly with a new round of daggers twenty yards away—well out of Vivian's line of sight.

Jacob opened his mouth to shout Vivian's name but only got as far as the initial *Vvv* sound when the first dagger sailed past Vivian's cheek nearly close enough to pierce her ear.

That is, the dagger *would* have sailed past her cheek.

Without pausing, Vivian snatched the handle out of thin air, sliced open the wax seal on the letter she was holding, then sent the dagger flying on in the original direction it had been heading.

The blade hit the bull's-eye with a clink of metal-on-metal as Vivian's blade knocked Kuni's previous dagger off the target.

"Um," said Marjorie. "What?"

"She's the Wynchesteriest of us all," breathed Adrian in stupefaction.

"And she doesn't even *like* Wynchesters," Marjorie added.

"We're growing on her," Jacob assured his sister once he regained his breath. "And possibly a bad influence."

"Did I hit it?" called Kuni as she spun back around to check the target.

"No," Jacob answered in disbelief. "Vivian did."

"Does she even realize she hit it?" asked Marjorie in wonder.

"Kuni!" Vivian yelled, the breeze fluttering her freshly opened letter in her face as she cupped her hands to her mouth. "Do you prefer whipstitch or French hems?"

"Are those foodstuffs or new dances?" Kuni called back, baffled.

Vivian held the letter over her eyes to block out the sun as she looked Kuni up and down. She nodded to herself, then turned to jog back inside the house.

Kuni shrugged, as if having already forgotten the encounter, then let loose with a fresh throwing knife toward the target. Another bull's-eye—right next to Vivian's.

Jacob's heart might never return to normal.

"Am I the only one who has no idea what just happened?" asked Marjorie.

"I never know what's happening," said Adrian.

Jacob glanced at his pocket watch. If he didn't hurry, he was going to be late for his poetry meeting. "Kuni, don't kill me! I'm crossing the garden."

He jogged across the wide grass to the house. Vivian was in the sitting room, calmly answering her correspondence.

"How the devil did you do that?" Jacob blurted out.

"Hm?" she murmured without looking up.

"You grabbed a knife from the air and hit a bull's-eye without looking!"

She held up an unfolded sheet of paper. "I needed to open my letter."

"But you..." he stammered. "We have letter openers! There was no need put yourself in harm's way—"

"Kuni can hit targets without looking at them," said Tommy. "Why shouldn't Vivian?"

Jacob goggled at his sister. Kuni was a Balcovian warrior who had been trained in armed combat since she could toddle. Vivian was an unpublished playwright who wrote rude comments to idiots in the newspaper.

"Kuni relies on her muscles' instinctive memory, gleaned from thousands or millions of past throws," said Philippa. "I imagine Vivian uses mathematics."

"Mathematics," Jacob repeated.

Philippa nodded. "It's theoretically possible to hit a target every time. All you have to do is take into consideration the weight, dimensions, and balance of the blade and its handle...the distance to and material of the target...the humidity and any associated wind resistance—"

"In less than a second?" Jacob demanded. "Instant calculations in the blink of an eye?"

"Just because you can't do sums doesn't mean Vivian can't," Tommy murmured.

The other three filed into the room from outside, Marjorie and Adrian with their arms full of wriggling shrews, and Kuni with a pile of razor-sharp daggers.

"Write faster," Kuni told Vivian. "You've got to come back outside to throw daggers with me before I have to leave for Kensington."

As much as Jacob wanted to watch over Vivian, he took advantage of his family's distraction to edge toward the door. Perhaps tonight, for the first time in years, no one would needle him about—

"Are you going to read your poetry to your friends?" Philippa asked.

He sighed. "No. Stop asking."

"Jacob says the only way he'd consider sharing his work is anonymously," Vivian murmured.

He sent her a repressive glance. "There's nothing wrong with that."

"If another identity makes you feel more comfortable in your own skin, then you should use it," said Tommy. "But if any disguise makes you feel worse, you should take it off right away."

Marjorie touched Jacob's shoulder. "Consider just for a moment how it might feel to have others appreciate your efforts."

Jacob grimaced. He didn't have to wonder what having avid

readers might be like. He was England's most celebrated reclusive poet...and no one knew it. Not his publisher, not the Dreamers Guild poetry group, and not even his own family.

Vivian followed him to the front door. "Don't be a coward."

He whirled to face her. "*What* did you just say?"

"You're so used to being Wynchester royalty, you've forgotten what reality is like for everyone else," she shot back unapologetically. "It's easy for you lot to take chances with other people's lives. Have you considered taking a risk of your own?"

He clenched his teeth. As it happened, he *did* imagine unveiling the truth. Often. Of shouting out to the world "Sir Gareth Jallow is Jacob Wynchester!"

And then what? Most likely, he wouldn't even be believed. Not by the Dreamers Guild, and definitely not by the world at large.

"You?" the public would sneer. "You're not a 'sir' anything. What makes you think your words are worth reading?"

"It's not that simple," he ground out.

Vivian folded her arms beneath her bosom. "I know what it's like to struggle and be smacked down, day after day, year after year, in harsher conditions than you've ever known. I almost *died* clawing my way to where I am today, and I'll be damned if some theater director's letter of rejection crushes my spirit now. What are you so afraid of? That some other aspiring poet dislikes your verse? Grow up."

Fury lanced through him. At her many erroneous assumptions... and at the ways in which her assumptions weren't all that erroneous.

Yes, at first he hadn't been certain of a positive public reaction. Not until multiple volumes and reprints started flying off the shelves. England loved a mirage. Jacob Wynchester wished they loved *him*.

He knew as well as Tommy did that sometimes it was the disguise that garnered respect, not the person inside the costume. Revealing his real identity didn't mean Jacob would automatically inherit

Jallow's fame and adulation. Admitting the truth might be the quickest way to ruin everything for them both.

"It's complicated," he said through gritted teeth.

"It's not complicated," said Vivian. "I have such conversations ten times a day. 'How do you do, I'm Vivian Henry, here's something I wrote.'"

"You write those words on paper," he said dismissively, hoping she would interpret his refusal as incapacitating shyness. "It's not the same as in person."

She looked amused. "Do you think I fail to knock on every theater's door in London every time I have a new script ready?"

Jacob had tried that tactic, too. In the beginning, and as recently as last year. Publishers laughed in his face without reading a single word of his work, if they bothered opening the door to him at all.

A decade of relentless rejection was what had spawned the "reclusive" Jallow to begin with. The lowest title (giving Jallow elevated status, yet keeping him somewhat humble) plus the inference of white skin (see: title) and an aspirational life of privilege (same).

Jacob was both thrilled that his scheme had worked, and disgusted to think his words were only considered valuable if written by a wealthy white man with a title.

He stared at Vivian. "If you know you're a talented playwright, yet receive nothing but rejection, then you ought to be more understanding about my position."

"Oh, I understand your position," she replied. "Since the moment you became prince of this palace, you've had anything you could desire delivered to you on a silver platter. Not only aren't you accustomed to hearing 'no,' you're not willing to try. You don't know what it's *like* to fail. A man without obstacles is champion of nothing."

He stalked outside and slammed the door without responding.

The hinges immediately reopened behind him.

"Try to fail tonight as spectacularly as you are able," she called out. "Your talent is worth the risk. *You're* worth it. No matter what any naysayers opine. You can't conquer your fears if you don't face them!"

He swung himself into the carriage and slammed that door, too.

Communicating with publishers exclusively via post—and ignoring the public altogether—made Sir Gareth Jallow all the more believable as an eccentric artist. Rumors abounded that the poet was old or sickly or disabled, housebound and irascible. The public loved him all the more for it. Sir Gareth was a triumph. An inspiration.

No rumors whatsoever indicated Jallow might be thirty-two-year-old Jacob Wynchester, scribbling on an old notebook inside a barn. Nor would such an unveiling be greeted with applause.

If he somehow convinced the public at large that he was the man behind the magic, they would not thank him for pulling the wool from their eyes. Breathless respect for Sir Gareth would not extend to Jacob Wynchester.

Vivian didn't understand that the only way for him to have success was by never allowing anyone to peek behind the curtain.

And he did have success! Loads of it. What had once seemed an eye-watering inheritance from his adoptive father, Baron Vanderbean, now looked like a pittance. Sir Gareth Jallow was a household name.

Granted, it wasn't *Jacob's* name, but wasn't success its own reward, no matter how it came about?

Soon, the carriage pulled up at the meeting site for the Dreamers Guild. A privileged location. Jacob rubbed his face as he trudged up the walkway to the home of the second-most famous poet in England.

His colleagues believed Jacob to be luckless but hopeful, and filled every conversation with well-meaning but useless advice on which type of parchment or ink to use to catch a publisher's eye, or which popular poets it would behoove him to study.

Which inevitably led to them rhapsodizing over his fictional persona. Unlike Jacob, Sir Gareth was a genius! A treasure! More influential than Shakespeare! It was exhilarating and infuriating and embarrassing.

A man without obstacles is champion of nothing, echoed Vivian's voice in his ears. *Try to fail tonight as spectacularly as you are able. You're worth it.*

Tonight, the first half hour of the meeting was devoted to speculation that Percy Bysshe Shelley would return to London to perform a reading at Vauxhall Gardens. Although the others spoke dreamily about addressing a crowd of ten thousand, the reality of being rejected by an audience that large made Jacob want to burrow into a hole with his field voles. Though he'd once dreamed of being the star of a show, he now preferred remaining safe in the shadows.

"Who wants to read first?" asked the group's host.

Jacob didn't raise his hand.

A record quarter of the assembled poets managed to read a few lines before the conversation inevitably devolved into talk of Sir Gareth Jallow, whose newest volume of poetry was to be published the following week.

On this topic, tonight the group was evenly divided. Half believed Jallow the most brilliant mind of the century and couldn't wait to read the new collection. The other half scoffed that Jallow had become passé and overrated. Now that the common folk could quote him at will, Jallow's poems were no longer the esoteric domain of the literati.

Eventually the group wandered back on topic and managed to have the rest of the room share a few stanzas each between sips of sherry.

Everyone but Jacob. He'd refused their entreaties for so long, they no longer asked him.

Part of him wished to cling to life as it currently was. Another part of him recognized that Vivian was right. The only way to get what he didn't have was through change.

A strange, forgotten itch crawled along his skin. An itch to try. To be seen. To be heard.

To prove Vivian wrong about him.

To make her proud.

"Well," said one of the founding poets as the group finished the last bottle of sherry, "I suppose that's it until next week."

Jacob's friends began to clap each other on their backs and shrug into their coats.

Perhaps he wasn't ready to tell the whole world the full truth—Jacob might never be ready for that, no matter how idyllic the dream—but these were his colleagues. He'd known them for years.

If Jacob was ever going to fail spectacularly, he might as well do so here. Starting now.

"I could read a few lines," he blurted out.

The others blinked at him in amazement.

"I didn't know you were a poet!" said one of the newer members.

Had it been that long since anyone had asked Jacob if he wanted to read? Had the others believed him merely a hanger-on all this time, and not a fellow colleague, as he had felt about them?

"Of course we can take a moment for a junior member," one of the other poets said expansively, despite Jacob having been present for the original founding of the group, and every meeting since.

"What are you going to read?" asked one of the new faces.

Jacob hadn't actually prepared anything. He couldn't quite believe he was even doing this. Did he dare? Once his poetry group knew the truth, regardless of their reaction, the secret would be out there. This could be the beginning of the end.

The others watched him expectantly.

He cleared his throat. The journal in his pocket was full of unfinished poems—he certainly couldn't read any of that. But Jallow's upcoming book of poetry contained lines Jacob had toiled over countless times. He could probably quote all hundred pages by heart. He decided to go with the two-stanza poem on page sixty-six. Short. Visceral. Powerful.

"Something I've been working on," he said hoarsely. "It's called 'Irrational.'"

When he finished, the room was preternaturally silent. The others regarded him with expressions ranging from confusion to awe.

"Splendid!" The newest poets burst into spontaneous applause.

"Derivative at best," sniffed one of the old guard as he looked down his nose at Jacob. "It is one thing to admire a better talent, and another entirely to copy Jallow's style as if it were your own."

"I did no such thing," Jacob said evenly.

Those who had praised him before glanced at each other, their smiles fading.

"Rumor has it 'Sir Gareth Jallow' is a pseudonym," their host said with a hearty clap to Jacob's shoulder. "Maybe Mr. Wynchester really is Jallow."

The others joined in the laughter.

Jacob remained silent. Purposefully silent. Meaningfully silent. And then remembered that silence was far from spectacular. To fail spectacularly, he would need to say the words aloud. All of them.

"It's my pseudonym," he replied quietly. "I trust you will not reveal the secret."

The poets' laughter crumbled like week-old bread. The room went preternaturally silent.

"No," whispered their host. "Impossible."

Jacob shrugged. "You don't have to believe me now. But you'll find that poem halfway through the new volume of poetry releasing next week."

Each syllable of his murmured reply echoed through the room like cannon blasts.

"*Is* it possible?" squealed one of the new poets.

Jacob gave a tentative smile. "You'll find out one way or the other next week."

"Be serious," said one of the more famous poets, as if Jacob had just confirmed the existence of flying dragons. "Are you really—"

"Quote another!" begged one of the novices. "Anything. What's on page forty-two?"

So Jacob recited another poem. And another. And another. Until there could be no doubt.

He braced himself.

The resulting cacophony was deafening. And mixed.

His colleagues' reactions were neither as vicious as Jacob had feared, nor as laudatory as he had dreamed. The cruelest ones said this was precisely why they had never respected an over-esteemed blowhard like Jallow in the first place. His poetry was as fake as his identity, and just as disappointing.

In response, their host burst out laughing. This time, not at Jacob, but at his own doubt. He pulled Jacob into his arms for an embrace that was part hug, part garlic crusher.

In fury, those who had never liked Jallow—or who could not reconcile the veneration of their hero with the ordinary human before them—donned their top hats and abruptly left the meeting. Some without a single word of goodbye, and others with parting shots so sharp, Jacob would need more than Vivian's reinforced leather armor to shield himself from the wounds.

Half of those still present were visibly reserving judgment. Convinced by the evidence, but uncertain how to react to this new information.

The rest, however, had no such misgivings. They looked at Jacob as though he'd just admitted to taking his afternoon tea from the Holy Grail, when not slicing the accompanying cakes with the Excalibur sword.

"Out of the way," said a chap called William, previously the most renowned of all the poets present. "I owe Jacob a fist to the gut for hiding this from us all these years."

"Me next," called one of the others, and cuffed Jacob lightly on the back of the head. "Take that, Sir Pseudonym!"

Handshakes and good-natured chiding abounded as the other remaining poets crowded around Jacob.

"Obviously our meeting isn't adjourned just yet," said their host. "I'll ring for champagne. You're not going anywhere until we have the full story."

"It can't leave this room," Jacob said firmly. "Sir Gareth's identity must remain a secret."

Part of him worried that those who had already left would not be so faithful. The ever-humbling cut of logic, however, promised they'd be the last to spread the word. Either they didn't believe him in the first place, or they resented him for his accomplishment. They would never breathe a word that might make him *more* famous.

"If I had half the success you do," said their host, "I'd shout the truth to everyone who made the mistake of glancing in my direction."

Jacob shook his head. "Swear to me. No one can know, until and unless I choose to divulge my identity of my own free will."

They all gave their word, if reluctantly. Revealing Jallow's true identity would have been the coup of the year for any of them.

"Can I get a quote from you to help me promote my upcoming anthology?" asked one of the poets.

"Can you give advice on my drafts?" asked one of the novices.

"You buy the wine and champagne from now on," interjected William.

They all laughed.

Just like that, the room was restored to its easy, happy mood.

Rightness bubbled through Jacob's chest along with the champagne. He hadn't realized how much being acknowledged would mean to him. How badly he'd needed to be seen, to be believed, to be valued. He never wanted this sensation to end.

In the end, he hadn't needed anything more than his own words to prove himself. At least, not to his true friends. With the others, Jacob's confession had failed spectacularly—but now that was over. The sutures, removed. His scars would heal, and he would emerge stronger than ever.

Or at least be able to limp off in a new direction.

19

When Jacob awoke the next morning at dawn, he still felt as though he were living a dream. He'd read to his poetry group! He had confessed his nom de plume! Some had been happy for him, and some had been furious, but the world had not ended. If anything, the day seemed brighter than ever.

In high spirits, he cared for his animals in record time, bathed, and checked the clock. Still two and a half hours before he and his polecats were expected on the morning's first mission.

Normally, Jacob would have filled the time by scribbling in his poetry journal. But his nerves were still springing against his skin too much to allow him to sit alone in quiet contemplation.

He felt like celebrating. Like dancing. Like flying with his wings spread wide.

And he owed this new sensation to a single person. The one whose extremely annoying unsolicited opinions had driven him to push past his discomfort and risk being his true self, in front of witnesses, at least for a few moments.

Very well, his family had also been begging Jacob for years to share his poetry. But they didn't fully understand what it was like to be someone like him in a profession like this.

Vivian more than understood. She lived it. She breathed it. She fought against it tooth and nail every single day, never once flagging, much less conceding defeat. Vivian shared her words and her identity with pride. Damn the consequences, and to the devil with anyone who tried to keep her in the shadows.

Jacob hurried to the kitchen to pack a basket. He didn't know what time she tended to rise, but he hoped to catch her before she broke her fast so that they could do so together.

He also hoped to smooth things over from their last argument. She'd called him a coward hiding behind anonymity. And she'd accused him of becoming as pampered and careless as the selfsame spoiled lords he chafed against.

As much as it galled him to admit it, she had not been entirely wrong.

He rode a horse to her home because it was faster. No need to ring for a carriage when he could fetch a mount himself. Though it did make an awkward ride, with the basket balancing on his lap and his hat clutched in his fist because the wind kept flinging it from his head.

After tying his horse to a post, Jacob paused outside Vivian's door for a full minute to smooth the new wrinkles from his clothing and set his hat at a rakish angle. This gave him time to notice a small green leaf poking out from the thin crevice between the door and its jamb. He frowned. Only the edge was visible, and even that at ankle-height. Despite being low to the ground and almost out of sight, it did not seem a place a leaf would naturally find itself.

Which was why, when Vivian opened the door to welcome him in, Jacob's first words weren't *Good morning* as he had planned, but rather, "Why do you keep a leaf stuck in the crack of your door?"

"Habit," she replied without hesitation, as though his was a perfectly ordinary greeting. "It's to let me know if anyone has entered—or attempted to breach—my private space. In this case, I'm hoping to see if Quentin returns while I'm asleep or away."

In this case. And her explanation made sense. But she'd said *habit.* Who else had Vivian hoped—or worried—would breach her private space? Jacob's protective hackles rose.

"What's in the basket?" she asked. "If it's a badger, I must warn you, Rufus does not play well with others."

"It's not for Rufus," he said. "It's for you. For us. Something to break our fast, if you haven't done so already."

She looked at the basket as though his words made no sense.

It was at this point that Jacob realized he had indeed packed a receptacle capable of comfortably housing an entire family of wild badgers. Vivian could break her fast for the next three weeks with the contents of this basket.

"A light snack," he said, leaning into her perception of him as coddled, and lacking awareness of how common folk lived. "A pre-breakfast, as one does. Something small to tide us over until the lazy servant wenches finally cook up something worth—"

She rolled her eyes and took the basket from him. "Sit down and stop ruining this for me."

He sat. In the chair across from the attack badger. "Ruining what, exactly? You didn't even know I'd be coming to call."

Unless she'd somehow guessed that, too? Vivian *was* disturbingly perceptive.

"Whatever you brought, I intend to enjoy with gusto," she informed him. "And I hope you're not too hungry, because I haven't decided if I'll share. Aside from biscuits with your siblings, this is one of the few meals I've had in England that I didn't have to cook myself."

His heart twisted in empathy. And perhaps a little guilt. The circumstances of his birth were unlikely to be much better than hers, but Jacob's luck had changed dramatically for the better while he was still young.

When Baron Vanderbean had first adopted six unhappy orphans, the wide-eyed children had looked at that gargantuan house and their heaping portions of food the same way Vivian was eyeing the picnic basket now. But after twenty years—or possibly over the course of those first several months—excess had ceased to be astonishing and started to become part of ordinary life.

"Well?" he asked. "Aren't you going to eat your gift?"

Vivian's eyes sparkled. "Watch me."

She gathered the papers cluttering the small table into a pile and carried them to the sideboard with all the other stacks of paper. After passing a cleaning rag over the surface of the table, she opened the lid to the picnic basket and began removing its contents.

"Milk...tea...coffee...lemonade...chocolate...a bottle of wine?"

"I wouldn't presume to limit your morning libations," he murmured.

"Apples...pears...nectarines...grapes...mulberries...figs...honey...marmalade...a full loaf of still-warm bread, *and* a dozen toasted slices?"

"Fruit is good for you," he protested. "Bats like it. And bread is delicious."

"We've also got pork chops...sausages...cheese...boiled eggs... and what looks like three pies?"

"Tommy and Chloe both would disown me if I packed a picnic without pies. If you don't want one, I'll—"

"Oh, I want them." Vivian placed silverware and two plates on the table, then began to pile hers high. "Don't talk to me until I've licked my plate."

He smiled to himself and reached for the bread and marmalade.

Her reaction had been all that he could have hoped for. She'd accepted his presence without question, granting a peaceful ceasefire to their prior argument.

Jacob would not have been surprised to receive the opposite reaction. He had fully expected Vivian to be nosy and pushy and demand to know whatever it was that he wasn't ready to tell her. Instead, she seemed content to wait until he was comfortable—which might be never.

"There." She shoved her empty plate away from her. "That was—oh, blast."

The plate banged into her spoon and sent it flying to the floor.

Jacob started to move his chair back in order to retrieve the fallen piece of silverware for her.

"No, no." She waved a hand. "That's what badgers are for. Rufus? Spoon."

Rufus lifted his black-and-white-striped snout from the scrap of carpet he'd been resting on and peered around the kitchen as if waking slowly. Obediently, he yawned, hobbled forth while occasionally stretching a rear leg, scooped up the lost spoon in his mouth, and delivered it to Vivian's waiting hand.

"You're bamming me," said Jacob. "You trained a wild badger to fetch fallen silverware?"

"No," Vivian answered. "I trained him to fetch pencils, which is far more practical. Rufus was bright enough to extrapolate from there." She scratched behind the badger's ears. He wiggled his arse and sat on her feet. She stroked his back. "Who's a crafty little beast? Is it you, Rufus? Is it you?"

Jacob suspected the clever one was Vivian. She was as flashy and competent and confident as his siblings, and she wasn't even a Wynchester. If *Vivian* had been Sir Gareth Jallow, she'd have told the world by now.

Instead, she remained frustratingly unpublished. Jacob wondered how many of her plays would have sold in a blink if she'd submitted them as *Sir* Vivian Henry instead of "Miss." Probably all of them. Vivian might be more famous than Jallow by now...if she'd given in instead of fighting back.

Which one of them had made the right choice? *Was* there a right choice? Because of their individual decisions, the rich one got richer, and the poor one stayed poor. Regardless of merit.

Life definitely wasn't fair.

Jacob couldn't help but suffer another pang of guilt. Financially, he could have afforded to stick to her morals. If he never earned a single penny as a poet, his quality of life would not change. Whereas if anyone had bothered to pay Vivian a fraction of what she was worth, she wouldn't be performing multiple jobs and still living off her cousin's mercy.

"Please," he said. "Allow me to help clean the dishes."

"Is this a dream?" She clutched her chest, then pinched her arm. "Will I awaken in a few moments to my usual life of an empty pantry and a pile of housework?"

"Don't celebrate yet," he warned her. "I've never washed proper dishes."

She frowned at his word choice. "What does that mean? You previously washed improper dishes? Makeshift items no one could reasonably mistake for plates and bowls? Or that you've never taken a cloth to a piece of porcelain in your life?"

"Yes," he answered, then changed the subject. "I didn't mean to interrupt whatever you were doing when I arrived. Were you working on a new play?"

"Answering advice letters," she said with a rueful sigh. "They're the only people willing to pay me for my words. Unfortunately, that only buys paper, pencils, and postage."

He glanced over his shoulder. "You mentioned Quentin has a trust…"

"And he gives me an allowance from it. My pin money covers my clothing and anything else I might need."

"Does it?" Jacob said with skepticism. "And is the money really a gift if you work as maid and cook and nanny and tutor and probably valet as well?"

She pressed her lips together. "Would I like to receive all those salaries? Of course. Who wouldn't? But Quentin's quarterly dividends aren't nearly the sum you must be imagining. If he could afford to hire staff, he would. We wouldn't be living *here*. As soon I sell a play and establish a solid career for myself..."

Jacob held his tongue. He wondered how long she'd been telling herself that recognition and riches—or at least a living wage that allowed her a full night's sleep once in a while—were right around the corner. Probably for years. Maybe her whole life. And here she was. Living here. Like this. Somehow still confident and hopeful.

"I *will* sell a play," Vivian said hotly, as though she could read Jacob's mind. "But...it's impossible to predict when that might be. In the meantime, I hope Quentin returns before the rent is due."

Jacob looked at her sharply. "You can't pay your rent?"

"With what I earn answering anonymous letters sent to the newspaper? Either you have no idea how much rents cost, or you vastly overestimate how periodicals compensate their contributors."

Probably both were true. Jacob had never paid rent. He didn't have a house the first several years of his life, then moved in with Baron Vanderbean, who had built the Wynchester siblings' Islington residence months before they had become a family.

Jacob's only experiences with earning money were a circus that had paid almost nothing, his failed publishing attempts as Mr. Wynchester, and his subsequent career as Jallow, which had rocketed far beyond his wildest dreams.

He was embarrassed to admit that although he'd meant it when he'd said Vivian should earn the wages of maid and cook and governess and any other roles she provided, Jacob actually hadn't the least notion what those positions might earn. He wasn't even certain if

Chloe still managed the Wynchester family's books, or if she'd passed the task on to someone else.

Would Vivian's newspaper income be enough to afford a small room of her own? Probably not. Servants lived with the families they served for a reason. Without her cousin's trust money, Vivian would either be out on the streets or toiling just as much as she did now for some other wealthy employer. Either way, there would be no free time for penning plays.

"I can cover the cost of your—" he began.

"Quentin would never allow me to be evicted," Vivian said. "He'll show up any day now."

Jacob hoped so.

Then again, Quentin hadn't made any attempt to communicate with his increasingly worried cousin. Jacob's siblings frequently traveled far and wide on a moment's notice for many of their justice missions, but they would *never* disappear for days without a word.

The lad was either pathologically self-centered and incredibly inconsiderate…or something else was going on.

Jacob had never hoped harder for a lad to bear the personality traits of young and thoughtless.

"How did it go at the meeting last night?" Vivian asked.

He couldn't hide the grin that threatened to take over his face. "I faced my fears."

"And lived to tell the tale!" She clapped her hands. "Well done."

"You might give decent advice once in a while," he teased.

"Why don't you let me read some of your work? I'm a playwright, not a poet, but I can spot talent a mile away."

"No, thank you," he said hastily.

He'd known the Dreamers Guild for years, and Vivian for less than a fortnight. If Jacob wasn't yet ready to tell his siblings, he certainly wasn't going to divulge his second identity to a client. Much less the world at large. Not when a secret that big would turn his life—and half of England—upside down.

"I'm not so scary," she coaxed.

She was absolutely that scary.

Her steadfast confidence in her own opinions was another reason he'd rather she never read a single word of his poetry. Vivian was literally paid to be right about other people. If *she* found Jacob's poems unworthy, it would wound him more than all the countrywide praise.

She dragged her chair closer. "You won't allow me to read your poetry because you think it's bad? Or because you're afraid it's *good*, and I'll have no choice but insist you share it with the world?"

He tightened his lips rather than respond.

"Don't block yourself from success," she said with surprising gentleness. "The fact that you're audacious enough to create something from nothing makes you exceptional."

Inarguably, Sir Gareth Jallow had indeed received exceptional success. But was his fame fully deserved? Or was the pretentious "sir" and the mystery of his reclusive persona doing more to sell books than the actual content inside?

"Why don't you let me read *your* work?" he countered, hoping to deflect attention from himself and perhaps even inflict a sliver of the same doubt and nervousness upon Vivian.

She shrugged and gestured to the sideboard. "Read anything you want. I'll take over the dishes."

He stared at her. "Read your work right now? In front of you?"

"Or take a script home. I have duplicate copies of everything, remember?"

Could she truly be that nonchalant about something she'd poured her heart into?

Jacob dried his hands and crossed to the sideboard. She didn't stop him. He scooped up an entire pile of manuscripts. Rather than tense in anticipation of his impending first reaction, she turned toward the sink. He started with the topmost page. She wasn't even watching him.

By the third line, he'd forgotten all about Vivian. He forgot he was standing in a tiny kitchen. He forgot his sausages were over on the table growing cold. He forgot he lived in this world at all. Instead, he turned the pages faster and faster, snorting at the witty dialogue and holding his breath at all the moments of drama and suspense.

When he reached the end of Act One, he glanced up in awe. She still wasn't peering at him, watching for any sign of approval or censure. She'd actually finished clearing the dishes and tidying the entire kitchen. He'd been too lost in her play to notice.

"I was going to help with that."

She shrugged. "Reading is more important than housework."

All right, then. Rather than continue to Act Two, he flipped through the stack, pausing at random to skim whatever lines happened to appear.

Every single page was brilliant, even without context. The humor, the swift pace, the action. She was the prima donna of playwrights... or would be, if anyone with a brain gave her half a chance.

"You sent these plays out?" he asked.

She nodded and joined him at the sideboard. "To every theater manager in the country."

He considered. "What if you didn't?"

She frowned. "If I've garnered no interest whatsoever when maximizing my chances, why would I purposefully minimize them?"

"You wouldn't be," he said. "Trust me on this. You are a logical person, but most of the world is not. Sometimes the only way to win is by resorting to a bit of trickery."

"No," she said flatly. "I'll be published on my own merit or not at all."

"Not *bad* trickery," he assured her. "Normal trickery. The sort everyone uses every day."

"It's not true success if I cheat my way to the top. What did I tell you about obstacles?"

"No, it's...Look. Why do society hostesses rent expensive pineapples to display as centerpieces at their dinner parties?"

"Because the rich have absolutely nothing else to do with their time and money? If I had a pineapple, I'd eat it."

"And they might, too, if pineapples weren't so exotic and rare that they cost more than a horse. Pineapple motifs are carved all over stately homes because their scarcity implies status, and everyone wants a little bit more of that."

She sighed. "What does tropical fruit have to do with my plays?"

"Be the pineapple," Jacob coaxed, edging closer. "Intriguingly unusual and irresistibly sweet. Research each theater manager before sending a query, and be sure to imply that their most hated rival not only has shown interest, but also is actively trying to keep this manuscript out of your target's hands. He'll not only snap it up, but also insist on exclusivity."

"It's not that easy," said Vivian. "Perhaps you and your family can feel good about making up lies to manipulate people everywhere you go, but I want to earn my accolades."

That cut closer than she knew.

"It's not lying...exactly," said Jacob. "It's worth a try, at least."

All right, yes, it obviously involved a wee bit of lying. And some manipulation. But that didn't make it a bad idea. Not when mutton-heads all over England were rejecting plays this excellent, unopened and unread.

Jacob hadn't the least doubt that if one of those theater managers actually read so much as the opening page, they'd be prepared to duel at dawn for the right to perform Vivian Henry's theatrical debut.

"If you won't use human nature to your benefit, then you can't expect footlights and confetti from a total stranger," he told her. "*I know you're talented enough to be a star overnight, but no one else knows it.* That's why apprenticeships—"

She looked unimpressed. "Why should I play apprentice to someone who cannot write as well as I do?"

"Because that's how the world operates." He slid the stack of plays back onto the sideboard behind her hips. "Working one's way up the ranks is a necessary step. You could take a volunteer position—"

"I ought to be paid for my labor!"

"Of course you should. But these are the facts. You would hear the same advice if you wished to be a baker or a blacksmith. In many cases, masters are well paid for training apprentices. That path may currently be out of your means—"

"And out of the question," she ground out with obvious frustration. "I don't want to waste my time and money copying someone else's words for the next five years, when I'm ready *now*—"

She jabbed her finger into his chest for emphasis.

He caught it and trapped her hand to his chest.

She glared at him in consternation.

"You don't have to convince me that you're worthy," he said softly. "I already know that you deserve everything you want."

Her eyes widened and her lips parted. She did not remove her hand from beneath his. The air crackled with awareness.

He could feel his heart fluttering against her palm as he lowered his head toward hers, fully expecting to be pushed away and rejected.

She was the great and talented Vivian Henry. The woman whose name crossed everyone's breakfast table every morning. The lady with all the answers.

He was just Jacob.

"You're taking too long," she murmured against his lips. "Kiss me before I die of anticipation."

He wasted no time in heeding her advice.

Their hips bumped against the sideboard, sending reams of neatly stacked plays flying. Neither of them paused. Vivian's hands laced tight behind Jacob's neck, and his own arms wrapped gently about her, cradling her close without trapping her to him. She tasted like success. Like the perfect opening line to a poem.

He *liked* that they'd both taken the first move together. He liked that she chose to kiss him. That she tasted like pies and marmalade. He liked that she argued with him. That she shared her thoughts and struggles.

He only wished *he* had the answer she sought. The ability to wave a magic wand and grant her the opportunity to shine, like the star she was destined to be—if only people would look and see what was right before their eyes.

His heart gave a little jump of excitement. Jacob Wynchester might not be able to do much about theater managers' prejudices, but Sir Gareth Jallow...now *there* was a chap with a fair bit of influence.

Jacob had never leveraged his alternate persona's fame in the pursuit of literary favors, but he supposed it was no different from Tommy utilizing any of her infinite disguises in the pursuit of justice. And the unfair prejudice against Vivian was an obvious injustice.

Unlike Tommy, Jacob couldn't claim he'd be bending the rules to help a "client." Vivian meant more to him than that. He didn't want her to disappear from his life the moment her cousin came home.

But even if she did...even if all the future held for them were a few fond memories...at least he could offer a little help up the ladder she very much deserved to climb.

She'd made her opposition to trickery clear—but his praise was no sham. He'd be telling the full and honest truth about what a talented and worthy writer she was. He'd shout it from the rooftops, if he could.

Though he shouldn't mention any plans to Vivian quite yet. First of all, Jacob wasn't certain what, exactly, he could pull off. Nor did he want her to think he was being benevolent in order to curry favor with her, or to make her feel beholden to him in any way. He'd rather be anonymous and know deep inside his heart that he'd done everything he could to help her achieve her dreams.

But that was a project for later. Right now, the only thing he wanted from life was to keep kissing the clever, talented woman here in his arms.

20

iv was breaking her most sacred rule:

> <u>No romantic entanglements</u> until a successful playwright career is well established.

After years of being certain she didn't even *like* Wynchesters, she couldn't quite fathom how she'd wound up in this one's embrace.

Except for the part where she'd wrapped her arms about his neck and pulled him close.

Their entanglement wasn't a *romance*, Viv assured herself. This was just a kiss. Men dished out kisses all the time without it meaning any particular commitment. Surely, she could be just as nonchalant.

But Jacob was a maddeningly good kisser, damn him. His lips were warm and inviting, his taste sweet and forbidden. He emanated heat like a fire on a winter's day: comforting, yet dangerous to touch.

Here she was, doing plenty of touching. Not merely approaching the fire but stoking the flames. Pressing her entire body against him, from bosom to hips. Not that he was complaining. All physical signs indicated he would be happy to lean her back across this sideboard and take her right here, with the scattered piles of her failed plays as a mattress. At least the pages would be used for something.

But Viv was now the playwright of her own life. The architect of her own success or ruin. She could stop this kiss before it went too far. She could exit this embrace any time she pleased.

The surprise twist was that she didn't want to stop. She not only liked Jacob's kisses, she liked *him* far more than she wished to admit.

His soulful eyes and slow smile and strong body—those elements were why every woman he passed took a second glance. Viv had seen beyond that.

She had been in his home. In his barn. In his arms. She knew how kindhearted he was, how insightful, how stubborn and clever.

He'd never voiced it, but she also understood deep in her marrow how it felt to be good at something, to have drive and tenacity, to have a calling, only to be overlooked or dismissed out of hand because of the prejudices of those in power.

She would *rather* have in common that they were the two most famous writers in England—or the world!

Which unfortunately reminded her that in order to earn that someday, she needed to stop kissing this delicious man and return to real life. With far more regret than she dared to show, Viv untangled her hands from behind Jacob's neck and lowered her lips from his.

"I..." she began, flustered to have momentarily forgotten all of her best objections.

He nodded. "Me, too."

Had he read her mind? Or did he think she meant something else entirely?

Jacob dropped to a crouch, swiftly gathering all of the fallen papers before she had a chance to clean up her own mess.

"Set them anywhere," she said. "They'll take hours to put in order, and there's no sense bothering. No one wants to read them."

"I do," he answered. "I'll put them in order for you."

"You don't have to," she said quickly.

His brown eyes were gentle.

"I want to," he said simply, his voice soft and warm. "Let me do something for you, just this once. You can tell yourself it's a blatant selfish bid for free reading material at any cost."

She snorted, despite herself. "That doesn't even make sense. Besides, you and your entire family are already doing things for me. Finding Quentin is far more important than reading my plays or... anything else we might have been doing."

He arched his brows. "What else might we do?"

Her neck heated. His kiss wasn't one she would be forgetting soon—or ever. A kiss like that would turn up in her next ten plays, right along with the happy endings she couldn't manage to write for herself in the real world. A kiss like that deserved footlights and fireworks and a standing ovation. She'd be replaying it in her dreams for the rest of her life.

"I've forgotten the entire incident," she assured him. "As though it never happened. Two strangers, staying strange. I mean celibate. I mean separate." Good God, what was this jumble of word soup flowing from her mouth? "I'm busy, you're busy," she babbled. "Don't let me keep you from your tasks."

His eyes glittered with amusement, as though *The lady doth protest too much, methinks* was on the tip of his tongue.

"Don't you dare say a word," she muttered. "Walk away while we both still can."

He tucked the thick sheaf of papers under one muscular arm and held out the other elbow. "Aren't we going in the same direction? I have to infiltrate a monastery within the hour, but if you'd rather not join our next planning session..."

She grabbed his arm as if he were saving her from drowning. Not because she wanted to touch him again. She was almost completely over that unquenchable impulse. But mostly because finding her cousin was her highest priority, which meant being on hand to hear any news or craft any strategies.

He handed her the stack of papers. "You'll have to hold these."

She frowned up at him. "Nobody has to hold them. They'll be fine lying between us in the carriage."

He grinned. "I didn't bring a carriage."

"What—" She followed him out the front door to discover a lone gray horse tied to an iron post. "You didn't even bring a *saddle*?"

"Be glad I didn't, or we wouldn't both fit. Do you want to grab onto me from behind, or do you want to sit on my lap?"

Her face was on fire. Her entire body was on fire. Should she slap him now, or after she ravished him atop his stallion?

"Behind you," she said swiftly. That had to be safest. She could hide her burning face and all the rest of her body. As she pressed herself tightly against him. Nipples and thighs and all. Purely for safety's sake.

Soon, the wind whipped past them as Jacob flew through the cobblestone streets. Her notebook and the jumbled plays were safe in a leather satchel, the long strap of which looped across her torso. A torso that would have been glued against his back, if her ankle-length skirts hadn't prevented her from riding astride.

Viv would be lying if she denied that a large part of her wished to channel Lady Godiva, and ride this horse naked—if it meant pressing her body more fully against Jacob's.

God help her, she was smitten.

This morning's breakfast had been the first time in Viv's adult life that someone had helped her, unasked, without expecting her to do something for them in return.

Even the one great kindness of her youth had not been without strings attached. After Aunt Kamia abandoned an orphaned ten-year-old girl to suffer the rest of her life in slavery, Viv's aunt had finally rescued her from that horrid plantation...in exchange for a different kind of servitude.

Jacob's kindnesses were given freely. The only thing he wanted was to make her happy. Viv had no idea how to respond to that.

And Lord knew, she wouldn't erase the kiss they'd shared for anything.

The horse soon slowed to a stop.

"We're here," Jacob said cheerfully.

Viv wasn't sure if this was good news or bad news. The end of the ride meant she no longer had an excuse to press her cheek against his warm back and wrap her arms tightly around his chiseled stomach. At least, she imagined it was chiseled. He was wearing too many layers of clothing for her to have been able to execute a subtle investigation to her satisfaction.

She lifted her head and peeled her arms from his abdomen.

He slipped down from the horse without dislodging her in the slightest and held out his hands. "Can you descend on your own, or would you like me to catch you?"

Both. Viv could jump from heights much higher than this and land on her feet, but she'd be damned if she'd waste an opportunity to have Jacob's hands on her body again.

As he lowered her to the ground with care, hoofbeats thundered up behind them.

She glanced over her shoulder just as a messenger on horseback pulled to a stop beside Jacob.

"Letter for the Wynchester family," said the lad.

Jacob held out his hand. "I'm a Wynchester."

"Note that *he* is using a saddle," Viv whispered behind her hand.

Jacob's eyes sparkled. "You liked the ride."

She'd like a different kind of ride even better. Maybe tonight, when the work was done...

The messenger approached without meeting their eyes. The moment the letter was in Jacob's hand, the footman tore off down the road as if the hounds of hell were after him.

Viv frowned. "In an awful big hurry, wasn't he?"

Jacob shrugged. "Footmen generally have more tasks assigned than they have time to do them."

"Footmen generally are on foot," she pointed out. "Hence the name. Idle lords famously spend hundreds of pounds wagering over how fast and how far their footmen can run. That messenger was on horseback."

"Maybe his employer isn't a numbskull." Jacob handed his own horse off to one of the Wynchester servants with thanks and a smile.

"Did you recognize his livery?"

"I didn't even notice his uniform," he said with a chuckle. "You must be confusing me with my brother Graham. Who, like you, always thinks everyone else is up to something."

"They usually are," she muttered.

"Do you know what I wouldn't mind getting up to?"

She smiled. "Please tell me you're thinking what I'm thinking."

He widened his eyes innocently. "Biscuits. I wager Cook has fresh ones in the oven."

She stifled a snort of laughter. "Are you bamming me? You're hungry again, after that breakfast we just had?"

They bickered playfully up the front walk and into the house, stopping only when they reached the sitting room and half a dozen faces turned in their direction.

"Oh, it's you two," said Graham. "I heard horses. I'm waiting for news on the Rainsford case."

"I think it just arrived. As we were heading in, a footman handed me a note addressed to…" Jacob's voice cut off as he glanced for the first time at the letter in his hand.

Viv felt the sudden tension emanating from his body. Her own flesh ran cold in response.

Marjorie rose to her feet. "Something's wrong."

"Another rejection?" asked Adrian. "Don't take it so hard. Honestly, Marjorie and I could fashion for you as many printed and bound books as you like, completely indistinguishable from—"

"Addressed to all of us," Jacob said. "'Wynchester Family.' There's a smear of red in one corner. It almost looks like...dried blood."

"It's not blood," said Philippa, her voice shaking. "Is it?"

Marjorie plucked the letter from Jacob's hand and scanned it. "I recognize the handwriting. This is from that hoaxer who claimed to have kidnapped Horace Wynchester."

"What?" asked Viv, startled.

"There's nothing to fear," Philippa assured her. "There is no Horace Wynchester."

"But there is blood," Marjorie said softly. "Jacob's right."

A heavy silence filled the room.

"Why is there blood?" Viv whispered. "Is that normal?"

"Was the messenger bleeding?" asked Graham.

Viv was ashamed to admit she hadn't noticed. Her eyes had been on Jacob.

"We receive heaps of utter nonsense," he said. "It could be nothing."

"It *is* nothing," said Philippa. "There's no Horace, therefore there's no problem. Throw that letter into the fire with the others."

Viv looked at the cold fireplace. "There is no fire."

"It's symbolic," Jacob murmured. "May is too warm for a fire. We'll turn it into ash in October."

"You lot are no fun at all," said Marjorie. "At the least, we ought to read the hoax before we burn it. I told you the silly ones belong in a special album."

Jacob took the letter back from his sister and broke the seal. "It says:

Dear Wynchester Family,

You do not appear to understand the gravity of your situation. If you do not cease investigating at once, your brother Horace will die.
 See below for proof that his blood still flows... for now."

Viv's flesh went cold.

"Dramatic," said Marjorie. "What proof did he send?"

Jacob held up the letter so they could all see. "A bloody thumbprint."

"That's commitment to the ruse," Philippa said, impressed. "A hoaxer cutting his own thumb, in the hopes that we would believe—"

"No," Viv gasped. "There's a scar on that thumb."

Jacob squinted at the dried blood. "It could be where he cut himself. Or just a smudge. Besides, what does it matter if—"

"I *know* that thumb." She fumbled open the leather satchel and pulled out her notebook. There, on an otherwise neatly printed page, was the blackberry-preserves thumbprint Quentin had accidentally made the day they'd argued and he'd stormed off, never to return.

Marjorie's wide blue eyes leapt from one print to the other.

"Identical," she breathed. "This print belongs to..."

"My cousin." Viv's voice cracked.

Philippa's brow creased. "Quentin faked his own abduction?"

Viv shook her head. She jabbed a trembling finger at the parchment. "Quentin faints at the sight of blood. Someone did this to him. You have to help. Someone *has* him. This is no hoax. Some malefactor has kidnapped my cousin and is willing to torture him to make us do as he demands."

21

*O*iv had never in her life felt weak at the sight of blood...until her mother was killed in front of her. The renewed panic and terror caused by the sight of her cousin's coerced thumbprint cut her off at the knees.

Jacob wrapped his free arm about her waist to give her strength. "Philippa, where's Tommy?"

"On the Badcock case." Philippa's face was pale.

"As soon as she's back home, we need her on this. Graham, summon the others. Chloe and Faircliffe might be at home preparing remarks for tonight's parliamentary session—"

"No, they're out handling the Sadler affair. I just rang for—" Graham sprinted over to meet the liveried footman just entering the room. "Norbert, wonderful. Please go to this address posthaste, and don't return without the duke and duchess. Let them know it is an emergency. Send someone else to fetch Stephen and Elizabeth. There's no time to waste."

The footman's eyes widened, but he hurried off to do as asked without hesitation or question.

Marjorie reached for Adrian's hand. "I can't believe Quentin's disappearance and the Horace hoax are the same case."

"*Why* are they the same case?" Philippa said in bafflement. "Nobody has been Horace since Tommy was courting me, years ago. Even the dullest of villains cannot possibly have mistaken Quentin for her."

"Who is Horace?" Viv asked. "How could Quentin be confused with someone who doesn't exist?"

Jacob explained, "Before our adoptive father, Baron Vanderbean, passed away, he created a fictitious heir called Horace Wynchester, who has now become the current Baron Vanderbean. Or would be, if there was one." He dropped to his knees before the unlit fireplace. "I'll find the original letter."

"Wait...Horace Wynchester is Baron Vanderbean?" Viv repeated in horror. "Then how didn't you know Quentin had been kidnapped? We've been wasting time following other cases while my adolescent cousin—"

"Wasting time!" Marjorie threw her hands up. "Every case is a priority, and there are more of them than there are of us. Even a middling effort to juggle all the open threads simultaneously is unsustainable—"

"Mixed metaphor," murmured Philippa. "But accurate."

"You know what isn't accurate?" Viv drew a folded letter from her bodice with shaking fingers. "Your false claim that Quentin was *safe*."

"When Graham's informant interviewed Newt—" Jacob began.

"Why didn't Graham go himself?" Viv demanded.

"Because he's assigned to fifty other cases! Why didn't *you* go yourself, Miss I-Can-Deduce-the-Truth-in-One-Glance?"

Viv's teeth clicked shut. She'd almost snapped that she would have gone if she'd known the address, but there was no doubt the Wynchesters would have escorted her straight to Newt's door if she'd bothered to ask where he lived.

Jacob was right. If Viv's great talent was her ability to see right through people, then the only explanation for her oversight was that she subconsciously couldn't handle the possibility of Quentin's blithe assurances of his safety being horribly *wrong*.

With him gone, Viv had been sliding close to a state of debilitating panic. She'd really, really needed it to be true that Quentin was all right.

That was her excuse. But what was theirs?

"You never told me Baron Vanderbean had been kidnapped!"

"Why would we?" Marjorie said, baffled. "There is no Baron Vanderbean."

"The rest of the world doesn't know that. That's what makes it a good disguise. I told you, Quentin sometimes used that identity."

"You didn't tell *me* that," Jacob burst out. "Pertinent information I could have used from the first day!"

"I did tell you," she protested. "I said he was dressed as a baron earlier in the day, though his friends assured me that mission had ended. *I* didn't know the ruse was relevant, but *you*…"

Jacob made a pained expression and scrubbed his face with his hand.

Viv poked his chest. "We had an entire conversation about Quentin's disguises, and how his secret society longs to be exactly like all of you. A club whose members you exhaustively interviewed. The same day I came for help, those lads must have given you every detail of the Baron Vanderbean mission and more. You lot would've *known* Baron Vanderbean was Horace Wynchester!"

"We…didn't actually…interview his friends that day." Graham didn't meet her eyes. "I do recall you mentioning the clothing he'd been wearing the day of his disappearance—"

"She did," said Marjorie. "I included the blue frock coat and waistcoat in my sketch. Vivian said Quentin thought it made him look Balcovian, though his clothing didn't once make me think of Baron Vanderbean. Tommy never wore anything like that when she was pretending to be Horace, either."

Viv nodded. "That's essentially what Kuni said, when I mentioned

Quentin's antics to her, too. Graham, you were right there when we discussed this! Your wife said a real Balcovian baron would wear pink."

Between the club members swearing Quentin's mission was long over, and the costume itself being laughably inaccurate, Viv had no reason to think anyone believed her young cousin to be a baron.

If only she'd known about the kidnapping!

"None of us were thinking about the hoax," said Adrian. "We'd already dismissed it as nonsense well before we met you. We were juggling so many real cases, there was no room left in our brains for extraneous details."

Viv's volume rose. "Extraneous?"

Even if they at first believed the kidnapping letter was a hoax, one of the Wynchesters should have connected the two together.

Her voice shook with fury. "You all knew Quentin had been pretending to be your imaginary brother! I also mentioned his disguise to Tommy and Philippa when we were talking about costumes. I reminded them my cousin often dressed like a Wynchester, and said to go ask Graham for the particulars. Although Quentin's club members are too loyal to him to tell me anything, they wouldn't hesitate to give the mighty Wynchesters every detail of Quentin's mission. Where he went, what he was wearing, what he was trying to accomplish..."

Jacob and Graham exchanged stricken expressions. Viv's heart stopped. "You didn't *ask* his friends for the information I didn't have about the mission Quentin had been undertaking before he disappeared?"

"We didn't interview them at all," Graham mumbled. "You had already done so, and seemed to think no one but Newt had any notion of where Quentin might be—"

"Didn't interview them?" she spluttered in disbelief.

"We didn't have time! I sent informants to watch their houses and report back on any activity, but the only bodies I could spare for that were children too young to be conducting interviews. As soon as we clear a few more cases, I planned to send a more experienced team…"

Viv was going to burst into tears. Or go on a murderous rampage. Or shatter into a million heartsick pieces.

Jacob reached for her hand.

She jerked out of reach. "Don't touch me. I want nothing to do with any of you, except for you to finally take Quentin's disappearance seriously. Find him. Please."

"We will," said Jacob.

She no longer believed him. He'd promised her before. "I should never have trusted you to follow through. I would have dragged your entire family by the ear to each of those lads' houses if it had occurred to me for one second that you wouldn't interview the best witnesses we have."

If the Wynchesters had interviewed the club members as promised, the entire secret society would have stationed itself in the siblings' sitting room to aid in the hunt for Quentin-as-Horace. There wouldn't be a bloody fingerprint on a ransom note.

"Don't panic," said Marjorie. "We have clues. The latest letter, for one. Blast, I wish I'd seen who brought it. Did you get a good look at the messenger?"

Jacob shook his head. "I'm so sorry. I wasn't paying any attention to…If I'd known the kidnapping wasn't a hoax, I would have been on the watch for further missives."

Graham winced in agreement. "We could have stationed someone to follow that footman back to his employer. Vivian, we're *all* sorry. We all deeply regret our lack of adequate resources, and can assure you that from this moment—"

"Five foot eleven," she blurted.

He blinked at her. "What?"

"The messenger. White, freckled, large mole on his right cheek, light brown hair, dark brown eyes," she rattled off. "Thirteen stone, give or take half a pound. Gap-toothed. Left-handed. Slightly myopic. Old cricket injury in his knee. Not an employee of the post office. Livery in shades of mustard and brown. White wig in need of fresh curls."

"Got it." Marjorie grabbed her sketchbook and pencils. Her drawing came to life as Viv recounted as many details as she could recall.

"With luck, the kidnapper used his own man, or at least a traceable messenger service," said Philippa.

"Old cricket injury in his knee?" Adrian repeated. "How the devil can you know—"

"Parse the magic later," interrupted Graham as he scribbled notes. "What about you, Jacob? What did you see?"

"Average…footman?" Jacob guessed. "Honestly, I scarcely glanced his way. I was helping Vivian down from my horse because we'd ridden in together—"

"I heard two horses," Graham said. "The other one belonged to the messenger?"

Jacob's face cleared. "Cleveland Bay. Older stallion, with a primarily reddish-brown coat. Black lower legs, mane, and tail. Sixteen hands high, fourteen hundred pounds. Early signs of arthritis in his hind legs. Likely a retired coach horse."

"Hackney carriage?" Graham asked.

Jacob shook his head. "Too expensive for ordinary hackney drivers, and too big and slow for fashionable bucks racing light phaetons. Think stage-coaches, Royal Mail, and the wealthiest families who can afford fine horses for their coach-and-four."

"I'll sketch the horse, too," said Marjorie.

"I'll make copies of everything," said Adrian.

Graham nodded. "I'll distribute these throughout London as fast as you can make them."

"What can I do?" asked Philippa.

A WALTZ ON THE WILD SIDE

"If they find out he's *not* a Wynchester..." Viv ventured, her voice shaky.

Horror flooded Jacob's face.

"What's happening?" asked Philippa. "Isn't Quentin in less danger if the kidnapper realizes he's not one of us?"

"No." Graham scrubbed a hand over his face. "Whatever the blackmailer wants, he thinks abducting a Wynchester gives him leverage. That's what makes 'Horace' a valuable hostage. If Quentin admits he isn't part of our family, he becomes nothing more than an ordinary Black boy."

"Disposable," Viv whispered.

"No," Jacob said firmly, giving her arm a squeeze. "I swear we'll find him first."

Viv wanted to believe him so badly.

"Why exactly was Quentin disguised as Horace?" Philippa asked. "And yes, I realize we'd have the answer to this if we'd interviewed the club members. In the interest of saving time, please tell us everything you know."

Viv swallowed. "I didn't ask. He's always disguising himself as someone or another, in the pursuit of one of his alleged cases. I never ask about those, either. I thought it was folly. I didn't want to show too much interest, because I was trying my damnedest to get him to stop."

"You wanted him to leave the club?"

"I wanted all of the lads to cease pretending to have the Wynchester reputation and resources before it got one of them killed." She swallowed hard. "I told Quentin your family was dangerous..."

"We didn't force him to impersonate Horace," Philippa protested.

"You don't have to. You're larger than life, like all his heroes. Lads see the Duke of Wellington and want to be a soldier, never comprehending the odds of returning from battle alive, much less with honors."

"None of us have *died* during a mission!"

"That's not the only danger. A Wynchester gets arrested more often than the average person washes his teeth, yet there's been no consequences for any of you."

"Our lawyers—"

"Exactly. Your money, your connections, your name, your status. Quentin and his friends don't have any of that. Can you look me in the eye and tell me with a straight face that his life would be in any less danger if he'd been captured by the authorities for a robbery instead of abducted by the kidnapper?"

Philippa looked horrified, but she could not refute Viv's point.

"We have another clue," Jacob interrupted quietly. "Quentin's letter to Vivian. He intended to spy on a Lord S."

"Who is Lord S?" asked Marjorie.

"I've no idea," Viv said hoarsely, wishing once again that she'd interrogated Quentin within an inch of his life every time he mentioned his stupid club. Then again, perhaps that would only have drawn a wedge between them sooner, and she wouldn't even have his coded letter to parse.

"You have *no* idea?" Adrian asked. "I thought Ask Vivian had all the answers."

"I don't have any of the answers," she whispered. "I never have. I'm faking it, just like Quentin. We're both doing the best we can."

"You have the answers quite a lot of the time," Jacob said. "I read your column, and so does half of London."

Graham nodded. "Thanks to your description, Marjorie and Adrian's sketches will help us find the messenger, who with luck can lead us to the kidnapper."

"Which could take days or weeks," Viv said. "We need to act now. Who do you think it might be?"

Jacob's nose wrinkled. "Wealthy, thinks his desires trump

everyone else, wouldn't know a Wynchester if one punched him in the face...Sounds like an aristocrat to me."

"Lord S," said Viv. "It has to be."

"The Marquess of Leisterdale," blurted Philippa. "Right?"

Adrian frowned. "I thought we decided Leisterdale was Olivebury's nemesis, not ours. Those two are polar opposites in Parliament. A rivalry makes sense. Whereas Horace Wynchester is Balcovian. He couldn't vote even if he were real."

Graham sent Viv a look. "I thought Quentin didn't have an accent?"

"He has a British one," she answered. "Not like mine. He was born here."

"This kidnapper did absolutely no reconnaissance whatsoever," Philippa muttered.

"He didn't have to," Marjorie pointed out. "Not if Quentin walked up to him and said, 'I'm Horace Wynchester, how do you do?'"

"He's been practicing his disguises," Viv said. "We took cosmetics classes at the theater. And I try to teach him to sew."

Philippa said, "I imagine you never dreamed a raffish waistcoat or false wrinkles would one day put his life in danger."

Viv tried not to scream. "Aren't you listening? It was my constant nightmare. Why do you think I object so hard to your law-breaking, lies, and dangerous exploits? A wealthy, well-connected family like you can get away with treason, but a boy like Quentin would face prison for breathing near the wrong person."

Jacob looked baffled. "You despise my family, but you helped Quentin to imitate us?"

"I love my cousin. There's little I wouldn't do for him."

"Should you? The way he works you to the bone, I'm surprised you manage to write a single sentence. You aren't the least bit resentful to become your cousin's dependent and guardian all at once?"

"Resentful?" she repeated. "He rescued *me*."

Jacob frowned. "What does that mean?"

She pressed her lips together and shook her head. "Concentrate on Quentin, not me. There are more important interviews to conduct."

"I'll visit Newt at once," said Graham. "Right now and in person. I'll extract every drop of information about Lord S that he can give us and report back within the hour. We'll interview all the club members this very night."

Viv's stomach roiled. She'd imagined her innocent young cousin had staged an elaborate plot to manipulate her into befriending the Wynchesters…when all along, Quentin had been *kidnapped*. Trapped. In danger. Fearing for his life.

Trusting his all-knowing cousin would find him. A woman who'd spent the day reading her mail and kissing Jacob Wynchester.

She would never forgive herself.

22

As Graham rushed out of the house, Viv prayed for Quentin's health and safety.

Jacob stepped closer. "The Lord S hypothesis makes sense."

Philippa nodded. "Maybe that's why Quentin was taken. He isn't experienced at espionage—and our villain definitely seems the sort to be breaking laws he wouldn't wish witnesses to observe. If a man like that caught Quentin in the wrong place at the wrong time, we're lucky..."

We're lucky he didn't kill him.

The words hung in the air, unspoken and deadly. Viv thanked the gods Quentin was still alive...for now. She *had* to bring him back home, safe and sound.

Mr. Randall appeared in the doorway. "Apologies for the interruption. A young boy just brought a letter addressed to Mr. Olivebury."

Marjorie groaned. "Can one of our cases leave us alone for just a moment?"

Jacob hurried over to read the letter, then confirmed, "The blackmailer again. Instructing Mr. Olivebury to quash all talk of voting reform in the House of Commons—and warning Olivebury not to come to us for aid under any circumstances."

"We don't have time to aid," muttered Adrian.

"Wait," said Viv. "Can I see that letter?"

Jacob handed it to her. "What are you thinking?"

Marjorie's eyes lit up. "Handwriting!"

Viv placed the blackmailer's letter onto the table next to the kidnapper's letter. "Do you see what I see?"

"Both are written by the same person," crowed Marjorie.

"Then the thief was never Mrs. Olivebury," said Jacob. "She might have motive to remove a portrait of a mistress, but she has no reason to kidnap Quentin."

"If anything, a politically minded woman like her would blackmail Parliament in *favor* of suffrage," Viv agreed.

"So we're back to Lord S," Jacob said. "Aristocrats who oppose giving commoners the vote."

"Does this put Philippa's Marquess of Leisterdale theory back into play?" Adrian asked.

She flipped through her notes. "Inconclusive. Leisterdale was one of dozens of lords present in London for each of the dates of the blackmail letters, the kidnapping letters, and the Olivebury robbery."

Jacob tapped his chin. "Can correspondence sent to Ask Vivian be traced?"

"Not by me. Each incoming letter is stripped of names and addresses, and is assigned a temporary number instead. I have to return the whole thing with my replies. A clerk at the newspaper sends my answers and the original letters to the associated party."

"And every clerk at every newspaper is overworked and underpaid," Jacob said with a groan. "Our few informants barely have time to glance up from their desks. I doubt any extra records are kept. There's simply no time, much less storage space. Nonetheless, we'll see what Graham can do."

"Maybe there's something I can do," said Viv. "I have a daily column that we know the kidnapper reads. Now that three different cases have combined into one, we also know more about the villain than we did before. Perhaps through my column, I can convince him that I am a likeminded soul of great influence and spur him to send me another letter."

"Won't it arrive in the clerk's handwriting?" Adrian said doubtfully.

"We already have samples of his handwriting," Viv pointed out.

"What we need is for him to give up a clue that leads us to Quentin."

"It's a marvelous idea," said Jacob. "Will the paper allow you to print any text that you like?"

Viv made a face. "Only direct replies to letters received."

"Done," said Marjorie. "I'll have a sufficiently vague query in the clerk's hands before Graham is back from Newt's. You'll be able to reply however you please."

Viv nodded. "With luck, my answer will be printed in tomorrow morning's edition."

"Which gives us time to try and install someone at the clerk's office to trace any future correspondence from the kidnapper."

"Or to bribe the clerk himself," Jacob added, then grimaced. "There we go again, thoughtlessly committing multiple crimes at once—"

"Find Quentin," Viv said hoarsely. "Use every privilege and resource at your disposal. We'll debate the legalities once he's home safe."

"All right," said Marjorie. "We reconvene in an hour, once Graham's home and the others have arrived. Meanwhile, we all have tasks to attend to—"

"What am I supposed to do?" asked Viv. "Stare at the walls?"

"Draft your bait for Lord S," Jacob suggested.

"And then what? Should we confront the Marquess of Leisterdale?"

"We don't know that he's involved," Jacob reminded her. "If he *is* behind this, he may be prepared for a counterattack. We don't want to do anything that might risk Quentin's safety. As hard as it sounds, the best thing you can do right now is wait for further developments."

"I can't sit still, I'll go mad. I need to clear my head." She spun toward the door. "I'm going for a walk."

Jacob rushed to block her path, then held out his elbow. "I'll accompany you."

23

Jacob didn't believe for a minute that Vivian had decided this was the best moment to have a promenade. Or rather, she probably *did* need to clear her head, which he presumed was currently swirling with the exact sort of desperate, rash actions she normally cautioned against.

"Where to?" he asked suspiciously.

"Hyde Park," she answered. "I've heard it's the most popular place to stroll after noon, but I've always been too busy to see it firsthand."

Not precisely the response Jacob had been expecting. A brisk walk up and down the Islington street in front of them would have been more convenient. To visit Hyde Park and back within the hour would require a carriage. On the other hand, she was right: the crowds would provide more of a distraction, which was perhaps what she truly needed.

And if Viv thought it a likely place to "accidentally" stumble across Lord Leisterdale, she was thankfully mistaken. Leisterdale's gout kept him from participating in promenades. He'd attended the spectacle in an open-top barouche precisely once, a fortnight ago, when his son first returned home from their Caribbean planation. Leisterdale's dedication to outdated politics kept him at his escritoire drafting arguments instead of rubbing shoulders with the young and beautiful, or the socially aspirational.

"We stay in the carriage," Jacob warned Vivian. "You haven't seen traffic like an afternoon promenade, and we want to be home in time to hear Graham's news."

She nodded, her unfocused gaze facing the general direction of the carriage window, though Jacob doubted she registered any buildings that passed outside of it.

Her spine snapped upright the moment they reached the famous gates, her brown eyes suddenly sharp and bright. Their carriage joined the long queue of conveyances inching forward amongst waves of well-heeled pedestrians.

Jacob narrowed his eyes. "Who are you looking for?"

"No one." She scanned the dense crowd of fashionable lords and ladies like a hawk hunting its next meal.

"Vivian," he warned.

She gasped and leaned across his lap to tap at his window. "Look! It's Lord Uppington!"

"Leave him be," Jacob advised. "We can't just march up to Leisterdale's son and start asking questions about whether his father is engaging in blackmail and abduction."

"Watch me," Vivian replied. "If Uppington's father kidnapped Quentin, I'm putting an end to it this very day."

"As much as we want to find your cousin, we cannot leap to conclusions. Let's say Philippa is right, and our enemy is Leisterdale. His heir could be a party to the crimes as well, in which case he's not going to tell us anything. Or he may have no idea what his father has done. Or both men could be completely innocent, and we're on the wrong track altogether."

"'Completely innocent'? Tell that to the enslaved people toiling on their sugar plantations."

"Innocent of this particular abduction," he clarified. "There's a place in hell awaiting both of them. But so far, we've no evidence linking any specific lord to your cousin's disappearance. And whoever it is could be working with accomplices or intermediaries."

Jacob could only imagine how he would feel if someone in his own family was being held hostage. He, too, would be ready to smash any wall and burn any bridge to rescue those he loved from danger.

He touched her arm gently. "Whoever has Quentin, we'll find him."

"But will we find him in time?" Vivian asked bleakly.

She launched herself from the carriage, leaving Jacob to scramble after her.

"Vivian, wait!" he hissed as he sprinted to catch up. "If anyone is to confront him, it should be Chloe and Faircliffe. They'd be the most likely to gain a peer's confidence and the least likely to cause suspicion. We can discuss a strategy in the Planning Parlor—"

Vivian put on speed as she threaded the crowd. Jacob stayed on her heels. A few faces glanced at them askance, but most ignored them altogether.

The aristocrats, the nouveau riche, and those who aspired to be one or the other ambled along at an unhurried stroll, content to see and be seen at their leisure. They'd promenade here for hours, moving at a snail's pace as they called out greetings and bussed cheeks and fluttered fans and loudly mentioned their hunting lodges or theater boxes or personal invitations to coveted soirées.

Vivian shot past all of them.

"There he is!" She stormed straight into the sea of lordlings, who parted in her wake. "Lord Uppington! I humbly request a brief moment of your time."

Upon sight of her, the earl's lip curled and he deliberately turned his back.

"Shite," Jacob muttered. This was the opposite of subtle.

Undaunted, Vivian pressed forward. "Please, my lord, just a few seconds to—"

Holding his body stiff and regal, Uppington shoved his nose higher into the air and dramatically refused to glance her way.

"Please." Her voice cracked. "I'm begging you."

The tips of her outstretched fingertips brushed the elbow of the earl's fine coat.

Quick as lightning, Uppington slapped her hand away, then scrubbed at his own hand and elbow with a monogrammed white handkerchief as though he had been irrevocably soiled from the brief contact.

Vivian's face went completely blank as she lowered her slapped hand back to her side.

Jacob put his arms around her and turned her away from Uppington, whose fawning cronies crowded against their white knight as though he'd emerged victorious from a battle with a grotesque monster.

There was nothing Jacob wanted to do more than plant his fist right in the middle of Uppington's smug, self-important face.

He knew better than to attempt such retaliation in front of this audience, however. Although "earl" was merely a courtesy title until Uppington inherited his father's marquessate, a Black man assaulting the son of a rich white lord in a public park would not end well for Jacob.

Wynchester or not.

Nor would Jacob risk accidental injury to Vivian due to proximity.

"We'll interview him," he murmured softly as he coaxed her back toward the carriage. "Perhaps no lord in that family would lower themselves to speak to *us*, but we're not the only weapons at our disposal. Chloe and Faircliffe will handle them both, and if there are any clues to glean—"

Vivian let Jacob tuck her back into the carriage with an uncharacteristic silence far more worrying than a well-deserved rant would have been. Either she was still reeling from Uppington's hateful treatment of her, or she was plotting his untimely demise.

Probably both.

"I remember him," she said quietly as she leaned her head against the carriage door.

Jacob's eyebrows shot up. "You know Uppington?"

"I know men like him." She didn't look up. "I was born on Demerara. Born to a slave, which made me one, too. Property of Viscount Ayleswick, like a boot or a used handkerchief."

A handkerchief like the one Uppington had used to "clean" her touch from his white skin.

Jacob cupped his hand over hers.

She met his eyes. "Reality was inescapable. I spent every moment of every day and every night focused only on survival. Mine, and others."

He put the pieces together. "When you first came for help, you mentioned Viscount Ayleswick was Quentin's father."

She nodded. "Lord Ayleswick was enamored with my mother's sister. Or rather, he took Aunt Kamia as mistress, like it or not, whenever he visited from London. It didn't take long for her belly to grow."

Jacob's jaw tightened.

"I thought it was a cruel disaster, but Aunt Kamia saw a way out. Rather than allow her child to be born into the same mean life that she and the rest of us had, she convinced Ayleswick to take her and his soon-to-be bastard child to England."

His heart went cold. "Leaving her own sister and enslaved ten-year-old niece behind?"

"Saving one of us was better than saving none of us. We didn't blame her for choosing survival."

Not blame, no. The horrific situation wasn't Aunt Kamia's fault. But Jacob could only imagine how complicated Vivian's feelings were. Then and now.

"A year later," she continued, "before my mother succumbed to a brutal punishment, she told me to find my own way. No matter what it took. Never to back down, no matter who or what I faced. She said it was better to die giving your best effort to thrive than to live under someone else's thumb."

Jacob paused. "Your mother was punished to death?"

"She wanted to lead an uprising. It might have worked if she hadn't been caught recruiting co-conspirators before she could hold the final meeting. Ayleswick's plantation overseer tried to make an example of her."

"I'm guessing his attempt didn't work?"

Viv gave a brittle smile. "I became the plantation's worst nightmare. I undermined everything I could and eventually organized an almost-successful uprising. There were too many of us involved to punish us all, but I knew I wouldn't be spared. I had dared to break the rules—and would die for my boldness, just like my mother."

"How did you get out alive?"

"Quentin," she said with a wan smile. "I told you he rescued me. I ended up on a boat instead of in a casket. Summoned to England by Lord Ayleswick, at my aunt's request. It took years, but she managed to save another child, too."

"That's when you became your cousin's governess?"

"Companion, first. Aunt Kamia taught me to read and write. That changed my life as much as leaving Demerara. I was insatiable. Read everything I could get my hands on. For all the good it did." She winced. "When Quentin needed me most, I couldn't save him."

"You will," Jacob said firmly. "It's not over yet."

She blinked rapidly and turned her head away.

"I'd never presume to know what it was like back then, but I'm here for you now." He lifted her hands in his, caressing the skin softly with the pads of his thumbs. "You're not alone."

She did not respond aloud but leaned back into his chest and allowed him to embrace her for the remainder of the journey.

When they arrived at the Wynchester home, the others were disappointed but unsurprised to learn a bigot like Leisterdale had raised a son like Uppington.

"I'll run him through with a sword," said Elizabeth.

"*We'll* go," Faircliffe said firmly, exchanging a glance with his wife.

"You're his father's political enemy," Stephen reminded him. "Why would he speak to you?"

"Because I'm a duke," Faircliffe replied.

Chloe handed her sleeping baby to Kuni and took Faircliffe's hand. "We'll intercept him as soon as he returns home and need no longer posture in front of his friends. We'll return posthaste."

Jacob wished he could take Vivian's hand. Kiss her, hold her, comfort her. But what she really needed was the safe return of her cousin. And a modicum of respect from the world around them.

Graham rushed through the door moments after Chloe and Faircliffe had left.

"Do you have Lord S's identity?" Vivian asked breathlessly.

He shook his head. "Newt doesn't know it. The club has apparently been trying to identify lords who abuse their power to squelch protests ever since the Peterloo Massacre. 'Lord S' stands for 'suffrage.'"

Marjorie handed him a tall stack of missives. "These were delivered while you were gone."

Graham scanned their contents eagerly, then sighed. "The messenger you two saw doesn't work for Leisterdale, nor matches anyone employed at any lord's London residence."

"Maybe he was in disguise," said Tommy.

"Or not related at all," said Philippa. "Not sending one of his own footmen to deliver the blackmail message doesn't prove Leisterdale's innocence. It does mean our enemy is clever enough not to leave a line of obvious clues leading back to his door."

Adrian nodded. "Blackmailing Olivebury to vote a certain way, abducting 'Horace Wynchester' to keep us from investigating..."

"What do you think?" Tommy asked Vivian. "How would you write it?"

"You don't want to know how I'd edit this ending," she said darkly.

"*I* want to know," said Elizabeth. "I adore the sight of our enemies' blood."

Vivian sighed. "I just want to see Quentin again. Alive."

Jacob wished he could hug her. Or pull her cousin's precise location out of a hat. The truth was, an unsettling percentage of their open cases at the moment were going exactly like this: nowhere.

Back when they used to only have one case at a time, justice was served swiftly. But with more fame came more clients, and with more clients came more conundrums: Taking on everyone's problems meant having time for no one's. But how could they turn any of their deserving clients away?

Vivian trudged in silence to the chair he'd come to think of as hers at the siblings' worktable. She shoved aside her growing pile of unread Ask Vivian correspondence, and sharpened a fresh quill.

"Time to pen the bait?" he asked.

She nodded grimly. "A worm for a worm."

Jacob wished he could help. A glance at his pocket watch indicated a bit of time remained before his next mission. He remembered he hadn't yet put Vivian's jumbled plays back in order. This was his chance to start.

At first, it was like matching up the pieces of a puzzle. He liked to begin with the edge pieces. If the last line of dialogue at the bottom of a page said "I wish to—" then he knew the first word on the following page ought to be a verb. I wish to *go*, I wish to *unmask*, I wish to *rescue*.

Once all the verbs were matched, he moved on to the next likely phrases, then the next, until only the trickiest matches were left: pages that began or ended with a complete sentence, thus leaving no obvious clue as to their mate.

Fortunately by then, there were few loose sheets left, and the remaining scripts were quickly complete.

He could've completed his task in half the time, if scanning for a stray verb hadn't turned into reading the rest of the sentence. Which then required knowing the other characters' sharp or witty comeback, leading to page after page being read compulsively. Out of order or not, Vivian's writing was engaging and highly entertaining. It was a true miscarriage of justice not to have these plays performed for the public at large. It was a moral imperative to help.

Until Graham's extended network of spies and informants turned up a new lead to follow, there wasn't much Jacob could do to find Vivian's kidnapped cousin. But although he could not fully save the day at this precise moment, he could at least attempt to distract her from the spiral of panic, and perhaps even tempt a smile back to her lips. Or another kiss.

He drew a fresh plume and a clean sheet of parchment from the communal supplies in the center of the table and began drafting his own anonymous letter to his favorite advice column. Who would know better how best to woo a woman like Vivian than Vivian herself?

Once finished, Jacob folded the paper and sealed it with wax. He'd copy the publisher's address from the newspaper when Vivian wasn't there to see his interest in her column and divine what he was up to. It might take weeks for her to respond. That was all right with Jacob. He was eager, but not in a rush. Some of the best things took time.

Before either of them could consider a proper courtship, multiple issues needed to be resolved. The first was to bring home Quentin. The second was to help Vivian achieve her potential as a playwright.

Of the two tasks, the latter was the most straightforward and already in the works. He'd sent off several notes as Sir Gareth Jallow and was waiting to see who would jump first.

Vivian was a phenomenal playwright. She just needed someone to believe in her. *Jacob* believed in her. And he would not rest until everyone else realized what they'd been overlooking.

Whether she would have any time to spare for Jacob once she was rich and famous and her cousin was home safe and sound...well.

That was when he would need to heed Ask Vivian's advice.

After his mission, Jacob returned the weasels to the barn and rejoined his siblings seconds before Chloe and Faircliffe burst back into the sitting room.

Well, Chloe did the bursting—Faircliffe was more of an "impassive expression and proper posture" sort of duke. Nonetheless, he strode quickly to keep pace with his wife.

Vivian leapt to his feet. "You weren't gone long at all. Did Uppington refuse to speak to you, too?"

"He practically knocked his own retinue asunder to make room for us." Chloe rolled her eyes. "Then lowered his voice to ensure no one overheard our actual words."

"The earl actually divulged something useful?" Vivian asked in surprise.

Chloe made a face. "Uppington heavily implied that the Marquess of Leisterdale would do anything to maintain his privileges."

"Which isn't exactly news," Faircliffe put in. "Leisterdale stands atop his bench an hour a day in Parliament, crowing about the need to conserve power within the aristocracy. His speeches about nobility's innate superiority have appeared in political pamphlets for years."

"It *is* a popular sentiment amongst the upper classes," Jacob pointed out.

Chloe sighed. "Uppington said he fears the marquess may take drastic measures. His exact words were, 'Who knows what lengths my father would go to if he thought he would get away with it?'"

"Lords get away with everything," Vivian said. "They should all be in prison. Present duke excluded."

"I appreciate the clemency," murmured Faircliffe. "I hope to always be worthy of it."

"Unfortunately," Chloe continued, "'my father is a ruthless man' is not as helpful as 'here's evidence my father committed this specific crime.' Parliament is full of ruthless men who would take drastic measures if they believed they could get away with it."

"And then what?" Vivian asked. "Where is justice? Even if we pull Quentin out of Leisterdale's attic in front of two hundred witnesses, no consequences at all will happen to a peer of the realm."

Elizabeth drew her sword. "I'll happen to him."

"You'd better not," Vivian warned her. "A marquess can claim 'privilege of peerage' to escape prosecution, but an untitled woman cannot claim any rights at all."

"First things first," said Jacob. "We find evidence, we rescue Quentin, and *then* we plot appropriate revenge against the guilty party."

"All right, then." Vivian lifted the advice column letter she'd been writing. "Let's hope the shark takes the bait."

24

For the next twenty-four hours, Jacob did his best to buoy Vivian out of panic over her cousin's safety. Although he couldn't assuage her fears as he wished—Vivian had every reason to be worried—Jacob did possess a prodigious number of distractions.

The tasks he normally undertook alone, from the care and training of his animals to their deployment wherever his siblings needed them, he now performed with Vivian at his side.

While they waited for the newspaper to forward Marjorie's letter to trigger the trap. While a footman hand-delivered Vivian's prewritten response to the paper at top speed. While they waited to find out whether the bait would print in the next morning's column.

Elation, to see it there in black and white at the breakfast table. Followed by a grueling morning doing their utmost to concentrate on cases while praying the kidnapper would not only take time to read the carefully crafted words but also be compelled to respond.

"Graham has no way to track the origins of the newspaper's incoming post," Jacob reminded her. The busy building received constant missives and deliveries from postmen and footmen sent from all over England. "But if our kidnapper bites, we have operatives stationed to follow your response from the clerk's desk all the way into our enemy's hands."

"I know," said Vivian, flashing him a tight but grateful smile.

Her sharp mind didn't need Jacob to reiterate their situation, but the worry lines on her face eased every time he reminded her that they had a plan, and they were executing it.

He tried not to hover when the newspaper finally forwarded the first batch of the day's new Ask Vivian queries. But he was close enough to hear her sharp intake of breath and feel the vise-grip on his arm when the letter arrived.

"He wrote back," she whispered, clutching the unfolded page in one hand, letting the rest of the queries tumble unceremoniously to the floor.

Jacob's heart leapt in relief. "You did it!"

"Not quite yet," she reminded him. "This is only the first…all right, more like sixteenth step in the plan. Once we see who receives my reply, we can rescue Quentin. And *then* we'll have won."

He was proud of her, nonetheless. The bait and trap were her idea, and a clever one. By combining the Wynchesters' resources with Vivian's resourcefulness, the nightmare could soon be at an end.

She tapped her quill to her cheek as she formulated her response. "It doesn't matter what I write, correct? All we need to know is who is expecting this reply."

Jacob hoped that was true. "Better to plan for contingencies, just in case. If something unexpected happens and we cannot determine the author this time, we'll need him to keep writing back."

She nodded, stared blankly at the ceiling for a brief moment, then began to write. Jacob rang the bell pull to have a footman at the ready, then changed his mind and summoned his fastest horse instead. He'd deliver this missive himself.

As soon as the letter dried, Vivian placed it in hands. "Go."

He went, flying through the streets like an arrow shot from a bow. Outside the newspaper's office, he glimpsed three faces he recognized as Graham's spies. One disguised as a beggar, one as a street sweeper, and one hawking bruised fruit from a basket of old apples.

Which meant at least a dozen more, in and outside of the office, were invisible even to a trained eye.

Vivian was glued to the front window when he rode back up the gravel path. She ran out of the house to greet him before he'd even handed off his horse.

"We wait again," he said. "Are you coming to the smelting operation with me?"

"I can't," she whispered, barely meeting Jacob's eyes from constantly looking over his shoulder. "What if Graham has news?"

He didn't have the heart to tell her there was no way to foretell how quickly the clerk would forward Vivian's reply. With luck, it had already begun. Without luck, it could take hours...if the overworked employee even had time for it today.

Jacob squeezed her hand and set off for his mission alone, though his mind never strayed from Vivian. He wrapped up matters as fast as possible and sped back to the house just in time to see a messenger sprinting up the road toward the Wynchester residence.

This time, he recognized the lad as one of Graham's informants.

Graham, Vivian, and every sibling presently at home rushed out-of-doors to intercept the informant.

"He's waiting on news from twenty different cases," Tommy cautioned Vivian.

"Twenty-five," corrected Graham. "But this is the one that we want."

The young lad was out of breath by the time he reached them, and at first his words were nearly unintelligible between his ragged, panting breaths. "We couldn't...tell for certain...the final recipient..."

Vivian sagged against Jacob's chest with a little moan.

"...but after changing...many hands...," the lad continued, "...a man without...proper livery...snuck it through the servants' entrance... of this address."

Graham snatched the paper out of the boy's hand, then jerked his head up with satisfaction. "Leisterdale's house."

Tommy gasped. "Philippa was right!"

"And so was Lord Uppington," said Elizabeth. "His father would absolutely resort to any measures and expect to get away with it."

"Now that we know," began Marjorie.

Vivian's eyes flashed. "Let's go get Quentin."

Jacob wanted to swing her into his arms and kiss her.

"We can't just march in," said Marjorie. "The marquess would never let all twelve adult Wynchesters through the door to start searching his house."

All twelve. Jacob wondered what Vivian thought of being included as part of the family. She did not flinch at the insinuation, but merely looked around them expectantly, awaiting their next steps.

"We aren't ready yet for the kidnapper to know we've unmasked him," Jacob cautioned. "A cornered beast is likely to act rashly, and we cannot risk endangering Quentin."

Especially since their enemy already felt comfortable slicing into his hostage's skin, just to send a message. The sight of a mob of Wynchesters would not only prove they'd disobeyed his clear warning, but it could also spur the kidnapper to retaliate even more violently.

"So what, then?" asked Vivian. "We go to the authorities? They didn't care before, and they'll do even less now, if we point our fingers at a peer of the realm."

"Chloe and Faircliffe could drop by for a chat, like we did with Olivebury," Tommy suggested.

"We knew which room to search then," Graham pointed out. "We don't even know which floor to start with this time."

"We don't have to know," said Jacob. "All we need are a few masks."

Vivian looked at him as if he had hung the moon. "You have a plan?"

"Yes. I just need to grab something from the barn."

"Is it the Highland Tiger?" Elizabeth asked. "Because if you won't let me sever the villain's neck with my sword, you should at least allow *someone* to claw his face off."

"I'll be happy to do it," Vivian murmured, flashing her fingernails. She turned to Jacob. "When do we leave?"

They arrived at the Leisterdales' street in a trio of previously unmarked coaches to which Marjorie had affixed a large ROYAL EXTERMINATORS sign and crest. One team would head straight to the target's residence, while the other two teams distracted the neighbors for verisimilitude.

In the first carriage, Jacob opened the basket Tommy had packed and handed out the four masks.

These weren't ordinary masks. They were the large-beaked sort used by medieval doctors to ward against the Black Plague. The trio didn't look like Wynchesters. They looked like giant black-leather crows, bursting up from Hell.

The Marquess of Leisterdale's butler nearly suffered an apoplexy at the sight of them.

"Wh-what?" he stammered in lieu of a greeting.

"We're the Royal Exterminators," Graham announced smoothly, flashing a gold-embossed calling card Adrian had created for this purpose. "This entire crescent has been declared a public health hazard. You're to remain indoors with every door and window latched until the bat outbreak is under control."

"We don't have any bats," said the butler.

Jacob pointed over his shoulder. "Then what's that behind you?"

Screams sounded throughout the house as Jacob's trained *Myotis mystacinus* streamed in through the open windows. The whiskered bats with their long brown fur began swooping and diving from one room to the next.

The butler gasped and scurried backward until his back flattened against the nearest wall.

Jacob held up his basket—empty, save for an extra mask and leather cloak to hide Quentin's identity as they smuggled him out. "We'll handle the bats. You man the door."

Before the butler could argue, Jacob and Vivian brushed past him into the house.

Graham remained at the entrance, to keep an eye out in case the Marquess of Leisterdale returned home earlier than expected.

"We have at least a few hours to search," Vivian whispered. "Right?"

Jacob kept his voice hushed as well, careful not to be overheard. "Leisterdale is at his club, and tends to drink and gamble there past midnight, yes. But even if Graham keeps the footmen from sneaking out and sending word of trouble at home, the neighbors will have seen our grand entrance. We have to work fast."

Her foot-long pointed black-leather beak sliced through the air as she nodded her understanding. "Do you have Tommy's map of the rooms?"

He tapped his pocket. "Right here. Do you need it now?"

She shook her head. "I memorized it. You take this floor, and I'll take the other?"

"Meet you back here in thirty minutes. If you need the bats to follow you—"

"I remember the commands." But she hesitated rather than turn toward the stairs.

Jacob wished he could see her face. Hell, he wished he could kiss her. But he'd save that for an hour from now, when they were all celebrating back at the Wynchester home with cakes and champagne.

He touched the tip of his beak to hers. "Let's go find Quentin."

She sucked in an audible breath and raced up the stairs.

Jacob allowed himself a small smile. Whether she liked it or not, Vivian indeed made a formidable Wynchester. Convincing in costume, memorizing maps and animal commands with ease...If only she could see how much *good* they could do if they worked together!

But there would be time to convince her his family was worth joining after they'd rescued her cousin.

Jacob hurried down the corridor, entering every room he passed. As he went, maids shrieked and stampeded out of the house to flee the low-flying bats. He peeked into pantries and tested walls for secret passages. Jacob doubted the marquess would have had the foresight to install hidden chambers in his Mayfair town home, but the Royal Exterminator ruse was only going to work once.

This was their chance to find Vivian's cousin.

As he searched, Jacob murmured commands to his bats, sending the furry tempest a few yards farther ahead, so as to clear each space of servants before Jacob slipped in to search it. Screams and fleeing footsteps preceded him every time.

Unfortunately, it only took twenty of his allotted thirty minutes to determine there were no faux Wynchesters tied to a chair on the ground floor. Jacob hoped Vivian was having better luck upstairs, where the sleeping quarters were located.

He and a dozen swooping bats hurried to the stairs to join her—only for Vivian to come trudging down before he'd even made it halfway up.

Her voice was bleak. "No sign of Quentin ever having been here."

"Did you check behind the—"

"Yes." Her voice wobbled. "My cousin isn't here. He never was. The Marquess of Leisterdale—"

"—is a very rich and powerful man," Jacob finished, his voice hushed. Despite the chaos, they shouldn't discuss their suspicions here. "Follow my lead, and we'll reconvene in the carriage."

He flipped open the lid to the basket and rushed down the stairs, giving the bats the signal to gather inside the wicker receptacle. By the time Jacob reached the front door, all dozen furry little mammals were perched inside the hamper.

As he strode through the entryway, Jacob tilted the bat-basket toward the butler, who stifled a shriek and cowered against the far wall to let Jacob and Vivian pass.

"Jolly good, then," Graham said briskly. "Give us a call if you experience another outbreak."

"Another...outbreak?" gasped the butler.

In seconds, Graham, Jacob, and Vivian were back inside the carriage. They ripped off their hot, heavy masks as the horses whisked them back toward Islington.

"He'd been moved?" asked Graham.

"Never there." Vivian stared at Jacob darkly, as though it were his fault the villain had been wise enough not to store his hostage in his primary residence.

"Leisterdale has more than one house in the country," Jacob reminded her. "Quentin could be at one of those."

"The marquess also has more than one plantation," she said, her voice unsteady. "Quentin could be at one of *those*."

One glance at the glossiness in Vivian's brown eyes was all it took for Jacob to realize this was a visceral fear. Vivian's own escape had been pure luck. Although slavery was finally illegal here on English soil, a sugar-plantation-owning lord depraved enough to kidnap an eighteen-year-old lad in order to sway the vote in Parliament was unlikely to have moral scruples about how best to dispose of a young Black hostage.

Her eyes were panicked. "We should have been watching the docks instead of the crescents..."

Jacob pulled her into his arms and held her tight. He could

imagine her terror. Vivian had *lived* the nightmare. She knew exactly what would await her cousin.

Jacob couldn't allow that to happen.

"We'll find him," he promised, his voice rough against the back of her ear. "I understand why that would be your worst fear, but remember, there is no evidence to indicate Quentin is no longer in the area. He was here to give that thumbprint."

Over her shoulder, Jacob exchanged urgent glances with his brother, who nodded to signal he'd deploy any spare spies he could find to lift every rock and check every ship's manifest.

"It sounds crass," Graham said softly, "but your cousin loses value as a hostage if he cannot easily be produced for the ransom. We have every reason to believe he's still in England, and probably here in London. Possibly at an accomplice's residence. We *will* find him. It's only a matter of time."

Jacob murmured, "And the moment the kidnapper mentions a price for ransom, we'll pay it and make the exchange at once. Quentin's safety is our priority."

Vivian shuddered in Jacob's arms, then went still for a long moment before straightening away from him.

She gave a stoic nod. "You're right. I *know* you're right. Emotions can overtake my heart, but my brain still recognizes logic. Leisterdale wants a certain act to pass before he asks for ransom money, and until he achieves that goal, it's in his best interest to keep my cousin healthy and close by. We don't know how much time that gives us, but Quentin should still be alive…for now."

Jacob held her hand in his, rubbing the soft warm skin with his thumb.

Vivian flashed him a grateful smile. As the horses clopped along, her spine regained its straightness. The panic melted away, replaced by what Jacob had come to think of as her *plotting furiously* expression. The Wynchesters might be worn thin, but Vivian carried a one-woman Planning Parlor in her brain at all times. If there were any overlooked clues, Vivian would spot them.

When the carriage reached Islington, the available family members piled out of the home and jogged up to the carriage in the hopes of being the first to welcome Quentin.

Vivian remained silent while Jacob explained why they didn't have him.

Marjorie took one look at her face and hugged her.

"Let's go indoors." Elizabeth gestured toward the sky. "It's going to rain."

"And Cook made lime biscuits," said Marjorie.

Graham blinked at her. "*Lime?*"

Vivian spun to stare at Jacob. "Like the ones my mother made in Demerara?"

"I hope they resemble them a little bit. I don't have a recipe."

"Then how did you know—"

"You mention them no less than seven times in your plays. I figured they had to be your favorites. Cook tried her best, but if they're not quite right, I do hope you'll forgive me."

Vivian threw her arms about him and pressed her cheek to his chest. "You're trying. I see you trying. I appreciate all of your efforts."

You're trying was not quite the same as *You're achieving your goal of making me happy*, but he hoped it was at least progress in the right direction.

He held her close for as long as she let him.

When they stepped into the siblings' sitting room, Philippa waved a hand toward the table. "Jacob, I almost forgot. Some post came for you while you were out."

Jacob sifted through the pile of correspondence, his spirits rising. He tossed all but one of the letters aside, then broke the seal and scanned the contents. What he read inside made his heart attempt to burst from his chest.

"Vivian," he began, trying and failing to contain his excitement.

Her eyes narrowed. "What is it?"

"Nothing bad," he said quickly. "Something wonderful. Your dramatic play about suffrage reform will be produced on Drury Lane!"

Huzzahs of joy rang around the room.

From every mouth except Vivian's.

Her forehead lined with confusion. "Why would a theater manager inform you rather than me?"

"Well..." Jacob shoved the letter into his pocket, belatedly realizing he did not in fact have a good explanation that didn't involve unmasking himself as Sir Gareth Jallow. "I...That is to say, you're aware that I have friends who are writers of some renown..."

"Poets, not playwrights."

His cravat felt too tight. "Yes, well, professional scribes of considerable fame and status. One such individual put in a good word for you at the Olympic Theatre—"

"Why would they do that?"

"Why would...someone...champion you to the theater?" Jacob swallowed. He'd hoped she would be too overjoyed at this once-in-a-lifetime opportunity to worry about how, precisely, it had come about. "You know I've read your plays. They're wonderful. You're an excellent writer, which is the very topic my weekly group discusses."

Vivian narrowed her eyes. The rest of his siblings were smiling and nodding. He'd waxed poetic about Vivian's abilities to them, too.

"Given your stellar talent," he pushed on, "of course I would rave about your work as an example of criminally overlooked craftsmanship. If an individual then took it upon himself to—"

"Who authorized you to interfere on my behalf without so much as enquiring whether I wished for such intervention?" she snapped.

Jacob halted. Though his lips moved like a fish, no sound escaped. His siblings watched avidly.

"Who has the biscuits?" Graham whispered.

"Here." Marjorie passed them down the line.

Jacob kept his focus on Vivian and tried again. "Remember, word of mouth isn't trickery. It's a good and natural thing. Opining you deserve to be published is simply stating the truth. You believe the odds are stacked against you, and you're correct. You know you're at a huge disadvantage. So why not accept help when you can?"

"Please listen to my words." Vivian poked her finger into his lapel. "I haven't worked this hard to become an annoying favor some theater manager must suffer through solely to curry the blessing of some white male poet."

"Er," he said.

"I *sent* that play to the manager of the Olympic. He said never to contact him again. This has nothing to do with me being good at what I do. It's not about my work at all."

"The manager now realizes—"

"—that he has a big important friend who said *do this*. Your manager didn't have a choice. He'll appreciate my work even less now." Her eyes glinted with anger. "This is yet another way Wynchesters are dangerous. You act rashly in others' names, even when they don't want you to. And then people like me are left to suffer the consequences. At best, this theater manager will throw on a halfhearted afternoon performance and call the favor fulfilled."

"But if otherwise your play wasn't going to be performed at all—"

"I want my work to be performed by choice! Only by earning the honor on my own merit will I ever be taken seriously as a playwright."

"You said yourself, that plan is not working. You've been trying for years—"

"And I'll keep trying for decades more! Eventually, someone will have to recognize good work when they see it."

"You don't believe that any more than I do," said Jacob. "You *know* the world isn't fair."

"I want it to be," Vivian said achingly. "I need there to be hope, not just for me, but for all the others who...Doing everything in my power *has* to be enough to make a difference."

"Does it? You couldn't leave Demerara on your own power," he pointed out. "Sometimes we have to accept help in order to realize our—"

"Is this where you wax poetic about your angelic Baron Vanderbean, the white man who saved you all and delivered you to lives of wealth and privilege?"

"I wasn't going to," Jacob said. "But now that you brought it up, that's a brilliant point. Without Bean sharing his considerable advantages without hesitation, many of us would still be—"

"One question," she interrupted. "Did your precious baron abduct you against your will and arrange your future without your knowledge or consent? Or did he present options, and allow you to choose what you'd like to do with your life?"

"Choice," the siblings chorused together.

Vivian's eyes flashed. "Yet you didn't think I deserved the same consideration a lord gave a small child?"

"You're being melodramatic," said Jacob. "I—"

"Oof," said Tommy. "You just lost *this* argument."

"Erase that phrase from your vocabulary," Philippa agreed with a wince. "Just because you might react differently doesn't make someone else's feelings invalid."

Vivian crossed her arms. "*Would* you react differently? If all it takes to be published is for one of your important friends to whisper into the right ear, then why aren't there volumes of Jacob Wynchester's poetry in bookstores all over England?"

"It's complicated," he hedged. "Listen—"

"Why should I? You don't seem particularly inclined to listen to *me*. I suppose I'm too melodramatic."

"Told you that was a mistake," Tommy murmured.

"Listen," Jacob said again, even though it was clearly the wrong thing to say. He wasn't skilled at talking to people. He needed time to hone his words. Most of which ended up in the fireplace for a reason. "I'm not an old white baron. I'm just a man trying to help a friend. If you don't want your play to be performed, then say so, and I'll let the theater manager know to take it off the schedule."

"If you do that," Vivian said quietly, "neither he nor any other theater manager in England will consider my work ever again. Rejecting this opportunity, no matter how insincerely granted, would blackball my name."

He swallowed.

"You give me no choice," she continued, her eyes glossy. "All I wanted was choices. The freedom to live my life on my own terms. You took that from me."

That…was not the gift he'd been trying to give. Jacob desperately glanced at his siblings for help.

They all became extraordinarily absorbed with inspecting the biscuits on their plates.

"All I asked of you was to help me find my cousin." Vivian's entire body seemed to vibrate with rage and hurt. "Achieve that if you can, but please don't do me any more favors. It's late. I'll see myself home."

Before Jacob could figure out how to salvage the situation, Vivian strode from the sitting room toward the front door.

It was raining now, just as Elizabeth had predicted. Outside the front window, Vivian walked with her head high as though she didn't even notice the cold drizzle.

Or perhaps it was the best way to hide the tears on her face.

25

The next morning, after another sleepless night, Viv forced her feet back toward the Wynchester home. She couldn't remember the last time she'd held such conflicted feelings about anything or anyone. Usually her convictions were strong and sure. Giving advice was easy. She wished Parliament would listen to *her* counsel. The world could be a better place in the blink of an eye.

But right now, Viv's personal and professional worlds were upside-down. Jacob's unexpected meddling had made her dream come true in the most galling way. She was furious with him and indebted to him and in a panic about how to make the most of what paltry attention might come her way.

If she hadn't gone to the Wynchesters, she wouldn't have met Jacob. If she never met him, she wouldn't have broken her rule about kissing. If she hadn't kissed him, maybe he wouldn't have bypassed her express desires and tried to arrange her career himself.

But she couldn't wish him to Hades. If she hadn't broken half a dozen other rules and joined the previously disdained Wynchester crew on their justice-seeking missions…she wouldn't have the least idea what had happened to her kidnapped cousin, or the remotest chance of rescuing him.

Somehow, over the past few weeks, keeping life divided in easy boxes of Good and Bad, Right and Wrong, had become exponentially harder.

By the time she reached the Wynchesters' front door, she still hadn't managed to sort things out. But she flashed their kind-eyed butler her best smile. Mr. Randall had let her in when she'd had nowhere else to turn. Unfortunately, her troubles had only increased since then.

Viv would decide how to handle what was left of her career on her own, but her best hope for Quentin's safe return still lay with the team in this house.

She girded her loins and strode into the sibling sitting room. Today, only Jacob, Graham, and Marjorie were present.

Upon her arrival, Jacob leaped up from a sofa filled with kittens. "We have every place the Marquess of Leisterdale owns or goes in England under constant surveillance. The moment there's any sign of Quentin or other suspicious activity, we'll know about it."

"We also acquired samples of Leisterdale's handwriting," added Graham. "The hand he uses to draft bills in Parliament doesn't match the letters sent to us or to Olivebury."

"Unsurprising," Viv pointed out. "Anyone with half a brain would disguise his handwriting."

"Or have an accomplice do the writing," Jacob agreed. "Such as whomever Leisterdale has hired to watch over Quentin."

"Probably yet another haughty, entitled extremist who views Black people and commoners as expendable," Philippa said. "Leisterdale boasts about his vast collection of slaves on his sugar plantations, and argues vehemently any time abolition is mentioned in Parliament."

Jacob nodded. "And someone who thinks of other humans as disposable tools would not hesitate to kidnap one, if it furthered his own aims."

"Like many English peers with lucrative 'investments' in the Caribbean, Leisterdale quite openly delights in abducting innocents," Viv said, her voice shaking. "No one volunteers to become his chattel."

Philippa expression was grave. "Most lords openly oppose abolition. The few willing to hear Faircliffe's views on the subject would only consider relinquishing slavery if paid handsomely for the loss of their so-called property."

"And how much would the recently freed slaves receive?" Jacob asked sardonically.

"Nothing," Philippa replied softly. "When suggested, the topic is dismissed altogether."

"Of course the hostages performing all the work would receive nothing." Fury spread through Viv's veins. "Those lords are our 'betters.' Just ask them."

Graham handed Viv a newspaper. "According to the gossip columns, there was a public row last night at Leisterdale's club. He engaged in a screaming match about the evils of suffrage, and threatened a powerful marquess to his face if the marquess didn't vote to protect lords' rights."

"Lords' rights," she muttered in disgust. "He has the right to bend over and receive my boot up his arse."

Marjorie leaned forward. "The question is, how do we unmask him?"

"No," said Jacob. "The question is, how do we rescue Vivian's cousin?"

Viv thought it over. "No new demands means there's nothing we can currently do to encourage Leisterdale to release Quentin on his own. Blackmail, not kidnapping, was the original goal. Quentin must have witnessed a robbery."

"That would do it," Marjorie agreed. "Leisterdale must believe he can easily sway the House of Lords. What he needs is for Olivebury to convince the House of Commons to vote against suffrage."

Jacob nodded. "Chloe and Faircliffe spend every spare moment preparing speeches and arguments, so it's reasonable to assume poor

Olivebury would need to do the same—particularly if he's expected to argue against his own belief system. No matter how fanatical Leisterdale is about whatever nonsensical way he believes wealthy white aristocrats are oppressed, he must realize this task won't be easy for Olivebury."

Graham nodded. "Abducting the baron was likely an impulsive act. Leisterdale needed to ensure his blackmail had enough time to generate the desired results. Kidnapping your cousin was an unintended side effect in an attempt to control *us*."

Jacob turned to Viv, his eyes tortured. "I'm so sorry."

"We're all sorry," said Marjorie. "More than words can say."

In unison, all three Wynchesters touched their fingers to their chests and lifted their palms to the sky.

Viv let out a long breath. It was past time to stop holding them responsible for everything. As much as she'd—rightfully—feared that Quentin copying the rule-breaking Wynchesters would lead straight to misery, her cousin's decisions weren't anyone's fault but his own. She could not continue to blame Jacob and his siblings.

"Leisterdale wouldn't have captured a fictional Wynchester if Quentin hadn't been running around pretending to be a man that doesn't exist," she admitted. "I guess this is what it took for him to learn his lesson about lying, spying, and bending rules."

"I love lying, spying, and bending rules," Marjorie said with a happy sigh. "If it helps others."

Viv looked at her sharply. "You wouldn't love it if such behavior got you abducted by a scoundrel."

"Precisely how I met my husband." Marjorie's mouth fell open and she clapped her hands with glee. "Maybe Quentin will return home with a betrothed at his side."

"Sorry," Jacob whispered again, as purring kittens crawled over his lap. "She never stops matchmaking."

"Is that what you want?" Philippa asked. "For Quentin to view our family as dangerous scoundrels of poor character?"

Viv had used those exact words any number of times when referring to the Wynchesters. Gallingly, Quentin was right: coming to know them had caused her to readjust her opinions.

Her fears about naïve young people copying the Wynchesters' antics willy-nilly had clearly not been unwarranted. They *were* reckless. They *were* unattainably privileged.

And they did make an irreplaceable difference in the lives of ordinary citizens, who would have no recourse or hope if it weren't for this one-of-a-kind family.

"I want Quentin to think before he acts," she said at last. "Actions have consequences."

Marjorie nodded. "For example, he set out to impersonate a Wynchester, which resulted in…successfully impersonating a Wynchester."

Viv shot her a dark look. Quentin was exactly the sort of high-spirited young lad who was probably cackling to himself over the stories he would be able to tell about the time he was held hostage after being mistaken for a Wynchester. He'd trot this tale out to anyone who would listen, until they all had it memorized. Other than fainting at the sight of his own blood, the bounder was likely having the adventure of a lifetime.

As long as his captors were treating him like a Balcovian baron, and not the orphaned bastard of a Black mistress.

"He's fine," Jacob said quickly, as though he could read the emotions crossing Viv's face.

"You don't know that," she replied, as evenly as she could.

"Leisterdale's original plan was to be a thief, not a hotel," Philippa said. "Unless your script included detailed instructions on how to manage a long-term abduction, Leisterdale may be at a loss as to what to do with your cousin."

Oh, Lord. Viv covered her face with her hands. She'd forgotten that it was her own damn plays that had spelled out how to steal and blackmail and kidnap in the first place.

Leisterdale wasn't the mastermind. *She* was.

"The prisoner in my play was well treated," she said in relief. "The kidnapper sent proof of captivity, and the grieving parents fell right in line."

Marjorie lowered her plate of cakes. "You wrote a play about abducting children?"

"Children are taken all the time," Viv said defensively. "*I* give them a happy ending. The kidnapper goes to prison, and the children return home to their parents. Besides, that script was a private exercise written for my own entertainment, not as a manual for malefactors."

"No one is to blame for this but Leisterdale," Jacob assured her.

"And the corrupt hierarchy that grants him immunity for his crimes," Viv muttered.

"Privilege of peerage isn't immunity," Graham corrected her. "At least, not completely. Peers cannot be arrested in civil suits, but they *can* face trial for criminal charges."

"Judged by a jury of his fellow House of Lords, who are singularly unlikely to condemn one of their own. Particularly if they agree with Leisterdale's motivation." Viv snorted in disgust. "Few peers lose a single day of freedom for their crimes. Whereas commoners can be executed for stealing a sheep, or pickpocketing a single shilling."

"Trust me," said Graham. "Chloe is planning to reform that next. She and Faircliffe have a list of—"

"Talking about us?" asked a female voice.

Viv twisted in her seat to see the duke and duchess enter the room, the baby gnawing on her shoulder.

"We're discussing the hundred-and-fifty items you hope to strike from the current list of hanging offenses," Graham said.

"We're up to one hundred and sixty-three," Chloe said with a smile. "I'm still negotiating."

Marjorie handed the baby a biscuit.

Chloe turned to Viv. "While Graham's team hunts for the missing painting and your cousin, why don't you return to our house with us and help us hone our arguments for tonight's parliamentary session?"

Viv blinked at her. It wasn't the first time the duchess had offered such a thing, but it was the first time Viv realized the offer was very serious.

"We can discuss more than that," added the duke. "After we enact voting reform, I am open to other worthy causes."

"Why don't you abolish slavery, while you're at it?" said Viv. "If it's illegal in England, it should be illegal on British soil worldwide."

Faircliffe held up his hands. "I agree with you, but we must tackle one thing at a time."

"Why must we?" Viv demanded. "I reject that binary. We should burn down all the injustices at once."

She was being a little sarcastic...and one hundred percent earnest. Most of her plays and all of her dreams were about reform of one type or another. She normally wouldn't hold her breath expecting some wealthy aristocrat to fight on her behalf, but until now she'd also never beheld one who flopped into an armchair in front of her as an equal.

If *anyone* could turn the House of Lords on its head and bring about real change, that duke was Faircliffe. In fact, even if Leisterdale's blackmail had worked on Olivebury, Viv wouldn't be surprised if Faircliffe stopped the act cold in the House of Lords.

"I'll help," Viv said swiftly. "Those issues are dear to my heart."

When Faircliffe swept into Westminster, he'd be as eloquent as a preacher on Sunday morning. He'd gain so many disciples the debates would be over in a single session.

"Splendid." The duke looked relieved, as though he'd feared Viv might dismiss *him* out of hand. "I'll take all the aid I can get."

No one else seemed to think anything of the unlikely partnership.

As they fell into easy conversation, Viv was forced to admit the Duke of Faircliffe wasn't remotely the snooty, self-serving prig she'd imagined all lords to be. After having been dismissed at first glance her whole life, Viv ought to know better than to assume that any one person was necessarily representative of whatever category they belonged to.

To be sure, some—perhaps most—men of great wealth were as evil as could be imagined. But the fact that aristocrats like Faircliffe existed, that he had allies in the House of Lords and even more in the House of Commons…It gave her hope that maybe she might actually see real and good change in her lifetime.

She accepted a cake from Marjorie. Tart lime and sugary sweetness exploded on Viv's tongue. For a brief moment, she was transported back in time. To the aroma of a freshly opened oven and the comforting warmth of her mother's arms. It tasted like the beloved hug she'd dreamed of for so long. It felt like family.

Regardless of their methods, there could be no confusion as to which side of the battle the Wynchesters belonged to. They fought for justice, always. Equality. Fairness. Representation.

Her gaze slid to Jacob, whose lap was hidden beneath a blanket of wiggling felines.

He gave a crooked smile and held one out. "Kitten?"

She took that, too. Its paws tickled her palm and its little pink tongue was rough against her skin. "What's its name?"

"Princess Poppy."

She petted the cat's soft fur. While she was being magnanimous, Jacob wasn't a monster, either. Much like the duke, Jacob had tried to use his colleagues' privileged status to help lift Viv up, too.

His heart had been in a good place. She appreciated the purity of his intentions. She just wished they could have worked toward a goal together, instead of him assuming he knew best.

Rich, coming from the woman who was literally paid to assume she knew best.

"If you're accepting everything anyone offers," said Chloe with a twinkle in her eye, "want to mind Dory for the night? I haven't slept four hours in a row since giving birth."

The duke snatched his son from his wife's arms before Viv could answer.

"He shan't spend a single night away from me until he goes to Eton." Faircliffe kissed the baby's brow. "And even then, I might stow away with him."

Chloe fluttered her eyelashes at him. "And then I might get *eight* hours of sleep."

Faircliffe blinked in sudden understanding, then held the baby toward Viv. "Want to mind Dory for the night?"

Viv grinned and lifted the kitten on her lap. "I can't even take Princess Poppy home. I have an attack badger who doesn't like visitors."

The mention of Rufus made her recall Jacob's most recent visit, when he'd brought over breakfast. The badger hadn't attacked him once. Perhaps Rufus had come to see Jacob as part of the family, too.

Viv wrapping herself around Jacob and devouring his kisses would certainly give that impression. She closed her eyes as she stroked the kitten and remembered what it had been like to run her greedy hands over Jacob's body, press her own to his chest and hips, open her mouth to his. It had been, without question, the best breakfast she'd ever had.

But was one perfect morning worth the risk of a lifetime?

26

That evening, when Jacob entered the supper room, his entire family squawked and flapped their arms and roosted precariously on their seats like a coop full of chickens trying to conceal their eggs from a fox.

"Not suspicious at all," he informed them.

No one made eye contact.

"Mmm, these are delicious pies," Tommy announced to the room in general, taking a comically big bite.

"I thought he'd be in the barn longer," Marjorie whispered behind her hand to Adrian. "Doesn't he train the ferrets on Tuesday evenings?"

Graham sent her a pointed look, then ducked back behind his open newspaper.

"All right." Jacob crossed his arms rather than head to the sideboard for a plate of food. "What's happening?"

"Nothing," Philippa said, far too quickly. "Nothing Wynchestery is happening to any Wynchesters. Don't worry about it."

"If it's nothing," Jacob said, "then why would I worry about it?"

"You shouldn't," said Kuni. "It has nothing to do with y—"

Thunk.

All heads swiveled toward the noise.

"Er..." Marjorie's face bloomed with color. "Jacob, I think I hear an...antelope. Across the street. Outside. You should go check on it."

He gritted his teeth and stalked around the table toward her chair.

Tommy covered her face with her hand. "An *antelope?*"

"I panicked," Marjorie muttered. "At least I didn't say dolphin."

A book lay on its side in the crevice between her chair and Adrian's.

A familiar-looking book.

One that had just been published that morning.

"What's this?" Jacob asked as he scooped it up.

A silly question, given that he was the only person present who knew the real answer.

"You don't like to hear anyone speak *J-A-L-L-O-W*'s name," Philippa blurted out. "So we try to hold our discussions of his work in private—"

"You lot have a secret *reading circle* you've been hiding from me?" he said in shock.

"We can't tell you about it if we can't say the words," Kuni pointed out. "A completely silent reading circle has no reason to gather at all."

"Wine," said Philippa.

"Biscuits," said Marjorie.

"I'd attend a wine-and-biscuits circle," Adrian agreed.

"Add pies and I'm there," said Tommy.

Graham stayed hidden behind his newspaper.

Jacob handed the book of poetry back to his sister. "Each of you bought your own copy?"

"We all wanted to be the first to read it," Philippa admitted. "You might not think much of Sir Gareth, but he's one of my favorite poets."

Irrationally, Jacob's instinctive reaction was irritation to discover he wasn't the very favorite.

Followed at once by the conviction that if Philippa—who was not a professional poet—had found faults in his work, then it was surely riddled with errors and incompetencies that his actual artistic peers would rightfully sneer at. Indicating Jacob's pathetic attempts at verse should never have been published at all.

"I deserve all the awards" and "Readers should throw rotten tomatoes in my face" might *sound* like opposites, but no writer of Jacob's acquaintance had any problem fully believing both things at any given moment.

He was dying to ask which of Jallow's poems she liked best. Instead, he announced, "I'm going to the barn."

"You just came from the barn," Marjorie said.

"You didn't have supper yet," said Tommy. "We have pies."

Jacob stalked from the room.

Graham jogged after him. "Wait."

Jacob waited. In part because he loved his brother, and in part out of habit.

Graham was the de facto head of the Wynchester family, despite not having been a member of it a single day longer than Jacob. They'd both spent their childhoods working for the same circus—though their experiences there had been wildly different.

Graham, the star of the show. Lit up in lights, to thunderous applause.

Jacob, out of sight. In the tents with the animals. Treated like one.

"I'm sorry about the poetry balderdash," Graham said remorsefully.

That was the other thing about Jacob's adopted brother. Despite all Graham's advantages—

> *public adoration*
> *an incredible wife*
> *acrobatic talent*
> *natural leadership*
> *an endless circle of friends and acquaintances*

lighter skin from his white father (which allowed Graham more privileges in British society)

the presence of a loving mother during Graham's infancy and most of his childhood

—despite all of that, Graham was still dependably, unfailingly, *nice.*

He had never once seen or treated Jacob as lesser. Which made Jacob feel that much worse any time he felt the tiniest flash of resentment.

If Jacob wanted to be head of the household—which they both knew he did not—Graham would have stepped aside without hesitation. If Jacob wished to command an army of spies or leap across London from rooftop to rooftop, Graham would relinquish his best shoes and his best men in a heartbeat.

But Jacob didn't want Graham's life. Jacob wanted his own life. Success at what *he* was talented at. A woman to love him for who *he* was.

And...all right, yes, maybe an adoring public. People for whom his face and his name were enough.

"It's so much easier for you," Jacob blurted out.

Graham blinked. "For me, personally? Or 'you' as a collective, meaning me and all of our other siblings?"

It was Jacob's turn to blink. "For most of you, probably, though in that exact moment, I was indeed referring to you personally. Everything has always been easier for you."

He sounded like they were eight years old again. He wished he hadn't spoken. What was the point? Graham would deny it. Jacob certainly wouldn't pull the scabs off old wounds that should have healed years ago to explain—

"I know," Graham said softly. "I'm sorry."

Damn it. There he went being bloody kind and understanding again. Like everyone else in the world, Jacob had no choice but to love his brother.

"I'm sorry, too," he admitted. "I shouldn't have stormed out like that."

"You're a poet," Graham said simply. "You're supposed to be moody and sensitive. If anything, you're not playing your role hard enough. Next time, flip over the table and then swig straight from a bottle of brandy on your way out."

"What if I prefer milk?" Jacob asked, deadpan.

"Milk takes a bit of an edge off the drama," Graham reproached him. "Think whiskey or gin. 'Blue ruin' is certainly a dramatic name for a liquor. Maybe work with Vivian on this one. As a playwright, I'm sure she can script you a satisfying ending."

"If fictional," Jacob added dryly.

"Not necessarily." Graham handed him a sealed missive. "This came for you."

Jacob hefted the letter. The handwriting on the front was unfamiliar.

"Perhaps it's a publisher," Graham said earnestly. "Perhaps you are about to become as famous as Jallow."

Right.

"Thank you," was all Jacob said aloud. "I'll read it later."

As soon as he was safe in the privacy of his barn, Jacob broke the seal and shook open the letter. The interior was neatly lined with a familiar hand he instantly recognized. He ought to, given he'd read a dozen scripts written by this author. His heart beat faster.

Receiving a response from Ask Vivian hadn't taken nearly as long as he'd expected. With everything going on with Leisterdale and her cousin, he hadn't expected her to spare a thought for her column. Of course she'd managed a hundred tasks at once. She probably had to. She received so much correspondence, the pile never seemed to diminish.

Ask Vivian wasn't the only one. According to Jacob's publisher, Sir Gareth received so much post that the stacks of unopened letters filled an entire wardrobe. Part of him longed to know what the messages said. And part of him much preferred to die in ignorance.

His publisher held on to reader correspondence for the time being, though they were unlikely to store it forever. But what was the alternative? Jacob couldn't have Jallow's mail forwarded home without his siblings catching on. Hundreds or thousands of letters would be a little suspicious. Nor could Jacob attend to his correspondence at his publisher, given they had no notion who the man was behind the pseudonym. If they even realized it *was* a pseudonym.

This letter, however, was one he could not wait to read.

Dear Loveless in London,

You ask how to woo a woman you aren't certain is ready to be courted. The first question therefore must be: Have you considered waiting until she is ready? Contrary to popular belief, not all unwed women are sitting around wishing for a man to fill up their vapid, empty lives.

Which leads me to the second point: The best way to learn a woman's preferences is to ask her yourself. Your friends and your family's opinions are irrelevant. Not even strangers with advice columns. Why?

I could tell you that my ideal courtship would include quiet time to read or write in companionable silence. That I prefer potted basil

> *to snipped roses, because basil is useful and the blooms are so pretty. I might confess that I'd take lemonade with a sprig of mint in it over the fanciest sherry. Or that I prefer lazy picnics to long walks in the park. It is rare that I have the luxury to do absolutely nothing.*
>
> *None of that is of any use to you, because all women are different people. Yours might wish to go fishing, or to the opera, or to volunteer at a hospital together. Perhaps she'd love a handmade crown of flowers from you, or perhaps fresh daisies make her nose itch.*
>
> *Perhaps she doesn't want anything from you at all, except your time and attention. To feel like you truly see her. That you're listening. That you understand her. That you respect her. That you admire her just as she is. That she is loved.*
>
> *Give that to a woman, and you may find she desires you just as you are, too. No glass slippers or white stallions riding into the sunset required.*
>
> *Good luck,*
Vivian

The response was both better and worse than Jacob had hoped for. On the one hand, she'd practically given him the script for planning a perfect night. On the other hand, her instructions were clear to wait until the woman was ready to be courted, which meant there was nothing Jacob could do for now.

When would Vivian welcome a suitor? Not until after her cousin had returned safely, that much was obvious. But after that? Not until her career was riding high, she'd said, but there was no guarantee when that day would come either. Especially if she wouldn't let him help. Er, interfere.

Jacob would wait as long as it took, but he'd rather do so at Vivian's side, as her partner, rather than as an afterthought somewhere in the shadows behind her.

A knock sounded on the barn door.

He fumbled to fold the letter and tuck it safely out of sight in his waistcoat pocket before his family could burst in with more commentary on Sir Gareth Jallow.

But when he opened the door, Vivian was on the other side.

Warmth suffused Jacob's body. The mere sight of her made him so happy, he had to tamp down the urge to grin like a loon. "Back from the Faircliffes already?"

"Parliament started. Chloe talked me into watching part of the session from a ghastly hole in the attic, and I barely escaped with my sanity intact." Vivian stepped inside the barn. "What are you doing?"

"I was about to feed the snakes. They're calmer when they have full bellies."

"Poisonous snakes?"

"Not all of them." At her crestfallen expression, he added wryly, "Hoping to attack me with them for meddling in your career, unsolicited?"

"It would have a certain poetic justice," she replied.

She was teasing.

He hoped.

"I really am sorry," he began again.

"And I really am trying to forgive you," she interrupted. "You need to understand that my frustration stems from more than one thoughtless act. I was born a *possession*. For two long decades, I didn't have the *right* to live a life I wanted."

He was horrified. "I don't think of you as—"

"You and your family have a long history of not thinking at all. You're so busy saving the day for the client *du jour*, there's no room in your brains or your lives to consider everyone else in the periphery. Starry-eyed people like Quentin try to be just like you, and we see how that went."

"That's…" True.

"As for my career," she continued, "you Wynchesters are so enamored with your heroic personas that you swept in to wreak destruction without pausing to ask or to even wonder what it was that I wanted."

"I shouldn't have had to wonder," he admitted. "You told me, out loud, time and again. I didn't listen."

"Exactly." Her lip trembled. "I may be your client, but please remember that the case is rescuing Quentin, not overruling my free will. If we're to be friends after this is over—"

He took her hands. "I hope to be more than friends."

"Then you have to accept me as a whole human, not as a project. To your eyes, I might have been taking the long way, but it was *my* path to take."

"You're right," he said. "I really am sorry."

"I accept your apology." She paused. "We'll drop the topic now that we've discussed it, but please understand…If my autonomy is trampled again, I shall not keep having this same argument with you. I'd rather forge a new path than entrust my heart to someone who doesn't care enough to listen to me."

"That's fair," he agreed. "And I vow to be fairer in the future as well. I can't promise to be perfect, but I *can* swear that I value your dreams and goals and brain, and will never be so carelessly highhanded again. You *should* have the right to live your life as you please, not in the manner someone else imposes on you."

"Thank you," she said softly. "I wish everyone had that luxury."

"I'll fight for that, too," he promised. "And as for lads like your cousin, I wondered if we might—" Jacob cut off mid-thought when he glimpsed the edge of a book tucked beneath her arm. "Don't tell me you're part of my family's secret poetry cabal, too!"

"Their what?" Vivian stared at him, then seemed to recall the leather volume nestled in her armpit. "Oh, you mean this? It's the latest collection by—"

"Jallow, yes, I have eyes. But why are you carrying it around? I thought you didn't even read that drivel."

"I hadn't, until today. On my way here, I passed three different bookshops with lines out the door as long as the Serpentine. All eagerly waiting to get their hands on this book."

"You stood in one of those queues?" he asked in disbelief.

"I didn't have to," she admitted. "I told Philippa I was curious to know what all the fuss was about, and she said she'd ordered more than enough for her entire reading circle, and she would be happy to give one of the extras to me."

"Of course she did," Jacob muttered. Philippa had probably ordered enough copies to replace every cobblestone in London with a copy of Jallow's poems.

Perhaps the contents would be improved with a few hoof marks and horse droppings.

"Don't read it," he said impulsively. "Life's too short for—"

"'Shards of piety stabbing from each disappointed glance'?"

"Shards of *pity*," he corrected automatically, then wished he hadn't. Someone who hated Jallow as much as he claimed to would not already have memorized lines that were published for the first time mere hours ago.

"I cannot believe you!" She shoved his chest so hard he stumbled backward.

"What—"

She held up the book and shook it. "Did you lie about being a fan, or about who wrote this?"

"I...No...Wait." What had even made her suspect the truth? Curse her ability to glance at someone and know everything about them! After the conversation they'd just had, he certainly couldn't lie to her face. "Both? I said it was complicated."

"Of all the pudding-headed..." She looked down at the book, then up at him. "Why would you hide this?"

"I..."

"Why wouldn't you want your name on the title page?"

That one was easier to answer. "No one would *put* my name on the cover. Being militant with your morals is all well and good for you, but if I wanted to see my words in print in my lifetime...Sometimes you have to work within the system, not against it."

Her lip curled. "So you pretend to be a wealthy, titled, white man?"

"You do if you want to hear 'yes,'" he said defensively. "Let me Ask Vivian: Would I have had more luck pretending to be an orphaned Black female immigrant from Demerara?"

"This book isn't luck. It's false pretenses. It's—"

"—selling thousands of copies before breakfast. You might not like my methods, but you cannot claim that I didn't win the game."

"*You* didn't win at all. Sir Gareth Jallow is the one who—" She gasped and held the book away from her as though it had taken on a horrendous odor. "Is your nom de plume the fictional artiste whose nepotism I should thank for getting my play staged on Drury Lane?"

"Um." He cast about for a response capable of diffusing the situation. "You said we were done with that topic."

"You lied to my face about that, too?" She shook the book at him. "You've been lying to me for *weeks*?"

"It wasn't personal," he protested. "Technically, I've been lying to *everyone's* faces...and eyes...and reading spectacles. For the past five years. Long before I met you."

She hurled the book at his face.

He caught it reflexively, then tossed it onto a pile of hay.

"Look," he began, though he suspected no man who had ever led off with that word had ever successfully won their argument against a woman. "I bent the rules, but you cannot play righteous. You don't want the rules to apply to you, either. You just break them differently."

She huffed. "I never—"

"Really? You insist on being fully and openly yourself, even when you know that way lies rejection. If it's only for men, you're first in line, petticoat and all. Only for white people? There you are anyway, beautiful Black skin on display. Something offered only for the privileged few or the educated elite? There's Vivian, insisting on being given the same consideration—"

"I *should* be given the same consideration as anyone else!"

"Of course you should. We both should. But I chose to wear the sheep suit, whilst you keep trying to waltz into the herd as a wolf."

"No. I reject your metaphor. *I'm* not the dangerous one. They are the wolves and I am the sheep. They may respect you whilst you hide in your wolf-suit, but a lamb like me? They'd happily eat me alive. As for you..."

He braced himself.

She glowered at him. "You're a capital fool."

"We've established that," he muttered.

"And an exceptional poet."

He blinked. "What?"

She strode to the block of hay and swiped up the book of poetry. "I only read the first twenty pages, and already I cannot believe I ever let you so much as glance at my scripts. You must think I'm the most amateurish—"

"*What*? Vivian, I've literally never read anything so entertaining or emotional or witty—"

"Have you read anything by Sir Gareth? Because that man can write." She stabbed her finger in the center of the leather cover. "It should be *your* name here, Jacob. You did this. You deserve the praise."

His throat no longer seemed to work.

"These are your words," she said softly, pressing the book into his hands. "You deserve the fame."

His fingers clutched the volume. "Wouldn't you take pride in your plays being produced all over England, even if the public believed them to be written by Lady Whipplesnout?"

"No," she said simply. "I'm proud of what I've written, even if it never leaves my kitchen. I don't want some fictional Lady Whipplesnout to achieve fame and fortune. It means nothing if no one knows it's me. If the page doesn't bear my name, it's not my achievement."

"I disagree." He gestured around the barn. "Every rehabilitated animal who leaves here able to survive is an achievement, though no evidence of my involvement is left behind. There's just as much poetry in the flap of a no-longer-broken wing as there is in the pages of this book. This barn is my theater, and these animals the only audience I need."

"Bollocks," she said. "Everyone dreams of bowing in the footlights to the thundering of applause."

"Maybe you do. I've tried that. It isn't for me."

"How do you know? A pseudonym isn't the same as—"

"One of my first memories is stumbling in a tent crowded with onlookers. I forgot my line. They pelted me with whatever was in their hands, and roared with glee at how wretched I looked dripping with rubbish. I've never forgotten the sound of their laughter."

Vivian looked appalled. "Where on earth—"

"The same circus where I met Graham. He grew up there, too, though he became a talented acrobat and the star of the show. The circus manager said I wasn't interesting enough to scare up a single farthing. He relegated me to the animal tent so that paying customers wouldn't have to look at me. Told me I belonged in a barn because I wasn't better than an animal myself."

"Oh, Jacob. Of course you're better than…"

He gestured around them. "Better than who and where I am?"

"Better than a cruel, greedy circus manager," she said firmly. "There's nothing wrong with loving animals or working in a barn. There's nothing wrong with Jacob Wynchester, animal trainer *and* poet extraordinaire. You don't belong in the shadows."

"I like the shadows."

"You're scared of the light, which is different. You're talented, Jacob. Truly the most extraordinary person I've ever met. It hurts my heart to be the sole keeper of that knowledge. I want the world to know how marvelous you are."

Her compliments made his throat feel tight, so he pushed them away. Along with the realization that those old dreams hadn't died after all. He *did* want to stand on center stage, and hear the audience applaud for him. Not for his brother. Not for a nom de plume.

Ordinary Jacob Wynchester. Who was maybe a little bit extraordinary after all.

You can't conquer your fears if you don't face them, Vivian had once said.

For her, maybe he would try.

27

Viv dropped her pencil back onto her kitchen table only when her fingers cramped up too much to continue holding on any longer.

If she couldn't sleep anyway due to her worries about Quentin, she'd inadvertently been handed the best distraction on the planet: The theater manager would soon be casting her suffrage reform play.

He might not be expecting Viv's ten-page outline detailing her best suggestions on cast, costumes, acting, stage decorations, timing, and audience participation, but if he adopted even a quarter of her advice, it might actually be a good performance.

She stretched out her indented and sore fingers before picking up the pencil again.

Viv still hadn't quite recovered from the shock that Jacob was Jallow…and that he didn't see anything wrong with the subterfuge. Or maybe part of him did, and that was why he had hidden the truth even from his own family.

For her part, Viv needed to believe that skill and effort were enough. That it was possible for people to get what they deserved without artifice. She took each rejection as a personal challenge. The world could do its best to keep her down, but each slap in the face only made her try harder.

The pencil fumbled from her clumsy, swollen fingers. She sighed rather than bend to collect it from where it had rolled off the table and across the floor, likely breaking the freshly sharpened nib in the process. Rufus would fetch it.

She couldn't entirely blame Jacob for not taking her same route. She had no doubt that he'd tried hard to make it as a poet as his true self. Then likely glanced around at his poetry group and thought *My work would be in shops and lending libraries across the country by now if I were one of them.* Which would naturally lead to the next logical thought: *Who's to say I'm not? It's words on paper. Nobody has to know.*

Sir Gareth had probably been an experiment. Jacob likely anticipated more favorable reception than he'd received on his own, but no one could ever have predicted his pseudonym would soon be sweeping across England, building a following as dense and fanatic as those who worshipped royalty.

Viv understood all that. How you might try a thing, and have that thing get away from you.

What she couldn't understand was keeping the lie going, long after it was necessary. There could be no arguing that Jacob's words hadn't resonated with his countrymen and women. The author of those poems was indisputably talented, no matter whether he was called Sir Gareth or Mr. Wynchester. It was time for Jacob to accept the accolades he was due.

Which was why she hadn't yet left her home this morning. She'd commissioned a gift for him, but it wouldn't be ready until—ah! She leapt to her feet and grabbed her spencer from its wooden hook. After bending to give Rufus a final pat goodbye, she tossed her recovered pencil onto the pile of notes for her play. The play Jacob had arranged to be performed onstage, written by Miss Vivian Henry.

If only he believed in himself half as much as he believed in her!

She hurried out the door and off toward Fleet Street, tying on her ducal bonnet as she walked. Maybe Jacob was starting to have more faith in himself as a talented writer. He hadn't lied when she guessed the truth. And he didn't ask her not to tell anyone else. Maybe he was starting to come around.

Jacob knew who he was and how hard he worked, but was scared to let others know. He needed an easy way to bridge the gap.

She would help.

"Here you are, then," said the shop assistant.

"Thank you." Viv tucked her small parcel into her reticule, then turned her feet toward Islington.

She could hardly wait for the world to know both of their names. Mr. Jacob Wynchester, poet. Miss Vivian Henry, playwright.

It would be easier for him than for her, of course. Male, British, handsome, wealthy, already a proven talent. Every person who knew Sir Gareth Jallow's name could just as easily learn Jacob's. They likely already *did* know it, but in his role as Wynchester rather than poet. He was already famous, no matter what happened next.

For her, everything was riding on a single night's performance. If her script failed to impress, she might never be given a second chance.

That was always going to be true, but she'd imagined at least having the advantage of a theater manager who believed in her. Someone who had chosen her script from a stack of hundreds. Someone who would do everything in his power to make her opening night a roaring success.

The theater manager doing the favor for Jallow hadn't even responded to Viv's letters. His assistant had confirmed the date of the show, but there had been no grand welcome, no invitation to put their minds together, no information about what plans or progress they were making.

"They don't have a plan," she muttered under her breath. "I will send them the plan."

Giving advice was easy.

It was whether the recipient would accept any of it that was always in question.

Before she could bang the Wynchesters' knocker, the butler opened the door wide. The corners of his blue eyes crinkled in his usual friendly smile.

"Welcome, Miss Henry, do come in."

"Thank you, Mr. Randall. How do you do this morning?"

"Very well, indeed. A bit of a late start for you, isn't it? There might be a few lime cakes left in the sitting room. I believe you know your way."

"I do, of course, but—are the others there? Specifically Jacob?"

"I believe he's in the garden, teaching a hawk to speak French."

Of course he was.

Viv thanked the butler and hurried through the house, bypassing the sitting room and the dining room and a dozen other doors and parlors until she reached the servants' entrance in the rear that led to the garden.

Before opening the door, she stopped to straighten her skirts and smooth her bodice and fluff her bonnet. She might not be *ready* for a romance until her career was stable and her cousin was back home... but she also wasn't a big enough fool to repel the handsome gentleman with the big heart and the stray hedgehog collection.

Assuring herself she was as presentable as could be expected after a sleepless night and a two-mile walk, Viv stepped outside into the Wynchesters' garden.

Six-foot-high stone walls delineated the sides of the property. The barn was in the very rear, but there was no need to go that far today. Jacob was crouched beside a flowerbed, holding an ungloved hand out toward a bird of prey.

The tawny sparrow hawk was perched on the lowest branch of the nearest tree, watching Jacob intently from two enormous black eyes deep set within an absolute explosion of fluffy brown feathers. The bird looked soft and cuddly, but Viv was not fooled. That cotton-fluffiness hid a two-foot wingspan, and talons that could rip a fleeing squirrel in two.

She held perfectly still so as not to interrupt.

"*Venez à moi*," Jacob coaxed. "*Je vous offre une souris. Venez, venez, venez.*"

The hawk rustled its feathers and let out a lusty hoot.

Nothing else moved.

Jacob sighed and glanced over his shoulder at Viv. "*Viendras-tu?*"

"*Mais bien sûr.*" She hid her smile as she walked over to join him. "Mr. Sparrowhawk isn't responding to *come here* yet?"

The hawk let out another hoot and flew directly to Jacob's outstretched hand.

"Only in English," he answered wryly. "I think I've learned more hawk language than Athena has learned French."

"Oh?" Viv arched her brows. "And what has Athena been saying?"

"Mostly 'Why did you interrupt my day for this?' and 'You lied about having a mouse in your pocket, I'm not falling for your tricks.'"

"You scoundrel," she scolded him. "One should always carry a mouse in one's pocket."

He brightened. "Do you have a mouse on you?"

"Of course." Viv lifted her bulging reticule.

He clutched his free hand to his chest. "See that, Athena? I told you the perfect woman exists. She is both our fantasies come to life."

Viv was overcome with the desire to kiss Jacob right then and there. She restrained herself out of respect for Athena. Today Viv had been jesting. There was not in fact a mouse inside her reticule. Only Sally. Maintaining a safe distance was perhaps the wiser course.

"*Envolez-vous!*" Jacob told the hawk.

Athena stared at him in silence, then let out an ear-splitting shriek.

"Oh, go off to bed, then." He gave his wrist a flick.

The hawk flapped her wings, hovering inches above Jacob's unprotected fingers, then soared up into the sky before banking hard and circling back to swoop inside the upper bird-window of the barn.

Jacob brushed off his hands. "What can I do for you?"

"I came to do something for *you*."

His eyes sparkled. "Does it involve kissing?"

"No," she said firmly. "No kissing until Quentin is safe and sound."

Jacob's eyes widened with interest. "And then we'll enjoy unlimited kissing?"

"Don't make assumptions," she said haughtily, then grinned. "Yes. I do plan to enjoy it."

"How do I know if I will?" he asked, all innocence. "Perhaps I forgot what our previous kisses were like. A small reminder would help to reorient me. Maybe a taste of tongue, then perhaps a little squeeze or two of your—"

"I'm only giving in to shut you up," she informed him as she pressed her lips to his.

"Mmrmph," was the only response, his lips smashing against hers as he wrapped his arms about her and hauled her close.

The next thing Viv knew, her spine pressed against the trunk of a tree, while the front of her body was plastered against an equally strong and hard surface. If they weren't standing in full view of anyone peering out the rear windows, she would take this opportunity to run her hands over Jacob's hot muscled form. Perhaps indulge in a squeeze or two of his derrière, and pretend she thought that was what he had been asking for.

With regret, she broke the kiss and slipped out of his embrace.

Before he could tempt her into another kiss, she lifted her heavy reticule. "Hold out your hand."

"I don't eat mice," he told her solemnly. "But do you know what I *could* eat?"

She ignored him and dumped the newest contents of her reticule into his palm.

Two twine-wrapped stacks of freshly cut white cardstock tumbled into his hand.

His brow furrowed. "What's this?"

"Don't tell me the great poet forgot how to read," she teased.

"Are these...calling cards?" He turned over the first stack and read aloud, "*Jacob Wynchester, Poet*. Vivian, I told you—"

"Look at the other one."

He turned over the second stack. "*Jacob Wynchester, Animal Trainer.*"

"They're both you," she explained. "Two sides of the same man. Use them or not, but be proud of who you are."

He made a face. "The public may laud Sir Gareth Jallow, but absolutely no one cares what I do in my barn."

"Your happy clients do," she reminded him. "But that's not why you do it, is it?"

He folded his arms over his chest. "This is where you take one glance at me speaking French to a hawk, and suddenly you can decipher all the secrets locked inside my heart?"

"I didn't need to see the hawk," she answered. "You tame the most dangerous animals in the wild and bend them to your will because you *can't* do so to the ruling class in the real world. Dominance over animals, rehabilitating the hurt, training the ignored...That is how you take back your power and prove to yourself you can control at least part of your world."

"That...is a good guess." He lowered his arms. "I don't think I've ever analyzed my motives before. Now that you've put it like that, it's hard not to read it that way. I've always wanted to provide support and shelter to strays like me who wouldn't otherwise have safe homes."

"It's noble."

"It's not naïve?"

"Then we both are," she told him. "It took a while for me to see how alike we are. We believe that determination and hard work are enough to effect meaningful change. I'm trying to change the world one stage performance at a time, whilst you do it with the aid of your woodland creatures whenever anyone has a problem that needs resolving."

"Hidden inside a barn or behind a pseudonym," he added self-deprecatingly.

She pointed at the calling cards in his hands. "You don't have to hide if you don't want to."

He seemed to consider this, then tucked the still-knotted cards out of sight in his pocket before reaching for her hands. "Would you rather kiss an animal trainer or a poet?"

"I don't have to choose. I get to have both, every time I kiss Jacob Wynchester."

He lifted her fingers to his lips. "All I want is to give you everything you dream of."

"I dream of giving myself whatever I want, through hard work and pure gumption."

"You could do that," he agreed, still kissing her fingers. "But you don't have to. There's an option called being part of a team, in which both parties can rely on the other."

"Gasp," she said blankly. "Never heard of it."

He nodded. "I made it up myself. I shall call the phenomenon... 'friendship.'"

"Humph. Do you kiss all your friends' fingertips?"

"Just Byron's," he answered, blinking angelically at her roll of the eyes. He lowered his voice. "I've an idea. You and I can share a special title, provisionally called 'Friendship with kissing and other unmentionable delights.' I warn you, it is a gateway to ever more decadent highs."

She raised her brows. "*Un*mentionable delights, you say? I thought you were a poet. Never say you lack the words to express yourself."

"Oh, I can express anything you wish me to express," he assured her. "I can express all night long. If you need my ejaculations verbally, I do require three to six working weeks per stanza to properly draft and revise the word choice and rhythm. But if expressing myself with my body counts, I'd be happy to lay you down right here on this grass...Or incline against this tree..."

"I am tempted," she admitted. "But I cannot think about romance while Quentin is still held hostage somewhere."

"Could you think about courtship after he's safe?" Jacob asked. "That is, might I woo you with the intention of something more permanent?"

She closed her mouth. Of course not. It was against her rules. Then again, she was the one who had written that rule. And as he'd pointed out...some words were meant to be edited. Why prevent the possibility of a happy ending?

"Find Quentin," she said, "and then I will be ready to consider a suitor."

"Specifically me?" Jacob prompted, brown eyes sparkling.

She kissed him. "Try your best."

28

As much as Jacob wished he could stay in the rear garden kissing Vivian all day, the family's other cases also needed him. He sent Tiglet to the dockyard with Kuni, dispatched Piffle, the crow, to a rooftop in Billingsgate with an urgent message for Graham, and accompanied the voles to the Custom House to assist with Tommy and Philippa's mission.

None of it truly received his full attention.

Even as he coordinated the polecats and the mongoose, his mind remained with Vivian, and their stolen moments in the garden. She had agreed to let him woo her! Hopefully. Conditionally. Just as soon as he and his siblings rescued her cousin.

Jacob had already been anxious to find Quentin, but now he was even more eager. Unfortunately, their best leads were proving slow. Leisterdale possessed several cottages and hunting lodges throughout England. Although they'd managed to place an informant to watch each location, amassing a team to infiltrate and search each site in person was far from achievable with their current resources.

Complicating matters was the simple fact that Leisterdale needn't house his hostage on one of his own properties at all. Restraining an eighteen-year-old in an ordinary inn would not go unnoticed for long, but the marquess had more than enough spare coin to rent rooms or even a whole house for the purpose, using a false name to avoid detection. If Jacob had managed to hide his pseudonym from the entire world for years on end, Leisterdale would have no problem paying rent through a third party until Parliament voted against suffrage.

Therefore, they were prioritizing targets. Leisterdale had to communicate with whichever lackey was holding Quentin captive. Informants followed the marquess, his employees, and his associates. Intercepted messages and listened to conversations at his club. Searched Leisterdale's financial records and business dealings.

Jacob had no doubt there was bound to be a breakthrough very soon. And when that happened, he intended to be ready. Not only to save his client's cousin, but also to woo Vivian.

He released the last of the ospreys, then leaned his shoulders against the side of the barn. He pulled out the two stacks of calling cards Vivian had commissioned for him.

JACOB WYNCHESTER, ANIMAL TRAINER

That was self-evident. He had not advertised his services outside of the family because there was barely enough time to manage his rescues and the upkeep and training and the family's many missions. Calling cards were a sweet idea, but he wouldn't be needing them.

He slid the first stack back into his pocket and turned his gaze to the other.

JACOB WYNCHESTER, POET

Well...that one was certainly less self-evident. Outside of the family and Jacob's poetry group, the only people who knew he'd even attempted to string a few words together were the publishers who had repeatedly declined to work with him over the past decade. He continued to send an inquiry once or twice a year in his own name, but all that ever generated was more kindling for the fire.

When he'd invented Sir Gareth Jallow, Jacob hadn't expected much to come of it. Landing the first publisher he queried had been an ironic surprise. Even then, he'd expected a printing of a few hundred copies, most of which would languish unsold. After which, even a fake "Sir" wouldn't be offered a second contract.

Jacob had planned to purchase five copies of his own pseudonymous poetry collection and gift them to his then-unwed siblings at Christmastide. He'd regale them with the humorous tale of how he'd done everything possible to get published but found no future in it.

Marjorie would have immediately forged a duplicate book with Jacob's name instead of Jallow's. Elizabeth would have wasted no time unsheathing her sword to knight Jacob properly so that the pseudonym wasn't a complete lie. Chloe would have hugged him and said she viscerally understood what it was like to put yourself out there again and again, only to be overlooked. Tommy would have offered him a conciliatory pie. Graham would have been the only one who attempted to read any of the poems.

None of that had happened.

Instead of the fizzle Jacob had been expecting, Sir Gareth shot to instant fame. A second, larger printing later that year. Months later, a third. Weeks later, a fourth. By Christmastide, his siblings already owned copies of Jallow's book, and the opportunity for a *haha-look-at-this-silly-thing-I-did* unveiling was no longer possible.

The longer he waited, the less likely he could ever come clean.

It was a lie all of London believed. Then a lie all of England believed. A lie so big it felt like it was happening to someone else. Perhaps separating himself from his nom de plume was Jacob's way of coping with the unexpected consequences of what had seemed like an insignificant deception. *He* wasn't a famous writer. Sir Gareth Jallow was.

Except the calling cards in his hands read, *Jacob Wynchester, Poet.*

He wondered what Vivian expected him to do about it. In his shoes, she probably would send out ten poems a day to every single publisher in Britain until they published her bloody poetry or committed her to an asylum.

Every so often, Jacob sent fresh work in his own name to Jallow's publisher, who didn't read a word of it. Jacob knew this to be true, because the same poems in his solicitation later appeared in Jallow's subsequent anthology, and no one at the publishing house so much as raised an eyebrow.

Maybe written queries were the wrong approach. His publisher had been begging to meet Sir Gareth for years. Mr. Pagett wouldn't be expecting Jacob of course, but they'd exchanged so many letters over the years, Jacob felt like he knew his publisher. Mr. Pagett seemed a friendly sort.

Perhaps all Jacob needed to do to stand out was to step up and meet with him in person. Face his fears.

He glanced at his pocket watch. Two hours until Zeus, the mastiff, and Hippogriff, the goshawk, would be needed for Elizabeth and Stephen's newest mission. Technically enough time to walk the two and a half miles each way to meet with Pagett, if the publisher were available and Jacob were granted prompt access. A wait was more likely. If he was going to go, he needed swifter transportation.

Before he could talk himself out of it, Jacob saddled Sheepshanks and set off. Upon arrival, he tied his horse at the closest available iron post, then strode up to the publisher's huge front doors.

Belatedly, Jacob realized he might have given a better first impression if he'd dressed in his dinner-soirée best. But it was three o'clock in the afternoon on Fleet Street, not the twilit ballrooms of Almack's. His clean buckskins, tan waistcoat, and trim blue coat tailored to his form would have been more impressive if he'd remembered to take off his leather apron.

He tossed the apron behind a bush before he knocked on the door.

A white lad with blond hair and tortoiseshell spectacles swung open the door with a welcoming smile...that faded upon sight of Jacob.

"We're not buying anything," said the lad.

"I'm not selling anything."

"We're not hiring new employees, either."

"I'm not applying for a post. I'm here to see Mr. Pagett. Can you take me to him, please?"

"He's not receiving at the moment."

"You didn't ask him."

"I'm authorized to use my good judgment." The lad began to close the door.

Jacob blocked it with his boot. "Please. My name is—"

"Mr. Pagett is too busy to entertain presumptuous strangers. Now, if you'll kindly step aside?"

Jacob did not step aside. A bolt of stubbornness stiffened his spine. "I'm not a stranger. You don't even know my name. I receive holiday greetings every year from Mr. and Mrs. Pagett, full of anecdotes about their daughter's new poodle and their—"

The lad laughed harshly. "As Mr. Pagett's apprentice, I handle his correspondence myself. I am certain he has sent no such thing to the likes of you. Now, if you'll allow me to return to my post—"

Footsteps rushed up from behind Jacob, heralding a virago in a raffish green bonnet.

"If you were at all competent in your post, you would have recognized that you were in the presence of a great writer, perhaps the finest poet England has ever known—"

"*Vivian?*" Jacob blurted out in surprise and horror. "What the devil are you doing here?"

She winced. "I—"

Taking advantage of the momentary distraction, the lad shoved Jacob's chest, pushing him off balance. The apprentice slammed the door shut in both their faces, leaving Jacob and Vivian abandoned on the exterior step.

"He put his hands on you," she spluttered. "He pushed you! I saw it!"

Jacob ground his teeth and wished he'd fallen into a bottomless hole. As if it weren't mortifying enough to be disrespected by his own publisher, Vivian had witnessed the entire encounter. Including the humiliating moment the most successful poet in Britain had been pushed around by a snot-nosed lad, as though Jacob were a mangy stray nosing around for scraps.

There was *fail spectacularly*, and then there was…*this*.

"What the devil," he repeated through clenched teeth, "are you doing here?"

She held up a sheaf of parchment. "I ran out of paper whilst enumerating my production suggestions for the manager of the Olympic Theatre. As I was exiting that stationer's shop"—she pointed over her shoulder—"I glimpsed you here."

He closed his eyes.

"I fully confess I should not have eavesdropped," she said quickly. "I just…It occurred to me that you might be using the new calling cards for the first time, and I didn't want to miss the moment."

"We didn't get that far," Jacob said dryly.

"Did you tell him you were Sir Gareth Jallow?"

He held up the calling cards. "I'm not Jallow, remember?"

"That's right. You deserve to make it as yourself." She twined her fingers with his. "Why don't you duck around the corner for a moment? That way, you can deny any knowledge of how some publisher's young assistant was beaten into a whimpering mess by a woman."

Jacob let out an angry breath and felt a fragment of his embarrassment vanish with it. To Vivian's eyes, he hadn't been summarily humiliated by a lad almost half his age. In her eyes, Jacob was a hero. A brave warrior daring to show his face where it was not wanted. Unafraid to face his fears, to confront the obstacles in his path.

But he didn't want to be the loser who tried and failed.

He wanted to be the hero worthy of capturing her heart.

29

As much as Viv yearned to bang on the publisher's door until the scornful apprentice reappeared so she could brain him with her boot, a stint in gaol for assaulting an Englishman would not improve her circumstances or Jacob's.

So she gnashed her teeth, clenched her fists, and furiously scripted a satisfying alternate ending in her head as they rode together to the Wynchester residence.

> **Viv**: Do you know who you've disrespected?
>
> **Publisher**: [in dawning horror] Sir Gareth Jallow?
>
> **Viv**: Mr. Jacob Wynchester!
>
> **Spontaneous flock of Demeraran chickens**: [pecks holes in every sheet of paper and gums up every printing press with rivers of chicken shite]

Outwardly, Jacob voiced no anger or even mentioned what had happened. A casual onlooker might have thought him unbothered—or at least worn down to apathy after a lifetime of worse incidents—but Viv was close enough to feel the stiffness in his spine and the tightly coiled tautness of his muscles.

If that hateful wretch had only known whom he was speaking to! Of course, having to be a prize-winning poet of nationwide fame in order to be treated like a human was just as heinous. If the bar for acceptance was so high that even Sir Gareth had doors slammed in his face, how could anyone else have the ghost of a chance?

As Jacob handed Viv down from the horse, a suspicion formed.

"When you arranged for my play to be performed, what specifically did you say about the playwright?"

"That you are very talented and that they would be fools not to host your debut."

"You said that about Miss Vivian Henry?" she asked as she followed him up to the house. "Or 'V. Henry,' scribe of undisclosed sex who will be assumed to be masculine?"

"I praised Miss Vivian Henry."

And the theater manager had said yes?

"What else did you say about me?" she insisted. "Do they know—"

"I did not lie," he replied evenly. "If your question is whether I preemptively described you as a formerly enslaved immigrant Black female maid-of-all-work and advice columnist from Demerara, the answer is no, those topics didn't come up. In the interest of expediency, I refrained from unnecessarily volunteering an overabundance of irrelevant details."

"Who I am is *very* relevant," Viv said. "It's a play about equality and suffrage. I'm uniquely qualified to depict the reality of—"

Jacob spun around on the front step.

"At the time, I wanted them to say *yes*," he burst out. "If you prefer, I can dash off a letter right now detailing all the ways you are not the sort of person those in power usually lend a public stage to, and that they ought to rethink their decision. At which point, he will cancel the whole thing. Is that what you want?"

"No," she admitted in a small voice.

Without Jacob's aid—and a few crucial omissions—Viv wouldn't have this opportunity at all, and she knew it. Her stage debut might not be unfolding the way it did in her dreams, but she was intelligent enough to know that now that it was done, the only path was forward.

"All I wanted was to give you a chance," Jacob said tightly.

"I know," she said. "You took a risk mentioning my gender at all. The female playwrights who do exist do not much resemble me."

"Your gender is not the risk. Suffrage is. The subject matter of your play may endanger the theater's future. Ordinary civilians are being massacred on the street for wanting the right to vote. Participating in this performance may be seen as the equivalent of taking up arms against the government and the aristocracy."

That was true, too. Putting on a pro-suffrage play written by a playwright of any color or sex would be wildly polemic, to say the least. The theater manager wasn't doing a simple favor in the name of nepotism. He was committing an act of sedition.

This one-night performance could very well alienate the wealthier half of the clientele. The manager could be ruined, and his entire theater forced to close permanently, all because a few stage actors had dared to repeat words Viv had written.

Her play had more than potential. It had *power*.

All thanks to Jacob using his own privilege, and measuring how far he could push on the first step. He'd given her a three-hour show. It was up to her to make the most of it.

Mr. Randall opened the front door. "Welcome home. There are cinnamon-raisin cakes in the oven."

Viv appreciated the innocuous new subject to latch on to. She realized she and Jacob had been standing on the front step arguing for several minutes. The butler must have waited for a lull in the debate rather than awkwardly interrupt them.

"Whatever you're paying him, it isn't enough," she murmured to Jacob.

"I gave the entire household a raise in salary last week."

"And we're always open to more." Mr. Randall winked at Viv.

"You're welcome here any time, Miss Henry."

She grinned at him.

"Shall I ring for those cakes?" the butler asked.

"I don't have time for a biscuit," said Jacob. "I have to get Hippogriff and Zeus to Elizabeth and Stephen."

"Shall I go with you?" Viv asked.

His deep brown eyes warmed, and he offered her his arm without hesitation.

Zeus turned out to be an enormous mastiff who weighed twice as much as Viv. Nonetheless, he seemed to think he was a tiny lapdog.

Jacob grinned at her from the opposite side of the carriage as they navigated the narrow dirt roads. "Zeus likes you! You still have all your limbs. Well done."

"He's drooling a puddle into my skirts," she said repressively, the severity of which was ruined by the fact that she hadn't yet stopped petting him. Every time she scratched behind the mastiff's ears, his tongue lolled out of his mouth and he whacked Jacob in the legs with his strong beige tail.

"Remember," Jacob said as the carriage pulled up at an overgrown field across from a busy warehouse. "We're not to stay. We're only to ensure the animals are in place—"

"I remember," Viv said. "It was a fifteen-minute carriage ride, and you explained the plan in great detail. Hippogriff will fly home on his own, and Elizabeth will handle Zeus."

"Whatever you do," he added, "don't go anywhere near Stephen. Or go anywhere Stephen might have also gone. Around him, cushions might be filled with poison darts and the floor might turn to lava."

She gave the mastiff another scratch. "Will Zeus be safe?"

"He'll be the only one left standing," Jacob promised. "Stephen won't even need his machines."

"Then why go through the trouble of sneaking them in and installing them?"

"Panache." Jacob gave a dramatic shudder. "You should see what he wants to do to my barn."

She snorted. "You would never let him anywhere near your—"

"There's the sign!" He pointed at a thin column of green smoke rising from the opposite side of the roof.

"How did they turn smoke *green*?" Viv asked in awe.

"Stephen and his devices," Jacob said with a fond shake of his head. "Having a mad genius in the family can be quite useful."

"What do we do?"

"We? Nothing. It's Zeus and Hippogriff's battle now." He flung open the carriage door and released the hawk into the sky.

Zeus bounded out onto the field. Hippogriff soared up, dove straight through the green smoke, and disappeared. For a dog the size of a pony, Zeus was surprisingly silent as he tore off over the tall grass and leapt through an open ground-floor window.

"Good Lord," Viv breathed. "I cannot imagine the havoc that dog is wreaking right now."

"Stephen and Elizabeth are causing even more," Jacob said confidently as he gave the signal for the driver to turn the carriage back toward town.

Viv expected Jacob to gaze out the window at whatever chaos they might glimpse as they drove away. Instead, he laced his hands behind his neck and stretched out his legs, crossing them at the ankle.

He looked positively delicious. Viv, on the other hand, was a wrinkled mess of drool and dog hair. It was a good thing she'd told him there'd be no more courting until her cousin had been rescued, or she'd be tempted to take a page from Zeus's book and leap onto Jacob's lap.

Disheveled or not, he'd probably still let her.

He was dangerous like that.

"So," he said. "In the mood for a cinnamon-raisin cake?"

Her stomach growled. Or maybe those were the butterflies in her belly. Could imaginary butterflies growl? Jacob could probably teach them to. The safest thing to do was to stay away, and not distract him from finding Quentin.

But once her cousin was home, all bets were off. She *dared* Jacob to lounge nonchalantly in front of her then and see what happened!

He raised his eyebrows seductively. "If cinnamon-raisin is not to your liking, I can offer you—"

"The Duke of Faircliffe," she blurted out.

Jacob blinked. "Not what I had in mind."

"He—Chloe—invited me back to help with their speeches. His Grace's speeches. I have three pages of notes in my reticule that I could send by post, but they're expecting me to discuss each point in person—"

"All right, all right." Jacob's expression was amused, rather than irritated. He slid the panel to inform the driver of the new destination. "When you're done helping, have them send you wherever you need to go in one of their carriages."

"I can walk home," she said.

"I know you can. But you shouldn't have to when your feet are tired from all the walking you already did today. If you're shy about ordering a duke about, I'll send this carriage back to you as soon as I arrive home."

This idea cheered Viv up immensely. "I can order a duke around?"

"Faircliffe responds appropriately to reasonable requests. And unreasonable ones, if his wife or child is asking. There's nothing he wouldn't do for Chloe and Dorian."

"What about you? Do you want children someday?" Viv bit her tongue as soon as the question was out. No courting meant more than no kisses. It meant no asking questions that betrayed her hope for marital compatibility in the future.

Jacob took a long moment to consider the question before replying.

"I used to think the answer was no," he said at last. "I have a large family already, not to mention hordes of animals that pass in and out of my barn every year. A baby is a tremendous responsibility. Humans are the only species that's completely helpless for years."

"I've seen how protective you are of wildcats and pythons," Viv acknowledged.

"And those can take care of themselves," he agreed. "I guess they'd have to. It would be hard not to spend every minute watching over my baby."

"That's impossible for anyone to do. You need sleep, for one. Plus, there are clients who need your help with missions."

"You see my conundrum."

"You could hire a nanny," she suggested.

"I want an army of nannies. Round-the-clock shifts. Armed with playthings and sweetmeats."

"So you have thought about it. Presumably, this theoretical baby would not drop into your arms from a crane or spring forth from the sea?"

"A wife. Yes. One does tend to lead to the other." He tilted his head. "Unless I were to adopt, which I am not opposed to. Our home does have an awful lot of empty bedchambers to fill."

"You wish to avoid marriage altogether?"

"Not at all," he said softly. "I would very much like a wife. Whether she'd want…"

The carriage stopped suddenly, throwing them off-balance.

He turned toward the window. "What in the...Why, the duke's coach just stopped in front of ours! His driver halted so abruptly, our horses nearly trampled into their wheels. What the devil is Faircliffe about?"

"We arrived at the same time," said Viv. "Maybe he didn't see us behind him. Is the door to their home wide open? I see—"

Chloe.

The Duchess of Faircliffe was up ahead. She'd fled from her house in stocking feet with her infant clutched in her arms, her face pale as milk and her brown eyes wild.

Viv scrambled from the carriage as fast as she could, with Jacob right behind her.

"Chloe," she called out. "Are you all right?"

A foolish question. The duchess was very far from all right.

Faircliffe was faster, sprinting across the grass to gather his wife and baby in his arms. He was clearly as lost as Viv and Jacob were, but he wrapped his arms around Chloe and pressed a kiss to the top of her bare head, his face confused and his eyes afraid.

A maid trudged out the door, sobbing, a valise in her hand and her gaze never leaving her shoes.

"Chloe, what's going on?" Faircliffe murmured, his tone calm but urgent. "Where's Hastings?"

"He quit his post," said the maid without looking up. "I was dismissed from mine."

"Hastings *quit*?" Faircliffe goggled at the maid. "He's been butler here since I was a child. Chloe, darling, please. What on earth has happened?"

"Take Dory," she mumbled. "Hold him tight."

Faircliffe did as instructed. Viv and Jacob flanked his sides.

"This is what happened." Chloe pulled a folded piece of parchment from her bosom. The paper rattled in her shaking fingers as she handed it to Viv. "You read it. I can't look at that again."

The two men crowded over Viv's shoulders as she unfolded the note.

You're lucky the cradle was empty.
If you don't want it to stay that way,
no more rhetoric about voting reform.

Viv's mouth fell open.

"Where did you find this?" Faircliffe demanded, his voice as shaky as Chloe's fingers.

"In Dory's cradle." Tears streamed down her cheeks. "Leisterdale was in our *home*. In Dory's *nursery*. If I hadn't been taking a nap with the baby in our room..."

Dory gurgled, oblivious to the shocked adults surrounding him.

"I don't understand," said Viv. "How did the kidnapper get inside your house?"

"He said 'May I come in?'" Chloe answered bitterly. "And our butler let him in."

"Hastings let a madman walk into our home?" Faircliffe said in disbelief.

"Let me guess," Jacob said, his tone ironic. "Your unwelcome visitor didn't 'look' like an undesirable. He looked like what he is: a lord. White, wealthy, male, upper-class accent...How am I doing?"

Chloe took an unsteady breath. "That's exactly it. Leisterdale didn't even offer a calling card. To our butler's credit, Hastings left him in the parlor while he went to find me. Only the soulless blackguard didn't stay there. Leisterdale strolled through our home as if he owned it. And then when *this* worthless creature—"

The maid cringed.

"—passed him in the corridor, he asked bold as brass where to find the nursery, and she *told* him. Then carried on her way as if nothing at all was amiss."

"He seemed important," she mumbled. "Like you said, a lord or some such. I reckoned he was a friend of Your Graces, if he had the run of the house like that."

"You think we're the sort of parents who would grant strange men access to Dory's nursery, as long as they have a title?"

"I don't know, Your Grace. I *wasn't* thinking. He was such a fine gentleman, and I just…wanted to be helpful."

"You wanted to help a kidnapper, you mean?" Chloe's face was bright red.

The maid burst into tears and hobbled down the road, dragging her valise after her.

"Wait," Viv called out to stop her.

"I'm sacked," the maid called out without slowing. "They can keep my last month's wages."

"Run after her," Viv told Jacob.

"No, let her go." Chloe pressed her wet cheek against her baby's soft night rail. "I want nothing to do with her."

"You'd better," said Viv.

Chloe's eyes flashed. "Who do you think you are to tell me how I should feel and act when my flesh and blood was…almost…kidnapped."

Her sharp voice trailed off as she realized Viv had a very good idea indeed how that might feel.

"I know you're angry and scared," Viv said softly. "But you can't send away the only eyewitnesses to Leisterdale's latest attempted abduction."

"Shite." Jacob took off running after the maid.

"Find Hastings, too!" called out Faircliffe.

Without slowing, Jacob touched his hand to his chest and lifted his fingers to the sky.

Viv reread the ominous note. She barely restrained herself from crumpling the threat in her fist.

Jacob was one of the most famous poets in England, and he wasn't allowed across the threshold of his own publisher.

Whereas some well-heeled blackmailer with the right clothes, color, and accent was allowed to waltz into a duke's town home and nearly steal a baby without anyone blinking.

30

Õiv and the Wynchesters gathered downstairs in the drawing room to interview the Faircliffes' maid for future testimony against Leisterdale.

The maid sobbed through the entire process. Hannah was desperate to help but felt useless. She couldn't even confirm the villain's identity. "I'm so sorry. I failed the entire family. I never glanced up at the visitor's eyes or even looked at him directly."

"The blackguard was probably counting on that," Marjorie said in disgust. "Lords are used to servants shrinking and cowing before him, heads lowered in deference the entire time."

Hannah nodded. "The only thing I saw were his boots."

"Let me guess." Stephen's lip curled. "Champagne-shined?"

"Brand-new," Hannah answered. "As if they'd barely been worn."

"One must look one's best when kidnapping a baby," Tommy said with contempt. "He probably purchases a new ensemble every day and then throws it out, so that he's always more fashionable than everyone around him."

Chloe's forehead creased. "Actually, no, that can't be right. Leisterdale's clothing is expensive, of course, but he's hardly the popinjay of Parliament. He hasn't changed his wardrobe in years."

"Perhaps he sent a footman or other lackey?" guessed Stephen.

Tommy shook her head. "A servant doesn't move with the same bearing as a lord."

Viv turned back to Hannah. "You didn't look closely, but you must have some idea of the man's body shape or a vague sense of whether he was young or old."

She made a face. "Medium age and medium body?"

Marjorie sighed at the still-blank open page of her sketchbook. "Not tall or short, or fat or thin, or old or young. Just new shoes and a limp."

Hannah frowned in confusion. "Limp?"

"Leisterdale has a touch of gout," Chloe explained. "His limp isn't pronounced, but if you were staring at his feet, you must have noticed."

"No limp," Hannah said with renewed confidence. "He was in excellent form. He moved so lightly, he could have been a fencer."

This time, the Wynchesters exchanged concerned glances. As meager as the description was, it did not match Leisterdale.

"Maybe…his co-conspirator is also a lord?" Viv guessed.

"Describe the boots," Tommy said suddenly. "Marjorie will sketch them. I know all the best bootmakers. One of them will recognize their own work."

Marjorie's pencil flew over her paper. Soon, she ripped the completed sheet from the sketchbook and handed it to Tommy, who tilted her head as she considered the craftsmanship.

"Thank you, Hannah," said Faircliffe. "You can go now. One of our carriages is waiting out front to take you to a boardinghouse. The first month's rent has been paid in full, and your final wages are in this pouch."

The maid scrambled to her feet and made a deep curtsey. "Thank you, Your Grace. I'm so sorry. I hope you catch him. I…" She swallowed hard and then ran from the room.

"That was fair of you," Kuni said. "I'm not sure I could have forgiven her."

"She'll never have her post back," Faircliffe said grimly, "but her crime was deferring to rank rather than good judgment, which one could argue is what the working classes have been instructed to do for centuries."

"You *have* argued that," Chloe said. "Many times. Voting isn't the only reform we're hoping to make. But first things first. Would someone please—"

"I'm going now." Tommy sprang to her feet, sketch in hand. "If I hurry, I can interview the five most fashionable bootmakers before nightfall."

"Will that be enough to find Quentin before something worse happens?" Viv asked, terrified her cousin's case had reverted back to nowhere. And the villain's crimes were escalating.

The Faircliffes had just had a serious scare, but their baby was fine. Quentin, on the other hand...

"We'll get him back home safely." Jacob squeezed her hand. "I swear to you."

As he touched his free hand to his heart, all the other Wynchesters did the same. In unison, they lifted their fingertips toward the sky.

"You made that sign earlier," she told him. "What does it mean?"

"It's our way of swearing something all the way to our bones," Tommy explained. "We will not rest until your cousin is safe at home."

"Even if I have to put a sword through Leisterdale's chest myself," Elizabeth added.

Viv was unsure whether to take Elizabeth's threat at face value, but she certainly did not intend to stop her. If ever a man deserved a swift trip to hell...

Before anyone else could speak, Mr. Randall walked in with the Faircliffes' erstwhile butler, Hastings, at his side.

"Oh, thank God," the duke breathed. "Hastings will have noticed more than boots."

"Don't leave yet," Marjorie called out to Tommy. "I'll have a few more details in just a moment."

"Did you see the caller?" Viv blurted out.

The butler glanced at her quizzically. "He stood an arm's length away from me for several minutes."

"Can you describe him?" Marjorie asked.

"Late twenties, the build of an equestrian, a pompous air. About this tall"—Hastings gestured just above his own head—"with blue eyes, curling blond hair, and a close-lipped smile."

"Nose length and width?" Marjorie's pencil flew over the page. "Any bumps in the bridge, or freckles and birthmarks?"

Even without watching the sketch bloom into sight, Viv recognized every detail Hastings recalled. It was the lordling in the park who had scrubbed off her touch with a white handkerchief.

Just as Marjorie held up the sketch for the room to see, Viv ground out, "Lord Uppington."

"'My father might have done it,'" Chloe parroted in a mocking falsetto. "Scoundrel. It was him the whole time."

"Or both of them," Viv added.

"Hastings, please take your post back," said Faircliffe. "We clearly need you."

"And no one needs Lord Uppington," Elizabeth said. "I'll sharpen my sword."

"Make it two," Jacob said. "Whether they're working together or not, the Marquess of Leisterdale groomed his son to follow in his footsteps. Both men wish to rule society from a golden throne, rather than be beholden to those they feel beneath them."

"Why wasn't this a priority?" Viv whirled toward Graham in anger. "You said you had spies following Leisterdale's known associates. Wouldn't his despicable *son* count?"

"I did have Uppington followed," Graham protested, then winced.

"As much as we could. I told you, we've been stretched past our breaking point. Because we'd been checking ships' manifests for signs of Quentin, I just found out an hour ago that the date of Uppington's return to England was misquoted in the newspaper. But it is true that since his arrival, he's spent every moment drinking with his friends, visiting his mistress, and promenading in Hyde Park."

"Wait. Uppington's date of return was misprinted by how much?"

Graham handed her a folded missive from his breast pocket. "Two months. He spent that time at a friend's home in York before coming to London, which is why no one realized he was back."

"Two *months*?" Viv repeated, staring at the message. "Uppington had plenty of time to write to my column and plot his burglary and blackmail. There was no need to be in London until he was ready to act."

"It also explains the mistaken identity," Jacob said. "After living an ocean away for several years, no wonder the earl believed Quentin to be Horace in the first place," Jacob said. "Uppington wasn't around when Tommy played the baron, so he wouldn't know Quentin looks nothing like Horace."

Graham nodded. "After abducting a hostage, Uppington couldn't run around asking strange questions about a baron no one else had thought about in years. Given the stakes, he wouldn't have wanted to look ignorant *or* suspicious."

"Yes, yes, your deductions are brilliant," Viv burst out. "But now that we know Lord Uppington has Quentin, why are we still standing here? Shouldn't we be searching his residence?"

"We did so weeks ago. Nothing there. I've kept his lodgings under watch, but so far my informants haven't reported anything amiss. The moment I receive word of the slightest hint of suspicious activity—"

Viv rubbed her temples, then froze. "What about Miss Yates, the best-paid courtesan in London? Did we search *her* residence?"

Graham's eyes widened.

"How did you miss that?" she burst out.

He stepped back, hands raised. "We believed our enemy to be his father, remember? Nonetheless, I did search the son's residence, and planned to extend the hunt beyond Leisterdale's confederates to anyone who had ever been acquainted with any of his cronies. Then the Boyton affair went sideways, which took my best scouts. The next day, I had to divert even more resources when the Landrake and Merther cases imploded across town—"

"All right, there was no one to help," Viv said, her heart beating so fast she was dizzy. "Meanwhile, Uppington has been visiting Miss Yates regularly? It's the perfect cover. The opposite of suspicious—clandestine visits to a well-paid mistress is what the world expects of a lord. What better place to conceal a hostage? Quentin *must* be inside that house."

The entire family sprang to their feet at once. "Let's go and get him."

31

Oiv spun toward the corridor leading to the Wynchesters' front door. With luck, the carriage was ready and waiting.

"We can't all show up at once like a big mob," Philippa warned.

"Why the devil not?" Chloe demanded. "That's where Uppington is keeping Vivian's cousin hostage, and likely where he planned to take my son!"

"What pretext should we use?" asked Adrian.

"No pretext." Elizabeth gripped the handle of her sword stick. "We burn the place to the ground."

"After we remove Quentin safely," Jacob said firmly.

"Maybe we *should* go as a riotous mob," Stephen said slowly. "The confusion could help. Whoever answers our knock won't be expecting to find a duke, a duchess, a baby, a Balcovian warrioress, a sword-wielding berserker, a Demeraran playwright, an acrobat, five hundred wild ferrets—"

"We take your point," said Chloe. "Let's do it."

"Riotous mobs are dangerous places to be," Philippa reminded them all. "After Peterloo, we'll be lucky if we make it up to the door en masse before authorities descend upon us to cut us down."

"Authorities!" exclaimed Tommy. "Exactly what we need. I'll meet you in the carriage!"

She sprinted from the room before anyone could ask questions.

"We're about to break all the rules we can think of," Jacob warned

Viv in a soft murmur. "And probably several laws. Are you all right with this?"

Her hands shook, but her voice was steady. "To get my cousin back safely, I'll break anything I have to."

Within minutes, they were piling into a trio of carriages. Chloe would stay inside the third one with her baby while the others undertook the rescue mission.

"How did your stable hands ready the coaches so quickly?" Viv asked Jacob in surprise.

"I've had them stay ready since the kidnapping attempt on Dorian," he explained. "I wanted to ensure we would be prepared for anything at a moment's notice."

"I'm coming," called Tommy. "Wait for me!"

She raced across the lawn toward the carriages dressed in a natty uniform of blue trousers, blue tailcoat with brass buttons, black hat, brown side whiskers, white cravat and gloves, and the signature ruby waistcoat of the Bow Street Horse Patrol.

"Isn't the Horse Patrol meant to prevent highway robbery?" asked Elizabeth.

"This knave stole Vivian's cousin," Tommy replied as she launched herself into the coach. "We intend to put a stop to it."

When the trio of carriages pulled up on South Street where Miss Yates lived, the horses barely had time to slow before the Wynchester family began spilling out of their coaches like dice from a cup.

They indeed looked like a colorful mob straight out of the pages of one of Viv's plays. Instead of painting them as the villains, however, this time Viv couldn't be more pleased to have them on her side. She was proud to be amongst them.

From the first moment, they'd welcomed her with open arms and without hesitation. Perhaps that itself had contributed to her unease. Viv was so accustomed to being ignored or ridiculed or punished that she perceived kindness as a sly trick meant to lower her habitual defenses so that the inevitable blow could strike harder.

She admired the Wynchesters' big hearts and indefatigable teamwork in the pursuit of justice. They knew the world was unfairly tilted in their favor, so they used their wealth and privilege to lift up others however they could. No matter what it cost them.

Her feet bolted across the pavement, along with ten other pairs of boots and the paws of a gigantic mastiff, who had been given some of Quentin's old clothes to sniff. Overhead flapped the three-foot wingspans of a dozen screeching hawks, each diving intermittently as though ready to carry Uppington away and drop him into the sea.

Tommy dashed ahead of the pack to bang upon the door.

Elizabeth drew her sword. Twin daggers appeared in Kuni's fists. Viv retrieved her tarantula from her reticule and placed it on her shoulder.

The door opened the barest of cracks.

"Horse Patrol," chirped Tommy, and kicked in the door.

Zeus bounded in first, knocking aside whomever guarded the entrance, and likely toppling tables and chairs as he skated through the house.

The rest of the Wynchesters poured in right behind, with Viv on the front lines.

"Quentin!" She shouted until her voice grew hoarse. "Quentin!"

"You cannot barge into a private residence," stammered Miss Yates, whose countenance had gone deathly pale at the sight of them.

They were in the right spot. They just had to find him.

Viv and the other Wynchesters spread out. While most searched for Quentin, a few Wynchesters peeked beneath cushions and behind furniture for signs of the scandalous Olivebury painting in order to put a stop to the parliamentary vote manipulation altogether.

"Found it!" crowed Stephen, emerging from a side room with a rolled canvas waving in his hand.

Elizabeth pumped her sword in the air.

At the moment, Viv was more concerned about locating her cousin. He had to be here. And please God, unharmed.

Zeus clattered into the kitchen and gave a mighty woof so loud it shook the walls.

Viv came running.

A cook and a maid stood with their spines flush against tall shelves of pots and spices. Both of their panicked, guilty gazes looked everywhere except at the pantry in the corner.

"Don't you dare run off," Viv growled. She took the tarantula from her shoulder and set it on the floor. "Watch them, Sally."

The maids shrieked and clutched each other.

Viv spun to the pantry and tried the door handle.

Locked.

"Quentin!" she screamed, her throat tight and raw. "Quentin, can you hear me?"

A muffled groan was barely audible on the other side.

"Out of the way," Kuni commanded.

"Quentin, get back!" Viv called, fully expecting Kuni to break down the door with one kick.

Instead, Kuni slid a hatpin and the tip of her dagger into the keyhole. In seconds, the door sprang open.

Quentin was standing on the other side, his hands tied behind his back and his mouth gagged with a handkerchief.

As his eyes widened with confusion and recognition, Viv raced forward to tug the gag from his mouth. "Are you all right?"

"My whiskers are itchy," he replied. "I haven't been able to shave all month. And my hair needs new twists. Wait, are these people… Are you with…"

His whiskers were itchy! Viv let out a choking laugh and threw her arms around him. With her sword, Elizabeth sliced through the rings of rope around his wrists. All of a sudden, after four long weeks, Viv's baby cousin was finally hugging her back.

"You're really safe," she choked out. "I was so afraid..."

"Are these really the Wynchesters?" Quentin whispered without letting go of her.

She nodded.

"Quick," he hissed frantically. "Shave me. I have to look my best!"

She lifted her disbelieving face from his chest to stare at his patchy, shaggy chin. "Quentin, I am not going to search this house for soap and a razor."

He glared at her with such adolescent *what-good-are-you* outrage that Viv knew right then and there her cousin was going to be all right.

"This reunion is sickeningly sweet," said Elizabeth, "but we should take it on the road."

Right.

Viv grabbed Quentin's hand. She hurried him out of the pantry and through the house to the waiting carriages. Or at least, tried to hurry him. Although he hadn't been tied to a chair, he'd spent several weeks in a space not much larger than a water closet, and his legs were no longer used to making large strides.

Tommy pulled the door to Miss Yates's residence shut, then launched herself into Viv's carriage just as the horses began to move.

Quentin's eyes bulged at Tommy. "Shouldn't you have made an arrest?"

"I'm not really the Horse Patrol," she replied, and peeled off her whiskers.

Quentin squealed in delight. *Squealed.* Like a happy pig.

"Tommy Wynchester?" he blurted out, slack-jawed.

"Here." She handed him the whiskers. "You need these more than I do."

"Yes, that's Tommy," Viv confirmed. "And next to me is Jacob."

Quentin leaned forward, elbows on knees and eyes bright with stars. "Do you really have a kangaroo?"

"I do not," Jacob said with a chuckle.

Quentin looked like he was going to cry.

"I do have dozens of trained raptors, scores of venomous snakes, several wildcats, and an antbear my brother and I stole from the Tower of London," Jacob added.

"I knew you would!" Quentin beamed at him, then whispered, "What's an antbear?"

"I'll show you," Jacob promised.

Quentin turned to Viv with his mouth hanging open, as if seeking confirmation that she'd just heard the same three words he had heard.

"He'll really show you," she confirmed. "You'll love it."

Quentin threw his arms around her and squeezed so tight the air whooshed from her lungs. "I love *you*, Viv. I knew if anyone could bring the Wynchesters to my aid, it would be my cousin."

She hugged him back as hard as she could. It was good to have him home—and even better to know that he'd never doubted her. "I missed you so much."

He released her and grinned into her face. "I bet it killed you to need anyone's help. Especially the Wynchesters."

"Vivian helped us, actually," Jacob corrected him.

Quentin's eyes widened. "Helped...you?"

"She's been assisting with clients for weeks," Tommy confirmed. "We've resolved dozens of cases thanks to your cousin's creative contingency plans."

Viv had to catch Quentin before he tumbled to the carriage floor. He gazed up at her, slack-jawed and starry-eyed.

"You have been helping the real-life Wynchesters!" he half-whispered, half-shrieked, then seemed to realize he was still inside one of their coaches. "And now I've met two of them myself! My friends are never going to believe this."

"There's more than two of us," said Jacob. "You can meet the others back at our house."

"I'm going to your house?" Quentin looked as though he might swoon.

"You're a Wynchester, aren't you?" Tommy said wryly.

Quentin started. "What do you—oh." He had the grace to look somewhat abashed. "You mean Horace. I suppose that wasn't well done of me."

"I think you've been punished more than enough for that deception," said Jacob.

Viv drew a shaky breath. "I'm sorry I didn't rescue you sooner, Quentin. I tried everything in my power. I went to the Bow Street Runners—"

"Useless," said Tommy, in her Bow Street uniform.

"Newbury's a good sort," Jacob objected.

Viv recognized that name. "He's the only one who actually listened to me. Until I came to you."

Jacob gave her fingers a squeeze, then kissed the back of her hand.

Quentin made a garbled sound, as if his head were moments away from exploding.

"How did you do it?" he demanded, awestruck. Then his face cleared. "I guess you really do know everything."

"If I've learned anything, it's that I know nothing." Viv smiled at her cousin. "I always knew I didn't have all the answers, but I believed I *ought* to have them. So I tried my best. Just like you were doing."

His expression filled with shock. "You're not angry with me for masquerading as Horace and getting kidnapped?"

"You're an idiot," she said fondly, "but a good-hearted one. I suppose I can think of worse people to emulate than the Wynchesters."

"You *can*?" Quentin stared at her.

"Within reason," she said quickly. "They're not perfect."

"Pretty close, though, with you on the team," Tommy said.

She and Jacob began talking over each other at once, detailing the ways in which Viv had aided the family in their various missions, and how it was her recollection of a line in a month-old newspaper article that had helped lead them to the right doorstep today.

"You're practically a Wynchester yourself, Viv," Quentin breathed in reverence.

"As good as family," Tommy agreed. "Her seat is next to mine in the sibling sitting room."

"In fact," said Jacob, "how would you both like to spend the night tonight, as our honored guests?"

Quentin turned pleading eyes to Viv. "Can we?"

She arched a brow at Jacob. He was a sweetheart, and he *might* be trying to ease Quentin's transition from being held hostage back to the real world.

Or Jacob might be remembering her promise that he could court her as soon as her cousin had been found.

Jacob smiled innocently.

Viv narrowed her eyes.

His smile widened.

"Better borrow a good book from Philippa," Tommy told Quentin. "I wouldn't expect to see your cousin again until well after noon tomorrow."

Quentin's eyes goggled as his head swiveled back and forth between Viv and Jacob.

"Tommy is teasing," Viv said quickly. "Er...somewhat teasing. Jacob is indeed romancing me—"

Quentin grabbed his chest and flailed against the carriage squab.

"—but I will be spending the night with you, of course. You

remain my highest priority. I doubt you've eaten or slept well since you've been gone. Why don't we take tonight to relax at home? We'll settle down on our own, then tomorrow afternoon—"

"Cousin, are you *bamming* me?" This time, Quentin's clasped hands bounced in supplication. "After a month stuck inside a pantry, I find myself making friends with real Wynchesters. I don't plan to sleep at all, lest I miss a single minute of it!"

Viv reached for his hands. "But I thought we could—"

Quentin grabbed her by the shoulders and spun her toward Jacob. "I'm willing to postpone further conversation with this Wynchester if the two of you have somewhere you'd rather be." He turned to Tommy. "I can't wait to hear every bit of the plan to rescue me. Did my clue help?"

Viv blinked. "What was your clue?"

Quentin held up his thumb proudly. "They tried to use another finger, but I made the print using the one with the scar."

Jacob raised his brows, impressed. "That was your idea?"

Viv arched one of her own. "You faint at the sight of blood."

"Which gave me time to come up with the plan," Quentin confirmed happily. "They'd pricked my index finger, so as soon as I regained consciousness, I smeared the blood onto my scarred thumb and pressed it onto the paper."

"That *was* a good clue," Tommy said admiringly. "Well done."

Quentin looked like he might explode into feathers.

"And yes, it gave us the break we needed," Jacob added. "My family wouldn't have known the significance, but your cousin put it together instantly."

"She's the smartest woman in the world," Quentin said proudly. "Except maybe for Philippa Wynchester. Will I get to meet her, too?"

"You can attend one of her reading circles if you like," Tommy said. "I'll help you with your disguise."

"Oh! And Graham? Can I meet him, too? I've collected so much intelligence for him over the years. Even more in the past few weeks. You wouldn't believe the things people say when they don't remember there's someone locked on the other side of the pantry door! For example—"

Viv and Jacob exchanged slow grins as Quentin prattled on happily to Tommy.

Although Viv had at first believed the best thing was for her and Quentin to have quiet time together tonight in the comfort and safety of their home, he did not want or need her hovering over him like a mama bird. Her cousin seemed to think her celebratory night would be better spent in Jacob's arms.

Viv wasn't used to taking Quentin's advice, but for once maybe her cousin was right.

There was a first time for everything.

32

Before he could whisk Vivian away in an attempt to enact his master plan, Jacob introduced her cousin to the rest of the Wynchester family and gave Quentin a tour of the barn.

Or tried to. Quentin wouldn't step one foot across the threshold into an enclosed area containing wildcats and venomous serpents. His own attempts at training pets had taught him wild animals were not his forte.

"You see how I ended up with the tarantula and the badger," Vivian murmured.

"Tarantula, I could understand," Jacob whispered back. "But badgers aren't venomous."

"Rufus gets quite peevish if his meals aren't served as quickly as he'd like."

"Don't we all?" Jacob answered with a grin, then turned to Quentin. "Speaking of food, I hear there are fresh pies and cakes inside. Shall we?"

All the others were gathered inside the sitting room. Quentin made Vivian point out which was "her" chair, and begged to have one assigned to him, too, if only for the night. Everyone was happy to play along.

"Oh nooo." Quentin looked as though he was going to be sick.

Vivian hurried to her cousin. "What is it?"

"I have to go home to gather my things, but I don't want to miss a single moment."

Some of the tenseness left Viv's shoulders and she rolled exasperated eyes in Jacob's direction.

"We can send a footman," he offered, amused.

"Or I can loan you what you need," said Tommy, sizing Quentin up with her eyes. "Are you feeling more dashing-rake-struck-by-ennui, or adventurous-sailor-about-to-embark-on-a-dangerous-mission?"

Quentin's eyes filled with delight.

As Tommy led him to her multiple dressing rooms filled with clothes and disguises, Quentin trailed after her like a newborn puppy.

"She's creating a monster," Vivian warned. "Now she'll never be rid of him."

"Who wants to be rid of him?" Jacob kissed her fingers again. "It's all harmless fun."

"Maybe now," she allowed. "But his abduction was hardly harmless. I don't suppose anything will happen to Uppington for all the laws he broke?"

"That depends on how successful Chloe is in convincing Uppington's mistress to testify against him, in exchange for sparing her own neck. She *was* harboring a hostage. Her servants were complicit as well."

"I can't blame the servants entirely," said Vivian. "Their livelihood depends on obeying a person with the power of depriving them of food and shelter."

"Couldn't Miss Yates make that same argument?" he pointed out.

"Not particularly. She's rich, from all accounts. And that roof over her head is in one of the fanciest neighborhoods in London."

He considered that. "Being in bed with a monster doesn't mean she's loyal to him. A lord who'd kidnap a man he believed to be a baron wouldn't hesitate to punish a mere courtesan for disobeying orders. Even if she wanted to walk away—or simply set Quentin free—she wouldn't have been able to."

"Power again," said Vivian. "Miss Yates can have anything she wants, except freedom from him."

"What do *you* want?" he asked softly. "The night is ours."

She bit her lip. "Are you certain that Quentin—"

"He's been locked in a nightmare for four weeks. Let his dreams come true tonight."

Vivian cocked her head to the side, then nodded.

Jacob cupped her cheek and rubbed the pad of his thumb against its soft warmth. With luck, a dream would come true for him, too. One in which he and Vivian spent far more than one night together.

"I have something I'd like to show you," he began haltingly. It was so important to get the next few minutes right. "But first, I have something I'd like to give you."

She folded her arms, eyes narrowing. "I'll bet you do."

"That, too," he admitted. "If and when you want it. But more important is a different sort of compatibility. Vivian, I want you to know how fervently I esteem and respect you. I can think of no greater honor than to be worthy of your time. Please indulge me by accepting a humble token that cannot begin to convey the depths of my admiration for who you are."

He held out a small rectangular package not larger than his hand, wrapped in a square of soft white silk and tied with a Balcovian pink ribbon.

Vivan's arms uncrossed to accept the parcel. Her palm bounced lightly as she felt its heft.

"If these are 'Miss Vivian Henry, playwright' calling cards," she warned, "I must warn you that I already own enough of those to paper every wall in this house."

He simply gestured for her to unwrap her gift.

She began to pluck at the pink bow, then froze with suspicion.

"If these are 'acceptance' letters from disgruntled theater managers you've browbeaten into performing my plays—"

Jacob arched his brows as if to say, *We'd know by now if you'd get on with it.*

Internally, however, every bone and vein trembled with fear that he still hadn't managed to get things right.

She unraveled the bow and tucked the ribbon into her bodice. The white silk fell away from its hidden treasure, revealing—

"Playing cards?" she exclaimed in surprise and confusion. "I do like a good game of patience, but I don't understand…"

"Look at them," he coaxed.

She handed him the scrap of silk, then held the deck to the light to view its intricate decorative pattern of limes and letters and badgers and spiders and quills and ink and theater curtains and breakfast feasts.

"You didn't purchase these," she said softly. "You commissioned them."

He held his breath.

She turned the deck over, face up in her palm. Instead of an ace, as was customary, decorative calligraphy filled the interior of the card:

> *Redeemable for the writing materials*
> *of the bearer's choice.*
> *If she so chooses.*

She snorted softly, then flipped to the next card:

> *Redeemable for the services of any member of staff*
> *to ease the bearer's burden or free the bearer's time.*
> *If she so chooses.*

Then the next:

> *Redeemable for the writing retreat of the bearer's*
> *choice: the temporary or dedicated use of a room*
> *or lodging, equipped to her specifications.*
> *If she so chooses.*

Then the next:

> *Instructions to Jacob Wynchester:*
> *Don't act. Just listen.*

She glanced up at him, her face full of questions.

He smiled hesitantly. "I didn't want to gift you something that would wear and fade with time. I want you to have whatever you need, whatever would most help. Even if—or especially if—that thing is me sitting still and shutting up."

She turned to the next card:

> *Redeemable for the services of the complete*
> *Wynchester siblings in conjunction with*
> *Philippa's extended book club,*
> *whose excellent penmanship and joint effort can*
> *produce a dozen copies of the bearer's*
> *play in two hours.*
> *If she so wishes.*

She touched her throat as a startled laugh burst free. "This would save me weeks of effort. I wouldn't even know how to choose which script to contribute."

"As fortune would have it," he said softly, "none of these cards are single-use. The ones involving me in particular can be redeemed as many times as you wish to do so."

She scanned the cards faster and faster, alternately gasping or snickering or shooting him an expression so tender, it warmed him to his toes.

He waited until she was finished before speaking again. "As with many things, you were right about me. The fatal flaw in my family is us assuming our first impulse is the right one. That because we've devised *a* solution, we must immediately execute it without further consideration."

"My assessment wasn't wrong," she said softly, "but I see now it was incomplete."

"There will always be room for improvement," he replied. "And I want you to know that I will be doing that work."

She glanced down at the cards in her hands, and fanned them across her lap, offer-side-up.

He pushed on. "I never want you to doubt again that I hear you. That I'm listening." He touched her cheek. "I long to make every moment of your life as bright and joyful as possible. But I will never again presume to know your needs or desires better than you."

She gazed up at him, her eyes unreadable.

He'd thought his lowest moment was when she'd witnessed him being rejected at the door by his own publisher. Instead, her ability to shrug off a constant barrage of *no* and keep on going had helped him realize that rejection wasn't a cause for shame. It was a badge of pride. Rejections meant you were *trying*. Not sitting at home whingeing about how lovely it would be if some miraculous fantasy were to come true, but out there in the world actively doing something about it.

"You are so talented, so tenacious, so deserving," he continued. "You are also brilliant and sweet and beautiful and loving and witty and optimistic and honorable. You're the most extraordinary woman

I've ever been blessed enough to meet. You deserve the best in life. All I can offer you is me."

She'd stolen his heart and, in return, given back pieces of himself he hadn't realized had gone missing. Confidence. Pride. Hope.

"Love, you are undeniably a whole, capable, self-sufficient person. Yet I will always be here for you, in whatever capacity you may need or wish. Just in case you'd like to face any portion of life together."

Her brown eyes shimmered.

"Keep the cards," he finished, his voice low. "Use them or don't. You'll know where to find me. In fact...might I convince you to spend the evening with me?"

She scooped up the cards and pressed them to her heart, then rewrapped them with care and placed them in her satchel.

"Spend the evening doing what?" she asked.

"Nothing at all," he replied simply, and offered his elbow.

She searched his eyes for a long moment, then took his arm. "All right, show me."

His heart gave a leap of victory. Time for the next phase to unfold.

Step one, according to Ask Vivian: Wait until the woman you wish to woo is ready to be courted. He'd shown his cards—literally—and she'd chosen to remain at his side.

Jacob's pulse beat faster as he took her not upstairs to his own private quarters, but to the opposite, partly used wing of the house, where he had spent days converting an empty room in the hopes of having this very chance. When they arrived, he opened the door and led her inside.

Soft light entered from a north-facing window, covered in gauzy marigold curtains. There was a small fireplace, in the event it proved necessary. A long sofa, deep enough for two to recline comfortably. A pair of cushioned armchairs, each with a cozy lap blanket curved over the back.

On either side of the window were floor-to-ceiling bookshelves, filled with plays and novels and biographies and instruction manuals. The other three walls were covered in thick green foliage up to his hip, broken only by a smattering of little white blossoms.

He turned to see what she thought.

Vivian breathed in deeply. Her forehead lined in confusion. "Does this room smell like...Are those potted plants *basil*?"

He grinned.

"Here you are, sir," said a voice from the doorway.

Jacob pulled Vivian aside to let the maids fill the tea table with lime biscuits, a picnic basket, and a large pitcher of freshly squeezed lemonade—garnished with a sprig of mint.

"You absolute scoundrel," she breathed, leaning against him and tilting her face up toward his. "*You're* 'Loveless in London'?"

"No handmade crown of flowers," he admitted, his insides warm with pleasure. "I wasn't sure if daisies made your nose itch."

The maids curtseyed and left the room, closing the door behind them.

"Do you remember what I said was most important of all?" Vivian asked.

He turned her so that he could gaze into her eyes while he held her close. "Time and attention. To really see you. To truly listen. To be understood and respected. To be admired, just as you are. To be loved."

Her lips parted.

He lowered his head to hers and kissed her. Telling her with every brush of his mouth, every lick of his tongue, that these were not idle words. He saw her. He heard her. He respected her. He loved her.

Her arms twined about his neck. She kissed him back just as fiercely. Only when they were both feverish and breathless did she lift her lips from his long enough to say, "Is this where you lead me to the sofa and ravish me just as I've dreamed?"

His heart leapt at the revelation that she, too, had longed for a physical connection. It took all his willpower to disentangle himself from her arms, stroll over to the bookshelf, and pluck a volume at random.

"You may claim the sofa if you like," he said guilelessly. "I'll take the armchair."

33

Never before had Viv so cursed her own damn words!

Her ideal courtship consisted of quiet time to read or write in companionable silence, she believed she'd said. Something about rarely having the luxury to do nothing.

It was true. Fully, completely, 100 percent true. And yet, a quill was the last thing she wanted to hold in her hands.

Drat this incorrigible man! He looked unconscionably attractive lounging in an armchair in the waning sunlight, immersed in a tome by—oh, who cared what he was reading? She wanted to yank the book from his hands and toss it into the fireplace. There was probably even a card in her pocket that explicitly gave her the freedom to do so.

That had been his first gift. Seeing her. Understanding her. And providing her with every freedom in his power.

Such as the freedom to glare at him while he pretended to be more interested in a book than being alone in a private parlor with her.

Well, two could play at that game, could they not?

To prove she categorically held no desire or intention of seducing the damnable poet-no-one-knew-was-Sir-Jallow lounging loose-limbed over in the armchair, she stuck her nose in the air and marched over to the bookshelves, intending to make believe she was happily ensconced in a book, just like him.

Her heart skidded.

The bounder had filled the shelves with things she actually *wanted* to read.

He hadn't been paying attention only to her. He had noted the titles and the authors of the volumes on her sparse shelf at home, and fleshed out an entire bookcase full of related works.

Jacob—or someone very knowledgeable on the subject—had even deduced key themes and motifs Viv enjoyed returning to and had filled the second bookcase with new-to-her authors. Volume after volume, begging to be read.

Utterly diabolical.

"Whose books are these?" she asked with suspicion.

"Hmm?" Jacob glanced up from his book, as though he'd forgotten she was in the room.

She scowled at him.

He grinned at her. "Mine. You can borrow as many as you like."

Viv harrumphed and turned back to the shelves. She didn't want to borrow a handful of books. She wanted to live right here, in this very room, until every word on every page was etched into her brain.

It took ten minutes to narrow the top contenders down to three. She carried them to the other armchair—she wasn't tempted by the sofa, either!—and curled her legs beneath her to pretend to read.

Hours disappeared without her noticing.

Suddenly, the novel was over, the picnic between them was half gone, and her hopelessly wrinkled skirt was littered with lime-biscuit crumbs.

She'd read an entire book?

In one sitting?

The faint shimmer behind the diaphanous curtains looked like moonlight. She'd missed the sunset completely. A low fire burned behind the grate. Just enough to warm the edge of chill from the air. It and the candles gave the room a soft, golden-orange glow.

Jacob's novel was on the tea table beside them. His arms folded loosely over his flat stomach, and his legs stretched out toward the fire. His eyes were closed.

"Jacob," she whispered, so softly even she could barely hear herself.

His eyes flew open at once. "Shall I light another sconce for you?"

"Do you know when the last time was that I read a whole book in one day?"

He shook his head. "Tell me."

"I can't. It's never happened before. This was a first."

He smiled. "You can read another if you like."

"I actually don't think I want to," she said, surprising herself. "I want to give that book a chance to live inside my head for a little while before I replace those characters with someone else."

"Shall I ring for more biscuits?"

"I'm stuffed."

"More lemonade?"

"No, thank you."

"More basil?"

She snickered. "What are you going to do with all these plants?"

He shrugged. "The books are mine. The basil's yours."

Viv hauled herself out of the chair, wincing at her stiff muscles. She crossed to the closest plant and popped one of the aromatic leaves into her mouth.

Delicious. Just as she knew it would be.

She turned back to Jacob. He was watching her, his eyes sensual and heavy-lidded.

"What now?"

He raised his brows. "I don't know. We reached the end of the advice letter. You tell me what happens next."

"I suppose," she said slowly, "it wouldn't be too dreadful if you were to kiss me."

His eyes glittered. "All right. I'd like that."

But he didn't move.

She crossed her arms. "Well?"

"Tell me what you desire." His dark brown eyes tracked her. "Do you *want* me to pounce upon you like a hawk snatching up a dormouse? Or would you rather be the huntress, and me the prey?"

Viv blinked and lowered her arms to her sides. She was no stranger to amorous embraces but had always been the one pursued—whether she wished to be or not. Turning the tables, however voluntarily, held the thrill of the forbidden.

Of feminine power, rather than submission.

She took a tentative step closer. "I can tell you to do anything I wish?"

"You can try," he answered. "I am not a lapdog, panting to your every command."

"*Yet*." She hiked up her skirts enough to place her knees on either side of his hips. "Let us not forget, I trained a wild badger."

"That's true." He skimmed his hands up her thighs to the curve of her hips, then raised his face toward hers. "Are you going to train me, too?"

"No." She lowered her mouth until their noses nearly brushed. "I like you a little wild."

He hauled her hips closer to his and crushed his mouth to hers.

She sank against him, her sex rubbing against his through their clothes as their mouths locked together in kiss after kiss.

Had she thought her body was stiff after so much reading in one position? Her muscles felt liquid now, her bones quick as mercury. She poured herself over Jacob, swirling into him like melting chocolate, until all she could taste or feel was their bodies mixed together.

To think that her pride had almost deprived her of the warmth of this man's embrace! Not just in this moment, but all the times this past month when she'd worked or laughed or plotted by his side.

Most of his animals accepted her as one of their own. Even the Highland tiger gave up trying to maul her on sight. She had her own seat not just here on Jacob's lap, but also in the dining room, and the sitting room, and the Planning Parlor.

Viv had once believed that the only way she could make a difference was by sharing her words with the public at large. But over the past month, she'd contributed to multiple Wynchester missions and planning sessions. Helping England become a better place on a case-by-case basis. No single escapade might have changed the world, but she'd reunited families and salvaged homes and returned lost or stolen goods and prevented evictions and improved working conditions. One by one.

Not that her precious words were going unspoken. Thanks to Jacob, her play on suffrage would be performed the week after Marjorie and Adrian's fête in Vauxhall Gardens.

Perhaps no one would attend Viv's theater debut. And perhaps the performance would launch a political uprising capable of spurring England toward greater equality. She'd find out in a fortnight.

Her words were already being performed on an even more important stage. She and Chloe and the Duke of Faircliffe had worked out several moving speeches on the topics of abolition and suffrage and autonomy. Not just prepared arguments for the duke in the House of Lords, but for his ally Olivebury in the House of Commons as well.

So much good was underway, it made her dizzy.

Tonight, Viv fully intended to debauch the stuffing out of the handsome poet whose warm hands had slipped beneath her skirts to cup the bare skin of her derrière.

Without breaking the kiss, she loosened Jacob's cravat and tossed the fabric over her shoulder.

"That might have landed too near the fire," he murmured against her lips. "We're surrounded by books. Paper makes excellent kindling. We could be engulfed in flames at any moment."

She bit his lower lip. "Do you want me to stop and tidy up?"

"Let it burn." He captured her mouth in another kiss.

She unbuttoned his coat and pushed it from his shoulders. It slid from the chair and fell to the floor. Next thing to lose was his waistcoat. A gorgeous piece of jade-green silk. It went over her shoulder in the general direction of the cravat. Or the fire.

Now the only clothing covering his torso was the thin white cambric of his shirt. She tugged it up from his waistband, revealing his taut stomach muscles inch by inch. Then his powerful chest, and his wide shoulders.

When she reached his neck, she let the shirt hang off the top of his head, obstructing his vision.

"Vivian," he said repressively, the stern words muffled by a layer of linen.

She grinned to herself and lowered her mouth to his chest, flicking her tongue against one of his nipples.

He stiffened, then tightened his hold on her arse, rubbing her against him as she licked and suckled.

When at last she whipped the shirt from his head and over her shoulder, he rewarded her with a kiss—and punished her by floating his fingertips over the dampness between her legs, toying and teasing without ever giving her the satisfaction of penetration.

She wiggled against his hands, trying to force him to give her what she wanted. He kissed her lazily as her pulse rocketed out of control. Her muscles trembled with frustrated desire. She untwined her hands from his neck to lower her own bodice, spilling her bosom forth into his face.

He responded by taking a breast into his mouth, and at last rewarding her with the full pleasure of his fingers. She gasped and arched her back, riding his hand until she was so close to ecstasy she could taste it.

She'd come all over his hand another day. Right now, she wanted to feel his cock inside her.

Barely able to think, much less breathe fluidly, she fumbled with the fall of his breeches until enough buttons broke free that his member popped up to greet her. She arranged herself atop him without delay, easing down ever so slowly. He teased her with his hand between her legs and his mouth on her nipple.

Once joined, she imagined she was ravishing him the way she'd wanted to when he'd first shown up at her doorstep to give her a bareback ride on his stallion. Now *this* was the sort of ride she'd been after.

The pressure built within her until she was no longer in control of her own body. She gave everything over to him. Her breasts, her blood, her breath. Waves of pleasure shot through her as her muscles clenched around his member again and again.

The moment she finally sucked in a restorative breath, he lifted her from his hips, covering his cock with the folds of her skirt and bucking wildly.

When they were both still, she touched her forehead to his. "Did you just smear your seed inside my underdress?"

"I would've used my cravat, but you tossed it in a fire," he pointed out. "Then you plucked the buttons from my breeches. I'll have to walk up to my room with my shirt tied about my waist. It won't be suspicious at all."

"They would've caught on anyway at the wet stain on my skirt," she informed him. "Besides, who needs a cravat? Tommy doesn't usually wear one."

"My sister is a girl. Sometimes."

"Is she? I'd take her sartorial sense over Brummell's, any day."

"Does this mean you're going to burn all of my cravats?"

"Does that mean I'm allowed to enter your bedchamber?"

"I'll carry you there right now if you want."

"Your trousers would fall around your ankles. You're missing a few buttons."

"I'll go nude. You ought to do the same. Let's get you out of that stained dress and toss the whole thing into the fire."

"Wait a minute...I begin to suspect this ploy is not designed to get me up to your bedchamber after all. Once we're both naked, we'll be stuck in this private room with its overabundance of basil and conspicuously accommodating sofa."

"Oh, is there a sofa behind me? I'd completely forgotten. Show it to me. Perhaps I'll lie down for a nap."

"Mm-hm."

"You should lie down with me." His dark gaze seared her. "Do you know what would be even better than reading a book in one sitting?"

"Tell me."

"Reading a book in one sitting whilst I kneel before you to pleasure you."

Her mouth went dry. "Do you think I could concentrate on a single word?"

"Let's try it and find out," he suggested sweetly.

She narrowed her eyes. "You think I'll last about five minutes before I climb on top of your cock again."

He gasped. "That would be a shocking twist. I had you pegged for three minutes at the most."

"Words, words. How about some action?" She slid from his lap and tugged him to his feet. "Be a gentleman, and help a lady remove her dress."

He reached for her. "With pleasure."

34

Six days later, Viv—this time accompanied by Quentin!—strolled down a walking path, on their way to the Wynchester residence. Jacob had told them both that they were welcome to spend as many nights there as they pleased, but Viv had insisted her moonstruck cousin not take advantage of the Wynchesters' hospitality.

And maybe she wanted a chance to think, in private, away from the absolutely perfect book-filled basil jungle and the many temptations of Jacob's embrace.

Not that the distance had helped. There were only ever five thoughts in her head.

1: Gratitude that Quentin was home safe
2: How much Viv missed and wanted to be with Jacob
3: She also missed participating in the Wynchesters' missions, blast it all
4: Excitement about her script's impending stage debut one week hence
5: Longing for Jacob to receive the recognition he deserved

To this latter point, she'd vowed not to push him again. He'd learned to give her the time and space she needed, and she could do no less for him.

Much as she loved giving advice, solicited or otherwise, she had come to realize that her suggestions weren't necessarily the right answers, just different choices.

A pseudonym was not a moral failing. It simply meant Jacob was his own person, with his own desires and comfort to consider. Besides, the potential backlash from the duped public could end his career.

As for Viv's authorial future, her stage debut was next Saturday. The good news was that the theater manager had taken the majority of her instructions under consideration. The bad news was, he anticipated a sparse audience at best. Wealthy aristocrats who could afford theater tickets would never attend a spectacle arguing in favor of equality and suffrage. The poor who couldn't afford a ticket didn't need the lecture anyway. She was singing their song.

The rest of her thoughts were of Jacob, and her wish to be back in his arms. Or by his side. At his table, on his horse, in an armchair with a good book. She didn't care what they were doing, as long as they were together.

In the days since she'd been gone, he'd dropped by every day with a basket of breakfast and one of the potted plants from his basil jungle. In addition to gluttonous proportions of foodstuffs, each basket also contained another book she'd admired from his bookshelves.

As a result, Viv snuck in a moment here and there to read a paragraph or two, then inevitably lost track of time until she discovered herself on the very last page. The house had never been less orderly.

Indeed, she and Quentin had set out for their walk to the Wynchesters this morning a full thirty minutes later than planned.

Which led him to grumpily complain on the way that if Viv wasn't going to keep up with the laundry and have meals ready when he was hungry, maybe he ought to hire someone else.

She shocked him by responding, "Maybe you should."

He stared at her now, with his mouth hanging open as they hiked the last quarter mile. "You cannot mean that. Why should I hire a maid when I have you?"

"Because I'm not your maid," she answered simply. "I'm your cousin."

It had taken a basil jungle and the freedom to read an entire book in one sitting to make her realize how much of her own needs she'd given up in the pursuit of assisting others.

Jacob had asked for nothing at all, and in doing so, had set her free.

"B-but," Quentin spluttered.

"What if the theater manager asks me to write additional plays? What if I begin to receive offers to work all over England? Am I to tell paying clients that I cannot possibly pursue my life's dream because my fully grown cousin cannot fathom any other way to clean his unmentionables?"

Her cousin stared at her in shock, his brain thinking furiously.

"I've nowhere for a servant to sleep," he countered in triumph.

Viv raised her brows. "Did you think I would live in your guest chamber the rest of my life, regardless of how successful I became as a playwright? Or whether some handsome gentleman sweeps me off my feet to live in his castle?"

The expression on Quentin's face indicated he hadn't considered her future or her potential desire for independence at all. Now that she'd pointed out a few possibilities, it was becoming clear even to him that using her in place of an entire cadre of servants had never been a sustainable plan.

"But I've never lived without you," he said in a tiny voice that sounded just like how he'd been as a small boy.

"You have," she reminded him gently as they approached the Wynchesters' front door. "You were simply too young to remember. Now you're grown. You can make new memories. Perhaps find a trade, or make some profitable investments."

"*You're* the one with brains and talent," he burst out. "I'm no good to anyone!"

"What's this?" said Mr. Randall, watching them avidly from the open doorway. "The founder of the first official Wynchester satellite brigade fails to acknowledge his own worth and brilliance?"

"The...what?" stuttered Quentin.

"There you are!" chirped Marjorie. She reached out from behind the butler to tug Viv and Quentin into the house. "We were just talking about you."

"I wouldn't miss your art school's celebration for the world," Viv assured her. "I hope you don't mind the presumption that we might all go together."

"Of course we should," said Marjorie. "But we needn't head to Vauxhall for another hour. We've spent all morning discussing how best to handle satellite brigades like Quentin's."

"You keep using words," he stammered, baffled. "What do they mean?"

"It means," said Jacob, swooping in to peck Viv on the cheek, "if we'd known what you were up to, we could have helped sooner. Meanwhile, you and your friends were trying to act as an extension of us, but without the supportive framework we could provide."

"In other words," said Marjorie, "we can all assist each other. My siblings and I already field more cases than we have time to handle. More hands helping will be better for us and clients alike."

Jacob nodded. "Your team can call upon any or all Wynchesters, whenever you have need of one of our services—"

Quentin swayed, as if light-headed.

"—and we will assign appropriate missions for your crew to aid with. You'll earn a salary, and of course mission-related expenses will be covered. All of our resources will extend to your team, including maps, spies, access to lawyers, the Faircliffes' influence in Parliament, medical care, a full library, in-person training, and appropriate disguises."

His eyes met Viv's as though to say, *I listened to your words. I understood your concerns. You're right. We do have a responsibility to protect everyone our actions impact, not just our clients. Your cousin is in good hands. Our privileges are now his. Our influence will be positive from now on. We're a team.*

"If such an arrangement is acceptable to you, of course," Jacob added.

"Acceptable to me," Quentin echoed faintly.

Philippa led him to a vacant armchair and handed him a cup of chocolate.

Graham lowered the newspaper he'd been reading. "Such partnerships make sense. The more good people we can empower to stand up for others, the better."

"But I'm not a Wynchester," Quentin protested.

Elizabeth and Marjorie exchanged secretive smiles.

"You are if you want to be one," said Jacob. "Those who act like Wynchesters are Wynchesters. Your legal surname is irrelevant."

Quentin almost dropped his hot chocolate as he spun toward Viv. "I told you so!"

Tommy rushed forward to rescue his steaming cup and replaced it with a sturdy plate of pies.

The tips of Jacob's fingers touched Viv's.

"Remember when I said you balance us?" he asked quietly. "So does Quentin. So do his friends. Your advice was sound: Having the *right* impact is more important than hurling ourselves into a tempest without a thought to what else would be tossed asunder by the wind. By accepting help, we can do better for our clients. We can be better to each other...and to allies like Quentin."

She squeezed Jacob's hands. His was a thoughtful solution. Quentin and his friends were never going to cease copying the philanthropic actions of their idols. Like her, they needed the freedom to forge their own paths, even if their decisions weren't always what Viv would have liked. This way, they'd have a robust network of helping hands at their disposal. Support, in any way one might need it, at any time, no questions asked.

There would always be risks, but when it was spread amongst dozens of willing co-conspirators, each with their own skills and privileges and talents...They wouldn't just be a force for good. They'd be a force of nature.

It was enough to start a revolution.

Viv nodded. "Thank you for listening to me. We do make a good team, and now we'll be an even better one. Though I'm not sure we truly achieved justice in Quentin's case."

Graham handed her the newspaper he'd been reading. "Don't be so certain, until you've read tomorrow's edition of the *Times*. I managed to get my hands on an advance copy of the society pages. What you want to see is front and center."

Viv shook out the paper. Her jaw dropped at the bold title across the top:

DISGRACED ARISTOCRAT LORD UPPINGTON TO BE TRIED ON CHARGES OF BLACKMAIL, BURGLARY, AND KIDNAPPING

The article scornfully detailed the lengths to which fashionable Uppington and his plantation-owning father had gone, in order to keep the imbalance of power favoring the upper classes and subdue the will of their common countrymen.

She jerked her head up toward Jacob, eyes wide. "Will the earl sue for libel and defamation?"

"Any investigation would only further prove his involvement. The handkerchief you removed from Quentin's mouth was the cloth Uppington impulsively gagged him with during the abduction. His distinctive monogram is embroidered in the corner."

Exactly like the one Uppington had used to wipe Viv's touch from his aristocratic elbow.

"Couldn't he claim he'd lost a handkerchief months ago?"

"We don't need it," said Kuni. "Uppington's mistress, Miss Yates, and her entire staff are willing to bear full witness against him."

"Apparently, their working environment left much to be desired," Stephen said dryly. "The servants were coerced into their supporting roles as well."

"I'm shocked," said Elizabeth, pressing a hand to her bosom. "Shocked, I tell you."

"The best part," Adrian added, "is that Uppington merely has a courtesy title. He cannot claim 'privilege of peerage' to weasel out of the charges. His trial will be scandal fodder for months."

"And ruin his despicable father by association at the same time," Faircliffe concluded with satisfaction.

The loud sound of a popping cork made them all jump.

Tommy grinned as she held up a foaming bottle. "Pre-celebration champagne, family?"

35

An hour later, the teeming crowd at Vauxhall surprised Viv. She'd known Adrian and Marjorie's art studio had become something of an institution, and she'd known Marjorie had been tutoring and giving classes for years before she'd met Adrian. But Viv hadn't realized until now just how many lives Marjorie's art had touched.

At least a thousand people had paid the garden's four-shilling admission for the school's anniversary celebration. There were children, and parents, and grandparents. Former students, aspiring students, happy customers with framed art in their parlors, and hundreds of admirers who had browsed the various galleries and exhibitions over the years.

In fact, behind the raised wooden dais upon which stood twelve easels covered in dark cloth, a large section of the pleasure garden had been converted into a temporary gallery of sorts. Visitors could stroll through the walking paths and admire paintings and sculptures on loan from current and former art students. At least as many onlookers wandered the paths as sat before the stage awaiting the ceremony.

"It's time," Adrian said to Marjorie.

The Wynchester clan were to sit single file in reserved seating at the very front of the audience, before the grand dais.

Marjorie turned to Jacob. "Don't worry. We can introduce ourselves if you don't feel comfortable."

To Viv's surprise, Jacob shook his head and took a deep breath. "I'll do it."

Marjorie bounced on her feet in glee.

"Take the floor for as long as you like," she gushed, then somewhat lowered her voice to a stage whisper that could be heard all the way to the Dark Walk. "Feel free to announce anything you please."

"But maybe don't mention Leisterdale and Uppington just yet," Graham advised. "Best to wait until tomorrow's newspaper is on every breakfast table in London."

Jacob looked more likely to vomit than to smile. "I know what to say."

"Of course you do." Marjorie squeezed his arms. "You probably spent all night editing every word into perfection."

"Go on," said Tommy. "We'll cheer you on from the front row."

Jacob, Marjorie, and Adrian took the stage. Marjorie, gamboling like an excited bunny. Adrian, loping beside her. Jacob, as stiff-legged as if trudging to his own execution.

Viv could not have been prouder. She knew how hard this was for him. How brave he was being. Jacob feared the public's reaction. That he'd agreed at all was testament to how much he loved his sister.

Adrian handed Jacob a speaking-trumpet to amplify his voice.

"Oh, Lord," Viv murmured beneath her breath. "He's going to hate that."

Jacob indeed accepted the speaking-trumpet as though he'd just been handed a rotting corpse for Christmas. For a moment, Viv feared he might fling the trumpet aside and flee from the dais, never to emerge from his barn again.

But then he drew the trumpet to his lips and began to speak.

The crowd fell silent.

At first, Jacob's words were halting. Then he gained confidence and volume. His moving introduction of his sister and brother-in-law and their artistic endeavors in the community was so eloquent, it was practically a work of poetry. He had very much edited every word to perfection.

The entire audience was rapt. When he finished speaking, there was a moment of silence, as if the crowd had hoped he would go on talking forever. Followed by thunderous applause and whoops of congratulations.

"Before we continue," Marjorie said loudly, without any need of a speaking-trumpet, "is there anything else you'd like to get off your chest?"

Jacob shot her a sour look.

She squinted at him as though she could see through his flesh and bones to the soul beneath. "Go on, then. As long as you need."

His jaw tightened, but he turned back to the captive audience with determination.

"Most of you don't know me," he said into the speaking-trumpet. "Those who have heard of me most likely know me as…" He fished a small rectangle of cardstock from his pocket and held it up to the crowd. "Jacob Wynchester, Animal Trainer."

Viv shot upright in her chair and grabbed Quentin's arm. "I bought him those calling cards!"

Jacob flicked it into the crowd and pulled out a second calling card. "A select few in the audience might know me as Jacob Wynchester, Poet."

Viv wiggled in her chair. "I commissioned those for him, too!"

Scattered members of Jacob's poetry group shouted huzzah from somewhere deep in the crowd.

He tossed the second calling card across the sea of faces after its brother.

"What you probably don't realize"—his grip on the speaking-trumpet visibly tightened—"is that you might know me best by my other name."

All the air left Viv's lungs. Was he going to do it?

Oh, Lord, he was really going to do it!

"It is my honor and privilege to present you to my true self." He took a deep bow. "Formerly known as Sir Gareth Jallow."

The crowd lost their collective minds.

Excited female shrieks rang out.

A disbelieving male voice shouted, "Liar!"

"It's true!" members of the Dreamers Guild called out. "Sir Gareth is our good friend Jacob Wynchester."

It took the crowd mere seconds to pass the salacious whisper that personages no less than the most famous writers in Britain had confirmed Jacob's secret identity.

"I love you, Sir Gareth!" screamed a fanatic female voice.

"So do I!" added a fervent male shout.

Laughter punctuated the roar of whispers, along with several more cries of "I love you more!" and "Me, too!" further lightening the mood.

Now that the shock was starting to wear off—and the few opposed to Sir Gareth Jallow being Jacob Wynchester having seen themselves out—the audience was more enthusiastic than ever to bear firsthand witness to what was quickly becoming an historic moment. They'd recount this story at dinner parties for years to come.

Several enterprising youths darted forward to jostle for the fallen calling cards, which had seconds before been in Sir Gareth Jallow's very hands.

Viv exchanged grins with Marjorie, who winked from high upon the dais, as if she'd known all along what Jacob meant to do. Perhaps she had. Or perhaps she'd simply seen her brother's potential, and strove to give him a stage, just as Jacob was attempting to do for Viv's play.

"Marry me!" came an ear-splitting cry from not far behind Viv. Several other young women echoed the sentiment.

"My apologies, ladies," said Jacob, deadpan. "I'm taken. Or hope soon to be."

"I'll take you!" came a voice from the back.

Jacob's gaze was hot on Viv, who had forgotten how to breathe altogether. "Is it all right if I read aloud an as-yet-unpublished love poem?"

She nodded, her throat tight.

The crowd went wild.

Viv wagered most of them were cursing their ill luck to have left their writing implements at home. By morning, a thousand misquoted versions would be circulating throughout London.

But the only words she cared about were the ones Jacob said next.

He shook out a folded sheet of paper and began to read.

Each syllable of his love poetry washed over her like the warmth of the sun on a cool day. Sweet, sensual, irreverent, heartrending. Tears ran down her cheeks before he finished the final line.

Young ladies in the audience dropped like flies, swooning in unison.

Viv almost joined them.

"I didn't have a chance to rehearse this next bit." Jacob handed the speaking-trumpet to Adrian, then lowered himself to one knee so that he could lock eyes with Viv. This time, his words were only for her. "Before I get to the main question, I want you to know I would never force you to live in the same house with my siblings if you don't want to. Pick a place, and I'm there."

She frowned. "What about your animals?"

"I can afford to build another barn. What I can't afford is to lose you."

She glanced over his shoulder at his family.

"They don't want to lose you either," he added. "Your views balance us, in the best possible way. Together, we could have more impact and be better people than I'd ever imagined. But even that isn't your responsibility. If you never want to work another case again, that's your prerogative. I'm not asking you to come labor for the Wynchesters."

She bit her lip. "What are you asking me?"

"Right." Jacob cleared his throat, his face half-terrified, half-hopeful. He lowered his lips to kiss the back of her hand. "Miss Vivian Henry, formerly of Demerara, soon to be the most sought-after playwright in England, forever the owner of my heart. Would you do me the eternal honor of agreeing to be my wife?"

Her voice may have trembled, but it rang out clear and loud. "Of course I will."

All the Wynchesters cheered, causing whoops and huzzahs to spread through the crowd like ocean waves.

The happiest ending of all.

Jacob reached out his hand. Viv held on tight. He hauled her up onstage and swirled her in a circle, earning even more cheers from the adoring crowd.

"I love you so much," he murmured into her ear. "If you ever need more basil, or a passionate distraction while you read, you can always call on me."

She hiccup-laughed into his chest. "I love you more than all the soon-to-be heartbroken ladies in England combined."

"You do know what this means, don't you?" crowed Marjorie.

"We're going to have to teach Rufus to respect hedgehogs?" Viv guessed.

Elizabeth rushed onstage, sword drawn. "It means it's my turn to shine!"

The other Wynchesters were right behind her. Graham sent his sister a repressive look.

"I mean Vivian's turn." Elizabeth swung her sword with a lofty smile. "I merely provide the knighting services."

"You do not have to be inducted as an official Wynchester in front of half of London," Jacob murmured to Viv.

"Are you jesting?" She raised her brows. "My cousin would disown me on the spot if I failed to make the most of such a spectacle." She glanced out into the crowd. Quentin was being swarmed by his faux-Wynchester friends. They took turns hugging him and pointing at the stage, every one of them bouncing around like a litter of puppies.

"More importantly," Viv continued, "I *want* to be part of this family. Just tell me what I need to do."

"Kneel," Elizabeth commanded.

Viv knelt.

Elizabeth waved her sword at Jacob. "You, too."

"What in the...You don't have to knight *me*. I'm already a Wynchester."

Elizabeth gave another pointed jab of her sword. "This time, it's going to be a combination knighting and handfasting ceremony."

"Handfasting weddings aren't even legal outside of Scotland," Jacob muttered.

"Don't be such a rule-follower." Viv grabbed his hand and pulled him down to the dais with her. "I doubt the knighting part has a royal blessing, either."

"We're doing this again in a church," Jacob whispered.

"All that matters is what's in your hearts," Elizabeth informed them sternly.

"In that case..." Jacob kissed Viv's fingers, then raised their joined hands for the audience to see. "Please continue."

Encouraging whoops rang out all around them.

"Hold the speaking-trumpet up to my lips," Elizabeth ordered Stephen.

"I told you I could've made a machine for this," he muttered but did as his wife requested.

"Do you, Miss Vivian Henry," Elizabeth bellowed, "accept your place in the Wynchester family, to bend any rules and break any laws necessary in our noble pursuit to seek equality and battle injustice—"

"Elizabeth," Jacob said in warning, making meaningful eyes in Viv's direction.

"It's all right," Viv told him. "All things being equal, no one should have to suffer injustice. However, things are far from equal." She raised her voice. "Returning power to those who have been wronged is the best kind of trouble to cause."

"That's right!" yelled Quentin from the audience. "Everyone go and see my cousin's play next Saturday at the Olympic Theatre! Let's vote!"

"Damn it," muttered Jacob. "I meant to make that part of *my* speech."

"And also," Elizabeth bellowed, interrupting them. "Do you vow to put up with Jacob, for better or for worse, as long as you let him live?" She added, "He'll be impossible now that everyone knows he's Jallow."

"I will find it in my heart to accept him anyway," Viv said solemnly.

Jacob pinched her.

"Then by the power vested in me, by myself, and by every Wynchester sibling, as well as our honorary satellite Wynchesters, several of whom are present here today, as is an influential poetry group, unfortunately including only one Wynchester, which is you...Two of you, if we count both of your names—"

"Get on with it," Jacob murmured.

Elizabeth tapped her sword on both of his shoulders, then both of Viv's. "I pronounce you...handfasted official Wynchesters!"

The audience whooped and cheered.

"Welcome to the family," shouted Marjorie.

All the Wynchesters atop the dais touched their fingers to their hearts and raised them toward heaven. Viv did the same.

Quentin scrambled up on his chair to copy the motions along with his friends.

On the grass behind them, half of the cheering audience did the same, touching their hands to their chests and raising their fingers or their fists to the sky.

"Speaking-trumpet," Marjorie hissed, bouncing on her heels. "Please."

Stephen gave a long-suffering sigh, then swung the trumpet to his sister-in-law's lips.

"This could've been a machine," he grumbled.

"And now," Marjorie announced, "the grand unveiling of the official Wynchester family before-and-after portraits!"

She ran from easel to easel, whipping off the curtains draped over the canvases, to reveal twelve exquisite portraits.

To the left of each pair was a Wynchester sibling, between eight and eleven years of age. They looked far too young, yet world-weary. Skeptical, but achingly hopeful.

To the right was a contemporary portrait of each Wynchester as they were now. Grown, adult, safe, confident, happy. With the love of their life at their side.

"This would've been awkward if you hadn't said yes," Jacob murmured.

"Or if you hadn't asked," Viv whispered back.

"I saw your true colors the first day I met you," said Marjorie, smiling. "I knew I just had to wait until you two saw them for yourselves."

"Is *this* why you kept pushing me to find a wife?" Jacob said suspiciously. "Because you wanted to finish a series of unsolicited paintings in time for your public exhibition?"

"Anyway, no time to chat." Marjorie swiped the speaking-trumpet from Stephen's hands and faced the audience. "Enjoy your stroll amongst the students' artwork! Bid high, and take home your favorite pieces! We give lessons five days a week. You can sign the waiting list up here on the dais. There are cakes and punch awaiting you in the piazza. Thank you for coming!"

Quentin was the first to scramble onstage. He grabbed Viv's hands and danced her around the dais. "You're a Wynchester! A real Wynchester!"

"So are you," she reminded him. "Those who act like Wynchesters are Wynchesters."

He looked like he was going to swoon. "My friends are real Wynchesters now, too! Everything we've ever wanted will now come true. We're going to change the world!"

"Easy there," she said with a laugh. "We'll do what we can to help those who need it, but neither I nor anyone else can single-handedly improve the entire world."

"Of course we can," said Tommy, chewing a mouthful of pie. "Wynchesters do impossible things every day!"

EPILOGUE

The next Saturday, it was Jacob's turn to sit in the front row. This evening was the stage debut of Vivian's first publicly performed play: *Suffrage & Suffering*.

She'd worried no one would come to the show, but the Olympic Theatre was packed to the rafters. The Duke of Faircliffe had spent the past week telling every aristocrat who would listen that everyone who was anyone dared not fail to be seen here on opening night.

Those who had experienced the wild spectacle at Marjorie and Adrian's art school celebration also wouldn't miss an opportunity to see a play written by Mrs. "Sir-Gareth-Jallow" Wynchester.

All those witnesses had told everyone else they knew, which resulted in the theater manager needing to sell thousands more tickets than the theater could hold. Instead of a single-night debut, Vivian's drama about suffrage would own the stage for at least a fortnight.

Tonight, the current crowd displayed mixed reactions to the play's central theme. Women and commoners cheered and booed at all the right places, whilst the lords scowled down from their luxury boxes at the unflattering portraits painted of themselves onstage.

They might criticize the content in private tomorrow, but the play had already achieved its goal of giving context and voice for those who could not speak for themselves with votes, as well as for their allies in Parliament who could agitate for change.

When the actors and actresses took the stage for their final bow,

Jacob was the first on his feet to applaud them—by only a second. Half of the house stood up with him in an enthusiastic ovation.

The actors and actresses parted down the middle of the stage, to reveal none other than their playwright, Vivian, who looked dazed and overwhelmed at the sight of so many paying theater-goers on their feet applauding her work.

With shock, Vivian's wide brown eyes met Jacob's.

Rather than throw roses at her feet, he tossed fistfuls of basil leaves.

She burst out laughing and held out her hands to him. "Get up here, Sir Nepotism. Tonight is your achievement, too."

Jacob not only joined her onstage, but also waltzed her in a circle. Then he delivered a scandalous kiss, much to the delight of the audience.

"Champagne when we get home?" he murmured.

"How about the reading room?" she countered with a wicked sparkle in her eye. "I'm sure there's a good book or two whose pages you could distract me from."

He swung her into his arms. "Mmm, I'll give you something to write about."

She wrapped her arms about his neck and kissed him. "You already have, my love."

Acknowledgments

As always, this book would not exist without the support of many wonderful people. I was lucky enough to have two fabulous editors: Leah Hultenschmidt and Sam Brody. Thank you to the whole team at Forever, including Jordyn Penner, Dana Cuadrado, and Estelle Hallick. And to my brilliant agent, Lauren Abramo, for your wisdom, encouragement, and friendship.

My utmost gratitude goes to Rose Lerner, who makes every book better. Erica Monroe and my early reader crew—thank you so much for your feedback and enthusiasm.

Enormous thanks to intrepid assistant Laura Stout for being my indefatigable right hand, handling everything I cannot from Costa Rica.

All the cowriting and writer dates with Joy Club and Coven—you guys keep me grounded, and I love you for it. Lace, you keep me sane. Thanks to Shauna, Amalie, Darc, Bree, Liza, Evie, and Pintip for the texts from the trenches and mutual support.

Muchísimas gracias to Roy Prendas, who makes every single day happy ever after. Te adoro, mi guapoderoso.

And my biggest, most heartfelt thanks go to my amazing, wonderful readers. You're all so fun and funny and smart. I love your reviews and TikToks and Bookstagrams, and adore chatting with you in the Ridley.vip newsletter list, on social media, in person, and in our Historical Romance Book Club group on Facebook. Your enthusiasm makes the romance happen.

Thank you for everything!

About the Author

ERICA RIDLEY is a *New York Times* and *USA Today* bestselling author of historical romance novels. Her debut young adult horror novel, *The Protégée*, releases this summer. When not reading or writing, Erica can be found eating künefe in Türkiye, zip-lining through rainforests in Costa Rica, or getting hopelessly lost in the middle of Budapest.

You can learn more at:
EricaRidley.com
X @EricaRidley
Facebook.com/EricaRidley
Instagram @EricaRidley
TikTok @EricaRidley